Muffin
But Trouble

Books by Victoria Hamilton

A Gentlewoman's Guide to Murder

Vintage Kitchen Mysteries

A Deadly Grind
Bowled Over
Freezer I'll Shoot
No Mallets Intended
White Colander Crime
Leave It to Cleaver
No Grater Danger
Breaking the Mould

Merry Muffin Mysteries

Bran New Death
Muffin But Murder
Death of an English Muffin
Much Ado About Muffin
Muffin to Fear
Muffin But Trouble

Lady Anne Addison Mysteries

Lady Anne and the Howl in the Dark
Revenge of the Barbary Ghost
Curse of the Gypsy

Muffin
But Trouble

Victoria Hamilton

BEYOND THE PAGE
PUBLISHING

Beyond the Page Books
are published by
Beyond the Page Publishing
www.beyondthepagepub.com

ISBN: 978-1-950461-17-2

Muffin
But Trouble

Cast of Characters

Merry Grace Wynter: newish owner of a real American castle and muffin baker extraordinaire!

Virgil Grace: Her husband, former sheriff of Autumn Vale and now a private investigator.

Gogi Grace: Virgil's mom and the owner of Golden Acres Retirement Residence.

Lizzie Proctor: Merry's teen friend.

Alcina Eklund: Lizzie's best buddy.

Felice Eklund: Alcina's mother.

Pish Lincoln: Merry's best male friend and partner in a new venture.

Shilo Dinnegan McGill: Merry's best female friend, now married and with a baby.

Doc English: Irascible senior who is Merry's living link to her past.

Gordy Shute: Autumn Vale resident and local conspiracy theorist.

Hubert Dread: Resident of Golden Acres and teller of tall tales; Gordy Shute's great-uncle.

Hannah Moore: Autumn Vale librarian.

Zeke: Gordy Shute's best friend and Hannah's boyfriend.

Dewayne Lester: Virgil's PI partner and old friend.

Patricia Lester: Dewayne's newish wife and cake baker extraordinaire.

Sheriff Urquhart: Autumn Vale sheriff.

ADA Elisandre Trujillo: Local Assistant District Attorney and new girlfriend of Urquhart.

Janice Grover: Merry's eccentric opera-loving Autumn Vale friend.

Reverend John Maitland: Autumn Vale Methodist Church.

Marciela Maitland: Reverend Maitland's wife and church coordinator.

Muffin But Trouble

Arden Voorhees, aka the prophet: The Light and the Way Ministry head.
Mother Esther: the prophet's wife.
Barney: Ardent member of the Light and the Way Ministry.
Nathan Garrison: The Light and the Way Ministry member.
Mariah: "Sister-wife" of Barney.
Cecily Smith: Missing girl, a friend of Lizzie's.
Peaches: Gordy's "girlfriend."
Bob Taggart: Local trucker.
Mack: Local trucker.
Anokhi Auretius: Composer.
Sebastienne Marbaugh: Anokhi's daughter.
Grant Marbaugh: Sebastienne's husband.
Millicent, aka Phyllis Urquhart: Waitress in Ridley Ridge coffee shop, known as Millicent because she wore her predecessor's uniform.
Millicent; aka Cara Urquhart: Former waitress in Ridley Ridge coffee shop.
Liliana Bartholomew: Lexington Opera Company soprano.
Blaq Mojo, aka George Alan Bartholomew: Liliana's famous rapper son.
Leatrice Pugeot/Lynn Pugmire: Model and Merry's former boss in New York City.

Chapter One

"Jezebel!"

"Who, me?" I asked, pointing to my chest like I was playing a weirdly personal game of charades. I was the only female around at that moment except for an elderly woman pushing a rolling walker down the sidewalk along the line of mostly abandoned brick and boarded-up glass storefronts.

"Yes, you. *Jezebel!*" This time *he* — the shouter — pointed his finger at me, I suppose so there could be no further cause for confusion. "Harlot!" he yelped, wide-eyed and with a hint of a smile still tilting his lips upward at the corners. The elderly woman using the walker stopped and glared at the fellow. I shrugged my shoulders when I caught her eye. It was confusing.

Nothing like being called names on a Monday in mid-October in downtown Ridley Ridge. And the fellow who shouted at me had seemed such a *pleasant* dude at first, smiling and nodding, despite the sandwich-board sign he wore as he marched up and down the walk. He held another sign, a placard he hoisted high and proud announcing that all of Ridley Ridge was bound for Hell, its inhabitants the spawn of *Satin* (perhaps being born of a silkworm?), and were *condemmed* (yes, spelled that way) to *eternity* (those *n*s and *m*s will confuse you every time) in a lake of fire.

I may have called Ridley Ridge the center of hell, true — at times it does appear to be the cesspit of western New York State, with trash blowing along the street and doggie doo just waiting to be stepped in — but some of its inhabitants are lovely people and don't deserve such a heated fate. Others do, but that is sad, and I try not to reflect on sad things on lovely October mornings.

"Jezebel!" he said again, as if I had failed to hear the first time, or the second time.

I was glad to see the woman with the walker hustle away. This was not going in a good direction. I cocked my head and looked the fellow in the eye, shifting my purse up higher on my shoulder. "Now, you don't even know me." I opened my plastic container and held it out, temptingly, wafting the fragrance of home-baked goodies his way. "Maybe you're hungry. Or constipated. Have a bran muffin; it'll solve both problems."

1

"God has told me; you're going to hell," he said pleasantly, nodding earnestly. "You are abusing God's grace on earth. You're a made-up, pant-wearing Jezebel!"

Pant-wearing? Well, yes, I was wearing a pair of pinstripe Lane Bryant body-hugging slacks, with a tunic top and moto jacket. But women had been free to wear pants for decades now; how nineteen fifties of him to disapprove. And makeup . . . ? I don't leave home without it. How very odd to have verbal brimstone rained down upon me by such a seemingly mild-mannered dude. I pushed my hair out of my eyes—the fall breeze was stiffening—and observed him.

He was tall and maybe in his late thirties, clean-shaven, short-haired with just a scar marring his receding hairline, wearing a blue golf shirt with a local golf course logo under the sandwich board, chino pants and a newsboy-style hat set far back on his head. I don't know what I expected. Maybe a lifetime of reading cartoons with brimstone types wearing long robes, sandals and Methuselah beards was the problem. I'll confess to feeling such dissonance that I thought I was hearing sirens in my head, like a brain wave, until the *whoop* of a police car pulling up to the curb and letting the siren blare in one brief blast told me it was real.

A female police officer, short but looking like she could bench press me *and* the kooky doomsayer, got out of the car, gave the zealot a look of disgust, and turned to me. "Ma'am, is he bothering you?"

I closed and tucked my plastic tote of muffins under my arm. "He did call me a jezebel, but that's about it. Oh, and harlot! He did call me a harlot. Sticks and stones and all that." I smiled. "And he didn't want a muffin. I already asked."

"Darn." She seemed disappointed. Perhaps she would have liked it better if he'd hauled off and belted me. Tucking a stray lock of blonde hair behind her ear, she shrugged. "Well, if he lays a hand on you, or threatens you in *any* way, tell us." She turned to the street preacher, read his sign, and said, "Barney, I told you to lay off the crap. Now, why don't you take your illiterate sign, go back to your encampment and leave all of us be?"

"You, Miss Police Officer, are the worst of all among the lost women of Ridley Ridge," he said, waggling his finger at her, a smile plastered on his face. I could see now that he wore a cheery *Hi. My*

Name Is Barney. Ask me about Salvation badge on his sandwich board, like someone marketing pricey herbal diet aids. Only he was apparently selling eternal afterlife, not just lengthy life on earth. "Usurping a man's rightful place and wearing pants; disgusting," he said to the cop, leering at her square, trim frame in neatly pressed khaki.

"All the better to agitate righteous types like you, Barney," she said with a wry smile. "You should see me at the disco on a Friday night, dressed in sequins, waggling my tatas and bootie."

He grimaced. I grinned.

"You should leave now, or I'll cite you for loitering," she said. She looked up and down the sloping street. A few cars passed, and one honked a horn. She raised her hand in acknowledgment. A man came out of the liquor store across the street and hustled away, clutching a paper bag under his arm; she watched him for a moment, then turned back to the fellow. "I've told you before to stop harassing folks. I won't be so nice next time."

"It's against nature and God's plan," Barney said, as if she had not spoken. "Wearing pants . . ." A woman and child walked past. He rested his sign in the crook of his elbow, smiled at the little girl, took a wrapped candy out of his pocket and gave it to her, along with a pamphlet. The mother snatched the candy away and threw it on the ground with the pamphlet, earning a glowering sneer from the proselytizer. He turned back to the cop and said, "My wife will *never* do that, wear pants, get a job. She knows her place, to provide for me whatever I so desire."

He was trying to anger her; I could see it in his eyes. He was spoiling for a fight. I wondered . . . did he really believe the crap he was spewing, or was it just a way to be contrary? When she didn't respond, he went on, his tone conversational, smile still firmly in place: "I can't believe they gave you a gun. What would happen if you were having your monthly troubles? You might shoot someone for looking at you wrong. That gun should be in the hands of your husband so he can keep you in line."

"I'll tell my husband that when we go out for target practice this weekend and I beat him on bull's-eyes. He'll laugh his ass off. Now go on . . . *go*," she said sternly. "Beat it! Out of town. I have a badge and a gun; I'm not afraid to use either."

That slimy smile, worse than any sneer, wedged on his unpleasantly moist mouth, he nodded, then waved to a fellow nearby, who was stapling the pamphlets to telephone poles, and trotted over to him. They bent together, whispering. I squinted, thinking I recognized the guy who had joined him, but he turned away before I could get a good look. They hustled away together, quickening into a gallop as a van with the words "The Message is with Us— Follow Us to Salivation!" painted on the side pulled up to the curb.

Driving the van was an older man wearing a head wrap from which thick tendrils of long graying hair fluttered in the breeze. A woman slid open the side van door and beckoned to the two men; she was wearing a long dress down to her ankles and a kerchief over silver-threaded dark hair. The driver glanced at the police officer, then his glance slid away. His lip was curled like an inept Elvis impersonator, as if he had gotten downwind of a dead skunk.

Barney tossed his placard inside, then hoisted the sandwich board off of him and handed it in to the woman in the van. He climbed in after it, as did the other fellow.

"What's *his* problem?" I asked, about the guy who had called me a jezebel.

"Barney? Me," the officer said, turning to me after the van sped off. "*And* you, and the whole of our sex who don't conform to ankle-length dresses, long hair and modestly downturned gazes. We are to procreate, work for our master, and nothing more. That is the mission of the Light and the Way Ministry."

"They're a church in town?"

"Nah. It's a cult of sorts. Or so I think. They have a twenty-acre patch of land about halfway between Ridley Ridge and Autumn Vale. Been there two years, give or take."

"How have I not heard of them before now?"

"They started out quiet, but they're getting bolder. Barney started this crap downtown after we chased him out of the bus station a couple of months ago. He used to harass folks there, especially arrivals, so we kicked him out. But he says the public sidewalk is free for all to use."

"Being shouted at and told I'm a jezebel is not a pleasant experience. It doesn't particularly bother me, but I can see that some women would find it . . . unsettling. Maybe even threatening."

"I wish we could get them to stay on their own little patch of land. Apparently at first they had a place in town, then a house on some farmland, and now a full-on encampment: huts, tents, lean-tos. I've driven past it. Their leader—or whatever you want to call him, their guru, or oracle or prophet, that guy driving the van—is a local, and so are some of the followers. But they've been gathering converts from all over, from what I understand. I wasn't here when it started. They got caught up in some movement a few years back."

Her speech was staccato, punctuated by her shifting gaze as she noticed everything: every pedestrian, every car, every flick of a curtain along the quiet streetscape. "For a while after they moved out of Ridley Ridge they were content to stay in their little campground, only coming into town for supplies. We wrote them off as survivalist kooks at first—you know, preppers—but their numbers have increased enough that we're starting to take notice."

"What can you do, though?"

"Sheriff Baxter is assembling a task force. The ATF are interested."

"ATF? Why them?"

"Well, I'll guarantee you it isn't the A, and it isn't the T."

Firearms. I shivered. I don't like guns. I've calmed down some about weapons, because my husband, Virgil, being a former cop, is very good with guns and practices regularly. He has a locked gun case in our house that I try to ignore. But I was born and raised a city girl, and guns still make me uneasy. "Do you truly think they've got guns?"

She shrugged, looking unconvinced. "Maybe. Sheriff Baxter is concerned they're stockpiling an arsenal."

"Based on what?"

Her face shuttered and she touched her holstered gun, resting her hand on it. "I'm not at liberty to discuss that, ma'am."

"Oh well," I said, walking away with a cheerful wave. "Nothing to do with me!"

Right then I should have known; nothing good comes of being cheerful in Ridley Ridge. Saying it was none of my business was like a cosmic taunt, a dare to the universe to come mess with me. I continued about my business, taking the muffins I make and sell to the local coffee shop, the only living storefront in a dead zone of four other closed businesses. It's an old-fashioned place, clean enough but worn and tired-looking, like most of the inhabitants of Ridley Ridge. The arborite tables are scarred, the vinyl chairs split and spilling fibrous stuffing, and the tile floor stained and worn through to the subfloor in spots. Every once in a while a bit of black or white tile will work loose and skitter around like a hockey puck for a few weeks before someone notices and sweeps it up.

I said hello to the latest in a long line of waitresses at the coffee shop, announced my business, and sat down at the row of stools at the counter. She yelled back to the manager that I was there with muffins, then sat back down on her stool by the cash register to stare at her phone. She wasn't busy; there were two guys in the café, both eating breakfast. Quite a contrast to the coffee shop in my town, Autumn Vale, where this time of the morning there would be several lively groups slurping coffee, eating muffins and arguing over politics, religion, and some long-dead controversy over the Brotherhood of the Falcon fraternal order hall outside of town. "Have you met that fellow, Barney, the guy who marches around up and down the street with religious signs?" I asked.

Millicent—she was the third waitress in as many months to wear the uniform, a knee-length blue polyester dress that looked like it came from the seventies and was three sizes too big for her, stitched with a name patch that said *Millicent* in flowing script—nodded laconically, not looking up from her phone. "Yeah. Him and a bunch of other loony tunes have been hanging around for a few years now. Started out keeping to themselves, but they've been getting more social."

"So I understand from the lady cop." I cringed a little at myself; *lady cop*? Haven't I learned not to say stuff like that?

She set down her phone and leaned across the counter. One blue eye wandered, but one fixed on me and met my gaze. "A few of 'em came into church a week ago. Reverend Maitland was so excited at that many new congregants you could almost see him counting the tithe."

I knew the church she spoke of, the Autumn Vale Methodist Church, which was outside of my town in a pretty valley. I also knew the reverend and his wife. "They came to a service? That must have raised a few eyebrows." I pictured the sneering fellow and others of his ilk lining pews in the cobblestone country chapel. If they spoke their thoughts on women, Graciela, the reverend's wife, would have had a few choice words for them.

Millicent the Third snickered. "Alls they did was listen and pass the offering plate without adding anything to it. After the service, as folks were filing out, they stood outside and handed each person a pamphlet saying they were all going to hell for supporting a church that had been commandeered by—" She paused, looked around, leaned further across the counter, and whispered, "Feminists, harlots, adulteresses, drug addicts and alcoholics."

She slid a pamphlet across the counter to me and I looked down at it. It was crudely done, with a yawning pit and cartoony flames leaping up and seizing some women who were wearing short skirts and drinking cocktails. Someone had been watching too many reruns of *Sex and the City*.

"Wow. Just now a member of the group called me a jezebel because I'm wearing pants. The officer warned him and he took off in a painted van."

"That painted van!" The man who spoke was at a table near the coffee counter. He was a rough-looking dude, in baggie blue jeans and stained jean jacket, muttonchops, dirty graying hair with a red ball cap jammed on. He was eating the hungry man's breakfast (breakfast is an all-day event in most local diners, coffee shops and cafés) of pancakes swimming in faux maple syrup, sausages, bacon, ham, three eggs and canned beans, all on a platter the size of a hubcap. He wiped his mouth with a napkin, the rough brown paper scraping against his three-day growth of beard, and shook his head. "They got all kinds of crap written on that van. You seen it up close?"

I shook my head.

"Have *you*, Mack?" Millicent asked.

"Sure have. I know those folks all too well. I picked up a hitcher one day—not supposed to do that, trucking for Atlantic Produce, but . . ." He shrugged. "Hate to see folks walkin' on the highway. Anyways, I took a little side trip to give him a lift to their camp—it ain't too far from my farm—and saw that van. They got stuff in big letters, but they also got stuff written and painted all over it. I grew up in the church, an' I seen a lot of stuff I recognized, like the Sacred Heart, and crosses, Mother Mary, bits of lyrics . . . you know, 'Shall We Gather at the River,' and the 'Old Rugged Cross.'"

"Do you know the people there?" I asked.

"I've met a few of 'em," he said grudgingly, a worried look on his craggy face, acne scars on his fleshy cheeks, but kindness in his washed-out blue eyes. "They're, you know, the dregs. The . . . I dunno. The folks who don't fit anywhere else."

"Bullcrap," growled another man, sitting at a different table. "I've met 'em too. Bunch o' religious nuts and commies," he said.

The first trucker said, "Bob, I got no beef with you; us truckers gotta stick together. But you know 'em a *whole* lot better'n you're letting on, amiright?" He stood and threw a twenty on the table. "I gotta go. Fresh lettuce waits for no man, y'know?" He tromped out, the plastic aglets of his boot laces flopping with a ticking sound on the tile floor, and the bells over the door chiming as he exited into the fall sunshine.

Bob, skinnier than Mack and tougher-looking, but about the same age and with the same shaggy graying hair, gave an ugly look at the door, then his gaze swung around and he met my eyes. He wiped his hands on his black Harley-Davidson T-shirt and looked me up and down, slowly. "Mack's got no right putting *me* down. He's the one who oughta not talk. Those folks out there . . . lotta stuff goes on, you know?"

"What do you mean?" Millicent asked.

"None o' your beeswax."

"Whatever. Hey, Bob . . . has Walt got time to look at my car?"

He shook his head, tossed back the last gulp of coffee, wiped his mouth, threw down a ten. "He's busy right now at the farm. Got some machinery he's fixing." He exited, the chimes jingling and the door slamming shut as a gust of wind caught it.

"Too bad about your car. Who is Walt?"

"Bob's brother. He's a welder by trade, but he's a pretty good mechanic, too."

"I always have Ford Hayes. He's the best mechanic around."

"Yeah, well, he charges, too. Walt will make deals . . . trade services for services, you know?" She winked and grabbed the tub of muffins.

As the waitress unloaded the fresh muffins into the coffee shop's own containers, the cook came out with the money they owed me, retrieved from Joe, the manager, who sat in the back room most of the time. I signed a receipt, thanked him, and he nodded and returned to his post in the kitchen. I held up the Light and the Way Ministry pamphlet. "All right if I keep this?" I asked Millicent. She nodded. I slipped it and the money into my purse, hoisted it on my shoulder and picked up my empty plastic tote. "Well, I suppose I'll go. What happened to the last Millicent, by the way?" I asked. "I was just getting used to her."

Millicent 3.0 shrugged. "Took off, I guess. Disappeared, anyway."

"Oh. That's too bad. What was her real name, anyway?"

"Cara Urquhart."

Another Urquhart; Ridley Ridge was riddled with Urquharts. "What's *your* real name?" I asked.

"Phyllis Urquhart."

"Any relation?"

"Cara is my second cousin, twice removed, or something like that," she said. "She always said she was going to leave one day and never come back." She shrugged. "I guess she finally did."

I nodded, smiled, and left. From Ridley Ridge I stopped in Autumn Vale to drop off a supply of homemade Merry's Muffins to the variety store/café and my mother-in-law's senior residence, Golden Acres. Gogi Grace—a pretty, well-dressed sixty-something widow—owns it and lives in her own suite there. I supply the kitchen with muffins for the tenants. I dawdled at the library for a couple of hours, talking to Hannah about her plans for the library, then paused at Binny's European Bakery for some Portuguese rolls; Binny Turner is the very first Autumn Vale resident I met when I entered the town what seems like a hundred years ago. She is delightfully taciturn, and an extremely talented baker.

I walked past the few shops on the main street and examined the window display of the newest, a yoga studio. It looked like they were set up to sell athleisure clothes, too, as well as yoga classes; I'd have to check that out, at some point. I may not exercise much, but I can wear the clothes. Shopping is my sport. After that, I bought two steaks from the newest business in town, a butcher's shop that was the logical outlet for a local farmer who has long sold meat from his own stock.

Business and shopping done, I headed home as the afternoon sun began to angle golden light through the trees.

Chapter Two

I drove home to my "estate," Wynter Castle and the property on which it sits. I know I've talked about the castle a lot in the past, how much I love its mellow gold stone and the grandeur of living in an honest-to-goodness American castle, built two hundred years ago by my Wynter ancestors. It's gorgeous, and I'm lucky. I still feel that every time I approach my home.

But . . . a lot has changed.

It's been a busy year or two. In fact, my second wedding anniversary was coming fast, two years married to Virgil Grace. I can honestly say time flies when you're having fun. As I drove through the new (vintage) ornate wrought iron gate, supported by stone pillars (built by a local craftsman), I smiled as I always do. I drove up the sloped winding road through the woods. To my right was the arboretum, or planned woods that my great-uncle had planted many, many years before, carrying on the work that his father and grandfather had started. Any moment the vista would open to reveal magnificent Wynter Castle. As bizarre as it seems, I'm so happy *not* to live there now.

Don't get me wrong; as I said, I'm grateful to own it. I *adore* it in all its grandeur, from the flagstone terrace to the big oak double doors and fabulous stained glass window, the ballroom and the gorgeous dining room, with gothic arched windows that face the arboretum. And I especially love the commercial kitchen that my late great-uncle installed in one of his renovation fits, when he was thinking the castle could be turned into a hotel.

I'm even more thrilled with the many ways my life has changed since that day over three years ago when I arrived to inspect my inheritance, guided there by then-sheriff Virgil Grace of the Autumn Vale sheriff's department, now my loving hubby and sexy PI. The castle had been in my family for two hundred years, give or take, and was passed to me by my great-uncle Melvyn Wynter, a man I met once when I was five, before he had a falling out with my widowed and tetchy mother.

Moving in and dealing with crisis after crisis, as well as a welter of new problems, joys and difficulties, financial and personal, taught me to embrace change. I've learned my lesson well. I lived in it for two years as my life and castle proved elastic, able to take in both of my best friends from New York City — Pish Lincoln, still living in the castle, and Shilo Dinnegan McGill, now married to a local realtor and refurbishing, baby on her hip (my goddaughter, Autumn Dinnegan McGill), a fabulous old Victorian monstrosity in the old part of Autumn Vale — as well as a multitude of new ones, too numerous to mention. The cast of characters in my life has grown like a one-woman show enlarged to a musical extravaganza.

I felt the peace of coming home wash over me as I passed my lovely castle, on the left, and continued past the big carriage house garage on my right, soon to be repurposed after years as a storage building. Other storage sheds and shacks dotted the landscape, most to be torn down eventually as we figured out what could be used and what needed to be discarded for our plans. In the distance was the planned enclave of period houses (two completely built so far, but with plots planned for five or so more) rescued from razing in Autumn Vale and beyond. We had no set title for the project yet, but I was thinking of an overall name of Wynter Woods.

At the end of the half-mile drive through my property I pulled up to our Craftsman beauty. In that, my human-sized home, I live now with Virgil Grace, my gorgeous and thrillingly sexy husband. A whole house to ourselves is enough for this former lifelong New Yorker made over into a staunch Autumn Valeite.

I grabbed the bags and empty muffin tubs from my backseat and struggled across the long covered porch and through the big dark wood double doors. If you've never seen a Craftsman home, I think it is probably the best designed house on earth: handsome, sturdy, built to last . . . kind of like Virgil and me, I suppose. We saved ours from demolition in Autumn Vale, where they are making way for a new complex that will eventually house the town council chambers, zoning offices, and various other local necessities. It had appeared to be in bad shape but was surprisingly solid, built in the nineteen twenties before the crash, lovingly crafted with oak floors and built-ins. It was the very first structure we moved to Wynter Woods, as plans for the property began to take shape.

The exterior is painted a moody olive green, with natural wood trim, and we do have a garage around the side-back that I rarely use. Virgil — who sold his ranch-style house in Autumn Vale, and paid for the renovations himself—wanted a garage, and he wanted it in front. I acknowledged the need for storage, but didn't want a garage, except maybe a detached one at the back. We compromised. I allowed the attached garage, but was adamant that it wasn't going to be at the front, spoiling the period look of my lovely work of art. So it is off to the side, near the back, with the front edge made to look like an extended wing of the house.

I rarely use it, but my husband insists I park the old Caddy—which I also inherited from my great-uncle—inside. I now drive a newer hybrid, and leave the garage for the small garden tractor with a snowplow and snowblower attachment (as well as mowing capability), the Caddy and Virgil's Hummer. Okay, so it's not a Hummer, but his latest vehicle is huge and heavy, an old beat-up Suburban, or something like that, his second souped-up vehicle, done over by Ford (short for Rutherford) Hayes, the best mechanic in four counties, as he will tell you himself. Virgil, his PI partner, Dewayne Lester, and elderly-but-spry Ford Hayes spend many a Sunday afternoon out in that garage chortling and murmuring about cars. I call Ford the car whisperer because he can get any vehicle moving with some grease, a wrench and muttered blandishments. He often says that it doesn't matter what a car looks like on the outside (the Suburban is dinged and rusted, perfect for surveillance in bad neighborhoods) but what's under the hood. It can look like a wreck and drive like a dream.

Virgil would be home soon. He had a meeting with his former deputy, who took his place as sheriff of Autumn Vale; I had an hour before he came home. He was going to grill the steaks on the flagstone patio, which faces my back woods (the Fairy Tale Forest, as I call it) and is almost exactly on the spot where we first made love.

I had time for a long, perfumed bath, and some soft, lovely clothes.

• • •

Virgil came home while I was still in the giant jetted bathtub I demanded when we renovated, we had a little watery fun, then dressed and descended, he wearing his beloved New York Rangers gear—the hockey team is his favorite, so he has the full pajama pants and hockey shirt ensemble—and I in my Lane Bryant tunic over leggings.

"By the way," he said into my ear, holding me from behind as I stood at the kitchen counter looking out over the back patio, "Urquhart is coming over after dinner."

"Okay." I turned in his arms and looped mine around his neck. "Is he still dating that nice girl, the assistant district attorney?"

He kissed me, which is rather nicer than the plain way I put it. He's a big guy, and freshly shaved (he needs to shave twice a day, some days, his beard comes in so fast) he is breathtakingly handsome. Heck, he's breathtakingly handsome with scruff, without scruff, in hunting clothes, hockey uniform, greasy jeans . . . however.

"ADA Elisandre Trujillo . . . he is," he murmured against my lips. "Why?"

"Maybe you should invite them over to dinner before it gets too cold. You can grill."

He pulled back, his brown-eyed gaze fixed on mine. "Really?" he said, his thick brows raised. "You *hate* him."

"I do not *hate* him!" I exclaimed, frustrated by my inability to shake that notion from everybody. Sheriff Urquhart of the Autumn Vale sheriff's department is someone I have had problems with in the past, but our relationship is getting better. "I don't hate him . . . *anymore*, at least. That woman is making him over to be almost human rather than a Terminator clone. But if you're going to be working with him again I want to be on good terms."

"How about Friday night?"

"Okay. Why is he coming over tonight?"

"He wants Dewayne and me to go over some cold cases. We talked about it briefly today, but he was too busy to get into it."

"Murders?"

"Mmmm, missing people, but yeah, also a couple of bodies found about three years ago, before you arrived. Near Ridley Ridge."

I frowned. "Ridley Ridge. Huh."

"Why 'huh'?"

"No reason. Not about murders, anyway." I debated saying anything; he looked suddenly tense. "I was there today," I said quickly to quell the worried look. "To deliver muffins to the coffee shop. I was confronted by a religious nut holding a despicable sign. That's all." He untensed, and I got it, suddenly. I sighed and patted his cheek. "My dear hubby, I am *not* still worried about your ex-wife." Kelly was the daughter of the sheriff of the county surrounding Ridley Ridge, Ben Baxter, and had recently moved home to sort her life out. She and Virgil had been separated for years in an acrimonious parting that had only in the last year or two, since our marriage, become less tense. "You can talk to her, you can help her move, you can have coffee with her . . . *whatever*. I am secure. You are mine, *mine* I say!" I threw my head back and laughed manically.

He kissed me deeply and I lost a few minutes.

"Invite Dewayne and Patricia to dinner, too," I murmured into his neck, intoxicated by more than the wine I had drunk. Heady stuff, my husband.

About eight or so Urquhart came over and he and my hubby sat in the great room, our living space off the kitchen and dining area. We have a big, U-shaped couch and a couple of chairs, a big-screen TV over a fireplace, and a large coffee table. They had laptops and notebooks spread out and were hunched over something. I drifted in and asked about his girlfriend. The man blushed. He *is* growing on me, I must say. He ducked his head and said she was great, and he appreciated the invite to dinner. He'd check with Ellie, as he called her.

"So what's this about missing people? Or murders?" I asked, sitting on the arm of the sofa by Virgil. He put his arm around my butt and caressed my leg.

The sheriff looked troubled, staring down at a map he had laid out on the coffee table. "I'm trying to get Ben to work with me on this problem. Locally we've had more than a half dozen missing girls or women in the last four years. Trouble is, from my aspect, most of them have been from his county so I've had to keep my hands off the problem. It's too many. I mean, one would be too many, but . . . you get it."

"I do," I said. "You expect some runaways, but not a half dozen in a short time period. Usually someone knows something, right?"

He nodded. Urquhart *is* handsome in a *Terminator 2*, T1000 way . . . you know, the cyborg from the movie *Terminator 2*? He is smooth and hard-jawed, tall and broad-shouldered, but I find him cold in a way my handsome husband has never been. I may be wrong, as Virgil has always claimed. He says Urquhart is shy and reticent, a very private person. Maybe he's right after all.

"There were a couple of murders a few years ago, and there was another girl found dead too, last year," he said.

Virgil nodded. "Yolanda Perkins. That, again, was over the line in Baxter's territory."

Urquhart sighed. "I know you tried to give Baxter a hand, but he wasn't having any of your help."

"We've had our differences over the years." Unspoken was the truth; Baxter has always let his personal feelings interfere in his police work.

"Is that a map of . . . of where the body was found?" I asked. I slid down next to Virgil.

"It's a map of *all* recent murders. See, here's Autumn Vale, in the lower area."

I saw the cluster of dots representing the murders I was involved with (not involved with committing, just involved with) and sighed. At least ours were all solved.

"There's Ridley Ridge; that's Connaught Line. Four years or so ago there were two girls found buried in a shallow grave along there," he said, pointing to a side road I had driven past a hundred times on my way in to Ridley Ridge. "The farmer who owns that land found them when he was repairing a fence. It made everyone uptight for a while. I was new on the force, then," Urquhart said to my husband.

"It was out of my jurisdiction," Virgil said. "I wish I could have worked better with Baxter but . . ." He shook his head. His former father-in-law had made trouble for him time and again, waging a constant war, trying to get Virgil removed from his elected position, and all over a misunderstanding among him, Kelly (Virgil's ex-wife) and Baxter, her father. "I'm glad you have a better relationship with him," he said to Urquhart.

The current sheriff of Autumn Vale nodded. "I grew up in Ridley Ridge. I think it helps. Poor Yolanda was found here," he said, pointing to a spot on the map. "Also along Connaught Line, but not buried, just on the edge of some sumacs and brush."

15

I examined the map. It seemed to be mostly flat farmland, with a few woodsy areas and streams. "Who found her body, this Yolanda Perkins?"

"It was a guy out walking his dog," Urquhart said. "He wasn't even on the land, that's what's weird. His dog is a hound and it took off over a field; when it didn't return to him, he went looking for it and found that poor girl in a pile of brush someone had tried to burn."

I shuddered. Such a grim topic. "And her murder has never been solved? Nor the other girls?"

"There wasn't much to go on by then, of Yolanda, anyway," Virgil said. "It took a long while to get an official ID on her, though everyone pretty much knew who it was."

Urquhart nodded. "A runaway. Everyone thought she had gone to California."

"I do remember hearing about it, but then it faded from the headlines," I said. "I know there were some 'Missing' posters at first, when she disappeared, and then a memorial set up when her dead body was found. We had some stuff going on at the same time; maybe that's why I don't remember all the details."

"She was a wayward kid from Ridley Ridge," Urquhart said. "Folks blamed her boyfriend, but I never thought he killed Yolanda. Poor guy still lives under a cloud and will unless we find the real killer."

"So what are the other girls' names, the six who are missing? Did I know any of them? I've been here over three years now."

He sighed and glanced down at his notebook. "Ashley Walker; she's been missing two years, a Ridley Ridge girl, fifteen when she disappeared. Madison Pinker, sixteen when she disappeared, missing over a year now. Delonda Henson, twenty, missing ten months. Glynnis Johnson and Cecily Smith, missing three months."

"Cecily," I exclaimed. "That's not a common name. One of Lizzie's friends from school was named Cecily. Is it the same girl?"

"I don't know."

"Have you checked out that cult encampment? Maybe some of them are out there."

Urquhart frowned and chewed on his lip. "Yeah, we thought of that. It's right here, on the map," he said, pointing to a green farmland area near Connaught and another road, gravel, it looked like. "That's Marker Road, between Connaught and Silver Creek Line. But it's private property and I don't have enough info to charge in there and take names. It's in Ben Baxter's county."

"But I interrupted you, Urquhart, when I asked about Cecily. That's five; there's one more. Who is that?"

He nodded, staring stonily at the sheet. "There's Cara Urquhart. She's been missing a few weeks now."

"Cara Urquhart . . . oh! She was a waitress at the coffee shop in Ridley Ridge. The current waitress told me she'd taken off. A relative?" I watched his face. It was twisted with emotion and he swiped at his eyes.

He nodded. "Niece. My oldest sister's oldest daughter."

"I'm *so* sorry," I said.

"We don't know where she is. It's not like her to not communicate with her mom. They've had some problems lately, and they had a big fight before she disappeared, but still . . ." He took a deep breath, stuffing down the emotion. I rose, knowing they would get no work done with me there. "I'll leave you two gentlemen to it," I said. "Good night, Urquhart. I hope you find your niece."

He nodded. "Yeah. I hope so too."

Chapter Three

We're working on big plans for my Wynter Woods property, but it goes beyond moving rescued homes and renovating them. We have a bigger goal; the working name is the Wynter Woods Performing Arts Center, though that is not official. It's going to be a home away from home for the Lexington Symphony Orchestra, which has a venue in New York City, of course, but either takes the summer off or tours. We will be their summer quarters, like Tanglewood is for the Boston Symphony Orchestra, and will include the Lexington Opera Company, which is Pish's real love. It's a grand scheme, all right, something that will make our area over into an arts hub and will, I hope, bring investment, jobs and eventually prosperity to Autumn Vale and beyond.

I worked all Tuesday with Pish on plans. We had already done much in the way of installing services for the performing arts center, and now had funding to start building, with the promise of enough to finish. Also, we had quite a few artists lined up to start. With the Lexington Symphony Orchestra and the Lexington Opera Company, including the opera singers Roma Toscano, Liliana Bartholomew and a few others, we had a good start at special events that we would be able to schedule once we had firm dates for building. This is a long-term project; it is not going to happen overnight. If we can do all the construction in one year that will be fortunate indeed.

Pish and I talked over my worries about alienating the local citizenry and agreed to discuss our fears with people like Gogi, who is both cultured and aware of local feelings, and Janice Grover, our offbeat opera-loving friend, who has been supremely helpful sourcing antiques and vintage items large and small for the castle renovation and my home. I felt like we were inching forward, but I was still worried. It was a big undertaking. After an exhausting day worrying about financial obligations, it is lovely to return home to my husband and our spacious but cozy home by the dark and mysterious woods at the end of my property.

I have become a homebody and love spending time with just Virgil in the evening, either watching TV or reading while he has the hockey game on. My husband is a true sports nut, but even more than *watching* sports he loves both playing and coaching, many sports but especially hockey. He played college and semipro growing up, and now plays recreational hockey in a men's league. I don't go to every game, but I was going this Tuesday night to support him against a difficult opponent. He's sexy, suited up for hockey, and it's worth it to sit in a cold arena for two hours to watch him play. He's good: strong, fast, strategic. And he's *so* in his element. He's a man of action, and never more so than when he's on the ice, winding up for a slapshot.

I see it as positive payback. He's been so good about all of the symphony orchestra and opera things I have going. He attends fund-raisers wearing a tuxedo when he must, he sometimes goes to New York City with me, and endlessly listens to me fret over it all. In return I hope my enjoyment of his games and even his coaching — watching him coach six-year-olds playing hockey is adorable — gives him back a little of the love and support he gives me every day.

We headed out into the coolish evening air and drove together in my car to the Johnson Memorial Arena, a big curved-roof building, like a glorified Quonset hut, part of a larger sports complex attached to a college two towns over, near Batavia. It is used for hockey most of the year, even in summer, but is occasionally repurposed for other things, like dirt bike competitions, monster truck shows and even horse shows and competitions. But from about September to May it is all hockey, all of the time, and is Virgil's team's home ice.

He grabbed his enormous hockey bag out of the trunk and we walked across the well-lit parking lot, parting at the doors with a kiss as he went off to the change rooms to suit up. There was a noisy game in progress, so I got a cup of the horrible coffee from the snack bar (when will I learn to bring my own?) and wandered along the bench seating area looking for a friendly face as the game was played. I spotted Graciela Maitland, the wife of the local Methodist reverend, and waved. She beckoned me, then returned her gaze to the rink.

I climbed the concrete bank of seating. Sound echoes in that building; the noise of shots, blades, shouts and cheering fills the space, reverberating off the high metal roof and ricocheting, amplifying. Some teams hire an organist to play the usual crowd-amping music. Between periods there is heavy rock music blasted through the sound system, a weird mix of metal and rock and modern pop, with a soupçon of rap and country thrown in. There is a particular smell and feel to a hockey rink, a pungent odor of popcorn, bad coffee, beer, sweaty men and women (there are plenty of women's leagues in Autumn Vale and Ridley Ridge, too, and those women do sweat hard!), ice and wood.

When I got up to Graciela's level I made my way toward her, slinking along the bench-style seating in the odd shuffle step common to all hockey wives, coffee in one hand, purse slung over my shoulder. "One of your kids playing?" I asked as I sat down beside her, plunking my purse (I didn't bring my good Birkin, but a disreputable khaki bag I use for many other occasions) on the floor between my feet. The Maitlands have two sons and three daughters, any one of whom could be on the ice.

"No, it's John who is playing!" she said of her husband. She leaped to her feet. "Go, John!" she screeched. "That's him," she said, pointing out a figure in a maroon and black uniform with the number 33 on his back and *Maitland* emblazoned above it. "He plays with an old-timers' league."

"Old-timers?"

"Yeah. I kid him about that. But he hates 'senior's league,' so old-timers it is!" Her gaze never left the ice as she talked.

I glanced up at the big square scoreboard that hung over center ice. It showed the two teams as Autumn Vale Valiants and the Ridley Ridge Rebels, so I knew who to cheer for. "I didn't know Reverend Maitland played!" I said, raising my voice over the ruckus.

"Between you and me he's not very good, but he's enthusiastic!" She jumped up again, cheering and shouting his name as he got a breakaway and raced down the ice, but then fanned on a shot.

I'm impressed I know the terminology and that "fanning" on the puck is when you go to hit it with your stick but miss. The game ended with the Rebels trouncing the Valiants seven to three. "Can't win 'em all," I said soothingly, expecting her to go to meet her husband at the door.

Instead she turned to me. "So, how is everything going?" she asked.

"Not terrible, I guess," I shouted over the sudden blare of Bon Jovi's "Livin' on a Prayer." The Zamboni machine chugged out to the ice from the far end and made its way around the surface. We had at least ten minutes between games.

She bit her lip and eyed me contemplatively. Graciela, dressed that night in a navy wool peacoat with a colorful scarf around her neck, is a lovely woman, the child of an African-American soldier and his Filipino bride. She was born in the Philippines but brought to America as a baby, in the sixties. She perennially has a smile on her round face, and her dark eyes are alight with good humor and kindness. She and John are a powerful force for good in Autumn Vale. Though I don't attend church, we have gotten to know each other fairly well at town meetings and events, and I always invite them to parties at the castle. After observing me for a long moment, she cocked her head to one side and said, "Sounds like things could be better."

I sighed and agreed. I unburdened myself of my worries about how the town was going to react to the performing arts center and the influx of people I hoped it would bring.

"Merry, you can't control everything. If I have learned anything as the wife of a reverend, you can only do what you want to do, with a good heart and good intentions, and adjust as things happen. If locals put up a fuss, I have faith that you'll find a way to bring them together. In fact . . ." She bit her lip again as she paused.

"Yes?"

In a rush, she leaned toward me and said, "I was talking about this to John the other day, but I never would have brought it up to you, except that this might help. Our church has a wonderful choir, which you would know if you attended. Your facility sounds like it's going to be magnificent. Maybe you could host our choir—and others of course, like the high school band and choir—for a night, a charity event to help the school arts program and the church choir fund. That would bring many locals to the center."

I sat, open-mouthed, as the idea took shape. The church choir. School choirs. Maybe . . . maybe a *festival* of choirs, to celebrate spring, or Thanksgiving, or Christmas. It was brilliant because it would bring locals to the facility to see that it would be their center too, not just for hoity-toity out-of-towners. "I *love* it. Let me run it past Pish."

"What are you saying about Pish?" John said as he approached, freshly showered, his sparse hair damp and slicked back. "Where *is* my favorite friend?" he asked.

I smiled up at the reverend, a slim, friendly-faced bespectacled gentleman, his kind face perpetually wreathed in a smile. Over warmed snifters of brandy he and Pish tend to have long abstract conversations about theology and church history, esoteric chats that leave me behind. Pish was raised in the Methodist church but left years ago when it became apparent that it was never going to be compatible with his life truth. John, like many Methodist reverends, was at odds with his church's exclusionary stand on sexual orientation, and it was a nonissue locally. Their conversations would be fascinating if I was smarter, or they were dumber. Pish occasionally comes to Virgil's games with me.

"He's home tonight. Reverend, do you have a moment?" I said.

His wife scooted over and he sat down between us. "Certainly, Merry."

"I've been hearing some stuff about this religious sect or cult or whatever out of town . . . you've heard of it, haven't you? I understand a group of them marched into your church a week ago Sunday and handed out pamphlets after service."

He exchanged a worried look with his wife. "The Light and the Way Ministry. Yes."

"What happened? How did you get them to leave?"

"I called the police. Sheriff Urquhart was most persuasive."

"Was it women and men?"

"Mostly men. There was one woman, an older lady in long skirts with a kerchief over her hair," Graciela interjected.

Likely the woman in the van, I thought. "I don't get the attraction of it to people. Why do you think folks join a group like that?"

"Some people want to be told what to believe and think. They don't want to have to do the work . . . *think* about their faith. That's what I believe, anyway. I've done some research. I also feel it gives the disenfranchised a sense of belonging." He told me what he had learned about how to tell a religious group from a cult, and then he said, "I've been worried about them for some time myself. I know several locals, even a few former congregants of mine, who have joined. I suppose I should say if they're adults, it's up to them what they do and believe, but I'm troubled."

"I'm a little worried too. Sheriff Urquhart and Virgil are

consulting with Sheriff Baxter to try to solve the cases of missing girls locally. I asked if some of them could be at that encampment, but he says he doesn't have any evidence indicating that, and without some evidence he can't go on the property without permission. So far they've turned away the police, Virgil told me after, and warned them to stay off their property." The Light and the Way members apparently took their privacy very seriously.

Graciela put her hand on her husband's knee. "John has been out there a few times to take food and clothes for the children, but there is often a man who won't let him come into the camp. He says it's private property and they don't want any false prophets."

"I got into the camp once, and spoke to a couple of children," John said, "but I didn't want to cause a ruckus, so I left when some men headed toward me."

A bunch of rowdy guys tromped into the stands, whistling and hooting, as Virgil and his teammates took to the ice. The rowdies, though, were fans of the opposing team and made their preference known. I recognized a few, and saw the truckers, Mack and Bob, I had seen in the coffee shop in Ridley Ridge the day before. The one named Mack had a younger woman with him. He kept her tucked under his arm even when he was banging his feet on the bleachers. She looked vaguely familiar, but I couldn't place her.

I watched her carefully, worried at how miserable she looked, but then my attention was drawn back to the action on the ice. I was joined by wives and girlfriends of some of the other players; they surrounded me chattering and laughing. The reverend and Graciela said good night and departed, with a shouted promise to talk in future.

The game proceeded. I leaped to my feet, spilled horrible coffee, and shouted just as much as the other women. Virgil is team captain and plays defense; he's good at it because he never stops moving, he's always aware of what is going on all over the ice (I think being a cop helped him, surprisingly enough) and his backward skating skills are amazing. In my humble opinion he is the best man on the team (of course) and this particular night he got two assists on goals. His team won.

I cheered, but the truck drivers and their friends booed loudly, which is to be expected. What wasn't expected or needed was one of them throwing his half-full beer cup onto the ice. A security guard approached, and they said they were leaving anyway.

I waited until that group had tromped their way out of the stands, then followed, hanging around at the front of the arena waiting for Virgil. Though he often goes out with his buddies for beer and wings after the game, on nights I attend he comes home with me. The truck driver with the girlfriend was at the front trash talking and saying he was going to whomp one of Virgil's teammates who had apparently, according to him, tripped the truck drivers' friend on the team. I knew which player he was talking about and didn't think that was going to happen. The guy in question is a gentle giant, but does not suffer fools gladly. In the coffee shop in Ridley Ridge Mack had seemed calm and sane enough, but amped up on arena beer and athletic bravado he was loud and boisterous.

I slipped by the guys to head to the entry to the hall that led back to the changing rooms. As I skittered past, I again noticed the girl. I caught her eye, wondering why she looked so forlorn, but her gaze slid away and she melted back, behind Mack. I had seen her before in some other background. I shook my head, unable to bring it to the front of my brain.

Spectators were coming in for the next game, crowding the entrance. It was a busy arena, and evening ice times were devoted to games, so spectators were a constant. Virgil's teammates were beginning to emerge from the hallway, scrubbed and wet-haired from showers. As I expected, Virgil's gigantic teammate defused the combative situation with a "friendly" choke hold that sent the trucker and his pals muttering away, the girl skittering with them as if she was eager to get away from the arena.

Virgil was the last to emerge from the dressing rooms, his head together with Urquhart. I suspect he joined because Virgil was team captain. I expected that they would be talking police matters, but they were actually talking hockey and parted with a fist bump. My hubby, his eyes gleaming with good health and high spirits, took me in his arms and gave me a long, lingering kiss, unfazed by a few of his teammates' good-natured catcalls. We walked out to the dark parking lot and headed home.

Chapter Four

Virgil was gone early the next morning. I was going to check in at the castle, and on my dear friend Pish Lincoln. We—meaning all of us, Pish, Virgil and I—had made many decisions in the last year and a half. One of my first was that although I love my castle, and my darling friend Pish thrives in the chaos, I was weary of living there. It has its drawbacks, and surprisingly, privacy is one of them. It's like a hotel, and we had a revolving door of weirdos for a while: friends came and went, but also we hosted a bickering crew of elderly ladies, one cruel but talented opera soprano, a cadre of ghost hunters and various others who passed through. When I saw several homes in Autumn Vale slated to be razed to make way for progress, I got the idea of taking one to be my new home, on my castle property but set apart from it. It afforded Virgil and me privacy, which I found soothing and delicious.

It's a bit of a distance, but I had my own reasons for walking all the way to the castle that Wednesday morning. Becket, my late uncle's ginger cat, who had survived for almost a year in the woods after my uncle's death, joined me as I donned rain boots—it had poured down during the night, and so it was a little spongy walking across the grass—and walked toward the castle. Not *toward*, in the normal way, I suppose. I was taking a circuitous route, first to view the work being done by Turner Construction. The last touch-ups were under way on the two houses we had already moved into place from their previous location in Autumn Vale. I stood and eyed the homes that were almost done, pulling my heavy sweater coat close about me against the quickening breeze and shivering.

There was a rather lovely Tudor-style brick and stone of moderate size. A young man, probably in his early twenties, was repointing the brick, filling with mortar the gaps caused by moving the structure, and it settling, as well as natural loss over the years. I moved slowly on to the next; the second home was an even smaller Cape Cod, with three dormer windows along the roof. A fellow nimbly trod the roof with a tool belt and hammer installing the last of the flashing along the dormer joints, after which he would finish with silicone caulking. I can't believe how much I now know about home construction, but I had learned a lot while ours was being moved onto the foundation and during the long process of making it fit for habitation.

Each house is set on a half-acre lot, and backs onto the far woods, distant enough away from Virgil and my house that we still felt we had our privacy. Both were beautiful. Once landscaping was done in the spring, when the first homeowners were scheduled to move in, it would begin to feel like a community. A man and woman consulted over spread-out plans. The woman was a local decorator and handywoman who was doing the interior painting and woodwork. The man was the Turner Construction project manager, a new guy Rusty Turner had brought in to manage the company for him, now that he is retired. I was happy with the new guy because he is responsive to my concerns. He had actually fired one worker, even though the guy was good enough at his job, because the fellow had harassed Shilo, shouting sexual innuendos and following her home, hanging around outside of her house until he was chased off by Shilo's husband, Jack.

I appreciated his rapid response, and that there was no hesitation in the firing. I waved to the two but did not interrupt.

I walked on down the lane that connected the row of houses; site prep had been completed for two more. Foundations were dug and cement poured; it had to cure and then the houses could be moved into place. Once that was done the interior renovation could continue all winter long. I approached one and eyed the giant hole in the ground. Becket jumped up and confidently walked along the board-enclosed poured concrete foundation, then jumped back down. Our little community was taking shape.

I have moments when I am unbearably excited about the enormous project we have undertaken, and many more moments when I'm scared to death. It's a wild ride, but like a roller coaster, once you're on, you don't get off. I'm in it for the duration, as is Pish.

Becket raced ahead, then leaped out at me from behind a clump of bushes as I strolled past. I laughed, the breeze carrying my laughter away, then picked him up, burying my face in his fur. He wriggled, squirming, and leaped down. I walked on. My property is large; it takes a half hour to stroll the length of it, longer when I meander. It's big enough that I don't think even now I have explored every acre. The enormous open area, within which the castle is centered, is rimmed on all sides with forest. For the first year I explored the forest along the road, which is a wonderful arboretum, a planned forest with a variety of natural American tree species. Early in my second year on my property, I explored the furthest treed area, what we call the Fairy Tale Forest. That was enough for a while . . . I've been a city girl my whole life. Conversion to a country girl is a slow and ongoing process.

I finally did a more thorough exploration with Virgil over this last spring and summer. The rest of the forest, this back acreage, is beautiful in a different way than the arboretum, wild and dark, deep and dense. It starts out relatively flat, but then in one section it climbs into a hilly area, with a stream running through it, and a small waterfall over a rock outcropping that I found when I followed the sound of splashing water. In spring there are the most amazing wildflowers in unexpected places: trilliums and lady slippers, May apples and dog's-tooth violets, all along old paths that may be dried up creek beds, locals tell me. It's all natural, acres of ash, maples and beech, among other trees.

We spotted a few problems. I enlisted the help of a local arborist, and he has done some preventative work to maintain the health of the trees. It's been expensive, but worth it in the long run. Everything related to our project and my property has been expensive. Without Pish's infusion of cash and planning abilities and connections I'd be bankrupt already. Unless our plans work that still may happen.

But now it was autumn, once again. The trees were turning, uneven as always, different species following their own time line, so there were leaves of green, gold, brown and scarlet. I strolled along the forest edge, down a path that was widening as vehicles were now using it. I came to a break in the trees and entered, following the newly cleared path that was kept high and dry with the copious use of mulch over a gravel bed. Fall in my forests is so beautiful; leaves were fluttering to the ground as birds chirped and flitted from branch to branch.

I wandered down the new forest lane as Becket trotted ahead of me. It was nice to be in the virtual silence. I hadn't slept well. Something troubled me; it harkened back to the conversation with

Urquhart about all the missing girls. So as Virgil snored beside me I stayed awake and worried about young women disappearing. It was troubling, and I needed a little forest to calm me. I could have walked in the Fairy Tale Forest behind my new home, but after my conversation with Graciela Maitland, our performing arts center was on my mind, so I decided to see if any progress had been made.

It was all Pish's idea. Besides becoming the summer performance venue for the symphony and opera company, we were going to become an artistic retreat and performance center, with up-to-date recording facilities, too. In summer we would host the LSO, but for the rest of the year we would have traveling troupes of Broadway shows, and many other concerts. Pish had grand and exciting plans for musical camps for kids, and all kinds of wonderful artistic endeavors. Without his vision it would not be happening.

The woods opened up to a huge clearing, an enormous three-plus-acre open area in the middle of the woods, now fully equipped with fiber optic, electrical, sanitary, plumbing and water, all the services that had to be created and buried before construction began. This had been accomplished after extensive dealings with the county for permissions and zoning. That in itself is a huge undertaking and has required an enormous amount of investigation, research, labor and money, all to accomplish an open space that looked like nothing had been done, though various pipes stick up out of the ground in strategic locations. Becket, who had trailed me this far, dashed off after a saucy red squirrel as blue jays shrieked in alarm, flitting from branch to branch in the trees bordering the opening. Sunlight streamed in, beaming on the leaf-strewn floor as I regarded it with an unsettling mixture of apprehension and exhilaration.

Pish and I had made three trips to New York over the last year and had found sponsors and benefactors, and had held fund-raising — with the considerable help of the Lexington Symphony Orchestra — so that now we have enough to begin construction of the performance hall. I hope to *hell* we're doing the right thing. In this enormous clearing in my beautiful autumnal woods, we are building a dome theater. This was far too big a job for Turner Construction so Pish was up to his eyeballs in bids, blueprints, schedules, and a million other small and large tasks.

I retraced my steps, emerged from the forest, again followed by

Becket, and headed along a worn and rutted footpath to the castle. Though Wynter Castle is the same as it has been since it was built two hundred years ago—timeless, built of mellow gold stone that warms me to see—the landscaping around it is now unrecognizable. That is one area in which, I'll freely admit, I do not shine. For the first two years I had absolutely no idea what to do with my huge American castle, set in a barren plot on a couple hundred acres of mostly flat, virtually untreed and unlandscaped acreage.

But Pish knew someone who knew a landscape artist who had had a nervous breakdown but needed to get back into this beloved art. That fellow, a modern-day Capability Brown (the most famous landscape artist of the eighteenth century), took six months and transformed the grounds. Pish and he spent long hours poring over landscape plans, seed catalogues, books on landscaping castles in Europe, and nursery catalogues of trees, shrubberies and the like. They hired dozens of locals, many of them teenagers, over the summer, and quite a few of the un- or underemployed. The result is a stunning transformation.

I circled to the front of the castle, as always, and paused, the autumn sunshine reflecting off the gold stone warm on my face. My barren castle is now beginning to look like it belongs in the landscape, rather than being dropped and abandoned by an alien race. Efren Roderick Bolden, the landscaper, had clustered some fast-growing evergreens in a few seemingly random places around the castle. Off to one side was a cleverly concealed parking area, something that would become necessary over time, but needed to be planned and installed now, rather than later. It was hidden by a row of a North American species of arborvitae, fast-growing white cedar. It made an effective screen to hide the ugly but necessary parking area. In front he had torn up (to my dismay at the time, though I see his point now) a lot of the flagstone—which he would reuse elsewhere—so he could create gardens to welcome visitors.

For a while it literally looked like the landscape had been bombed, and it brought back memories of the way I had first seen it, with giant holes dug in the landscape because of a rumor my eccentric uncle had buried treasure. But now the space has been transformed; there is a grand circular drive, with a grassy strip within the circle and a huge reclaimed fountain (from a mansion that had been razed to rubble) centered in that. It had required thousands of dollars' worth of piping and electricity, but now it was lovely, and the water tinkled and welcomed visitors who drove up the graveled drive. There were perennial gardens around the terrace, which stretched across the entire front and along the far side, where the ballroom opened out to it. Efren would like to use the reclaimed flagstone to complete the terrace along the other side, so the dining room would overlook it; tables and chairs could be placed there for al fresco dining. That part wasn't done yet, and the flagstone was piled alongside it.

This was all necessary because my castle would be the iconic centerpiece of the performance center. It will house, in its high-ceilinged bedrooms, the elite among the guests, hosted by Pish, of course. It was to be kind of a guesthouse to conductors and composers, performers and reviewers. The ballroom would be a reception area, and the dining room would host formal dinners. The castle would finally be revived and become what it was always meant to be, a grand estate.

To that end there are further plans afoot: a statuary garden; an Elizabethan knot garden using herbs; and a garden with box hedges in the shape of the initials of the place, WC. Pish and Efren convinced me that the drive should continue all the way back to the gorgeous carriage house garage, which was going to be renovated with the addition of a second floor to become quarters for summer band camps, ballet camps, and other learning opportunities. I shivered. It was so, so much: so much work, so much money, so *much*!

I grabbed one of the big double oak doors and pulled; it opened. That meant Pish was up and about. Becket raced in ahead of me and dashed up the stairs to have a good look around his domain for the first years of his life, when he lived with my reclusive uncle. Pausing, I changed from rubber boots to a pair of loafers I keep near the front door, and took in the tinkle of classical music over the sound system, which was the first thing Pish spent money on in the castle. Vivaldi; it was a good day.

But as I advanced toward the kitchen I heard voices raised in an argument. I followed the clamor and entered the long, professionally outfitted kitchen, where I always made the muffins, preferring to keep the ingredients, tubs, pans, and all the rest in one place.

"You're being dramatic," Pish said.

"I'm not! I *swear* to you, no one knows where Alcina is," Lizzie yelled. "It's spooky. I took Grandma's car and drove out to their old place, but it's abandoned . . . like, overgrown. And she hasn't been to school since the first few days of the new school year."

"Maybe they moved away," Pish said as I entered. Clad in his royal blue silk dressing gown, he shuffled over to the coffee press, yawning and pouring himself another cup of his custom blend.

"Hey, you two, quit the kvetching!" I said.

Lizzie and Pish both looked over, but then back at each other. "If that's the case, why didn't she tell me?" Lizzie complained. "I'm pretty much her only friend. She's been avoiding me, sure, and she was hanging out with a real bunch of losers, but we still talked once in a while on social media. But she's gone silent. It's like I've been ghosted."

"Maybe she was avoiding you because you called her new friends losers." Pish gave me a look, one of his *Here we go with the teen angst* looks.

"Hey, Lizzie, what's up?" I asked, though of course, having heard the rant I already knew.

We chatted for a while . . . or rather, she raved, going over the same stuff she had told Pish, and I listened. I love the kid, but she can be a bit intense at times. Lizzie, a few years ago, had been dragged to Autumn Vale by her mother, Emerald, who grew up here. She had taken Lizzie away when she was a toddler and hadn't been back, though Emerald's mother lives in town. Starting over in a new place, Lizzie rebelled and got in trouble, spray-painting her grandfather's tombstone, an act of anger at the world. Virgil, sheriff at the time, had given her a second chance; the sentence she served was community service at the retirement residence owned and operated by Virgil's mother. Lizzie had been volunteering at the retirement home, Golden Acres, ever since, though she years ago had fulfilled her hours.

When I arrived in Autumn Vale Lizzie was a misfit among the local teens, most of whom had grown up together from toddlerhood. So Alcina, who didn't go to the local school and was a few years younger than Lizzie, was once Lizzie's only friend. She is an odd, lovely, artistic girl, given to flights of fancy that had her building fairy homes that Lizzie photographed, and spending a lot of time flitting through the forest. She told everyone that her mother was deathly ill; I pictured her rather like a wraith, a literal Mimi fading away in her garret. But that was apparently an exaggeration, for the woman seemed fine whenever I saw her, though distracted by the impending doom of her marriage and the business of making a living, not so easy to do when you live off the grid on a plot of land from which you eke out an existence growing and selling produce, flowers and herbs.

So the plot of land was now abandoned, according to Lizzie. I knew that once Alcina's father left them for good, things went sour. Alcina was no longer homeschooled, or "unschooled," which is apparently a thing, and had to attend the local high school. That academic institution seems to be, from Lizzie's description, a combination of dystopian young adult fiction — think *The Hunger Games* — and a Sharks and Jets *West Side Story* dance-off, complete with knives. The two friends drifted apart as Alcina got in with a set of kids whose worst attributes, according again to my young friend Lizzie, was a penchant for short plaid kilts and aggressive eyeshadow.

"So I went away for a few weeks in the summer," Lizzie said, "with Aunt Bin to check out colleges, and I come back, and Alcina is nowhere to be found. I gave it some time. I figured she and her mom would be back, but nothing. Nada. Zipolla." She fiddled with her camera, which is never out of her hands. "What's up with that? Alcina and her mom have disappeared off the face of the earth, and I can't get anyone to listen to me," she said, throwing a moody look over at Pish, who had perched on a stool by the long trestle table that ran down much of the length of my castle kitchen, sipping the aromatic brew made from his expensive imported roast. Good coffee like his apparently spoils you for normal brew; I've seen his decaffeinated panic when he's out of it. I stick to grocery store brands for the most part.

I had made a pot of coffee and poured one for myself, then sipped it while I moved stuff around, tidying the seating area near the fireplace and adjusting the angle of the wing chairs in front of it. "Maybe they moved to Ridley Ridge?"

"I checked that out. Her mom got a job there for a while in the summer at the same bar where Mom works." Emerald, her mother, has a fitful work history. She's always trying new careers, but usually ends up back working as a cocktail waitress at the same lousy, seedy bar (which changed owners and names frequently) in that sad-sack town. "But Mom says she worked there a week in the kitchen, then disappeared. She had been talking about some new friends, a guy she had met in the bar when he marched in with a sign saying they were all going to hell."

"Oh, hey! I know who that is," I said, pausing in the act of pouring a second cup of my dark brew. "One of those guys yelled at me and called me a jezebel yesterday in downtown RiRi." Yeah, I know; Riri is supposed to be Rihanna, the gorgeous Barbadian singer, right? But locally RiRi is Ridley Ridge. They don't know from Rihanna. Musical preferences in that town tend toward Metallica and Korn.

"Called *you* a jezebel?" Pish said, frowning.

I told them the story, punctuated with laughter. But we sobered as the implications sank in. "If Alcina's mom has been lured into that cult, I'm genuinely worried."

Lizzie pushed her bushy mop of hair out of her eyes and fiddled with her camera. "Poor kid," she said about her friend. "Her mom has dragged her through so much crap lately."

I got up, turned the oven on, and began to ready my pans for the day's muffin baking. I had a new recipe I was dying to try before the holiday season arrived, a mandarin orange cranberry chocolate chip combo inspired by a treat my grandmother's English friend savored. If the recipe worked out, it might be a hit among my customers for winter!

A text chimed on my cell phone. It was Hannah, asking if she and Zeke could visit. They were worried about something and wanted to ask our opinion. I texted back, telling them I was at the castle. They were out and about and would be just a few minutes.

Hannah Moore, the Autumn Vale librarian, is one of my favorite people in the world. She carved her library out of an abandoned space on a tiny side street that was dreary to most but had become a haven for readers. Hannah is physically disabled, a tiny elfin woman who looks like a child until one sees the maturity in her eyes. She gets about in a motorized wheelchair, but once you get to know her,

her attributes make one forget the chair and anything else but her magnificent brain and heart. Though she has the appearance of a mouse, she has the courage and heart of a lion.

Zeke, her lifelong friend and current companion, was one half of an odd friendship; Zeke and Gordy Shute had once been my stalwart helpers with the grounds maintenance of the castle, but both had since gone on to other jobs. Hannah and Zeke's friendship deepened as she tutored him with lessons that helped him deal with his dyslexia, and had blossomed into something lovely and sweet and tender. I had always known he adored her, so it was no surprise. Zeke now lived with Hannah and her parents. Someday, maybe, they would marry.

Of course, as life changes, some folks get left behind. That is what had happened to Gordy, who always had trouble making friends, and who harbored odd conspiracy theories that he adamantly defended against external logic.

What could be worrying Hannah so much, I wondered, that they needed our opinions or help? I hoped it wasn't Gordy.

Chapter Five

I popped muffins into the oven, then cleaned up. Pish changed the music on the system to Brahms, then went up to get dressed. Lizzie headed out with Becket and her camera to walk the property; it was a gorgeous day, and she had photos to take. She was doing, against her mother's wishes, a gap year between high school and college, and her projects were intended to further her prestige and learning at photography school. She was documenting both aspects of the Wynter Woods property, the moving and reestablishing of old homes on my property, and the building of an arts community from the ground up. Emerald, her mother, was worried that Lizzie would lose focus, as she had, and never end up going to college.

I might have been similarly worried but I knew the ferocity of Lizzie's ambition, and her gap year was intended to further it. She would have one shot at this, and didn't want to be out of the loop. That's ostensibly why she was at the castle this fine morning; she was photographing our progress for a book that she and Pish were working on together, called *Building the Arts*, which was going to be about the transformation of Wynter Woods into a purpose-built Tanglewood-like arts community. She had consulted with Pish about what photos he wanted as the project began to ramp up, he had given her a list, and she was intent on getting a start, as well as taking photos of the progress on the moved houses.

I looked out the back window and watched Lizzie, on her way back from taking pictures. I couldn't even begin to imagine where life would take me in the next few years, except that I would always have my friends and my husband, and my home. It took me into my forties before I found lasting happiness—joy I had achieved before that was brief and fleeting—and now that I have it I'm holding on with both fists. No one and nothing will harm those I love, and the village I have come to call home.

And yet I am single-handedly responsible for many of the changes that will soon be wrought. We were almost ready to sign the first long-term leasehold: Blaq Mojo (birth name George Alan Bartholomew), a well-respected rapper and activist, was planning to lease one of our houses for his mother, one of the most famous opera divas of our time and the first African-American soprano for the

Lexington Opera, Liliana Bartholomew. They weren't going to arrive until near Christmas. For a time Liliana would stay in the castle. She and Mojo (as he is known to the public) hadn't decided on which house to lease yet; she wanted to have a look before committing herself.

There was a good chance that Mojo would invest in our performing arts center project, since he was interested in renting our recording facilities for his own use and that of his mother. He had visited the property and had checked out the town, and loved it all. His visit had caused a national stir among entertainment shows, and locally the young folks in Autumn Vale had been ecstatic. He had made a nice contribution to the school's music program, but he had done it on the sly, with no prior notice. He wasn't looking for kudos. His mother was similarly entranced by our project and the venue we were building. I like them both very much. Despite her over-whelming talent and impressive, majestic aura, she is one of the most down-to-earth opera singers I have ever met, and I have met a few.

Thinking about the lovely people we are attracting to our project helps when I feel overwhelmed. We'd sort it all out.

Lizzie came back in with Becket as Zeke and Hannah arrived. I could tell the two were worried. This was no ten-minute conversation. They joined Pish, Lizzie and me for lunch in the breakfast room. We ate soup with cheddar muffins, then we all retired to the small parlor, one of my favorite rooms.

"So what's up?" I asked.

She and Zeke sat, hand in hand, he in a wing chair and she in her mobility chair. "We're worried about Gordy," she said, glancing at Zeke, who watched her.

He turned to look at us. "I haven't seen Gordy in a while," he said, his acne-scarred face flushing with guilt. Zeke and Gordy had once shared an apartment over the top of Binny's bakery, which was owned by Turner Construction. "In the spring he let this guy, Nathan, move in, a guy who was working for Turner Construction."

The name was familiar. "Nathan . . . is that Nathan Garrison? I met him on the crew when they were putting up the foundation for the Tudor house." I flushed, feeling heat in my cheeks, angry at the memory. "He followed Shilo home from here early in the summer and sat in his car outside her and Jack's house until Jack chased him off. After that he kept harassing Shilo whenever Jack wasn't around, even after he was warned off by Sheriff Urquhart. I spoke to the new manager at Turner Construction, and he agreed to fire him."

It was common knowledge. "Yeah, that jerk," Zeke said.

"I didn't know he lived with you guys. How did they meet?"

"I guess they were at some bar, and Nathan and him got into some long conversation about . . . I don't know, one of the New World Order things that Gordy is always going on about."

That made sense. Anyone who would indulge Gordy's crank conspiracy theories was a-okay in his books. Most people shrugged and rolled their eyes when he got on one of his pet theories. It must have seemed like a connection to him. "So he let the guy move in?"

"Yup. Without even asking me."

"That's happened before."

Zeke sighed. "Yeah, he's a soft touch. I mean, I get it. I've done it too. We've had strangers crash on our couch too many times. But this guy . . . at first I didn't say anything about Nathan because I thought Binny had asked him to let him stay—you know, because Nathan worked for her dad—but no, it was Gordy's idea. So we had a fight and I moved out to the Moores' place, and I haven't seen him much since." He shrugged his shoulders in unease. He didn't normally talk so much in one stint, but Hannah was letting him continue, watching him anxiously, worry on her sweet narrow face.

"But now you don't know where he is?" I prompted, as it appeared he was done.

"Yeah. I stopped by at the apartment last week hoping to talk it through with Gordy. I miss him. We've been friends since . . . well, forever. But Binny says he had started spending time with Nathan out at some place between AV and RiRi. I guess he moved out and the apartment is empty. But now he's, like, d-disappeared."

"What do you mean, disappeared?" Pish and I said in chorus.

Zeke blinked once, his Adam's apple moved up and down his throat. "Like I said, he's gone. I guess this guy talked him into moving out to this compound, he called it." He sighed heavily. "Said something like, it was a place for the last real men in the world."

"Real men! As if." Hannah giggled, then bit her lip and looked away. "I didn't mean . . ." She shook her head.

I sent her a sympathetic glance. I got it, Gordy could be hard to take at times, especially recently, with his conspiracy theory talk.

"Binny didn't know anything about it and no one has seen him in town in weeks. Maybe months! I *thought* it was weird, that he was, like, *no*where," Zeke said. "I tried calling, but he's not answering his phone, and his voice mailbox is full, it says. I texted and . . . nothing. Used to be I'd see him once in a while in the coffee shop. I went to see his uncle, you know, the one he works for."

I nodded. Gordy worked for his Uncle Rich, a farmer, doing odd jobs and working the harvest, or whatever else needed doing on the farm. His Uncle Rich lived with his two sisters, Gordy's aunts.

"But Rich hasn't seen him either. I'm worried."

Unspoken was the *reason* we were all so worried; Gordy has a tenuous grasp on the world as it is. His great-uncle Hubert Dread, who lives at Golden Acres, is a humorist, but if you didn't know that you'd think he was a wing nut. Mr. Dread loves to tell tall tales, but he had not managed to convey to Gordy the tall part of the tale, in that they were not true. He is always sharing the latest conspiracy theory, and claimed, among other things, that Elvis was abducted by aliens and lived on Pluto, that so-called chemtrails are a government experiment to induce a docile populous, and that Autumn Vale was underlain by hundreds of miles of tunnels from its time as a World War Two experimental facility.

Most recognized the twinkle in Hubert's eye, but Gordy had always believed him implicitly and naïvely spread his wild theories to others, who laughed behind the poor fellow's back. And lately it seemed that he had spun off on his own. He'd been getting deeper and deeper into those conspiracy theories as an explanation for everything. It had started out harmless enough but had steadily become more frightening, to me, once he started talking about a New World Order, the Illuminati, and the coming apocalypse that was being planned by those who held power (Hint: reptiles in people suits were not out of the equation).

"Where he's gone sounds like the same place we think Alcina and her mom have moved," Lizzie said to me.

It did, and it sounded like the same place where the jezebel-caller had come from, where salvation was promised and the lure of belonging would collect the waifs and strays of the world. But for what purpose?

"We're worried, Merry," Hannah said softly. "But we're not sure what to do."

"I think it's time for a field trip, Lizzie," I said to my young friend. "I'm curious now, and if Gordy and Alcina and her mom are all there, I'd like to check into their welfare, see how they're all doing. What do you think?"

"Yup. And I'm taking my camera."

There was no time like the present. I set the muffins on racks to cool, then sent Zeke and Hannah back to Autumn Vale, she to open the library and he to work at Golden Acres on Gogi Grant's (aka, my beloved mother-in-law) computer system, which she had somehow mucked up with a bug.

While I did all that and tidied the kitchen, I let Lizzie retrieve my car from the house and pull it up to the front of the castle. I wasn't comfortable yet with her driving me in my new car down the highway, but we were working on it. She could drive me on the highway or in town when she stopped being distracted by every cool view and neat picture opportunity along the way.

From a chilly, dampish start, it had become one of those deceptive October days when it feels like summer is still in full swing. The air was humid from the previous night's rain, the sky was hazy, and there was a light breeze, soft puffs of air tossing my bangs. I assumed the driver's side, while Lizzie hopped around to the passenger's seat. She called one of her few school chums, another photography nerd, Julian Delvechio, who had some tenuous connection with the nutbars at the compound, and got directions, relayed to me in a minute-by-minute monologue.

"Julian says it's east of Sharon Road . . . dude, where is Sharon Road? Oh . . . west of the cemetery? Okay, Merry, go left there," she said, pointing. "Left! No . . . *left!*" She grabbed the steering wheel and jerked it left.

"Lizzie, there *is no left turn!*" I yelped as we careened off the road.

"Oh. Okay, right, then, go *right!*" she said as we settled. "Jeesh!"

I sighed heavily, rolled my eyes until they ached, and started the car again from the bottom of a ditch, where it had coasted as she frantically yelped in my ear and wrenched the steering wheel. *This* is why I don't let her drive; the concept of right and left are abstract to her, as is the notion of right-of-way. Stop signs she sees as mere suggestions, vague hints to be followed. Or not. "You keep threatening to get a tattoo?" I grumbled. "Now you're legal age. I'll pay for your first two; I'm going to get right and left tattooed on the backs of your hands!"

Smugly she said, with a smirking side glance, "Who's to say it would be my first tattoo?"

"What?" I screeched. "Where did you get a tattoo? When?" I slewed a look at her. Ever since I showed her my one tattoo (not saying where it is, but I got it on my honeymoon), she's been hell-bent on getting her own.

"Never mind," she said. "Don't freak out."

"Fine. Let's put a pin in this conversation." I backed up onto the road and headed at a sedate pace. "Put Julian on speaker phone." I cast a side glance at her and saw the rolled eyes — between the two of us we were going to sprain our eye sockets — and said, "Do it *now*, Lizzie, do *not* give me that look!"

Julian's voice erupted out of her cell phone, which she put in the bracket on my dash as she sat back, arms crossed over her chest, to sulk.

"Ms. Wynter?" His reedy voice intoned from the tiny speaker of the cell phone. "Where are you?"

"In the driver's seat of my car with a sulky Lizzie, who should know better than to grab at a steering wheel while someone is driving," I said, my tone taut with the aggravation I was still feeling. I took in a deep breath, threw her a look, which she lobbed back at me with a volley of teen sneer, which she would have to grow out of soon enough.

"No, dude, I mean, like . . . where *are* you?" Julian said. "Like, what road?"

I calmed myself, and told him. We were on Connaught Line, and he adroitly guided me the rest of the way; we had to turn off Connaught Line onto Marker Road. Marker Road . . . I recognized that from Urquhart's conversation two nights before, but I had never been down it. I drove, and Lizzie gradually came out of her sulk and bundled her riotous hair into a black scrunchie. I saw a thread of smoke as we approached what he assured me was the Light and the Way Ministry compound, where he had been a few times to buy weed, I suspected, given his evasiveness and knowing Julian. He broke the connection and I stared at the phone on the dash mount.

"That's what he does," Lizzie assured me, grabbing it from its holster. "It's like text. Nobody our age says goodbye."

"Fine, abandon civility along with a sense of direction and good music." I parked along the roadside, got out of the car and examined the scene. If I hadn't known what I was looking at I would have overlooked it completely. From the road there was a rise, and atop that a long sagging wire mesh fence, so old it was rusting out in spots. A lane crossed the ditch, and at the top was a wood and wire mesh gate. A faded *No Trespassing* sign—not very welcoming for a religious organization—was attached to a fencepost with a multitude of other hand-lettered signs. *The Light and the Way Ministry,* one announced. *You made it to salivation!* another boldly proclaimed. *All who seek salivation are wellcome!* yet another shrieked. That appeared to contradict the *No Trespassing* sign.

I *could* seek salvation, though maybe not salivation. It wouldn't hurt me to have a little insurance against future misdeeds. We climbed the rise. I examined the encampment in the distance, beginning about fifty yards back from the fence. At first I saw some weather-beaten sheds in the distance, and a few sagging tents. It could have been an off-season low-rent campground. But there were a couple of curling threads of smoke hanging in the hazy air, one drifting from a metal smokestack poking out of the corrugated tin roof of a long ramshackle shed.

"I guess this is it," I said. I could see people, but I was too far away to make any individual person out.

"Yeah, I guess so," Lizzie replied, joining me at the gate. She had her camera, of course, and began shooting pictures.

"I'm going in." I glanced over at Lizzie but she was busy snapping photos. "You can wait out here, if you'd prefer."

"*Hell* no," she said. "I came here to find Alcina."

She shimmied between the chained gate and the fence post. I tried the same, but it took more of a seismic event rather than a mere shimmy to get my thicker curves through. Under the chain, first one breast, then the other, and then my butt. Wiggle wiggle wiggle, like my dance floor moves, with Lizzie doubled over with laughter on the other side. And finally, with many pulls and tugs and a snagged blouse, I made it, straightened and dusted my jeans off, then looked along the trail, a beaten-down meandering pathway through long weeds.

"Let's see where this takes us," I said. It was like we were about to discover a lost tribe. I hoped they'd be friendly. I took the lead along the path, while Lizzie snapped photos. I was a little worried about that and finally said over my shoulder, "Maybe you'd better not take pictures until we see someone and talk to them. They may not like it." My advice was fated to be ignored, as usual.

We approached the encampment, a collection of buildings and tents, with women engaged in many tasks. In the center was an open firepit with a smoldering heap of ash in the middle. Wind kept whipping flutters of ash on the breeze. There were two Quonset huts toward the back, one painted blue and with a cross atop the barn-type doorway, and another painted red, with windows along the side. The paint was peeling and there was trash heaped along the wall—car tires, lumber, rotting piles of construction materials—as well as overgrown weeds everywhere, turned yellow and dried out this late in the year. Paths crisscrossed among these buildings.

Now that I was closer I could see that there were a couple more shacks farther back, both with cement block steps up into them, as well as a lean-to or three. An ancient rusted-out pickup truck was parked under a shelter by one particularly disreputable hut, farthest back of all the buildings. It appeared more deeply mired in the landscape than the others, with a special abandoned feel to it, like something out of a teen horror slasher flick. It was overtaken by ambitious brambles, bittersweet and blackberry bushes growing along the base and scrambling over the roof.

We were being watched. Multiple women had stopped in their tasks and were eyeing us uneasily, their attitude one of caution. Some darted glances over toward a lean gray-bearded man who lounged in the doorway of a hut that was to the right of the blue Quonset; he smoked a pipe and watched us. He wore a long robe like a dashiki, only plain colored, with the hood pulled up over his head. I stayed aware of him, just in case, not liking something about his stare.

I kept expecting to be confronted and warned off, as Reverend Maitland had been. But maybe being a woman helped. I shrugged off the uneasy feeling that crept up my spine. A group of children and women in a circle sang a song; it seemed tuneless and wordless, a nonsense chant. I thought that the women in that circle were our best chance of meeting someone who would give us information.

As we strolled in their direction, I took in the sights, smells and sounds. Someone was hammering. I paused and let my gaze travel. I saw a distant hut and a skinny fellow wearing a hoodie under a heavy jean jacket atop it, hammering roof tiles in various colors — leftovers, perhaps — in even rows. He looked somewhat familiar; I thought it might be Gordy.

I turned and watched the women for a minute. They had stopped chanting and were going off in twos and threes to work-stations, as the children scrambled off to hide, watching us from behind posts and buildings. One woman hauled a heavy pot to the ashy firepit and sat the pot on the ring of rocks, then headed off to get something else, her expression grim. Others headed to one of the Quonset huts. It seemed to me that they were aware of us but studiously avoiding us.

Who should I talk to? Lizzie, despite my warning, was strolling the encampment taking photos. That made me uneasy, but I'd handle any trouble as it came. I inhaled deeply. The pervading scent was woodsmoke, undercut by an odor of garbage drifting on the breeze. And cooking, and a soapy smell. And . . . my nose twitched. Body odor.

I whirled. "Gordy!" I squeaked, startled. The roofing fellow was indeed my friend and occasional employee, Gordy Shute. He had crept up on me so quickly I was startled, my heart pounding. Lizzie returned to my side and eyed our friend, examining him closely.

"Merry, how are you?"

I stared. Normally I would have reached out and hugged a friend I hadn't seen in a while, but I held back. He seemed . . . different. He met my gaze; he stood tall; he smiled.

Weird. His usual demeanor was so retiring, so shy. His gaze usually slid off into the distance and he never smiled. He always seemed too anxious to smile. Another guy approached and eyed Lizzie with smirking interest. I wanted to tell him to back off, but my teenage friend can look after herself. She stared him down and he looked away.

"I'm good, Gordy. Who is this?" I asked, though I thought I already knew. I recognized the lout.

"This is my buddy, Nathan," Gordy said.

Lizzie drifted away, looking back at me, and then escaping, a woman on a mission. I hoped she didn't get in trouble. "Hi, Nathan. You worked for Turner Construction." He was a nice-looking fellow, with a thick thatch of brown hair and big brown eyes. "I remember you working on the foundation of one of our houses at the castle."

He didn't say a word, just stared at me with a slight sneer on his lip. I supposed that he would know I was instrumental in getting him fired after he stalked Shilo.

"So, how are you, Gordy?" I asked, turning my attention back to my friend. "Zeke and Hannah haven't seen you in a while. They're worried about you." The breeze picked up again and flipped my long hair into my face. I picked stray hairs out of my lipstick.

"Why would *they* be worried?" Nathan asked. "They're the ones who ditched him."

I shifted my gaze and stared at him for a moment. He was about the same age as Gordy, and his face should have been pleasant-looking, except for that sneer and something in his eyes, an expression of . . . derision, I decided. I looked back to my friend. "You don't think that, do you, Gordy?"

"Yeah, well, they *did* ditch me. Too busy all the time. Last I saw him all I asked was if Zeke wanted to go play pinball but he was too busy. He didn't have time for me."

I was not prepared for this harsh answer from humble, sweet Gordy. "I don't know anything about that. I know that Zeke is worried because you two had an argument and he hasn't seen you since."

He shrugged. "He's got his life, I got mine. No big."

"But he's been your best friend your whole lives."

A glimmer of moisture in his eyes proved it was a big deal. He *did* care, but he didn't want to show it, especially in front of Nathan. Maybe there was hope. "They thought you might have moved out here, so I said I'd come and say hi. You and Nathan living together out here?"

"Yeah. Folks here get me. I'm not some weirdo."

I glanced over at Nathan and caught that look of derision on his face. I wasn't so sure that was true. A young girl drifted over, waited a yard away for Gordy to beckon, then joined him, sheltering under his left arm. Nathan watched the girl, a hungry look in his brown eyes. For all his good looks there was something off-kilter about him. Something unappealing. I noticed how the girl chose the opposite side of Gordy, away from Nathan, and when that fellow edged around to be beside her, she slipped around Gordy and nudged under his right arm instead.

"Who's this?" I asked.

"This is Peaches," he said, hugging her close. She looked up at him with a trusting gaze.

I stared. It was like an alien had abducted Gordy, installed new programming, and gently set him down in the Light and Way Ministry compound, full of confidence and charisma. "And she is . . . ?"

"My girlfriend," he said proudly, hugging her to him.

Chapter Six

Girlfriend? That was a first, as far as I knew. Gordy had never had much luck with the ladies.

Nathan's eyes flicked away and his lips firmed. I wondered how he felt about that; was he jealous of the relationship? And why, because of Peaches, that she had chosen Gordy over him, or because it took Gordy's time away from him?

"Hello, Peaches." I examined her; she was a pretty girl, slim, light brown hair almost down to her waist. She wore a long lavender dress over combat boots that looked too big for her.

She looked up at him and he nodded. Shyly, she looked in my direction, not meeting my eyes, and said, "Hi."

"How old are you, Peaches?"

"Why are you asking?" Gordy said.

I eyed him warily. There was an undertone of suspicion in his voice, and his expression had turned challenging. I turned my gaze back to her. "How *old* are you, Peaches?"

Her eyes widened, and she shook her head.

"I gotta get back to work," Gordy said. He twisted and pointed at the shack he was roofing. "I gotta get it roofed. We're getting married, and we'll need someplace warm for winter!"

"You're getting *married*?" I exclaimed. "Really?"

"Sure." He looked down at the young girl.

"What's so weird about that?" Nathan said, tension in his whole body. He looked pugnacious, ready for a fight. "It's every man's duty to procreate."

"Procreate. Is that what marriage is all about?" I turned away, done with him. "Gordy, are you sure about this? What does your Uncle Rich say?"

He shook his head. "I haven't seen him all summer."

"But you work for him. Doesn't he count on you during the harvest?"

Nathan said, "What's it to you?"

I took a deep, long breath, restraining a retort. Now was not the moment to start a quarrel.

"Peaches, you run along now," Gordy said to his girlfriend. He cupped his hand over her shoulder and gave her a gentle push. "Be a good girl and go on with the other women and make lunch." It was said with tender condescension, but she seemed not to mind or even notice anything wrong with his tone. She shot Nathan a wary look, then nodded and obediently drifted away, toward one of the Quonset huts.

"Gordy, I have to ask . . . are you sure about what you're doing. Are you . . . are you living with her now as man and wife?"

He huffed and gave me a stern look. "That wouldn't be right, Merry. We're not married yet. She lives with the women and kids, of course."

"And they live . . . where?"

He motioned to the red Quonset. "In the women's quarters, of course."

Everything was "of course," like I should know. "Okay. Well, that's all . . . okay."

"I gotta go," he said abruptly. "Tell Zeke I said hi." He turned away with Nathan and started walking back toward the shack they were roofing.

"Gordy, wait!"

He paused and turned back to me. He actually looked taller, I thought, and broader-shouldered, toughened by a summer of hard outdoor work. He held himself differently. I was worried and upset, but I couldn't figure out quite why. He looked happy, and healthy. He had a girlfriend and seemed balanced, sane, content. And *why* he was all those things were none of my business. However . . . "How are you, *really*? And what is this place?"

"My new home. Why, Merry? What's it to you?"

I was taken aback by his challenging tone. I frowned and examined his face. "It's not like you to . . . to divorce yourself from all your friends."

"Friends? *Sheeple*, you mean," he said, with the first hint of anger in his tone. "Can't tell them anything truthful, they all laugh." His eyes darkened. "They laugh at *me*. But when Armageddon begins, *we'll* have the last laugh."

Armageddon. That's what I was tuning into, what was worrying me; there was a coldness belying his smile, gentle voice and openness, a chill that had never been there before. "You . . . you can't be serious, Gordy. What do you mean, Armageddon, and the last laugh?"

"My eyes have been opened. I mean, I *knew* there was stuff not right in this world, like the way women are, and how they laugh at men, and torment them. But I never knew how to put it into words."

Nathan was right there with him. "Yeah, women got to know their place. And there's too much . . . too much of women being the boss of us. It's not right. It's not natural."

I felt sick, but steadfastly ignored Nathan, focusing on my friend. "Gordy, the other day I was harassed in Ridley Ridge by someone from here, a guy named Barney. He called me a *jezebel*. Is that okay with you? Him treating me that way?" My friend had turned his body away, as if unwilling to listen, but he flinched. "Gordy, I know you're listening to me. One of your fellow . . . campers, whatever you want to call them, called me a *jezebel* and berated me. You don't go along with that, do you?"

"No, of course not, I mean . . ." Gordy had turned back toward me and looked somewhat like his old self. He was troubled. He looked off into the distance, his gaze roaming over the odd collection of sheds and tents. "That's just Barney. It's the way he is. He's . . . he's a bit of a crackpot. Don't mind him."

"Don't *mind* him?" I said, my voice rising in anger. "I don't appreciate being berated on a public street and called a jezebel. I know you better than that; the Gordy I know would *never* allow that to be said to a woman. Do you hear yourself? He called me a jezebel. He *literally* said I was going to hell for wearing pants and makeup. Please tell me you don't believe that."

Nathan headed off at a trot toward the man still lounging in the door of the hut, watching us.

Gordy shook his head, sighed and shuffled his feet, a little of his old uncertainty drifting to the surface. The man who had been lounging in the doorway smoking now walked toward us, ambling, hands in his pockets, trailed by Nathan. I knew where I had seen him before; he was the driver of the van that picked up Barney.

"Look, Merry, I already said Barney is a crackpot," Gordy said swiftly, watching uneasily as the man approached. "Prophet Voorhees lets us all believe whatever we want, and —"

"Wait, what? *Prophet* Voorhees? Who or what is *that*?"

He sighed again, and then looked over his shoulder at the man ambling closer. "He brings us the word of God, the raw, masculine, unadulterated word of God. It's a hard world out there, Merry. He tells it like it is, you know, not like all the love and peace crap Reverend Maitland dishes out. The world's not like that and the prophet is honest about it, about how the government is against us, how we're being brainwashed in school and in church. He's . . . he's our leader."

"Your *leader*." This sounded more and more like a cult.

Gordy's stance had changed. He had appeared relaxed before, sure of himself, then a little uncertain, as he had in past, and now he looked tense. It was as though as the older man approached, he leached all of that pseudo confidence out of my friend. One thing I know for sure, if confidence is real, it remains unshaken no matter who is near, or who challenges you.

"Is that your Prophet Voorhees?" I nodded toward the tall, lanky man, now about thirty feet away, out of hearing, I hoped. Gordy, without looking, nodded. "Gordy, are you here of your own free will?"

"Of course I am!" He took in a deep breath and straightened up again. "Merry, you gotta stop worrying. I'm fine. Everything's *fine*. I gotta go." He turned away and strode off, but veered toward the fellow, who beckoned. I had thought his prophet was coming to talk to me, maybe to throw me off the property, but they walked away, heads bent toward each other, in the direction of Nathan, who stood by a hut.

The encounter had left me uneasy, unsure of how much time I had before the prophet turned ugly toward me. Where was Lizzie? I worried about her now, in this atmosphere. I strolled through the encampment. I was being watched, I could see it, but I could *feel* it too. My skin crawled. Where earlier it had been a relaxed atmosphere, now it seemed, since Prophet Voorhees had spoken with Gordy, tense and watchful. The children were gone, as were most of the women. A buzzer shrilled somewhere. Folks, including Nathan and Gordy, headed into the blue Quonset, the one with the cross atop it.

I caught up with Lizzie, who had managed to find a friend in the camp, a girl who had briefly attended the local high school, but who had dropped out.

"Merry, Alcina and her mom are here!" Lizzie exclaimed, after introducing me to Cecily, a chubby girl with blonde shoulder-length hair and big brown eyes. On her the dress similar to the ones worn by all the girls of the encampment was ill fitting and unflattering, the puffy sleeves jammed under a thick cardigan making her look like a football player.

"We met once," I said, remembering a school event a year or two ago. "You're . . . wait . . . you're Cecily *Smith*, aren't you?"

She looked warily at me and narrowed her eyes, but nodded. I had already made the connection the evening Urquhart was over; she was on the list of missing girls. How many others might be at the camp? I needed to find out, for Urquhart and Virgil's sake, but for the girls, too. "How did you come to live here?" I asked, eyeing the frumpy garment. I remembered when we met she had been wearing other unflattering clothes, too revealing and too tight; now she had gone in the opposite direction. The stylist in me longed to make her over. She didn't answer, just shuffled her feet anxiously. "Cecily, why are you here? This place seems so . . ." I shook my head, unsure how to proceed.

She shrugged.

"C'mon, Cec," Lizzie said, her tone both pleading and bossy. "Merry's cool. *Tell* her."

"My dad kicked me out of the house," she said in a bored monotone. "He's remarried, you know? And this new woman — Jessica — has her own kids, and he didn't want me around anymore. I was smoking pot and drinking. He said he'd had enough, so he kicked me out and burned all my stuff." She looked tired and was pale. "I was sleeping in the park in town when Barney told me I didn't have to live like that. He brought me here."

"And you've been living here ever since? Without telling your family?"

Her look hardened. "So what? They didn't want me. Why should I tell them where I am?" Her eyes widened. "You won't tattle, will you?"

Uh-oh. There was an ultimatum coming, I could feel it. Slowly, I said, "Cecily, it's only right to let your dad know where you are."

Her face reddened. She jammed her hands in her coat pocket and said, "You have to promise you won't tell. Or . . . or I'll go somewhere else. I'll run away."

"Cecily—"

"Promise, Merry," Lizzie said, turning and glaring at me. "You have to!"

I fidgeted and fumed. "I won't tell your father," I finally promised, then swiftly, so she didn't see the loophole, added, "Are you okay? Is anyone harming you?"

"No. It's . . . okay." The buzzer sounded again, an insistent shrill. "Look, I gotta go . . . the buzzer—"

"What about the buzzer?"

"It's service. We're supposed to go for prayers and meditation and to listen to lectures."

"Stay a minute. Answer some questions," I said, grasping her arm. I could feel tension radiating from her. "Look, you may not know this, but you're on a list of missing girls. So your dad *must* have reported your disappearance."

She looked uncertain. "He didn't want to be blamed if people noticed I was gone," she said finally.

"Maybe," I said. "But maybe he really is worried." I wanted to ask about other girls, but I didn't want to scare her off. "Can you tell us a bit about this place?"

As Lizzie shifted from foot to foot, her gaze sweeping over the encampment—looking for Alcina, I figured—I got more information from Cecily than I was able to extract from Gordy.

Prophet Voorhees was the leader of the group, which seemed to be a charismatic religious organization with loose affiliation to some online church, though Cecily didn't know what church it was. She no longer had her phone; Voorhees confiscated all tech when a new member arrived. That explained, I suppose, why Gordy had not responded to Zeke's phone calls or texts. The confiscation was supposed to be for a month, but as far as Cecily knew no one had a cell phone, tablet or computer.

Their days were broken up into sections of work, prayer, confessions, meetings, more work, more prayer, *more* meetings. The meetings, she said, were most often presided over by the prophet's wife, Mother Esther, and usually devoted to listening to taped recordings by a preacher from years ago. They lasted long into the night, sometimes *all* night.

That explained how weary she looked. It sounded like a classic example of brainwashing to me: keep people tired and bombard them with the information you want them to believe. I began to get this creepy crawly feeling up my spine, a tingling as I thought of a documentary I had recently watched on the Jonestown community mass suicide/murder. My mouth felt dry.

Discussion about their past was discouraged by Voorhees. You were supposed to leave your past behind when you joined, Cecily said, and focus all your thoughts and feelings on the group. The work was divided up along gender lines: men did physical labor like roofing, construction, going out into the community to work—some fellows worked for Turner Construction—while the women did the domestic labor in the community: sewing, cooking, gardening, cleaning, laundry—lots and lots of laundry—child-rearing, and teaching. Some of the women went somewhere else to clean, to make money, Cecily said. They were the trustworthy older women, and they did not blab to the younger girls.

"They complain about it all the time," Cecily said, rolling her eyes. "We work, but the other women say we don't work nearly hard enough."

"I saw kids . . . whose are those?"

"Some of the older women have kids. A few families joined the Light and the Way a couple of years ago, I guess," she said.

"Families? Where do *they* live?"

"Well, not together, of course," she said. She frowned, her thick brows knit. "I guess that probably sounds weird to you. I suppose I would think it was strange too, before coming here. I heard a couple of the women whispering. I guess the prophet and Mother Esther broke them up, made them sleep in different places. They're supposed to keep their eyes on God, or . . . or something."

"So families don't live together."

"Well, I mean, the women keep their kids, of course."

"Of course."

"Us younger girls get saddled with the kids a lot. It's supposed to get us ready for our lives." She sighed heavily. "The men go off and work, I don't know where. Some of them are construction workers, but there are others that go off and work at some farm, or some . . . I don't know . . . welding and stuff, and then come back and sleep in the men's quarters. That shack over there . . ." She pointed at a narrow shack, one of the ones with cinder block steps and junk piled along it.

I squinted into the distance, trying to figure it all out. "Do you have new people coming all the time?"

"Yeah, kind of. I mean, there are some guys who drift in to live for a while, then disappear again when life gets real and they get clued into the fact that we're not some free love and sex place, you know?"

Okay, so no free love and sex. Good to know. "But families join? Why?"

"Gordy says it's because the world is getting scary, and people are looking for a simpler way to live. He says when the end-times come, all that will be left are farmers and people who know how to live off the land."

"So you know Gordy?"

"Sure. I mean, I knew him from Autumn Vale. And here . . . the prophet likes him, so he has Gordy talk to us all, sometimes, in a meeting. He's shared lots of stuff about what is wrong in the world today, about how the government is using all of us, and how there is a Jewish conspiracy behind it all, and how they control all the governments in the west. He reads from some book called *The Protocols* of something or other."

I felt a wave of such overwhelming sadness and nausea that for a moment I thought I was going to toss my cookies. My friend, the young man I had relied on to take care of my property at times, the fellow I had trusted in my home . . . and he was spouting anti-Semitic garbage like that, conspiracy crap gleaned from discussions of a long-ago fake book, *The Protocols of the Elders of Zion*.

I had Jewish friends growing up, many of them in our building in New York City, where my mother and I lived with my nana. My grandmother was an honorary Jew, she always joked, dedicated to playing mahjong and baking babka, so I had heard one of her friends talking about the *Protocols* book; it was very old, and had been debunked time and again. It was *not* real and did *not* reveal a vast Jewish conspiracy to pervert the morals of Gentiles and so take over the world. And yet no debunking was ever enough. Sadly, there was not enough logic in the world for the dedicated conspiracy theorist.

However . . . I didn't take Gordy for a true bigot. He was confused, yes, and he had read without discernment too many 4Chan and 8Chan discussions, but it all seemed, with Gordy, to be jumbled into a big conspiracy muck ball. He wasn't clear on *any* of it, except that someone was in charge in this world, and it wasn't him. He was a helpless cog in a giant international wheel; disseminating conspiracy theories was him trying to take control of his own life.

"Cecily," I said gently, touching her shoulder, catching her eye and holding her gaze. "These people are not to be trusted. *Please* don't believe what they spout. You're smarter than that. And more rebellious. I know this may seem to hold answers to the confusion of life," I said, gesturing to the encampment at large. "But remember . . . you're isolated here, and they are in your ear twenty-four seven. They're trying to pull you in. The plain truth is, there is no grand overarching conspiracy. It's all in the heads of those who need to make sense of a confusing world. Please . . . don't be misled."

Wearily she shrugged and looked around anxiously. "But . . . the prophet calls Gordy his spiritual son, you know? He says Gordy is the kind of godly man all of us girls should be looking to marry."

"Okay. What makes this prophet the boss of you?"

She looked taken aback and opened her mouth, then closed it again.

As for me, my mind was whirling feverishly, trying to figure this place, this *movement*, out. It didn't seem real, any of it. I'm a pretty cynical soul. I believe that most online preachers, televangelists and cult leaders are in it for their own reasons, and those reasons have little or nothing to do with salvation. I don't think they believe the crap they spew, any more than *any* con man. So what was the prophet's takeaway in all of this? What was the scheme? There had to be *something* behind it beyond duping rubes into parting with their money and dedicating their labor and souls to his murky cause.

I asked a few more questions and Cecily said there had been several marriages, though she was not sure if they were legal in the eyes of the state. They were spiritual bonds, she said; the couples didn't even live together after the ceremony. She was supposed to get married as soon as Voorhees decided to whom she would be "sealed." *Did she want to get married?* I asked. She shrugged, too weary, it seemed, to have feelings one way or the other. As defiant as she was, and as reluctant to have me contact her father, she was clearly exhausted and uneasy. Her gaze kept traveling, as if she was scanning the horizon, afraid of trouble.

Not only was discussion about their past forbidden, I learned, but discussion about anything but what Voorhees said was actively discouraged, though he seemed to leave little time for chat anyway. Given what Barney, who Cecily admitted was a rabid skunk, had said to me and called me in RiRi, I asked her about how the women and girls of the community were treated.

"Okay. I guess," she said with a frown.

"What does that mean?"

"Well, as long as we follow the rules, it's all good. It's a bit of a relief, knowing that someone is looking out for you. I like some of the women," she said, the first spark of enthusiasm I had heard in her voice. "Some are mean, but others aren't. They're nice. It's kind of like having five moms."

"I can hardly deal with the one I have," said Lizzie, who had returned from one of her explorations. I shot her a look.

Voorhees had finally discovered me talking to Cecily and was coming toward us, his sweat-stained dashiki flapping about his legs, revealing dirty thermal leggings underneath. Great, just what I needed . . . a smelly prophet.

Chapter Seven

He joined us and put his arm over Cecily's shoulders. "Mrs. Merry Wynter Grace. Brother Gordy told me all about you."

Cecily stood silent and acquiescent, head down, boot-shod toe tracing circles in the dirt. Her weary meekness was troubling. The girl had been a spitfire, which is what got her into trouble so often; I remembered Lizzie regaling me with tales of Cecily's misdeeds. I'm not saying it's good to kick your teacher, the last offense that got her thrown out of school, but I didn't know all the details. "Did he?" I said in response to the prophet's comment. "And what did Gordy say?"

"He said that you had been very kind to him in the past, and had given him work. I want to thank you for that."

Well, wasn't that special? Like I had done the glorious prophet a personal favor. I examined him. He was tall, and gaunt, with a graying beard. He wore a head wrap and a hood over it, but there were stray tendrils of greasy gray hair escaping. He looked exactly like a prophet should look, I suppose. As off-putting as I found him, I saw something in his eyes, a wily intelligence, and a sense of humor. He was a personality to be reckoned with. If I were a teenager, kicked out of my house and afraid—young, vulnerable, alone—his strong personality might feel like safety to me. He exuded an aura of surety, a *follow me* kind of confidence. "*You're* thanking *me* for giving my friend, Gordy Shute, work?"

"I am," he said, his voice holding a tone of amusement. His breath, puffed out with every word, had a weird onion garlic odor to it. "It seems to me that despite some personal failings—Gordy tells me that you have a sad habit of failing to maintain a womanly submissive spirit, though you have married a suitably robust man— that you tried to help him. As his spiritual adviser I want to thank you for that. I think you may have set him on the path to our community."

Set him on the path . . . I opened my mouth then shut it. I was speechless. *A womanly submissive spirit?* I was dumbfounded. And *I* had set Gordy on the path to the Light and the Way Ministry? I sincerely hoped not. "Well, Mr. Voorhees, I feel you have a few personal failings of your own. The verbal attack on me on the streets of Ridley Ridge by one of your . . . *members*, a guy named Barney, was rude and borderline assault."

"Barney can be overly zealous, but he feels strongly that a woman's place is in the home. We feel that women are happier when they follow nature's dictates, and to be the center of the home is her natural place." He hugged Cecily to him. "That's not an outrageous belief, is it?"

I started counting to ten. *One, two, three . . .* many in society felt that a woman should have a submissive spirit and that her place was as the primary caretaker of children and the home. I suppose in some circles that is not an outrageous belief, even though I thought it was a load of horsepucky. *Four, five, six . . .* it was their right to believe so, and the women who followed had a right to do that, if that's what they wanted. *Seven, eight, nine . . .* it was none of my business what others believed or did not believe.

Ten. Counting hadn't helped; rage boiled over, and I felt my cheeks flaming red. "However, mister prophet, those *beliefs* don't sanction publicly berating anyone who doesn't follow them. You can believe whatever you want, but the moment you call me a jezebel or a harlot is the moment I consider if my boot will fit up your butt."

He nodded with a smirk, as if he'd scored a point for the home team. Cecily glanced up wide-eyed, with a terrified expression, as if I'd rabbit punched the pope in St. Peter's Square. "I hope you have a day filled with blessings," he said, his tone tauntingly gentle, his smile beatific. He led Cecily away.

"Cecily, if you want to leave, you can come with us!" I called out.

He paused and turned. "A reminder: this is private property, Mrs. Grace," he said, his voice still soft but underlain with steel. "I won't tolerate my children — or my brethren — being misled or lured away."

It was a warning, and I felt a little better hearing it, though it bothered me that Cecily meekly allowed herself to be led away. I had gotten under his skin, even if it was just a little. I belatedly realized that he not only knew I was married, but to whom. Interesting. Gordy must have filled him in on Virgil's past as sheriff of Autumn Vale.

Lizzie had drifted away again. I had lost my opportunity to ask Cecily if there were other girls from the list of the missing at this camp. However, having accomplished one of our goals, talking to Gordy, it was time to leave before we were kicked out. I began searching for Lizzie, hoping that perhaps she had found Alcina and her mother.

As I strolled, I could feel that I was being shunned; somehow the prophet's command had rippled through those few of his followers who were not enclosed in the Quonset hut. Whenever I asked a woman or child anything they shook their heads, as if I was speaking in tongues.

Finally, though, I found my young friend behind the red Quonset hut; she was speaking to Alcina's mother, Felice. I was relieved, and joined them.

"No, Lizzie, really . . . Alcina is fine!" Felice was saying, her expression smiling and serene. She was gowned in lavender, her blonde hair braided into a coronet. She looked like she had stepped out of *Little House on the Prairie*. "We're both *fine!*"

"But she's not going to school!" Lizzie griped.

"Not *that* school. You know how much she hated it." Alcina's mom, Felice Eklund, was delicate and pretty, and had a lovely lilting voice, soft as a pansy petal, but her tone now had an edge to it. "We have a school on-site. She's in class this minute."

Class? Did she mean the buzzer-commanded meeting? I was filled with dismay for Alcina. She had been homeschooled, or free-schooled, for most of her childhood. Free-schooling, as far as I understood, meant no specific curriculum and no set lessons or lesson times. That might seem like a recipe for trouble, and I had found Alcina to be a little odd, yes—a kind of ethereal, free butterfly of a child—but also intelligent in ways I couldn't quite grasp. She read widely and voraciously. There were definitely gaps in her knowledge, but she knew *how* to learn, and that, to me, is the biggest lesson a school can and should teach. From being a skeptic I had been converted to free-schooling's benefits, at least for *some* kids. Alcina was a poster child for the benefit of it.

"Okay, we know she didn't like the local school. She was too smart for it," I said with an acerbic edge to my voice. Too smart, and too odd, I thought, but did not say. Alcina was shy and fey, wild and wary, but the local high school had forced her into a groove; the more she tried to fit in, to find her place, the further from herself she got. "But I don't buy that this place and their 'school' are right for her either."

"Me neither," Lizzie said. "Why couldn't you stay on your farm and keep homeschooling Alcina? Why come here?"

"Do you know how hard that was? Trying to take care of everyone, trying to keep track of everyone? Everyone thought it was so easy, and I was sick a lot, and . . ." She shook her head in exasperation.

I examined her closely; on second look she didn't appear quite so well. She was pale and hollow-cheeked. She swallowed convulsively and swayed on her feet. I was alarmed. "Felice, how is Alcina *really*? You can tell us if there are any problems, or if you have any concerns."

"She's *fine*, Merry," Felice said. But her tone had a hysterical edge to it, a fearful tension.

"How are you?"

"I'm . . . fine!" she said, staring into the distance.

I looked over my shoulder, where her gaze had strayed. Barney was approaching. Felice, surprisingly, went to him and he put his arm around her. I was speechless.

"This is Barney," she said, putting her small white hand flat on his golf-shirted chest. From the edge of hysteria she had rebounded to a kind of bright and twinkly smileyness.

"We've met," I said tightly, trying to figure out their relationship.

He leaned his face down and she offered a long, lingering kiss. "He's my husband," she said defiantly.

"Oh, *hell* no! You're not even divorced from Alcina's dad yet!" Lizzie burst out, waving her hands around.

Felice's face colored delicately. "Spiritual marriage needs no permission from the state." She smiled up at her husband. "Barney has been so wonderful. He loves children, and he's *so* good to Alcina, so caring. He couldn't love her more if she was his own!"

Something was off, but I couldn't figure out what. She *seemed* happy—she was smiling and bright-eyed—and yet there were dark smudges under her eyes. Maybe the sleep deprivation that seemed to plague them all. Did I dare risk asking about the missing girls on Urquhart's list?

Another woman, considerably older than Felice with silver

threading her hair, tucked back in a kerchief, approached. "Barney, the prophet would like to speak with you."

He took her under his other arm and gave her the same long, lingering kiss, which she returned with enthusiasm.

Felice smiled at her, then looked at me with an almost defiant gaze. Her chin went up. "This is my sister-wife, Mariah."

Chapter Eight

All hell broke loose.

"Your *what?*" Lizzie shouted. "What are you, the freakin' Browns?"

For those who don't watch reality TV, that is apparently a notorious polygamous family who have or had (I'm not too clear on this; Lizzie filled me in on the reference later) a reality show.

Lizzie bolted forward and grabbed Felice's arm, tugging her to try to pull her away from Barney, while she shouted, "Take me to Alcina! Now!"

"Lizzie, stop!" I said in a low tone. My young friend is occasionally erratic and holds strong opinions. I was with her in spirit, but I had been surveying the landscape, poking my head around corners, watching to make sure we were not noticed. Any place that promoted Barney's beliefs was suspect to me. And I was right to be wary; things were getting dodgy.

Folks I had thought were safely tucked away in the Quonset hut meeting now appeared; a few men, bearded and beady-eyed, clustered in groups between the two Quonsets. Even Gordy appeared, looking alarmed. Some of the men ambled toward us. Gordy tried to delay them and at the same time comfort Peaches, who was weeping loudly. This was headed sideways, and I did not want Lizzie in trouble.

"Lizzie, you calm down now," Felice said with a tremor in her voice.

She looked frightened, and that worried me. She and Mariah (I had wondered if Mariah was the woman in the van I had seen in Ridley Ridge, but she was not, being a little younger and slimmer) clung to each other even as Lizzie still held on to Felice's arm, tugging at it, while Barney started chuckling, crossing his arms over his narrow chest. He clearly *deeply* enjoyed watching the two of us horrified by Felice's marital situation. Nothing could be accomplished with Lizzie shrieking at Barney and Felice, and him grinning back at us like a howler monkey, baring his teeth and haw-haw-hawing.

I grabbed Lizzie's hand and wrenched her fingers off Felice's slender arm — she likely left a bruise — then physically lifted my young friend away from the group. There was no alternative; I knew what I had to do. "We'll be leaving now," I said loudly, over the squawks of indignation from Lizzie. I'm bigger, stronger and meaner than she is, for all her teen bluster, so when I threaded my arm through hers and clamped her close to my body, she had to go, bumping alongside of me like a skiff tethered to a powerful tug, her camera bouncing against her chest until she steadied it with her free hand.

I led her away — she grumbled the whole time about civil rights and suffragettes and outdated stereotypical female roles — past the groups of men who watched, past Gordy and Peaches, and past the women and children who were streaming out of the meeting and gathering nearby. As I hauled Lizzie away I thought I saw Alcina hiding behind one of the bigger girls, but I was not going to pause to find out if it was her, not with a crowd of possibly angry men watching our every move. Felice said Alcina was fine, and she was, to my knowledge, a loving mother. I had to trust that.

I wove between the buildings, followed by the gathering crowd. The far fence looked even farther away than I had thought it. This was troubling. A day that had started with such promise was devolving into a brewing storm. I shivered as a breeze stirred, tossing treetops and riffling dead grass. I looked back over my shoulder.

Barney was there, among the men who were monitoring our progress with stony stares. I found him even creepier than I initially had when faced with him in Ridley Ridge, and I was worried. Alone, he was a loser shouting imprecations at women who could laugh in his face, but here, with the power of the whole cult behind him . . . I didn't like it. Even as he guffawed there was a mean glint in his eye that made me wary. Felice had looked in turn defiant, then alarmed, then frightened. Mariah seemed to offer her more consolation in the situation than Barney.

I thought that the group was gaining on me. No time to lose. "Come *on!*" I said to Lizzie, who was still resisting. "Lizzie, please . . . we can't do another thing for Alcina if they decide to beat us up or get a court order against us."

"I'm not happy about this, Merry."

"That makes two of us." I needed to think about this, how to contact Alcina personally — I had a definite feeling it wasn't going to be easy—and how to get her away from there. It wasn't going to happen in the middle of Lizzie's cyclone of fury. She had stopped resisting, but she was dead weight, stumbling along beside me like a drunken sorority girl after a frat party. I hauled her all the way back to the gate, beyond which I had parked the car. I pushed her through the gap between the padlocked gate and the fence and followed, pulling at my snagged blouse and ripping it away from the chain link it was caught on.

"Damn! This is a Michael Kors and now it's ruined."

Lizzie growled, "Boo fricken' hoo."

I marched her to the car and shoved her into the passenger side, slammed the car door and took the driver's seat. We were swiftly on the highway headed anywhere but there. Lizzie twisted awkwardly in the passenger's seat, her seat belt straining, so she could glare at me as she ranted and raved about Felice, Alcina, the encampment, and my own traitorous behavior hauling her away from there.

I drove and appeared to listen, nodding and uh-huhing occasionally, but my mind was disengaged. All the horrible things that man had said to me in town played back in my mind. I hated to think that Alcina, that lovely, delicate, true-minded sweet fairy child was now his "daughter"—I shuddered—and subjected to who knew what teachings in their school. I trusted Alcina's good sense to see the falsity of it all, but it must be hard on her. How could Felice allow it? I had thought of her as a good mother, but she was making me doubt it, as I thought of Alcina.

The only bright spot, as I saw it, was that in Ridley Ridge Barney had seemed truly kindly toward the child he had seen; maybe grown women were a bane, but children were safe from scrutiny. I hoped that was true and our young friend had nothing to fear.

I considered what I knew of Felice. With her husband and two children she had lived off the grid for a few years in an old gothic monstrosity of a farmhouse that, as far as I knew, the family still owned as the adults went through a divorce. The father was a long-distance truck driver and had supported his wife as she went through some kind of devastating illness from which she had apparently miraculously recovered. It was all odd, down to the fact that the dad had custody of their son, while she kept custody of Alcina.

I needed to find out more about this cult, with the new added twist of polygamy and what appeared to be underage marriage, if Gordy's determination to wed Peaches was anything to go by. And I was still worried . . . I hadn't had a chance to determine if there were any other of the missing girls on Urquhart's list at the camp, though I had seen some teen girls among the females gathered. Could the police use Cecily's presence, even though it was voluntary, to go onto the property to find out?

"So, what are we going to do about it?"

"What?" I said.

"Everything I said!" Lizzie shrieked in my ear, flinging her hands up in a gesture of ire. "What do you mean *what*? Weren't you *listening*?"

"Only dogs could have heard what you were saying," I said, glancing over at her as I turned onto the main street in Autumn Vale. "So settle down and tell me what you said in ten words or less." I could see her counting in her mind even as she fumed and glared out the car window.

"Okay, so . . . how do we get Alcina away from that band of raving lunatics?"

It was so exactly what I had been thinking that I smiled as I pulled up to Golden Acres and parked on the street. It was Lizzie's day to volunteer and I had promised to drop her off there after our field trip. I undid my seat belt and turned to look at her. "That's twelve words. Fourteen if you count *okay, so*. You could have left out *raving*."

"Ergh!" she growled. "I don't know what you're grinning about. This is serious."

"It is. And I was smiling because what you said is exactly what I was trying to figure out while I was *not* listening to you. I'm going to do some research, talk to Virgil, and we'll figure something out. I do *not* want that child there any longer than she has to be, but she's still underage and in Felice's care. We can't do anything that will be like kidnapping."

"To hell with that! I'm all for kidnapping," she said as she yanked her scrunchie out of her hair and rebundled it, trying to make it neater. She pulled a second scrunchie off her wrist and used both to restrain her riotous mop. "We can hide her in the castle. You've got an attic."

Wouldn't that look special to the outside world? I thought . . . *Crazy woman kidnaps adolescent and chains her in attic of haunted castle.* "Kiddo, I get it. I'm anxious too. But we have to do this right," I said, watching her. Her face, from being spotty and unformed, was narrowing into the planes of adulthood. She had grown up so much in the three years I had known her. I reached out and tucked a stray hair behind her ear. "Maybe we can get Alcina's father involved. He may not even know how she's living. But we have to go carefully. She doesn't appear to be in any immediate danger. *Promise* me you won't do anything stupid!"

"All right. Okay," she grunted, heaving herself out of the passenger's side, grabbing her backpack and camera from the back-seat and slamming the door shut.

"Hey, wait!" I pushed the button to roll down the windows. She leaned in. "You're coming out to the castle to take more pics of the carriage house before they start working on it?" She nodded. "Don't off-load the photos of the encampment. I'd like to see them. So let's talk. Text me."

I drove back to the heart of town, parked and headed on foot down a side street to the library, Hannah's haven, marked by a simple sign that dangles over the narrow sidewalk: *Autumn Vale Community Library.* It's kind of a dingy space, with concrete block walls painted gray, florescent lighting, tables filling the interior and shelves lining the walls. High windows allow in light but give no view of the outside. The library was open, and there were a few patrons, Helen Johnson among them.

"Helen, how nice to see you!" I said as she leaped up from where she was perusing a book on the Johnson family, one of the oldest in Autumn Vale, concurrent with the Wynter family, she had told me in the past. She's a neat older woman, always dressed in comfortable mall-ish clothes off the sale rack in J. C. Penney, or if she's splurging, Macy's. I hugged her and she grasped my arm in an iron-tight grip. We made small talk as I plotted how to escape her clutching hand, chatting mostly about her latest project with the church, a mission to some less-fortunate families living in the valley between Autumn Vale and Ridley Ridge. There had been local flooding in the spring, and a few of the families were still struggling to rebuild. Turner Construction had donated time and labor, but could only afford to do so much, so Reverend Maitland of the Methodist church was recruiting local fellows to help get the places ready for winter. Helen's husband, a retiree, was organizing, she told me.

"Zeke has promised to do some of their wiring so they will have access to the internet," Helen said, stealing a sly glance at Hannah and smiling. "He's such a blessing, that boy!"

Hannah's cheeks pinked, but, her nose in a book, she gave no other sign of hearing. Helen kept talking, and I kept nodding while trying to pull my arm out of her grasp. Her conversation required no other participation, since it consisted of things I had heard before, or that didn't matter to me.

Isadore Openshaw was there too, eating an apple as she read a book. She's a local eccentric. She was not born and raised in Autumn Vale, but came here to live with a relative who then died and left her his house, she being the only kin he had. She had been a teller at the bank run by my friend Janice Grover's husband, Simon, but she was caught up in the scandal that almost closed the bank and hadn't been back to work there since. After a long period of perilous unemployment, she found work at the local coffee shop bussing tables and washing dishes.

She keeps to herself. Isadore is a friend to Hannah because Hannah doesn't push. Instead, she pulls, asking Isadore for her help in the library. The woman shelves books, sorts donations, and also repairs damage, fixing dog-earred page corners and cleaning covers. Helen and Isadore have kind of an uneasy friendship, mostly one-sided, a determined effort on Helen's part to comfort the afflicted even when they don't want comforting. I do like Helen; she has a good heart. She also has a delicate sense of grievance, and an erratic attention to detail. I listen more than I want to because to pull away too soon is to upset that delicate sensibility.

I finally managed to extricate myself and she went back to her reading. Isadore hastily hid a grin as I glanced her way. I nodded to her and headed to Hannah, pulling a chair up next to her power wheelchair.

"Did you see Gordy?" she asked, setting her book aside.

I nodded. "I'm not going to sugarcoat it, Hannah. I'm worried." I quietly told her everything as she listened intently, occasionally interjecting a question. "Trouble is, he seems happier and more focused than he has since I've known him. How can we argue that he's better off away from them if that is the effect the place has had? And he says he's getting married. Peaches seems like a sweet girl, too." I shrugged.

"Peaches? Is that her real name?"

"Why?"

Hannah chewed her lip. "What did she look like?"

"Uh . . . well, I'd say she's fifteen, but she could be older. She was about five six, thin, with long, *long* light brown hair."

Hannah had been scanning her computer and tapping things in. She nodded and said, "Is one of these her?" She turned the monitor toward me. She was on a website of missing and exploited children.

Given Virgil and Urquhart's conversation of the other night, how could I have missed that possibility? I had been looking for some of the missing girls, and yet didn't even consider Peaches. Maybe it was because of my trust in Gordy; I know he would never intentionally exploit a young runaway, but still . . . I looked them over and lingered on one photo. It was of Madison Pinker, fourteen at the time of her disappearance from her home in a nearby small town, Pavilion, New York, over a year ago. Madison was one of the girls on Urquhart's list. I checked her date of birth; she'd be barely sixteen now.

"That could be her," I said, my voice tight as I pointed to the picture on the screen. "I only saw Peaches for a minute, and she's thinner than this girl. But the cheekbones and the eyes . . . kind of hollow." My heart was pounding. "What should we do?"

"How sure are you it's her?" Hannah said.

"Not sure at all," I murmured, staring at it. "I wish I was. This could be real bad for Gordy if it *is* her. She's underage and it's questionable how she got to the encampment." I met my friend's worried gaze. "Hannah, if it *is* Madison Pinker, Gordy could wind up in prison. I mean, he's twelve or more years older than this girl."

Hannah's eyes welled with tears, and one rolled down her cheek. "We have to do something," she whispered. "I've known Gordy my whole life. He'd never do anything wrong like this."

"Unless he didn't *understand* what he was doing was wrong. Hannah, he's always been super gullible. You know that. If someone talked to him long and hard, he could be convinced. One of the guys there said something about it being their duty to procreate; I know he has kind of a doomsday idea among the conspiracies he believes. If he thought this was the right thing, his duty to the earth . . ." I sighed, unsure of what to think, or what to do. "Gordy has never seemed to have that . . . that core of common sense to battle the far reaches of insane conspiracy theories." Hannah had stated aloud what I believed: Gordy would never do anything to hurt anyone else. That I knew, to the bottom of my heart. But as the unwitting tool of a user like the prophet . . . ? "We do have to do *something*."

"But what?" Hannah said, deep worry threading her tone. "What can we do without getting Gordy into trouble?"

That was the problem; I didn't know. "Normally I would just call in the police, but I am not sure it's that girl. Not sure *at all*, not even fifty percent. And if it's not . . . I could be wrong about Peaches's age. She could be twenty, for all I know. I can't let it go, though. I'll talk to Virgil about it." Given his and Urquhart's strong friendship, and their work on the missing girls project, he'd know what to do.

"That's a good idea," Hannah said with a sigh of relief. "I'll tell Zeke what you're doing."

I was mulling an idea, and finally said, "That encampment would be a dandy place for fugitives to hide out. I wonder, is there a way to check on that possibility?"

Hannah chewed her lip. "I don't know, Merry. Given how big the country is, and that someone could come from anywhere and end up here, it's unlikely we could be exhaustive, but we *could* start with the FBI list, I guess."

She found an online list of the FBI's most wanted, but I could see right away that it was going to be useless. There were *hundreds* of fugitives on the list, and I didn't know what I was looking for. It was an exercise in futility. "Gosh, so many wanted. Who knew there were this many fugitives on the streets? And some of these names! Bart Sampson, Aron Danger . . . look, there is literally a John Doe. Their real names sound like fake names."

Mug shots have to be the most misleading photography in the world, I thought, looking through the photo gallery of the wanted. My former employer, Leatrice Pugeot, had been arrested a couple of times for disorderly conduct—she was often drunk, stoned, or both—and it was hard to recognize the high fashion model in the blotchy, disheveled, cross-eyed mug shot. These guys, the most wanted — *mostly* guys, anyway, with the occasionally disgruntled-looking female — were a rogue's gallery of men sporting tattoos, a few with skinhead affiliations, and various piercings, even one eyebrow pierced. But mostly underneath the dirty hair they would have been pretty normal-looking dudes, despite the occasional facial scar from a fight with the cops, like one guy, the real John Doe, who had a gash in his forehead right up into his hair.

They had simply been caught and photographed on the worst day of their life. I sighed and shook my head, pushing away from the desk. "I don't know what I thought we'd stumble on to. Wishful thinking, I guess, that I'd find this so-called prophet on the list and be able to clear the whole camp and free Gordy, Felice, and Alcina."

"Free them from their own decisions? You know that wouldn't work, Merry," Hannah said gently. "We'll have to find another way to get Gordy back."

We left it at that. I exited the library, but as I walked down the street I felt a tap on my shoulder and whirled around. It was Isadore. She stood before me, her gaze sliding away from me to the street sign.

Finally I said, "Do you need anything?"

She nodded. "I want to help," she said, still looking off down the street, her prominent gooseberry green eyes shifting nervously.

"Help?"

"Help. With . . . with those people."

"At the compound?"

She nodded again. "I was driving an old lady to a doctor's appointment in Ridley Ridge," she said, her voice scratchy, like she was out of practice talking.

I know that for a modest sum she drives folks without cars; it's a side hustle for extra money to keep gas in and insurance on her car. Strictly speaking it isn't legal, but no one so far had complained or turned her in.

"This jackhole on the street there, in Ridley Ridge, a guy with a big sign, said I shouldn't be driving. *Women shouldn't drive*, he said."

I stifled a smile. Barney strikes again, I thought, pleasant chappie that he is. I waited, the best way to get more from Isadore. If you urge her on, sometimes she clams up and retreats.

"I told him to drop dead. I said, *this isn't Saudi Arabia, you know.* A van picked him up . . . Light and the Way, it said. Then I saw this sign on a post. That place . . . the compound place . . . they're looking for a bookkeeper." A ghost of a smile fluttered over her thin lips. "I could go and work for them. Find things out."

I was startled. Of all the things I had thought she might say, that was not among the possibilities. A bookkeeper? "I appreciate the offer or . . ." I shook my head, unsure if her taking the bookkeeping job was an offer to help me or what. Or *how.* "But Isadore, unless you're a member of the group it seems that they frown on outsiders."

She glowered. "They wouldn't advertise for a bookkeeper unless they were looking for an outsider. I can look after myself."

She had a point there. I hesitated, then said, "But given their feelings about women, how do you know the prophet would hire you?"

"They don't have much money, right?"

"I don't know but I'm assuming not. I can't even figure out why they need a bookkeeper."

She twisted her lips, screwing them up into a tight bud. Her glance flitted to meet mine, then slewed away, down the street. "Maybe they want to file for a church tax exemption with the IRS. To do that, they'd need their books in order."

She might be right; maybe the prophet had bigger plans than his ramshackle cultish compound. He wouldn't be the first leader to begin humbly and build an empire by promising a reward in heaven in exchange for all your money here on earth. And I had been wondering what his stake in it all was. Maybe there was some way to profit by being a prophet. "But what does any of this have to do with hiring a woman?"

"He'd assume a woman bookkeeper would work for less than a man."

She was right; bigots are usually hypocrites, too. "He'll assume a woman *should* work for less than a man." I paused, considering what Isadore was offering to do, though I still wasn't clear on her intent. She's an older woman of some indefinite age between fifty and seventy. It wouldn't be right to encourage her to go into a situation like that alone. "It seems dangerous to me."

She snorted, still looking off down the street. "They won't think I'm a threat."

"But what could you find out?"

"Won't know until I'm there."

I shook my head and crossed my arms. It was late in the afternoon. The weather had turned. In the northern states in October, we can go from midsummer heat to a wintry blast in hours, and the temperature was on a downward trend. A thread of niggling worry wormed through my stomach. "I can't stop you, Isadore, but I won't encourage you."

"It's my day off. I'll go out there now. I'll tell Hannah if I find anything out." She whirled and headed back into the library.

It was about four by the time I got to the castle. I pulled into the new paved parking area by the castle and picked a spot between Pish's shiny black Buick and a rental car. I had muffin orders for the next day and needed to get them started, as well as packaging up the muffins I had already baked. I entered the castle to find that Pish was giving a tour to a group of folks. These must be important people, I thought, because the huge vases were full of fresh flowers, gentle classical music tinkled through the sound system, and the place was spotless, gleaming and lovely. They had finished, it appeared, in the great hall, with light streaming through the elegant rose window.

"Ah, and as we finish up here is Merry Wynter herself!" He surged forward, giving me a kiss on both cheeks. "Smile, sweetheart; you look forlorn," he muttered in my ear. He looped his arm through mine and turned me, as I pasted on a big smile. "Merry, this is the legendary composer Anokhi Auretius. She was on her way home to the city from the west coast and made some time to visit us here, to talk about our plans."

"Ms. Wynter, pleasure to meet you." She was tall, with very dark skin that glowed in the multicolored light shed by our rose window. She wore an amazing couture dress with a capelet that emphasized wide shoulders. Her voice was melodic, like an oboe.

"Just Merry, please, Ms. Auretius." I held out my hand and she took it in both of hers. "Of course I know who this is, Pish." I met her gaze. "You were guest composer for the LSO back in the early two thousands. Pish took me to one of your concerts." Her work was experimental, and my untutored ear found some of it discordant, and yet . . . and yet I had ended the evening in tears, overcome with emotion. It was like the concert had taken me on a poignant journey, though I didn't understand it. Pish said her work is groundbreaking, and I trust his judgment.

"Call me Anokhi, please."

"Anokhi, it's an honor to have you here. I enjoy your work so much!"

"Thank you." She swiveled and gestured with one graceful sweep of her long-fingered hand. "This is my daughter, Sebastienne, and her husband, Grant."

The couple, she a fashion plate and he a pale cipher in tweed, looked solemn and nodded, then turned toward each other and whispered, the sound echoing in my great hall like wind through dried grass.

"Pish has graciously given us a tour of your lovely castle, and now we *must* be on our way. It was the briefest of stopovers, and now we head to the airport in Buffalo," Anokhi said, tucking a capacious Birkin bag (a design I had lusted over but couldn't afford) under her arm and looking toward the door.

"It was nice to meet you. Are you thinking of using our facility once it is built?"

She turned back to me. "I'll consider it. The Lexington has offered me another guest position in two years. I haven't agreed yet. Pish, if you'd be so kind as to send me the performance hall specs when you have them, it will help immeasurably."

"Of course, my dearest Anokhi. We're finalizing design specs now, working with a company that has constructed many performance halls." They embraced and did the triple cheek kiss.

We shook hands all around, and Pish walked them out as I headed to the kitchen. I put the muffins I had baked earlier into tubs. I then got out baking supplies. Again. Tomorrow was muffin delivery day, and I was behind, so I thought I'd make some extras and get ahead of myself. I got out my phone and looked at my muffin orders. The small business I run, making muffins for various Autumn Vale and Ridley Ridge cafés and other places, is not especially lucrative, but it *is* a way of connecting with the community and keeping in good with folks. What Pish and I were trying to do was causing waves among locals, so it behooved me to be a friendly public face.

I looked up as Pish entered the kitchen and filled the kettle. "She didn't seem overly impressed," I said, getting out mixing bowls and my new stand mixer. Five dozen bran, two dozen each of carrot and banana nut, and four dozen cheddar and herb muffins, coming up. I already had the cheddar muffins made, but needed to get busy with the rest. I would make the batter, put it into baking cups and freeze it. That way I could make as many or as few as I wanted at a time. All I'd have to do was come back to the castle and bake off what I needed to fill all the orders. I had new double ovens installed in the kitchen for that very reason, as well as the large commercial oven in the range my great-uncle Melvyn had installed. "Is everything okay with the performance hall? Are other artists wary?"

He shrugged wearily as he padded around the kitchen in his slippers and sweater. He put the kettle on the front burner and turned the knob; it lit with a *whoof*. He then got out the big teapot and some rooibos tea. He likes the earthy flavor of the African herbal brew, which he discovered while traveling. "I couldn't convey our vision and she doesn't trust the construction company specs. I think I need some renderings . . . expert drawings, a vision board. *Something*."

The theater design was a dome, which was the least expensive and best we could find. There were examples out there, built by the same company. But perhaps now was not the time for bracing suggestions. Maybe he needed a friend. I went to him, put my arms around him and laid my head on his shoulder. He stroked my back. "My darling Pish, you'll soldier through."

"I'm tired, my dearest."

"Maybe you need a vacation," I said, straightening and examining the lines around his eyes and the softening of his jawline. "Go to the city. Visit your mum. Attend the theater. Find a few scandalous boys to entertain you."

"I think I'm too old for scandalous boys now," he replied.

"You're *never* too old for scandalous boys." I kissed his cheek loudly, then went back to my batter.

He chuckled.

"If it makes you feel any better, make it a business trip. See

Roma," I said, naming Roma Toscana, the operatic soprano, who would be headlining our grand opening, whenever that happened. I loathe her; I think she is an emotional vampire and mean girl. However . . . she is Pish's friend and very talented so we make sickly sweet nicey-nice to each other. In his presence, anyway. "Maybe you can check in with the LSO's stage coordinator. He can help convince Anokhi to give us a chance. Or maybe Liliana can talk to her. She's on board. Do she and Anokhi know each other?"

"They do. It's a thought."

I knew he was worrying about how other artists would feel about our facility. Getting them to see our vision and commit time and resources to it was proving to be a tough sell in some cases. Pish was risking his own money, but also donors' money and the LSO's future. It was terrifying. "If you go to the city you can take a meeting with the construction company. There's nothing like face-to-face."

"Maybe," he said, picking up his mug of reddish brew. "Or maybe I need to buck up, buttercup, and stop whining." He kissed my forehead and headed out the door. "I'm going to make some calls to try to get the LSO creative director to speak with Anokhi."

I did what I had to do, and by the time I was done I had little muffin pucks frozen and a pail of resilient bran muffin batter in the fridge. I cleaned the kitchen, put on the dishwasher, then carried the stacked tubs of muffins for the next morning out to the car. Becket trailed me out and hopped into the passenger's seat, taking the lift, for once. We drove the short distance to the house.

I was finishing up some routine chores at home when my phone pinged. A text from Virgil. Something had come up, he said. He was coming home, but would probably be going out again almost immediately. I texted back that I would make him something to eat. I had something I needed to tell him, and hoped he was in a mood to listen.

A half hour later he came into the kitchen. I had made him a grilled Reuben, one of his favorites, and set it on the breakfast bar. "What's up?" I asked as I made him a cup of coffee.

He looked worried. "A girl was just found along the road."

I froze, a prickle along my spine, and everything I had intended to say flew out of my mind. "A girl? What do you mean?"

"Dead. A girl was found dead." He swiped his big hand over his face. "The poor kid . . . not more than fifteen or so, a pretty teenager, long brown hair, long dress, big coat . . . dead. Some folks leaving here found her."

Chapter Nine

"A teenage girl, dead?" My heart thudded and I felt sick. I collapsed on a stool opposite him. "And found by people from here? Virgil, what do you mean?"

"Pish had some visitors, right? From New York City?"

"Yes, Anokhi Auretius—she's a composer—and her daughter and son-in-law were here to tour the castle and talk to Pish about a possible guest composer residency once we have the Wynter Woods Performing Arts Center up and running. They left about . . . oh, four fifteen or so. They were heading to Buffalo to catch a flight back to the city. What happened?"

"They were driving along the highway when they saw what they thought was an injured or dead animal along the side of the road. It was already getting dark, but they stopped to help. It was a body or . . . a girl who would soon be a body."

"Oh, no . . . she was alive when they found her?"

He nodded.

"But she's dead now? That's . . . awful." My mind was racing. A teenage girl? Thank goodness I knew where Lizzie was or I'd be worried, though Virgil would have told me immediately if it was someone I knew. But wait . . . "This teenage girl had long brown hair? And a long dress?" I was thinking of Peaches, hoping it wasn't her.

"Yeah, why? Do you recognize the description?"

I told him about my visit to the compound, and meeting Peaches, Gordy's girlfriend. I told him everything, including finding Cecily Smith there, and that she was there voluntarily—they could take her off the missing list—and my fear of who Peaches might be. He ruminated on what I told him, gulping down his sandwich in wolfish bites. I refilled his coffee and buttered one of the mandarin orange cranberry chocolate chip muffins I had experimented with that morning. He ate it, nodding enthusiastically. I don't think I had ever tried a muffin recipe on him that he *didn't* like.

"Okay. I gotta go," he said, wiping his mouth and dusting crumbs from his hands.

I bolted up from my stool. "Wait, aren't you going to tell me more?"

"When I know more, I'll tell you what I can. But right now Baxter is up to his eyebrows, and it's not going well."

"What do you mean?"

He took me in his arms and gazed into my eyes, swiping strands of hair off my forehead. "Look, the reason I wanted to talk to you is, Baxter has made a few missteps and things with the New York folk aren't going well."

"What does that mean?"

"He's stepped in it good, it sounds like. Offended them with . . . implications."

"Implications? Like . . . they're involved somehow?"

He nodded. "Baxter swears he said no such thing. But now there are lawyers involved, and the composer woman is talking about how she's going to tell everyone back in the city how she was treated."

"Oh, crap." I put my forehead to his chest, then looked back up at him. "This is awful!"

"Baxter swears he didn't say anything of the kind, and it actually sounds like the composer and her daughter were cool at first, understanding that as the ones who found the body, they needed to stay and give statements. They've missed their flight, of course, but it doesn't sound like they made a fuss over that, at least at first. It's the son-in-law, Grant Marbaugh, who is making trouble. He's the one who called a lawyer, who is now on his way to Ridley Ridge airport by private plane."

The full implications began to sink in. Self-interest will assert itself. If this became a big stink, it could easily damage our fledgling performing arts center's reputation before it even held its opening. Anokhi Auretius was a big deal in the arts community; if she loudly complained of her treatment by the Ridley Ridge police, it would be hard to counteract.

But there was a dead teenage girl. There were parents somewhere who would learn of her death and be devastated. There were friends and family members who would never be the same. What if it was Peaches, the sweet girl I had seen hours before?

"Can I help in any way? Should Pish and I come and talk to Anokhi?"

"I may be able to smooth things over. That's why Baxter has

called me in." He kissed me thoroughly. "I wanted to give you the heads-up because I *may* need you or Pish. I'll call you later."

I called Pish and had a long discussion about what I had learned. We mulled it over, dissected it, told each other our worries, then at long last signed off. I went to bed alone except for Becket, who took the opportunity of Virgil being absent to snuggle. I buried my face in his fur and worried myself to sleep.

• • •

All hell broke loose the next morning. As Virgil (who had come home in the middle of the night) showered, his phone blew up with texts, voice messages and social media alerts. I sat on the closed toilet and read them to him, raising my voice over the splash of the multiple showerheads he had insisted on, as I had on the jetted tub.

The lawyer Marbaugh had summoned was a well-known New York City attorney who specialized in cases of racial discrimination and religious bias. He had a reputation for doggedly pursuing police forces, especially in cases of racism and racial profiling. I didn't know what to think; as much as I was not fond of Sheriff Baxter, I had never thought he might be a bigot. I hoped any problems or misunderstandings could be straightened out without a high-profile lawsuit against Sheriff Baxter and his sheriff's department.

I checked local news sites to see what reporters may have sniffed out. "Oh, no, Virgil!" I cried. "We discussed Baxter trying to involve the ATF in the problems they were having with the Light and the Way Ministry folks, right? Well, it looks like he couldn't get them, so he raided the compound himself, overnight!"

Virgil, water streaming down his face and over his chest, ducked out from behind the glass enclosure. "You've got to be joking."

"I'm not!" I said, holding up his man-size phone. Virgil does not like teeny devices, so his phone is almost tablet size. "It's on the *Ridley Ridge Record* site! He took someone—more than one person, it sounds like—into custody, but they don't say who he nabbed."

"Shit!" he yelled, hammering on the tile. "I told him to stay cool, to not go in guns blazing. He was talking crazy, like he was going to go in even if he couldn't get a warrant. Damn it!"

"Why would he do that? Is there a definite connection between the dead girl and the compound?"

Virgil wiped water and soap out of his eyes. "Nothing firm. When I left him at about one in the morning I thought I had him calmed down. He's just . . . he's getting . . . damn!" He slapped the tile wall again, splattering soapy water. That was a troublesome sign, since he generally doesn't go for displays of emotion. "I wish he listened to me!"

"When has Ben Baxter *ever* listened to you?" I said lightly, though my chest tightened with worry. If Virgil thought it was bad, it was bad. I worried that Gordy was among those detained. I worried that Peaches was the girl found dead. There was no confirmation of the dead girl's identity so far.

I texted Pish quickly, and he replied almost instantly. He had been in contact with the composer. Fortunately, Anokhi Auretius and her family had left Ridley Ridge and were already on a flight to New York City, not because of her son-in-law's lawyer, but just because there was no reason for them to be there once they had given their statements, as Baxter had said all along. The son-in-law had overreacted but Anokhi and her daughter had prevailed, she told Pish, and all had been smoothed out. If necessary, she was willing to make a public statement to that effect.

Virgil finished up his shower and I made him breakfast as he paced on the back patio, alternately screaming into his phone and listening intently, then scrolling through messages.

"Virgil, breakfast!" I yelled out the back door.

He came in and sat down to eggs, bacon, hash browns and pancakes. I knew him well enough to know he would be gone until evening, and when would he get a chance to eat decent food again? It would probably be awful sheriff's department coffee for the rest of the day.

I drank my coffee and waited, then as he slowed, I asked him, "Why the heck did Baxter raid the compound? What was he hoping to find? And what did he find that resulted in anyone being taken into custody?"

He mopped up egg yolk with toast and sighed, shaking his head. "I knew what he wanted to do; he was waiting for a warrant. With this murder investigation I advised him to put it on ice until we knew more. If we could prove that the victim was from the compound, we'd have more ammo going in and could broaden our search. As it was, he didn't have much, rumors and innuendo from some shaky sources." He chewed, swallowed, and slurped some coffee. "Historically, raids of so-called religious compounds haven't gone well."

I nodded. Every American knows about Ruby Ridge, and Branch Davidian, among others less famous. My husband had been reading up on it lately, worried about Ben's new fixation on the Light and the Way Ministry compound (after ignoring it for years) and fears that there was another Waco in the offing. From what we had discussed, I understood the concern; what all of those raids had in common was that the religious philosophy at the center of it had an end-of-times flavor. Virgil was right, though, in my opinion, in his advice to proceed with caution. "So . . . what did you find out about last night's raid?"

"Well, you already know that Baxter claimed to have information—and he won't tell me where he got it—that the so-called prophet had a cache of weapons."

"That's why he was trying to get the ATF involved."

"Day before yesterday they backed off, though, refused him assistance. I can only guess *they* didn't consider his info strong enough." He sighed heavily and rubbed the back of his neck, a sign he was deeply perturbed. "Ben's never been a Rambo whack job. He *must* have some reason for doing what he did, but I'm damned if I can figure it out. He truly was worried about letting it get too far until the place became a fortified compound."

I got up and poured myself another coffee as Becket wound around my legs. I opened another can of food for him—he had had first breakfast and would bug me until he had second breakfast, like some Middle-earth feline Hobbit—and then topped my coffee with milk. I sat down and gazed at Virgil. "But I was out there; I didn't see any hint of weapons. I could have told Ben that."

"You weren't inside any of the buildings though, right?"

I nodded. "I get it. But this is a muddle, husband. Are you going to get involved?" It could be messy.

"I am," he said, standing and stretching.

"Do you know, though . . . did they arrest anyone? Did they find anything?"

"As far as I know he detained a couple of the men, but he won't be able to hold them for long. I'll know more later, hon. I gotta go. Do you want help with the dishes?"

"That's what machines are for." I circled the breakfast bar and put my arms around him. "You do what you need to do. I'll be delivering muffins today. But Virgil . . ." I pushed my fingers through his thick dark hair and scratched his beard scruff along his jaw. "If you find out who that poor girl is, can you text me?" I was haunted with worry, and anxious that I had somehow missed some vital clue at the encampment. Could I have stopped what happened? I took a deep breath. We hadn't even established that the poor girl was from the Light and the Way compound. "And if Gordy was snapped up in the raid, can you let me know that, too? I'm worried about him."

"You know I'll do my best to help him if he's in trouble. But I don't think this raid netted Ben anything. I'll know more soon."

We kissed, a lovely, long lingering smooch that left me tingling, and he departed. I got dressed appropriately, in nice slacks and a belted cardigan over a tunic—the day was dramatically colder than the day before, and the gleaming sunlight had a chilly crystalline quality—then loaded muffin tubs in the car as Becket departed, no doubt heading to the woods for some huntin'. "Don't bring me any mice!" I called out. His tail flipped a jaunty wave and he disappeared around the corner of the house.

I drove past the castle. Pish had a videoconference that would take him most of the morning, which I knew from our dozen or so texts already that morning. The Anokhi situation was, indeed, calm; she had landed in New York, none the worse for wear. Anokhi told Pish that a very handsome fellow had arrived at the police station and sorted things out with the sheriff, after which they were free to go, and they had departed, making their way to Buffalo in plenty of time to catch the earliest flight to the city.

That very handsome fellow, for the uninformed, would have been my husband. It was after Virgil had done all of that work smoothing things over and finally left to return home that Sheriff Baxter had gone off his rocker and conducted a middle-of-the-night raid on the Light and the Way encampment.

I would catch up with Pish when I returned after lunch, which is when I decided I'd finish the rest of the muffins. I drove down the long curved lane and through the new stone pillars and to the highway, and thence to Autumn Vale. The town was buzzing with the news of the murder and the subsequent raid on the religious compound. I carried muffins into the coffee shop, which is reached by first walking through the variety store then up three steps to the coffee shop section, which appeared to be right out of an old movie, with original vinyl-covered chairs and scarred arborite tables. I plopped my tubs of muffins on the coffee counter and turned to view the diners, most of whom I knew by sight.

There was a town council meeting being held at one of the tables. My mother-in-law, Gogi, a newly elected member, was there, and while I lifted my hand in greeting and she waved back, she returned to her intense conversation with the other members. They had maps laid out, and seemed to be discussing the roads in and out of town. There were many local issues dividing the council, and that included arguments with township officials, who were dealing with increased truck traffic they blamed on Autumn Vale, though the town council disagreed vehemently, saying it had nothing to do with the town. They were attempting to prove it, and that was probably what they were discussing in the coffee shop. Maybe they should have been doing their business behind closed doors, but in Autumn Vale the coffee shop was as close to a public forum as you can get.

Such are the thorny local issues—roads and utilities and social services—that become major dramas.

But the more recent traumas occupied most of the villagers at the other tables, and the hum of conversation rose and fell, with the occasional Autumn Valeite becoming passionate enough to hammer on a table. Anyone who assumes they know what a person will think has never been in the middle of a small-town coffee shop argument. Both the murder and the raid by Sheriff Baxter were hot topics. Of course there was no argument about the murder, just drawn faces, worry over who was responsible, and pity for the girl's parents. But while there was consensus over the notion that those who lived at the Light and the Way Ministry compound were "a bunch of fruitcakes," there *was* argument over whether that made them dangerous nuts or not. There was equal representation on both sides.

I greeted Simon Grover, the now-retired husband of my opera-loving friend Janice Grover. He lifted one hand in a wave, then returned to his conversation with his tablemates. He loudly said that those Light and the Way people should have been run out of the area before having a chance to establish themselves. One of his Brotherhood of the Falcon buddies—that's one of those fraternal organizations endemic in small towns—insisted that America was a free country, not a commie land yet, thank God, and those religious nuts had every right to settle wherever they goldarned well pleased, as long as they followed the rules.

Isadore, silently, gloomily, clearing tables with a bus tray under one arm, caught my eye and motioned with her head. She needed to talk to me about something. I nodded and held up two fingers for two minutes. Mabel Thorpe, the manager of the coffee shop, was counting muffins—heaven forbid I should short them a banana nut muffin—and preparing a receipt for the money she was getting out of the till. She had dyed her short hair a new color . . . chartreuse, with stiff waves rippling back from her forehead.

I tuned back in to the conversations as Mabel recounted the money, which she would do twice more before counting it into my palm.

The prevailing opinion among most in the coffee shop was that Sheriff Baxter had mucked up the raid. A couple of people had been hurt—or claimed to be hurt, a nurse from the Ridley Ridge hospital said, a cynical edge to her tone, more stubbed toes than bleeding out—and no actual weapons had been found. A few men had been detained, but most had now been released without charges. It was vastly overblown. There were also some raised eyebrows over Sheriff Baxter's behavior of late, with hints of a mutiny among his deputies tossed into the mix.

I wondered what an equal conversation at the Ridley Ridge coffee shop would sound like.

As for the murder, no one yet had identified the dead girl, but there were plenty of raised brows and squinted eyes over her death. Maybe she was a hitchhiker. Maybe she was from some other part of the country, or state, or . . . from somewhere else. Unfortunately, there were also whispers that "outsiders" had found her. With those whispers came a whiff of blame, a hint of anger, and gazes slewed at me. I shifted uneasily; there had been a few murders in the three years or so I had been in Autumn Vale, but it wasn't like I had initiated the problem. In fact, I was responsible for solving several of them. I straightened, holding my head high, and met my friends and neighbors in the eye.

But bravado failed me and I slumped down on a stool, impatient for Mabel to be done so I could get out of there. I tapped my fingernails on the counter as I pondered Urquhart's list of missing young women; was the dead girl one of them? Virgil had, the minute I told him, shared the info with Dewayne that I had seen Cecily and that she was at the compound of her own free will, as far as I could tell. She had been kicked out of the house by her father, and had settled with the Light and the Way Ministry people in the wake of that familial disagreement. She was eighteen; no one could touch her.

I had also told him about Peaches, and about the photo I had seen of Madison Pinker, one of the missing girls. Peaches resembled her, I said, but I could not be sure. I was still sick with worry that she was the dead girl found along the highway. Virgil and Dewayne would follow up on it at some point with Urquhart and Baxter, but right now the murder and the raid would take precedence.

I nodded and smiled as a young woman I knew, the local lawyer's secretary, came in to buy take-out coffee. We chatted for a moment; their coffeemaker was on the fritz, which was the only reason she was buying takeout. She was an old friend of Hannah, and told me she was hoping Zeke was going to pop the question soon, so she could help plan a wedding. I took in a deep breath as she happily chattered, and glanced around the coffee shop. These people had become my friends and neighbors, and I was intimately involved in so many of the local goings-on. I had made friends. I had champions.

Then Pish and I had announced our plans. In our enthusiasm, we had expected that the news of our decision, to transform my castle and property into an arts community, would be welcomed with glad cries and gratitude. We saw the future and it was glorious: jobs, investment, new shops, new shoppers, new people.

What we had failed to appreciate was that we could not implant our vision into other people's brains. We couldn't force them to see how beneficial in the long run this would be for the town. And it was brought home to me that what I thought of as advantageous had another darker side. Property prices and taxes would inevitably go up. As for the shops I envisioned popping up to satisfy the tastes of the new people, would locals even be interested in what they had to sell? Would they be able to afford to shop there? And those people from New York City—musicians and writers and singers, fans of opera, literati and glitterati—meant that maybe Autumn Valeites would feel pushed out of their own friendly small-town ways. Would the new people blend with the old, or would there be a schism, an inevitable divide, with resentments building up on both sides?

Who *were* these people who would come? locals asked each other, these New Yorkers, and Los Angeleans, these coastal elite city people who would expect Autumn Vale to change overnight from their beloved home into some metropolis of wine-swilling, biscotti-munching, kale-growing artistes. I couldn't argue one truth: their town would inevitably change, and Valeites were not sure it would be for the better.

The secretary departed, laden with coffee in take-out cups and a bag of donuts. After Mabel paid me, I piled my muffin tubs together and, feeling lonely and out of sorts with the Autumn Vale community, headed to the door. Graciela had offered me an idea of how to begin to integrate our vision with our friends' lives. I would take her up on it.

I had almost forgotten Isadore. She waited for me outside, her gray hair still confined in a hairnet, pacing and muttering. She whirled and faced me. "I got the job, out there at that place," she said without any other greeting.

"You went out there? You weren't there when the sheriff raided it, were you?"

"'Course not, that was in the middle of the night. I was out there in the late afternoon."

"Of course, right . . . I knew that. So the prophet gave you the job. Did he tell you what he needed?"

She nodded. "Easy. He's got bookkeeping ledgers at some other place and he wants them tidied up, he said."

Tidied up . . . hmmm. "What did you think of him, of the prophet?"

"What d'you mean?"

"What do you think of him? What's he like?"

She looked mystified by my question. "I'll let you know if I find anything out." She turned to go back inside.

"Wait, Isadore . . . !" She could be exasperating. I had so many questions. "Did you see Gordy there?"

She nodded.

"Did he say anything to you?"

She shook her head.

"What did the place feel like to you?" She stared at me blankly. Maybe this wasn't going to help. She was not one to describe atmosphere, or her feelings about a place. I considered and asked, "Where did you go? Did anyone talk to you?"

"Yeah. The guy who runs the place—"

"The prophet."

"Yeah . . . him. He sat me down in this hut, no electricity or anything. And he told the woman who did the books to show me her system. Then he left. She didn't know anything about spread-sheets."

"Who is she?"

"Woman named Mariah."

"Aha! That's Barney's sister-wife," I said. "So they don't have a computer there?"

"Nope. Ledgers. I saw one of 'em. A mess."

"In what way?"

She screwed up her mouth and stared at the sky. "Things crossed out. Underlined."

"What kind of thing would ledgers for a place like that hold? I mean . . . ledgers for a religious community."

She stared at me and blinked. "You don't know anything about accounting, do you?"

"Guilty. Dumb it down."

"Don't know if I can," she said, and she was *not* teasing. She didn't know how to explain to me. She sighed. "They should have a general ledger that holds everything: assets, debits, credit, *everything*. Should cover income—tithes, donations, offerings—and expenses."

"Expenses like . . . ?"

"Mortgage—if they've got one—building costs, utilities, wages, gifts, food, support for congregants, since they live on-site."

"I get it. So . . . do you think the prophet may be planning to file for a tax exemption, like you mentioned?"

She frowned. "He didn't say that to me."

"Not yet, anyway. He may still." I was mystified by the whole bookkeeping thing. "Did you see where the prophet stays? Does he have his own hut?"

"It's someplace else where he keeps the ledgers, he said . . . that's all I know. I gotta go back out there."

"Someplace else? What does that mean?"

"He told me there was another place where the ledgers were kept. Someplace safe, he said. He told me next time to go further on Marker Road and turn off on Silver Creek Line. There's a place there, a house; he said I'd know it when I saw it from the *Trespassers Will Be Damned* sign on the gate."

That was a new one; quite the threat. "But he didn't tell you what the place was?"

She shrugged and grimaced. "Some place he lives, I guess. He called it his meditation center."

I frowned. He didn't even live with his congregants? Interesting. Thinking about the girl who had been found dead on the highway, I asked, "Did anything happen while you were there? I mean . . . was there any stir, or upset?"

She frowned and twisted her mouth, struggling to put something into words. Her gooseberry green eyes flickered with some emotion in their depths. "There was a big secret, it felt like, something . . . something going on."

She was struggling to put it into words and her gaze kept flicking away. She was uneasy talking this much.

"Like an undercurrent?" I said. "Something wrong that people weren't talking about?"

"I guess. Like I said, the prophet set me down to talk to the woman who did the books."

"Mariah," I filled in.

"She looked upset."

"In what way?"

"Like . . . like she'd been crying."

"Did she say why?"

Isadore shook her head. Intensely private herself, it was unlikely she'd ask what was bothering the woman. "Then that fellow who carries the sign—"

"Barney?" I said.

"Yeah. He came and got her. She said she wasn't finished, but he said to move her butt, that the prophet wanted to talk to her. She was to go to him right away."

Why would the prophet want to talk to Mariah when he had just told her to show Isadore her bookkeeping system? Interesting. "About what time was that, Isadore?"

"'Bout . . . I don't know. It was starting to get dark."

"How long had you been there?"

"Half hour."

"And you saw the prophet there the whole time?"

She shrugged. "I didn't follow him around, if that's what you mean."

"Okay." I could tell she had reached the end of her frayed tolerance for conversation. "Please, Isadore, be careful." I reached out and carefully, gently, hugged her. I let her go and she rocked back. "Maybe this isn't a good idea. Maybe you won't even *have* a job now that there was a raid on the place."

"I'll see tomorrow." She turned and stumped up the steps into the variety store.

I returned to my car and checked my phone. There was a terse text from Virgil. The murder victim had been identified.

Chapter Ten

He then texted *You saw a girl there, one on the list named Cecily Smith, right?*

Cecily? *She* was the victim? No!

It was like a punch to the gut. I stared at the text, then read the *next* line: Cecily, who was upset and crying, had told the deputies and Sheriff Baxter when they raided the camp that there was a girl missing, a girl named Glynnis Johnson. She had been there the day before but no one had seen her all that day. When she heard about a girl dead along the highway from the deputies who raided the camp, she got scared. There would be confirmation, but all the details matched, including the clothes Cecily told them Glynnis always wore. I was grateful the victim wasn't Cecily, Lizzie's friend, but still . . . a girl had been murdered.

Glynnis Johnson . . . she was on the missing girl list, as was Cecily, and both girls had gone missing at about the same time. To me, that made a strong connection between the Light and the Way Ministry and the missing girls, and a possible link to the murdered girls who had been found in the last few years. I was sure that Baxter, Urquhart, Virgil and Dewayne would have already made that connection and would be investigating it. I thought of all the men I had seen at the camp and knew there were others there, ones I hadn't seen. Was one of them a killer? And if so, why Glynnis?

The poor girl was found on the highway. Had she been running away from the cult, and had she been followed? Or had she been beaten in the camp and her body disposed of along the highway? I texted Virgil with what little I knew, and that Isadore had been at the encampment the day before the raid and had noted that there was a bit of a commotion, an older woman being hastily summoned by the prophet. That could have nothing to do with Glynnis, of course. I texted an additional note, asking if he knew if Cecily wanted to leave yet. I was more than uneasy about the girl still being at the encampment.

It was early, but I was tired already. Maybe I was overdue for a visit with my favorite nonagenarian, my substitute father/uncle/grandfather Doc English, the only fellow who had known most members of my family, including my actual grandfather, great-uncle and father. It's a complicated history, but my father had fallen out with his uncle over the accidental death of his father. That lasted until my father died, when I was five. My mother, a strong-willed social justice warrior, had visited Melvyn Wynter, my great-uncle, once, but they had a huge fight and she never spoke of him again, apparently throwing out his letters unopened. My memory of that long-ago visit as a five-year-old was kneeling in the backseat of the car waving to my uncle Melvyn out the back window.

Doc English had filled in lots of holes in my family history. He's failing, somewhat, lately. It scares me, how bad his health is getting, but I'm holding on to him tenaciously. He can't die, I've told him. I'm not ready to lose him. A visit and talk was just what the Doc ordered. I found him in the front living room of Golden Acres, which was once a house, but with a modern addition built on the back was now the retirement residence and long-term care home owned and operated by my mother-in-law.

"What's up, Doc?" I said, dropping onto the vinyl sofa beside him.

He let his bottle-bottom glasses slip down his beaky age-spotted nose and eyed me rheumily over the top edge while holding up his book. "Young lady, I'm reading philosophy and *Kant* be disturbed!" He tapped the book's cover, which is the only way I knew he was making a pun.

I groaned, then chuckled obediently. "Did anyone ever tell you you're a hoot?" I eyed him affectionately, from his balding age-spotted pate to his bandaged foot. "Feet giving you trouble still?"

"Whatya gonna do?" he said. "Diabetes is a bitch. Diabetes and gout combined are a bitch and a bastard."

"Mmm." It was meant to be a sympathetic noise. He'd been having trouble with wounds on his feet not healing, but at his age there was always something, he ofttimes said. As a medical doctor who took his training after World War Two on the GI Bill, he knew what to expect and he knew how to take care of it. Conversations between him and his physician invariably wandered off into medical lingo that left me scratching my head.

He grabbed a smudgy tablet from the side table and turned it on, his arthritic gnarled fingers tapping unsteadily at the screen. "What's this all about?" he asked, handing it over to me.

It was the front page of the *Ridley Ridge Record*. There were multiple local stories and some national: there had been a mosque bombing in Michigan, but no one had been injured; someone had been caught at the Canadian border smuggling drugs in a semi with specially welded compartments cunningly fitted into it; and the latest national job numbers were not encouraging. But the two stories that held my attention were strictly local: one was about the body found on the highway by renowned composer Anokhi Auretius, on her way to the airport after consulting with the owners about the new theater and recording facility being planned at infamous Wynter Castle; and another about Sheriff Baxter's unfortunate raid on the Light and the Way Ministry compound.

I clicked on and read both articles. The newspaper was highly critical of the sheriff's decisions, and quoted an unnamed ATF source as saying there was no proof the religious group was planning anything at all. Another source said the raid had netted nothing: no guns, no drugs, no crime. There was much more; the story had been updated to indicate that the dead girl was known to be a local runaway who had apparently been at the religious camp for some time, but, according to Prophet Voorhees, had left of her own free will that very day. What happened to her clearly happened in the outside world, not in their safe and sanctified compound. Though Voorhees had been detained for questioning, the paper said, he and others picked up during the raid were most likely going to be released. A civil liberties lawyer who had been in Ridley Ridge on another case (that was the one Anokhi's son-in-law had called in, no doubt!) had been about to book a flight out of the tiny local airport but had stayed when he heard about the raid. He gave an interview to the *Record* saying, among other things, that the prophet's civil rights had been trampled and a lawsuit against the sheriff's department and Sheriff Ben Baxter himself was a possibility.

The murder victim had now been identified as Glynnis Johnson, a local girl who had been missing for some months—reported so by her parents, assumed even by them to have run away after some family trouble—and was now known to have voluntarily joined the Light and the Way religious group. It gave a brief overview of her life, as well as the bald fact that she had been having problems at home, arguments with her parents over drugs (a dramatically increasing problem locally, I wasn't sure why) found in her room, and had lost her job at the hospital after stealing money out of fellow employees' purses. She had left home after an argument with her mother in June. The journalist had done a thorough job, and in a sidebar gave a brief list of signs someone may run off to join a cult—trouble at home or in their life, a sense of aimlessness, and low self-esteem being the top three items on the list.

It helped me understand Cecily's situation. I was filled with sadness for Glynnis and her family, who clearly loved her despite her problems. The photo used was one of Glynnis's mom sitting on what was presumably Glynnis's bed in her still-intact room, weeping on the shoulder of her distraught father. Pain clutched my heart; I knew too well the agony of losing someone, all the *what-ifs* and *should-haves*. "Why do you think I know anything about this?" I said, wiping the screen with the sleeve of my sweater. Everything Doc handled was smudgy, including his glasses. It was a wonder he saw anything.

"Don't you always?" he griped.

I admitted I might know something about both happenings. I told him about my connection to Anokhi, which he had already figured out, then I told him about my visit, with Lizzie, to the encampment, and my chat with Cecily. There was a list, I said, of missing girls from the area; Cecily and Glynnis were both on it. I wondered aloud if I could have helped Glynnis. What if I stayed longer at the encampment, or looked further? Was she still there somewhere, despite Cecily not seeing her that day? What if I'd gone into the structures, even the church Quonset? Had Glynnis run away from the cult, only to meet some bad dude on the highway, as she hitched, maybe even the killer who was murdering girls and young women over a several-year stretch? Reporters had been speculating that this murder was related to some in past years, spread out along the I-90 corridor from New York through Ohio and Michigan. It was one theory among many.

"Seems to me the simplest answer is the likeliest, someone from that place got to her."

I nodded and sighed. "But who? And how did she get to the highway, if that's the case?" I then griped about my worry about Gordy. "He's so different . . . confident, but not in a good way. He seems happy, and I *want* him to be happy, but . . ." I glanced over at Hubert Dread, who sat in the corner playing chess alone. "I wish Hubert had made it clearer to Gordy that he was joking about all of those stories he told."

"Getting so you can't even kid around," Doc griped. "Are we raisin' a generation of kids who can't figure out if something's real or not? Thought these millennials, or whatever you wanna call them, would know not to trust whatever's on the internet, but they're more gullible than I was before they shipped me to Europe. Who knew Gordy would take all that crap Hubert spouts as God's own truth?"

"I'm not blaming Hubert. Or at least . . . not totally. Gordy seems to believe we're in the end-times, or something like that." I remembered what the female cop in RiRi had said about the assumption that the group was made up of preppers, preparing for doomsday. It seemed that folks had been content to write the Light and the Way Ministry off as whatever flavor of lunatics they deemed least dangerous.

I frowned and twisted my mouth. Hmm. If you were up to no good, that could work to your advantage, everyone writing your group off as a lunatic fringe doomsday cult. I tucked that thought away to pursue another day.

"I don't know what to think, Doc. Gordy looks happier than I've ever seen him. That has to count for something, doesn't it?"

He shifted uneasily. "I don't know, Merry. Gordy's living in a fool's paradise, and I have to think it'll end badly for him."

"So what do you think I should do, Doc? He's an adult. I can't just march in and haul Gordy out by his ear."

"I know, I know," he griped. "Ain't nothing to be done, I suppose. I seen those fellas . . . those Light and the Way fellas . . . in Ridley Ridge. Why do you think they ain't in Autumn Vale?"

"I never thought of that. Why?"

"I know you don't like him, but Sheriff Urquhart caught one of 'em in front of the coffee shop harassin' women, callin' 'em jezebels and harlots and the like. He told the guy that if he ever caught him in Autumn Vale again, he'd tie his nads in a knot."

I coughed and laughed. That seemed so incredibly un-Urquhart-like that I had to think Doc had put his own colorful spin on the sheriff's words. I wondered briefly which of the Light and Wayers it was, Barney, or maybe Nathan? "I'm making my peace with the sheriff, Doc. He's growing on me. In fact, he and his new girlfriend are coming over Friday for steak. Do you want to come out?"

"I wish. Last time I tried to chew steak I had indigestion for a week." He grimaced. His teeth had been giving him a lot of trouble.

"Virgil would gladly grill you a sirloin burger."

He smiled and patted my hand. "That's okay, honey. Nowadays it's kinda too much to go out to eat. At least here if I fall asleep at the dinner table nobody minds. As long as I don't wake 'em up with my snoring."

I laughed, but left the room with some worry, pausing at the doorway to look back. He seemed so tired, and though he picked up his book again, he closed his eyes and nodded off. I felt my eyes prickle; I had just found him, and I wasn't ready to lose Doc yet. He was my only tenuous tie to the family I never knew.

Chapter Eleven

I delivered my muffins to the kitchen at Golden Acres, then headed back downtown, stopping at Binny's bakery for a moment.

Binny Turner is the very first person I met in Autumn Vale, that misty September morning a few years back. She is also Lizzie's aunt. Her brother, Tom, was Lizzie's father but was murdered before they ever had a chance to get to know each other. Binny tries to make it up to Lizzie, and the aunt and niece are fairly close, or as close as two explosive, sometimes tetchy women can be.

But there is no way around it . . . Binny is a bit of an odd duck, insisting on selling European delicacies only, whipped up in her custom-designed bakery, to the exclusion of other treats. You can buy profiteroles and baklava, cannoli and charlottes, croissants and éclairs, vol-au-vents and strudels, but you can't buy muffins or cookies. It's the way she runs things, and there is no point in complaining, though many still did. As a result, most of her sales are of her amazing breads, buns and biscuits instead of sweets. She's generous to a fault locally; the retirement home and local shelter get the best European day-old pastries anyone has ever tasted. Binny is a good person.

As I bought some of my guilty pleasures, her biscotti, which rivaled any I bought when I lived in New York City, and she boxed them up, we chatted over the hinged counter centered between two glass cases. I told her about seeing Gordy, to whom she had rented an apartment upstairs when he lived with Zeke. "I worry about him. Maybe I shouldn't, but I do. It's weird," I reflected. "He seems happier and more confident than I've ever seen him, and yet I'm worried."

She shrugged. "He's an adult, Merry. He's got a right to do whatever he wants."

"So people keep saying, even the ones who are as worried as I. Of course you're right. But he's such a lost lamb, you know?" I paused as she put a sticker over the flap of the bakery box. "There was a guy hanging around him. Zeke said there was some dude living with Gordy upstairs before he moved out, some guy from the Light and the Way Ministry. He worked for Turner Construction for a while."

"Sure. This was last June, right? Nathan was crashing on their couch, then Zeke and Gordy had an argument and Zeke left to move in with Hannah's folks."

"Nathan Garrison, right?" She nodded. "What is he like?" I asked, without going into how I knew him, as the creep who followed Shilo home from the castle and stalked her for a while.

"Quiet. Until he was outside on the street. He had a run-in with Urquhart when he started calling women things."

So it *was* him, not Barney! "Things like 'jezebel'?"

"Yeah. Urquhart threatened him, I heard. Garrison got snarky but backed down when some local roughneck threatened to clothesline him."

Maybe that explained Nathan's retreat to the Light and the Way Ministry compound. Autumn Vale was too tough a nut to crack, so they focused on RiRi. And like some cultish Pied Piper, Garrison led Gordy Shute out of Autumn Vale and to that Armageddon cult. "I can't figure out why our gentle Gordy likes him. I don't get it."

"Gordy always had trouble making friends, so he was never picky. He was lucky with Zeke, but other than that . . ." She grimaced. "I could tell you tales. Poor guy got beaten up and robbed more than once by 'friends' he made."

"What's your opinion of this Light and the Way Ministry group?"

"Bunch of weirdos. You won't catch *me* going out there. I stay clear away."

I headed back to the castle. Pish was done with his video-conference. I found him in his study, which he had furnished like a nineteenth-century gentleman's library, with lots of wood, leather, globes, books, and a set of cut-glass decanters that held the tipple he prefers, Maker's Mark bourbon. Becket was snoozing in his place of honor, a special pillow Pish had put in the deep sill of his study window, and my friend was at his desk, frowning at his computer screen.

"What's up?" I said, plopping down in the guest chair he keeps beside his green-leather-topped Sheraton desk.

After the videoconference he had a chat with Anokhi, making doubly sure she was okay after her shocking discovery. I could tell he was still worried that the awful experience she had would make it easier for her to reject our offer. "She's deeply concerned. I tried to reassure her about our area being safe and peaceful but she's rattled, for lack of a better description. And her treatment at the sheriff's office, while it did not reach what *she* considered offensive, was not reassuring."

"And her son-in-law called in an attorney, and not just any lawyer; I've heard the guy is a specialist in civil rights cases. Why is that?"

He tapped a pencil on the edge of the desk, his gaze clouded. "Grant is a problem. I have the feeling that Anokhi is not overly fond of him, but of course she didn't say that. She said that he is Sebastienne's husband, and as such she will not criticize him."

"That attorney stayed on, you know . . . he's involving himself in whatever men were held by Sheriff Baxter's deputies in the raid of the compound."

"Lucky for them."

"Did she describe what happened on the highway?"

He nodded and met my gaze. His eyes were watering. "It's so much worse than we heard, Merry! The poor child . . . they found her along the side of the road. She was beaten badly, but still alive!"

My heart thumped. "I heard that. But no one could save her. That's . . . awful. What did they do? What happened next?"

He took a deep, shuddering breath and told me all that Anokhi had said. They were on the highway heading toward the airport. Sebastienne was driving, her mother was in the passenger seat and her husband was in the back, working on his laptop. She saw what she thought was a pile of clothes in the ditch along the road, but something about it didn't seem right. Sebastienne had driven past, but at her mother's urging turned around and came back.

Anokhi was the first to get out, and discovered it was a young woman, and that she was breathing. While she tried to help the girl, Sebastienne made the 911 call. A female deputy from the Ridley Ridge sheriff's office was first on the scene and began to administer lifesaving measures. It's what Anokhi overheard that had upset Pish so much. Another officer arrived and the first thing he said was "Another one?" apparently referring to the beaten and dying girl.

I remembered what Urquhart had said about another girl found along the highway dead last year. Was this a serial killer case? I told Pish about it, then asked, "Did the officers say anything else?"

"They caught snatches of the conversation as they waited for the ambulance to arrive, but *Grant* claimed he overheard the police plotting to hide the murder."

"No! Pish, was he . . . was he *certain*?"

My friend drew in a long breath. "Anokhi sounded unsure."

I watched his face; he was troubled. "Pish, what is it?"

"Grant has been against Anokhi's wish to work with us on our center. He's been trying to get Sebastienne to talk her mother out of it."

"Why?"

He shrugged and shook his head. "I wish I knew."

"How do you know this?"

"I have a young friend who knows Grant well. He doesn't like the guy, but it's not beneficial to his position in the theater community to let his distaste be known. Grant gets in the way of his mother-in-law's work. He interferes, as I understand it. No one in the industry trusts him."

"When did you learn about that?"

"Some time ago. I was hoping it wasn't true."

"How do you think that applies to this?"

He paused, frowning. "I don't think we can trust what Grant says he overheard." He looked up and met my eyes. "He has too much motive to lie. Anokhi is upset about the whole thing, and I can *feel* her pulling away. Even if she doesn't believe Grant, it may seem too . . . complicated. A bad feeling. She believes in vibrations and auras, that kind of thing, and if this place seems doomed to her, she *will* decide against it."

I put my hand over his. I could feel how worried he was. I have begun second-guessing our decisions of late; this project is overwhelmingly complicated and scary. Was it too much stress for my friend? Was it putting his health in jeopardy? "Dear heart, if she *does* decide against our invitation to be our first guest composer-conductor, then we will find someone else. We have time. The grand opening isn't even planned until this time next year."

"You know as well as I do that planning is in place already for the next year or more of orchestra bookings. The LSO is fine — they trust me — but Anokhi is well regarded in the community and many people know she is considering our offer. If she says no, there *will* be gossip about why."

I took a deep breath. "Let's not borrow trouble. Let's find out what happened. I'll talk to Virgil; he may know more."

"I feel bad even thinking about this when a young woman is . . . is dead."

I understood completely. I felt the same, hating myself for worrying about the mundane when a life had been snuffed out. "The victim is one of the missing girls Virgil and Urquhart are helping Baxter investigate. Her name is Glynnis Johnson, and she was a member out at the Light and Way place. I may have even seen her while I was there."

He covered his face with his hands, sighed deeply, then raised his face again. "It's so awful. Who would hurt a girl so badly?"

I thought for a moment. "Did Anokhi say anything about what the young woman looked like? What had been done to her? Did the victim say anything?"

"The girl was in frightful shape: bruised all over, bloody, cuts, gashes. She had one sparkly barrette in her long hair, but it looked like the other had been torn out, along with a clump of hair. Her scalp was bleeding. Someone beat her *badly*. Anokhi said the only time she has ever seen anything like that was when she volunteered at a shelter and a young woman came in who had been beaten almost to death by her husband. She said it looked personal."

"Oh." I blinked.

"She said it sounded like the girl was saying . . . *am I safe?*"

That was heartbreaking. *Am I safe?* And then she died. "It sounds like she was trying to escape someone, or a situation." Once again I felt a suffocating wave of regret; if only I had spent more time at the compound, looked around, poked my head into buildings. Glynnis may have come away with Lizzie and me . . . *if* she was even still there. "You know, Glynnis was reported as missing by her parents, and all along she was out at that compound. But I wonder . . . I mean, when did she leave the Light and the Way? Had she left sometime before this happened? Was she sheltering somewhere else? I wish I could ask someone. Maybe I can contact Cecily. I hope this tragedy is solved quickly, for her family's sake." I stood. "I'm worried about Gordy, but in light of this, I'm even more concerned for Alcina and her mom. It's a hideous situation." I took in a deep breath and let it out slowly. "However, as banal as it sounds, I need to make more muffins." I bent over and kissed my dear friend on the forehead. "Come down and have a cup of tea with me. Please don't brood. If we can help, we will."

"When I'm done with this, I'll come," he said, waving his hand at his screen. "I'm typing up notes from the videoconference with the LSO chairmen."

I descended and Becket followed me, hoping, no doubt, for third breakfast, or first lunch, or something like that. I know I'm not supposed to have him in the kitchen; it's where I bake the muffins I sell to local businesses. But I tried keeping him out and it didn't work. If an inspector ever caught him in the kitchen I could lose my commercial kitchen license, but I'd handle that if it happened. Life is too short to worry over every single thing.

Five minutes later I heard hallooing and went from the kitchen to the grand front entrance; there I found Shilo taking off her jacket and slinging it over the carved end of the staircase banister. She had brought Lizzie with her. Lizzie's mother, Emerald, had gone to Batavia for a job interview of some sort with *their* car, Lizzie said, with rolled eyes and a snort of disapproval. And her grandmother was doing some shopping, and so needed *her* car.

"You didn't bring my goddaughter!" I said to my beautiful friend Shilo about her baby girl, Autumn, as I led them back to the kitchen.

"She's at home with Savannah," she said of her younger sister, who was staying with her for a while.

Shilo has a complicated family history, and had recently reanimated her relationship with her siblings. I had known her for twelve years, and the first ten of those she had never intimated that she had a huge family, but she did, more sisters and brothers than I could enumerate. This move to AV, marriage to a wonderful man, and motherhood had given her newfound courage, strength and surety. She had confronted her abusive past and was on speaking terms with her father again, though barely.

She was always gorgeous, in a dark, wild, Gypsy way, and she's still so beautiful, but in a different illuminated-from-within sense, since having Autumn. Even tired, with her messy dark hair in a bun on top of her head and baby goop on her shoulder, she was stunning.

I glanced over at Lizzie. "So . . . have you heard the latest?" I said, testing out her knowledge of the tragic recent events.

"About Glynnis? Yeah, I heard." She plopped down on one of the stools by the breakfast bar.

"Did you know her?"

She nodded, staring down at the counter, her eyes watering. "She was in my same grade but she quit school and disappeared around when Cecily took off, like, two weeks before grad. She was always talking about running away to New York. She was into fashion . . . always wore sparkly jewelry and clothes. She wanted to be a star." Lizzie looked up, one tear tracing a delicate path down her freckled, tanned cheek. "When she left town I joked about it. I said, *So maybe we'll see her in an acne commercial on TV. Ha-ha-ha!* I feel like such a jerk," she whispered, her voice broken and thick.

I circled the breakfast bar and hugged her, hard, feeling her sob, catching her breath. "Lizzie, you didn't do anything wrong," I murmured against her mop of frizzy hair. "We all make jokes. You couldn't know." I let her go and returned to my side of the breakfast bar. "How long ago was that?"

"June."

"Right; two weeks before graduation, so early June. If she was running away, she didn't get far." I sat down. Something was teasing my brain, something my mother used to talk about. She traveled a lot when she was young, and she told me about getting off a bus in San Francisco and being met by what she called Moonies—members of the Unification church, called Moonies because they followed Sun Myung Moon—who invited her to a seminar. She was pretty much isolated for two days and fed endless information about how joining the Moonies was the way to salvation. She bolted in the middle of the night, though she told me there was no *real* bar to leaving, just heavy pressure.

I wondered . . . had Glynnis intended to leave Ridley Ridge? Was she met at the bus station before leaving and convinced to go to the Light and the Way compound? I texted Virgil with the idea while Shilo comforted Lizzie.

"Anyway, I brought the photos out to you," Lizzie said, fishing around in her camera bag. "I transferred them to a flash drive for you, though, 'cause I figured you'd want to look at them on a bigger screen." She put a small flash drive on the countertop and slid it across to me.

"You're absolutely right," I said, and grabbed my huge Birkin bag; it's a lovely taupe and dark gray, bookbag style, and (don't tell anyone) is pre-owned, bought in a New York consignment shop on our last trip. I took out my tablet, one of those two-in-ones that are like a mini notebook computer, plugged the flash drive into it and sat down between my two friends.

Shilo's lovely face was shadowed by sadness. She's a highly emotional person and absorbs feelings, from joy to anguish, from anyone she is comforting or celebrating with. She had felt Lizzie's despair and mirrored it. But she also had additional insight from her new identity as a mother. "I can't imagine what that poor mother is going through right now . . . Glynnis Johnson's mother."

"Glynnis and her mom never got along," Lizzie said. "They fought all the time."

I thought of my own teenage years, and how I fought with my mother, my poor grandmother in the middle of so many of our battles. "It doesn't mean they didn't love each other, Lizzie."

"I know," she said gloomily. "I was thinking; Mrs. Johnson is probably extra sad because of that, you know, wishing she could get back all that time they fought."

Shilo and I both hugged her. It was so profoundly true.

"And even worse that Glynnis was so close this whole time," I said.

"We have *got* to get Alcina out of there, with or without her mother!" Lizzie said through gritted teeth.

I shared a worried look with Shilo. We both know what Lizzie is capable of, and I would not put a solo raid on the compound out of the question. "We don't know if Glynnis's death was caused by someone at the compound."

Lizzie gave me a look. "Right. And people say teenagers are naïve." She sniffed in disgust. "It was probably that creepy old prophet fellow. I'll bet Glynnis had all *kinds* of info on him."

"That's wild speculation, kiddo," I said, though it was an interesting notion. "What kind of girl was Glynnis? Like . . . smart? Dumb? Nosy? Quiet?"

"I didn't know her well," Lizzie said. "She was in trouble, I know that. She had worked at the hospital part-time, but got canned when they caught her rifling through someone's purse. And I think she was taking drugs."

"What's up with that? I'm hearing about drugs more and more locally. I mean, I know it's always been a problem, but . . . have you noticed an uptick in drug use?"

Lizzie frowned and shrugged. "I guess. I mean, my last two years at school it just seemed there was more partying, and more drugs. The last couple of years there was a big end-of-school bash somewhere in the country, and kids kept getting wasted. One of Julian's friends almost died."

"Well, that's troubling. What would attract Glynnis to the Light and the Way, do you think, I mean, given her wanting to be a star?" How did you get from wanting to be in show biz to belonging to a religious cult that frowned on makeup?

"I don't know. Maybe Cecily would. I mean, they must have spent a lot of time together out there, right?"

"Maybe. In any case, we can't jump to conclusions. We can't just decide it is the prophet to blame because we think he's creepy." Shilo looked hesitant for a moment. I caught the look. "Shilo, what is it? Do you know something?"

She bit her lip, looking about ten years younger than her early thirty-something. "I . . ." She sighed and shook her head.

"Honey, what is it?"

She took a deep breath, and her cheeks colored. "I've been volunteering at the women's shelter in Ridley Ridge. I heard they needed someone to paint their interior for free, and I was done with our house so . . ." She shrugged. "I took my paints and rags and went there to help."

Shilo has revealed an amazing hidden talent she didn't even know she had; she has transformed her and Jack's funky older house in Autumn Vale with hand-painted décor, including whole murals of butterflies and trees, vines, and in Autumn's room trees full of monkeys swinging from limb to limb. Every single monkey has a different expression. It's amazing.

"I didn't know you were doing that!" I watched her eyes; she was debating something. I thought of all the shelters I have ever visited—I did some volunteer work too when I lived in New York

City, after Miguel died — and how privacy-obsessed they rightfully are. "Shilo, did you learn or hear something at the shelter?" She nodded but stayed silent. I took a deep breath. "You can't say anything you heard there. I know that. But was it about the compound?"

She nodded.

"Was it about one of the men there?"

She nodded again. "Or . . . kind of. I can't . . . I can't say any more." Tears welled in her eyes. "I wish I could, but I can't! They'd never trust me again."

"I know, honey," I said, putting my arm around her shoulders and squeezing.

"What do you mean?" Lizzie yelped. "What if what she knows could solve Glynnis's murder?"

"What if she said something and it led to another woman getting killed?" I shot back.

She shut her mouth and nodded.

So . . . a woman had turned up at the shelter and said something about one of the men at the compound. That scared the hell out of me. Secretly I was with Lizzie, worried that staying silent would endanger the women and girls at the compound. I thought of Felice and Alcina under the thumb of that creep Barney, and I was even worried for Gordy . . . dumb, innocent Gordy, who trusted people to tell him the truth, and so could be swayed by anyone with an agenda. His lovely friend Nathan was a real gem.

One thing was for sure: I needed to get to Alcina, at least, and make sure she was safe. I needed to see if I could convince Felice that Barney was evil, and to leave him. It helped to know that a woman had gotten away from the compound and escaped to a shelter, but it meant that a man there had likely treated her very badly indeed.

Isadore had already started working there. Maybe now would be a good time to return to the compound, to make sure everyone was okay. Maybe with muffins for the kids. I'd think about it. As much as everyone was preaching to me about people's self-determination and their right to make their own decisions, I was leaning toward meddling, given how many of our dear friends were there and potentially in danger.

We spent some time looking over the pictures Lizzie had taken. I enlarged them on the screen, and we discovered a lot of information that I would be sharing with Virgil later. Even the shacks in back that had appeared abandoned were apparently inhabited. There were pictures of people going in and out of them, even the sagging dump furthest back from the encampment! It looked like Nathan was using that as his own little nest. I shuddered and shrugged him out of my mind, focusing instead on the groups of children and women. "Lizzie, did you meet any of these kids and women?" I said, idly making conversation as I examined faces, seeing if I recognized anyone.

"Yeah. I was looking for Alcina, you know? So I talked to a lot of them."

"How did they seem?"

"Okay, I guess. I mean, they were clean, and had food. There's some kind of root cellar where they store stuff."

"A root cellar? I didn't see that."

"Yeah, you access it from a door at the back of the red hut thingie . . . it's underneath."

"Hmph. Who knew?" All kinds of hidey-holes in that place.

"They don't get candy, or anything. I gave one a package of Tic Tacs and you'd think it was gold, the way they all crowded around."

Lizzie's camera is professional grade, and there were a few photos she had taken from an elevation. "How did you get these?"

"They've got, like, this raised clothesline pole, with a platform built around it, and from there it's easy to get on the roof of one of the huts. I took pictures all the way around."

"I see that." I squinted. "Look, there in the distance . . ." I used my fingers to expand the photo. Because the resolution was so high, it didn't get blurry. "There's a small shack by that grove of trees. It looks like it's about five hundred feet or so from the Quonset church. And there's another flat-roofed hut, larger," I said, pointing to it, "beyond that hill. It's like a quarter mile away; you can barely see it for the trees. It kind of looks like it's on the next road, in fact." I frowned. The next road . . . was that Silver Creek Line, where Isadore had been told to go to work on the ledgers? "That looks like an antenna sprouting from the top, maybe a *satellite* antenna."

"One of the kids I talked to said the prophet seems to know

everything that's going on, even though he never leaves the compound. He, like, hides out for hours 'meditating,' and then comes out with a new revelation. Like, he'll come out and say he had a revelation that the world is evil 'cause he learned from God there was another school shooting, or a politician caught with his pants down."

"I've never heard cable news called God before. So, a news item." I was jotting down notes, and I wrote myself a reminder to tell Virgil all of this, and also to get Zeke to look at the picture and see if he could tell me what it was. "More likely he spends all of his time hidden away smoking dope and watching *Jersey Shore* reruns."

"He's old. He probably watches *Beavis and Butt-Head*," Lizzie said.

A woman in the photo caught my eye and I drew in my breath in one swift gasp. I enlarged the photo and focused on the face. Was it . . . ? It *had* to be. Leatrice Pugeot, aka Lynn Pugmire! It was my archnemesis, the supermodel who had hired me as her personal assistant, then fired me, then ruined my career and life when she accused me of the theft of a necklace she probably pawned to buy oxy.

Chapter Twelve

I stared, squinted, enlarged, trying to be certain. "Shilo, look at this face!" I pointed. "Who is this?"

"Oh. *Oh!*" she yelped, almost falling from her stool. "That's Leatrice!"

"You see it too? I'm not imagining it, then." Holy crap. Holy *freaking* crap. I don't know how to explain Leatrice: she was my boss, my torment, and my saving grace, as much as it didn't feel like it at the time. In making so much trouble for me Leatrice had given me the greatest gift anyone ever could by forcing me to run away from New York City to my inherited property. She had kick-started this new life; until then I had been stuck in a tumultuous relationship with my lingering grief over my husband's death, and the effort to make a life or career for myself in the wake of it. I was furious with her and grateful, a weird mix.

But what was she doing at the religious compound of the Light and the Way? "I have to go out there. *Now*," I muttered, slapping the counter with the palm of my hand.

"Who is it? What are you talking about?" Lizzie asked.

"That woman, the one I've zoomed in on . . ." I pointed her out; she was sitting on an upturned pail in front of one of the huts, hands to her head, looking frail and frightened. "I know her. She's an addict, and usually unwell. She's not safe there. I have to get her out."

"I'm coming with you. I gotta find Alcina."

I took a deep breath and let it out, common sense taking over. "First, I have to call Virgil."

He didn't pick up. I started pacing and worrying, my footsteps echoing in the cavernous kitchen as the three of us tried to figure out how best to extricate a woman from that place. I didn't know if she would come with me. What would I do if she refused, or put up a fuss? Was I even right to charge in there to rescue her?

I made some calls to old New York friends. No one had seen Lynn in months. Finally I got my old friend Zee on the line. Zee is one of my last remaining contacts in the fashion world and knew Lynn well.

"Have you heard anything about Leatrice Pugeot?" I asked after the initial pleasantries.

"Aw, honey, don't tell me! She's dead, right? I figured it was just a matter of time."

"Not if the woman I saw is her." I briefly described Lynn's situation.

"Hmmm. Last I heard she was telling anyone who would listen that she was going upstate to stay with *you*."

"What?" I yelped.

"She said that you two had this big reunion when you were in town, and you were gonna come work for her again."

"*Not* true! None of it."

"She said she was going to stay at your castle—"

"Who told her about my castle?" I squawked.

"Don't look at me," she said with a warm chuckle. "You know what I think of Leatrice. I love her to death, and she was a hell of a model back in the day, but she is the *last* person I would trust with anything, even information. And I know how she burned you. I'd *never* tell her where you live. But honey, the woman does read—even if it's at a third-grade level—and there was that write-up in *Downtown* about you and Pish."

Downtown was a New York City magazine, and there had been a long-read piece about the castle and our plans for it. "And she said I had invited her out here?"

"She did."

"But I didn't!"

"I thought it was unlikely, but Pishy has a big heart and I thought he might've gotten to you . . . you know how he loves a stray."

Pish. *Pish!* Well, he *had* invited a ghost-hunting show to come and film at the castle without me knowing about it. *And* his wacky Auntie Lush, and her crew of demonic old ladies. How much more likely was it that he had invited our old friend, down-on-her-luck Leatrice, aka Lynn? "Maybe you're right. I gotta go, Zee."

"Don't be too hard on him!" she said with another chuckle.

I smiled. "Let's have lunch and catch up next time I'm in the city."

Pish wandered down and into the kitchen. Shilo bit her lip, and Lizzie's eyes widened. But I wasn't going to yell. I turned and gave him a hard stare. "Pish, have you seen Lynn Pugmire lately?" My voice was controlled but full of tension.

He stared at me puzzled, in the act of filling the kettle. "No, dear heart, I haven't seen her for years. You *know* I'd tell you if I had."

I nodded, relieved. That is what I'd already concluded. Pish is on my side. Always. He wouldn't have invited her to the castle.

"Why do you ask?"

"Shilo, show him the picture. Pish, tell me what you think."

Shilo did so, turning the tablet for him to see and repeating my close-up action of the woman in question. He, too, did the gasp. He looked up and met my gaze, searching my eyes. "Is that . . . ?"

"I don't know. But if it is—"

"We *have* to save her," he said.

"I know."

• • •

I had called Virgil again, and this time he picked up. Prophet Voorhees had been briefly detained, as had Barney and a couple other of the men; not Gordy, apparently. But the civil rights lawyer Grant Marbaugh had ordered up argued that the two men had been denied their basic rights and had been illegally detained and held. There was insufficient evidence to hold them on anything, even given Glynnis's connection to the compound. As much as I hated to admit it, I agreed. Baxter's raid on the compound, unjustified by any actual incriminating evidence supplied by the ATF, seemed oddly rushed and without basis.

So Voorhees and Barney were being released any moment, though Baxter was not rushing to comply. The civil rights lawyer was threatening a lawsuit. Virgil suspected that the lawyer would meet with the two men after they were released to see if they wanted to file charges, in which case they would likely hang out in Ridley Ridge for at least an hour or two, more if they decided to file charges against the sheriff and his department. Why was I asking about them?

I told him that I had seen a woman in a photo of the encampment who I thought might be Lynn. He knew exactly who I meant, of course, because I have bitched and moaned about her enough in the last three years. I sent him all of Lizzie's photos of the encampment while I told him about Zee's info, that last anyone heard, Lynn was heading for my castle. Even with everything that had gone down between us, I couldn't leave her there. She was emotionally and physically as fragile as a cracked eggshell. I didn't say to Virgil that there may be more than one rescue of a friend if we found Alcina, though taking her without Felice's consent would be illegal at the very least.

I was going in, I told him.

He freaked . . . I mean, *freaked*! I was *not* going in, he said, panic in his tone.

I got all stiff and snippy. I am too old to be told what to do by any man, woman or child. I *could* not leave Lynn there; that's all there was to it. I was a private citizen, and I was not going in alone. The worst that could happen on the Light and the Way Ministry compound was that I would be evicted for trespassing. If I could find Felice and get her to invite me to stick around, it wouldn't even be that.

Virgil, intelligent husband that he is, amended his previous statement. I was not going in there without him; he and Dewayne, his PI partner, would meet us there. I was relieved, I have to say, though my by-the-book ex-cop husband might not like what I was prepared to do.

I rushed around the kitchen and pantry, and then, armed with muffins and staples like powdered milk and soup—food items gave us an excuse to talk to the women, and for being there—Lizzie, Shilo, Pish and I headed out. Pish insisted on going along. If we found Lynn, it might require both of us to deal with her. It depended on whether she was clean or not. In the photo her expression was cloudy, hands on her head, fingers thrust into her unruly hair, her gaze focused on the distance. That could either mean she was sad or stoned.

Somehow, in my time at the compound, I had missed her.

We all piled into Pish's capacious car. I drove. I drove *fast*. But even so, as we turned onto Marker Road a big semi blew past me, laying on the horn and throwing up gravel onto Pish's pristine vehicle. I restrained myself from giving him the finger.

Virgil was, of course, as good as his word. He and Dewayne Lester, a stocky, balding fellow who was Virgil's shooting instructor at police college many years before, and a cop of many years before retiring and forming his own PI business, stood talking, awaiting us. I parked and we got out of the car, Virgil's thick brow quirking when he saw how many of us there were. It looked like a parade, not a rescue mission, he said.

We all greeted each other tensely. Shilo looked nervous. I watched her for a moment. "Shilo, maybe you should stay with the cars and be our lookout?"

But she saw right through that. "No way. Who knows which one of us Lynn will listen to? I was a model, and she was a model; I can talk to her. You and Lizzie have other . . . uh . . . problems." Thankfully she did not mention Alcina.

I nodded and turned to Virgil. He looked tired and grim. I put my arms around his waist and he did the same around mine, looking into my eyes.

His expression lightened a little. "How do you always make me feel better?"

"Because you know that I got you, babe," I said with a smirk.

He kissed me nicely, the PG version of our usual smooch, and let me go. "Okay, kiddies, Dewayne and I have news. Listen up."

Dewayne, with even deeper training and knowledge than my hubby, took command. "As you may know, Sheriff Ben Baxter raided this compound at oh-two-hundred hours and took into custody a few men, a couple that he kept for a time. He has now released both without charge. They will be coming back." He met each of our gazes, and stayed on me. "What are your reasons for coming out here?"

I took a deep breath. "We're not sure of any of this, Dewayne, but some of our friends are here. Also . . . I have reason to believe that a woman I know to have serious mental health issues is here mistakenly. I have heard from friends that she was coming to find me, but she may have fallen into the Light and the Way Ministry folks' hands."

"So we're here to extract her." He nodded. "The fellow named Barney has been chased out of the bus station in Ridley Ridge multiple times. If your friend traveled here by bus, she may have been intercepted."

"I'm not surprised. I don't know how she got here, but she doesn't drive. If Lynn showed up here on the bus she'd tell anyone who listened about me. If he befriended her and promised to take her to me, she'd have gone." My voice broke on the last word. Pish took my arm and squeezed. Shilo supported me on the other side.

"We'll find her, honey," Pish murmured.

"Dewayne, this is private property, I understand." I motioned to the *No Trespassing* sign. "I was told to leave last time I was here."

Virgil cleared his throat. "It *is* private property. The ministry owns a twenty-acre section, and the rest is farmland. The Light and the Way started, apparently, in a house in town, then moved to a rented farmhouse just outside of Ridley Ridge, but two years ago or so they bought this chunk of land."

"Property around here is not cheap, even undeveloped farmland. How could they afford that?" Shilo asked. "And who sold it to them?"

"The sale was private and didn't go through Jack, I can tell you that," Virgil said, flashing her a smile.

"I knew that," Shilo said. "Jack would have told me about it."

"So my point is . . . are we doing anything illegal? I don't want to get you guys in trouble," I said. "Like I said, the prophet guy told me to leave."

Dewayne turned his dark sloe-eyed gaze to me. "Do you think someone is in imminent danger?"

Shilo piped up: "Yes! I haven't been here before and so I've never been warned off. I saw the photo of someone on this land—someone I know who is vulnerable—and I believe she's in danger from herself and others."

Dewayne nodded. "That's enough to go in on. If we have reason to believe someone is in imminent danger, we can make a case to the police." He smiled grimly. "Sometimes it's easier to ask forgiveness than permission. I don't think Ben Baxter is going to vigorously pursue us. But let's be swift; I'd rather we're gone before Voorhees and Barney show up."

"Let's go," Virgil said. "Orderly, now, ladies and gent," he said, with a smile for Pish, who had been uncharacteristically quiet.

We all clambered up the hillside and through the locked gate, pushing our cloth bags of food ahead as we went. Dewayne led the way, Virgil followed us from behind. I stayed directly behind Dewayne. Lizzie, camera in hand, was clicking photos a mile a minute, weaving off the path, taking photos of us and the field across which we traversed. There was the encampment ahead, looking the same: laundry on the lines, a smoky fire in the open space. Women were gathered in groups by some of the huts, with children doing what kids do . . . running around after each other, playing tag, probably. Inevitably one fell and started shrieking, and a woman rushed over and picked him up, returning to the group with him on her shoulder.

One of the women in the group glanced over and saw us, and soon all eyes were turned toward us. Belatedly I realized we might look a little menacing. I pushed ahead of Dewayne, but he was having none of that. He made me stay behind. Another of the older women, the one I had seen the first time I was there and who had been in the van with Barney, Nathan and Voorhees in Ridley Ridge, broke away from the cluster and strode toward us.

"Who are you and what do you want?"

I stepped forward, taking a deep breath. "I'm sure you remember me," I said in my most placating tone. "I was here yesterday. We don't mean to intrude, but we have some concerns about folks we love who are living here." I had decided to focus on Alcina and Felice, first, because I didn't know how to ask about Lynn. But I'd keep my eyes open. "We'd like to see them, to be sure they're all right. We heard about the raid last night, and we want to help."

The woman looked with hostility to Dewayne and Virgil. "I don't want *them* here," she said.

I watched her. "I'm sorry, we haven't been introduced. My name is Merry Grace Wynter. This is my husband, Virgil Grace," I said, motioning to my hubby. He smiled, trying to look less intimidating. "Dewayne is our friend," I said, hand on his arm. I felt a muscle flex on his forearm; he was tense. "This is Lizzie," I said, pointing to the teen. "She was here with me yesterday. And this is Pish and Shilo. I was out here to talk to my friend Gordy Shute. Is he here? He can vouch for me."

Her expression was troubled, but not fearful, at least. That was a good start. I wondered how scary the raid had been for them all. It *must* have been terrifying, I realized, to have armed men march into camp in the middle of the night and seize Voorhees, Barney and others.

113

"Gordy is around here somewhere." Her glance slewed over to Dewayne, and she glared at him as she said to me, "Him and Nathan have been looking after things since the prophet and Barney were illegally seized."

Lizzie pushed forward. "I'm here looking for my friend Alcina. She's just a kid, so you better damn well hope she's okay. If I don't find her I'm calling the freakin' cops to arrest your asses."

The woman's gaze turned to my young friend, her expression one of disgust. "Shut up, you filthy-mouthed little mongrel!"

Chapter Thirteen

I gasped. It took me a long minute to process what she meant, but I got there, and I could see Dewayne had too, by the fury sparking in his eyes. I put my hand on his arm again and the muscle was leaping, a nerve pulsing under his skin. Lizzie, with her dark eyes and wild halo of frizzy hair, could be mistaken for mixed race. If I was right, that's what this woman was implying and I wanted to hit her, not for the assumption but for the disgust in her voice and the hatred in her eyes when she said it.

I held on to Dewayne's arm and grabbed Lizzie, pulling her back. I so wanted to tell the woman off, but what I wanted more was to actually find Alcina and hopefully get her out of there, and Lynn too. And I wanted a chance to ask Peaches if she was Madison Pinker, and to find out about Glynnis Johnson, whose death haunted me. But most of all, I needed to find Lynn. "She's worried about her friend," I said, my voice tight with suppressed loathing. "If she hears from the girl herself that she's okay, she'll leave peacefully. Won't you, Lizzie?" I gave my young friend a level look.

Lizzie sulkily nodded. She turned away and started clicking the camera, which distracted the woman.

"Stop taking pictures! This is private property."

Pish, the most diplomatic person in the world, stepped in between Lizzie and the woman, and the rest of us took the opportunity the distraction presented and headed toward the huts.

I saw a familiar face. "Cecily!" I said.

She was sitting with a group of women, some of whom had been crying. She said something to one of them, and stood, walking over to us. "Do you know what's going on?" she asked. "We don't know anything. Barney and the prophet aren't back yet, and some of the women are scared. What's going to happen to us?"

I put my arms around her and hugged. I wondered if she knew about Glynnis, and didn't know if I had the courage to tell her. "Honey, no matter what, you and the other women aren't in trouble," I said, hoping I was telling the truth. A cold wind whipped up, raising a dust cloud in the open area near the firepit, mixing with ashes. "I was worried too, so I brought out some stuff. Some muffins and dry goods." I handed the bags to her, and she gave them to a woman who had followed but stayed at a distance. "Who was that woman who came out to talk to us?"

"That is Mother Esther. She's the prophet's first wife."

"*First* wife; does he have others?"

Cecily shook her head. "Uh, no. He doesn't."

"Why not, if his religion believes in polygamy?"

She shrugged. I took her arm and pulled her away, keeping my eye on the others. It seemed that it was almost all women at the encampment, and that was a good thing. I didn't know how long we had before Barney and the prophet showed up, and I didn't particularly want to be there when they did, as I was intent on retrieving Lynn and getting her to safety. I wasn't sure why, but there was a panicky sensation in my chest, a feeling that we were coming to some sort of tipping point.

"Okay, you have to explain to me this multiple-wives thing," I said. Mother Esther surged past us to organize or forbid the sharing of the food we had brought. It was too late for that, of course; the kids had already got the tubs of muffins open and were sitting around on the dry ground devouring them with great relish.

"Plural wives is from the Bible, that's all I know," Cecily said. "Prophet Voorhees wants us to live as the original prophets lived, you know?"

"That doesn't make any sense. Do you think the original prophets lived as their cave-dwelling ancestors lived? Life moves forward, not backward," I said. "We learn, we grow, and hopefully we do better. I don't know why plural wives is a good thing, any more than plural husbands."

Cecily shrugged, her brow knit together. "Plural husbands . . . huh. I never thought of that."

"And if he believes it so fervently, why doesn't he have more than one wife?"

She shook her head. "I don't know. I don't *care*. The prophet said something about 'complex marriage' or something like that. I guess there was a community near here in the old days, way back, that had, like, free love and stuff."

"Way back? Like . . . the nineteen seventies?" I thought maybe she was referring to the free love generation of hippies my mother had always talked about fondly.

"No, like the eighteen hundreds. It was called the Oneida community, or something."

Learn something new every day, I thought, but did not say. It was not pertinent to the current situation. "It doesn't matter," I said impatiently, wanting to get on with things and worried about spending too much time on-site. "Look, we're here to help anyone who wants to leave."

Cecily looked nervous. "If I had anywhere else to go, I'd leave," she said softly, shifting from foot to foot. "I don't like this idea of getting married to some guy who already has a wife. It's weird." She wriggled her shoulders. "Or any guy. I mean, fu . . . dge that!"

Lizzie had approached quietly and listened in. "Cec, you don't *have* to stay here. You can come stay with me at my grandmother's."

The girl brightened and stood taller. "Really? You mean it?"

I wasn't going to interfere; that was between Lizzie and her grandmother, with whom she lived when she and her mother weren't getting along . . . in other words, most of the time. From then on, Cecily was our main guide. I saw Gordy still working on his roof, but fortunately his back was turned. I didn't think he had noticed us, which was good. I had other priorities and didn't want to talk to him right then. Virgil and Dewayne had disappeared past the huts. I had a sense that there was more on their minds than the missing girls, but it was better if they were out of sight. Two big, muscular men, one of them black, striding around the encampment would probably strangle my search. Their presence had appeared to rattle Mother Esther.

I assumed the two ex-cops had assessed the camp and decided we weren't in any danger, especially given we traveled in a pack. "Can you show us around, Cecily?" I asked, my nerves still on edge.

Mother Esther had also disappeared. Shilo was making friends with the women and children, something she would be very good at. If anyone could attract Alcina it would be Shilo, who has some kind of unspoken bond with the elusive, charming girl. Pish was MIA. Maybe he had made friends with Esther; if any gay man could get through to her, it would be him, with a charm offensive more powerful than bigotry. Lizzie and I followed Cecily, asking questions.

"How long have you been here, Cecily?" I asked, though we knew the answer.

"June," she said.

"So you came here directly when you left home? You told me you had been sleeping in the park when Barney offered you a place to stay."

"Yeah, but I'd only been there one night."

I led the way back through the encampment, threading between shacks, trying to figure out the one that might hold Lynn. "We're looking for Felice and Alcina Eklund, but I'm also wondering about someone else." I turned my face away from the wind and pulled some hair out of my mouth. "Was there another woman who arrived around the same time as you, give or take a few weeks? She would be in her late thirties, very thin, blonde hair, brown eyes, kind of vague at times?"

Cecily stopped and turned. "Do you mean Lynn?"

My heart leapt. "Yes, *Lynn!*" There was a loud buzzer. "Prayer time *again*?" I asked.

Cecily nodded, her cheeks flushing. "Every day, twice on Sundays. I have to go," she said, her voice strangled. "I can't linger."

Darn it. Gordy climbed down from the roof, and, with Nathan, was walking toward the cross-topped Quonset hut building, as were others. I hid from his view behind the wall of a hut. "Cecily, wait—"

"No, I have to go!" she said, her tone panicked. "If I don't Nathan will report me when the prophet comes back, don't you see?"

"But you're coming away with me!" Lizzie said, as perplexed as I was at Cecily's abrupt about-face.

"I w-want to, but when the prophet comes back, and Barney . . . Nathan will tell them. And your grandmother's place in town . . . they'll find me," she said, wringing her hands, looking terrified.

"And then what?" I asked. I was alarmed by her fear; it seemed so out of keeping with what I knew about the encampment so far. There hadn't appeared to be any physical punishment, or at least no one had mentioned it. I touched her arm. "Cecily, what is going on here? Has anyone hurt you?"

She shook her head.

"Tell me what you know. Was Glynnis Johnson here? Did you know she's dead?"

Her eyes widened. "It's true?" she cried.

"Yes. She was found out on the highway. What about other girls; have any of them disappeared from here?"

She still shook her head, then turned, running, her long skirts fluttering behind her like broken wings.

"Cecily, what about Lynn?" I yelled after her. But she didn't stop. "Damn! There is something seriously wrong here."

"I'm going into the meeting place and give them what for," Lizzie said, her cheeks suffused with a dark red, her hands fisted at her sides, her camera swinging on its long strap looped around her neck.

She is her grandmother's (a sturdy pugnacious woman) granddaughter, that's for sure. "No, you are *not*," I said, grabbing her arm before she could march off and give 'em hell. "Number one, you could endanger Alcina by barging in and making trouble. And number two . . . priorities. While they're all busy, we are going to search this place from top to bottom. If I know Lynn, she won't be attending any prayer meeting. I'm going to look for her, and so are you, and you're going to take photos of every place we go into."

The encampment was large, though, and I didn't know how long we had before Barney and Voorhees returned. The place felt deserted. Most of the huts were empty—including the one Nathan and Gordy had been roofing but had deserted when the buzzer sounded—but there was evidence that mostly women lived in them. I had no desire to search the women's belongings—that would be wrong on so many levels—but I did want to look for Lynn. So I entered every building, shelter and tent there was.

The tents flapped in the breeze. Somewhere a bird cried, like the caw or screech of a raven or blue jay. Winter was coming. How were they going to manage? Western New York State gets miserably cold in winter. And even the shelters and huts . . . they were poorly insulated, if at all, and there was a moldy smell in some of them. I remembered the elevated view of the camp Lizzie had taken, and some huts that even appeared abandoned to the elements, shut up and with boards nailed over windows. What kept all these women here, in these conditions, with *children*? Had child protection services seen how they were living?

One way or another they would see . . . the photos would document it.

There was a tiny hut back from the rest, not as far away as the abandoned-looking one I had been thinking of from the photos, but along the edge of a wilder tangle of bramble bushes and a refuse heap. I almost decided not to check it out, thinking Lynn must, after all, be at the meeting. The shack had broken windows covered in cardboard and the door, some planks nailed together, hung on one hinge. But I'm thorough. I led the way down a path, through long grass and weeds. I could hear something inside, and the hair on my arms stood up. It was voices . . . or at least one voice, and weeping.

I recognized that *weeping*. I had heard it every day of my life for two years. I shuddered, and strode up, banging on the door. "Lynn? Lynn, it's me, Merry! I've come to get you!"

The door flung open and fell off its one hinge, and there was Felice, Alcina's mother. She was crying and pressing her fist into her gut, but she stood back and pointed to the bed. "She's sick, and no one will help her. She's been impossible from the start. She's thrown things at people, and cursed them out . . . she even bit Mother Esther. Finally no one else would help her. But she's sick! Can *you* help?"

"That's what I'm here for," I said. "I know her. We're . . . we were friends."

I pushed past her. There, on a disheveled cot, was Leatrice . . . Lynn Pugmire, as she was born. She wept, shivered and shuddered, then coughed. She was thin . . . thinner than I had ever seen her, with bones that stuck out like razors under her skin. I got my phone out of my pocket and punched in a number.

"Virgil," I said when he answered. "I've found my friend, and . . . and I'm afraid she's d-dying!" I slumped onto the floor and began to cry.

Chapter Fourteen

Virgil was on his way, understanding through my blubbering where we were, approximately. I sent Lizzie outside to wait for them and flag them down, getting myself together with effort. I crouched down beside the disheveled sagging cot, wiping the tears from my cheek with the back of my hand.

The place smelled of rot, mold and vomit. There were two trays of food on the other cot, soup with congealed fat on the top, and sandwiches, the bread curling and desiccated. "Lynn, it's me, Merry," I said, pushing back her frowsy hair from a high forehead pallid and yet filmed with sweat. "Lynn . . . Leatrice," I said, not knowing which name she'd respond to. "It's me, honey, Merry Wynter. Can you hear me?" I examined her worriedly. Her eyes were open and staring, but unfocused. Her skin was dry, flaky, and coarse, like leather. Her scalp looked awful, the dermatitis she was prone to having flared up and leaving scaly patches. I'd bet she was dehydrated. There was also a sour smell clinging to her, like spoiled diapers. She wore a nightgown, of sorts, a long cotton shift, stained with numerous substances. My stomach turned. I looked to Felice. "How long has she been like this?"

"A few days. She won't eat." Felice rocked back and forth, fist pressing into her stomach as if she felt ill, as well she might with the odor in this place. "She hasn't been able to keep anything down, not even water today. Anything she eats or drinks she brings up." Felice's eyes welled, and tears began running down her cheeks. "Mother Esther made her an herbal tea, but that didn't help. Before today she was at least able to get out of bed by herself, but she hasn't been up at all today. Mother Esther said she was being stubborn and willful."

"She's sick," I said angrily. "*Anyone* could see that."

"I was told to leave her alone until she decided to get up. Mother Esther said she'd get up soon enough if we let her sulk, but I snuck here to see if she had eaten her lunch and wanted to go to the toilet, but she couldn't get up."

My phone pinged. It was Virgil.

"Sweetheart, I've busted open the gate and we're bringing Dewayne's Jeep to the encampment. I don't give a shit what goddamn Mother Esther or anyone else says even though she's squawking at us and flapping her arms like a chicken." His voice was rugged, and I had a sense that they were approaching over the bumpy ground. "We'll be there in less than five minutes. Have your friend ready to load in and we'll take her directly to the hospital."

I nodded, then muttered a teary yes. My husband is the best. I shoved the phone back in my bag. "Felice, we're taking Lynn to a hospital."

She looked tearily relieved and nodded. "She has a purse with some cards in it. She hid it before the prophet could take it away when she first came here. I knew, but I didn't say anything. I've been looking through it, trying to find a contact phone number or something. I was g-going to sneak off and call someone, but I d-didn't know who! I think there's ID in there, and a hospital card." She reached under the cot and pulled out an LV bag.

Louis Vuitton; that was definitely poor Lynn's! I put my hand on Felice's shoulder. "You're a good woman. If you and Alcina will come with us—"

"I want to but . . . I can't. Not yet."

I examined her face. "Why not?"

She shook her head, her eyes wide and frightened. She was scared, but I didn't have time to figure out why. "Was there a girl called Glynnis here?"

She nodded. "She left, a few days ago."

"She didn't *leave*, Felice," I said, my tone harsh.

"What do you mean?"

I was going to be the bearer of bad news, but maybe she needed a strong dose of reality to make up her mind. I could hear Dewayne's Jeep roaring close. Lynn's breathing was shallow; there was no time to lose. My search was over for today but I still desperately wanted to get Felice and Alcina to leave. I stood and put my hands on her shoulders, looking her in the eye. "Glynnis is *dead*. Murdered. Someone—probably someone here—beat her senseless and dropped her off on the highway to die."

Lizzie pushed the busted door aside and shoved the second cot toward the wall. As Dewayne backed the Jeep up to the hut, Virgil came in and knelt by Lynn. As a former cop, rescue is his thing and he is adept. He examined her eyes, felt her pulse, and nodded. "We can get her to the hospital a lot faster than if we call 911 and try to describe where we are. And she's not dying . . . not yet anyway. Another day or so and I don't know." He gently covered her frail body with a tattered blanket and pushed his arms under her shoulders and knees, picking her up as if she were a rag doll, hoisting her securely against his chest. He sidled out of the hut and lifted her into the backseat of the Jeep, climbing up in with her.

Felice was ashen and shaking. She shoved the purse at me and muttered that she had to go find Alcina. She scooted out the door and ran, bunching her skirts up in both hands, the material fluttering and flapping behind her. I pushed the car keys in my hand at Lizzie and said, "Find Pish and Shilo and tell them what's happening. I'm going with Lynn."

"Okay."

"And don't do anything on your own! Don't try to be a hero, Lizzie, I mean it," I said.

She had a pugnacious look, but finally nodded.

Virgil had made Lynn comfortable in the back of the Jeep, and had hopped out, taking Dewayne aside and muttering with him. He turned to me. "Okay, I'm going to drive, and you're coming with us, right?"

I nodded.

"Dewayne is staying back with these folks." He glanced around the encampment, or what we could see of it from our angle. "There is something not right about this place. I'll tell you more later, but right now, let's get going."

I climbed in back with Lynn, talking to her in low tones as Virgil took off, quickly, but trying to steer clear of bumps and ruts. We got to the highway, and the ride became smoother. Lynn didn't seem any better, but she wasn't any worse, and we were within minutes of professional help. I was grateful that Dewayne had stayed behind; he is as stalwart and as reliable a human as I have ever met, ex-army, ex-cop, current PI, and all-around good guy.

Virgil, while he drove, called ahead to the hospital and explained the situation. They know him from his time as sheriff of Autumn Vale, so it was a simple conversation. There was a team waiting outside the emergency room doors with a gurney. River Valley County Hospital is smallish but serves a large area and has a bustling emergency room. Fortunately it wasn't overly busy—too early for flu season—and they took Lynn in immediately. I wasn't going to complicate her story too much, especially not at first, but I did tell the doctor that I was her friend and had known her many years. She had no immediate family that I knew of. She was from New York City.

A nurse started an IV of fluids, given her severe dehydration, they then drew blood for tests. They peppered me with questions that I answered as well as I could, considering I hadn't seen her in three years. We told them where we found her, and I told the triage nurse—a young fellow named Rick—that I had been told by friends in the city that last they heard of her in the summer she was on her way to visit me, at Wynter Castle. The nurse's eyes gleamed with interest and he made a passing reference to the castle.

But he was all business and started the paperwork necessary. Her insurance was up-to-date; she would be admitted. She would need many tests to determine if there were underlying problems beyond severe dehydration. I told the physician of Lynn's inability to keep anything, even water, down, and her best guess was a gastrointestinal blockage or an infection.

I was sent into the hall while they worked, and I paced and worried. Virgil had been willing to stay with me but I was concerned for Pish, Lizzie and Shilo at the encampment. As we spoke Virgil received a tip from someone at the Ridley Ridge Sheriff's Department that Barney and Voorhees were on their way back to the Light and the Way, so I sent my husband back to the camp and told him to keep me informed.

After a couple of hours the doctor came out and said that though she was drowsy, she was awake and responsive. They had done numerous tests; her problems appeared to come from malnutrition and dehydration, mainly. She had, though, been in starvation mode, which meant that her body had no fat to use as energy. She was also therefore in severe ketoacidosis. They would not be releasing her for a few days, at the very least, as she needed a slow, controlled introduction of fluids and dietary elements.

I could see her, if I wanted, the physician said with a kind smile. Taking a deep breath, I entered, stopping just inside the door to look first. There was an IV in her arm with fluids going in, and she was being monitored for heart rate, blood pressure and oxygen levels. She was so frail she barely made a mound under the sheet and blanket on the bed, the head of which was propped up at an angle. This was not the first time I had seen her in a hospital bed. She had overdosed twice when I was working for her, and I never knew if it was by accident or on purpose.

I watched her breathe and thought about the past. I had been angry at her for so long I wasn't sure what I was now feeling: pity; worry. But I was still angry. So much of what was wrong in Lynn's life seemed self-inflicted. She burned through friendships and relationships, destroying them by lying, cheating, even stealing. Her manager had dumped her, weary of babysitting her every time he found her a job. She was destructive and ruined the lives of so many people, but . . . my heart relented. It was true that she had hurt me terribly, but by chasing me away she had sent me to a much better life, while hers continued in decline. The person she had hurt the worst was herself.

I could have pity. I was now in a better place to perhaps help her, but what I would *not* do is be dragged back into her whirlwind life. I approached the bed and said softly, "Lynn, can you hear me?"

She opened her eyes and looked up at me, focusing for the first time since we had gotten to her. "Merry." She reached out one bony hand and I took it, but it was limp, so I laid it back down on the cover gently. "Where am I?"

I knew the doctor had already told her that, but I told her again, and I told her where she had been. "Lynn, how did you get tangled up with the Light and the Way Ministry people?"

She blinked, her pale eyes wide with worry. "Are they . . . they aren't coming to get me, are they? Those men—"

"No, honey, it's me, Merry. You know you can trust me. Everything's going to be okay." I gently touched her shoulder.

She sighed, burrowed under the cover, turned on her side away from me and fell deeply asleep without answering my question.

• • •

I headed outside and blinked at the bright sunlight. After the drama and trauma, it felt like I had lived through a whole day. It should be midnight, but it was just midafternoon. I needed to see where my people were and what they were doing.

I called Virgil, but he didn't pick up. Worried, I called Lizzie, and *she* didn't pick up. Nor did Pish. Or Shilo. Frantic, I dialed Dewayne's number.

"'Lo?"

"Dewayne! Where *is* everyone?" I cried, pacing. "No one's answering their phone!" I had worked myself up into a lather.

He chuckled. "It's okay, Merry, it's all right. We're batting five hundred."

I relaxed at his warm laugh and took a deep breath. "What does that mean? You know better than to use sports analogies with me."

"As I understand it you went there looking for your friend, but also would have liked Lizzie's friend and her mom, and that girl Cecily, to come away with you. Two outta four ain't bad."

"Did Lizzie find Alcina? Did she come away with you?"

"No, looks like that'll have to wait. But you got your friend, and we convinced Cecily she was safe with us."

"Oh."

"Hey, don't sound so disappointed!"

"No, that's great. *Really*, Dewayne! I'm disappointed that Felice and Alcina didn't come away, but happy that Cecily did. Did Barney and Voorhees arrive?"

"Virge told you we got the warning, right? With our cargo—meaning Cecily—we didn't want to run into those two, so we took off. Didn't see them."

"Okay." I was deeply worried about Felice and Alcina, but I wasn't sure how much more we could do. We'd have to talk about it.

"Virge and me did find a little surprise out there before your call."

"Oh? What was it?"

"Guess."

"Come on, Dewayne, don't make me drag it out of you. What's up?"

"We were a little far afield, you know? A little reconnaissance. A friend of yours was on-site. I've seen her around town, but I can't say she's a friendly sort."

My jaw dropped open. "You saw Isadore?" I cried. "Where?"

"I'd rather not say on the phone. You're never gonna believe it all."

"Where are you all?"

"Well, Cecily knew Glynnis, so we took her to Sheriff Baxter, and she's in now being interviewed."

"Poor kid," I said. "She must be scared!"

"That's why Virge is in with her; she wouldn't let go of him."

"That explains why he's not answering his phone."

"I think she's got a bit of a crush on your man."

"I don't blame her."

"Isadore is being interviewed too." His voice had an odd tone.

"What's up with that?"

"Oh, nothing . . . but I've interviewed her type before. I'm not sure they'll get all the information she has. She's . . ." His voice drifted off, as if he didn't know how to finish the description.

"Yeah, I know: closed off, to say the least. She's not a talker. If you don't ask the right questions, you don't get all she knows. If I can help, or more likely Hannah . . . she'll talk to Hannah Moore. Anyway, okay. I know you can't really talk." I thought for a long minute and huddled into my sweater. "I'm at the hospital, but Lynn is sleeping now and is going to be staying, so I may as well go home. Anyone available with a car?"

"You need someone to pick you up?" he replied.

I heard my darling Pish's voice in the background. "Shilo and I can come get her," he said.

"Tell him that's good, Dewayne. And thank you for answering!"

"No prob. Give him half an hour."

"Okay. I'm going to the cafeteria to get a tea, but then I'll be near the outpatient exit sitting on a bench in the sun."

The cafeteria was a small, dimly lit dungeon in the basement. I ordered tea, and they gave me a pale imitation about the color of straw. As I was fixing it up with honey, I overheard a mention of the Light and the Way. Interesting. I half turned; it was two women in scrubs sitting at a table nearby. I skulked and took a seat, my back turned to them.

It took a moment to tune in, but it was an involved and indignant conversation about one of the women's sisters, who had become a plural wife to the rudest guy she had ever met, some dude who looked like a golfer but acted like a Bible thumper.

Barney; *had* to be. This must be Mariah they were speaking of.

The woman referred to her sister as Maria, though.

"I don't get her at all! She left her husband and took her son—he's a grown-up, for God's sake, but she still treats him like he's her little boo; I mean, she named her damn kid 'gift of God,' for crying out loud—and hooked up with this guy, the one who yells at women on the streets. Whata *creep!*"

The other woman murmured something.

"Didn't I just *try* to talk her out of it, but she's got this idear in her head, something about divine retribution on all the sinners, or something. Something about the hand of God, and the prophet getting rid of all the loose women. She always was strange but she's been getting weirder and weirder lately. We had a big blow-up and I said to her, I said, *Maria, aren't you one of them loose women, since you're still married and yet you're out there shacked up with a guy with two wives?* I said to her, I said, *Maria, don't you want your own man?* And she said no. *Having a sister-wife . . .*" The woman snorted there, in disbelief—"*is sooo much better,* she said! More hands to do chores. Someone to talk to. So I said to her . . . I said, *If I want someone to talk to I'll get a dog. Better than a damn man.*"

The other woman mumbled a question.

The sister of the sister-wife loudly swore and said, "Screw that! I know that fricken prophet, Arden Voorhees. That whole family is bonkers. Arden and his brother, Bardo . . . they were troublemakers when they were kids, back in the seventies, but I always thought it was Bardo who was the real jerk, and that Arden—he was like a baby bird, you know, fluffy thin hair, kind of a weak-looking sad sack—was okay. Bardo was in jail, but he got killed in some fight as soon as he got out. They found his body in the woods. Guy was beaten to a pulp." She paused as the other woman murmured something. "No, they never convicted anyone. Can you imagine? Anyway . . . Arden went off the deep end from that day forward. Turned into the lunatic you see now, out there."

The other woman asked a question, but her voice was still so soft I didn't catch it. However, the answer was loud and clear.

"Oh, I have no *doubt* Voorhees is behind that murder. That poor kid. Who else would have done it but the jerk who convinced her he was the freakin' be-all and end-all prophet of the world? Glynnis Johnson's death is Arden Voorhees's fault."

Chapter Fifteen

They both got up and left, after one checked her watch. I tossed the rest of my crap tea—it wasn't even worth drinking—and followed, finding my way out of the dungeon and back out to the sunshine, thinking deeply. Something was not right in that conversation. I'd have to find a quiet space and think it through.

Pish picked me up at the hospital. While I sat in the car he ran in to see Lynn, but she was still sleeping. He spoke to a nurse and was told we could come back during visiting hours, and could check in by phone any time. He was warned, though, that they were running more diagnostics on her, an EKG and a CT scan, so she would be out of her room on occasion.

As we drove home by a circuitous route to avoid going through town, Pish told me about his adventures at the encampment, which did indeed include a run-in with Mother Esther, who tried to dissuade Cecily from leaving. Her "persuasion"—a lengthy diatribe against our "kind of people"—almost worked; Cecily had seemed cowed by the woman. The argument was that we (Pish and myself in particular) had strayed so far from the path that we were dangerous to know.

Lizzie was the hero of the day, Pish said. As Cecily wavered, Lizzie told her that we were all good people, and that she should be free to choose who to befriend. She told Cecily that there was a place for her wherever she was.

If I had ever had a kid, I'd want her to be just like Lizzie.

Pish drove me all the way to my house and let me off. I collapsed, exhausted, on our roomy and soft sofa, with Becket sitting on my chest, not allowing me to move. I got texts, at least: Cecily, after talking to the police for hours, was staying with Lizzie at her grandmother's.

Virgil came home late. We made love, nice and slow, to some new soul music. Music has always provided the rhythm of my lovemaking. With Miguel it was Satie and Debussy. With Virgil it is funk or R&B or soul, from Marvin Gaye to Ella Mai. I'm happy that my two loves have/had such different tastes. Not everything has gone right in my life, but I do choose most excellent lovers.

I lay tucked under his arm after, and we talked softly in the velvety darkness. He filled in what Dewayne had hinted at. There was indeed a shelter quite a distance from the others in the encampment, as we had seen in Lizzie's photos. It was powered by generators and filled with gadgetry and junk food. Someone — probably Voorhees — had a fondness for frozen burritos, Confetti Pop-Tarts and Funyuns. That explained his garlicky oniony breath. There, Virgil and Dewayne suspected, in the lair, out of sight of the congregants, the prophet hung out in warmth and comfort. The two men had broken in to look around and discovered Isadore there snooping.

She warmed up to Dewayne more than him, my husband said with a laugh, and told our friend what she had figured out so far. After a good long look at the financial ledgers, which were mostly stored there, at the prophet's lair — she was supposed to work on them there and only there — she knew more than the prophet likely thought she would. She showed them the books and Dewayne took photos with his cell phone of some of the pages. The woman is smart and numbers speak to her in ways words speak to others. There was something illegal going on with the Light and the Way Ministry, she said.

But what?

The group's only income was supposed to be from the congregants' jobs — payment for which they were supposed to turn over — and any donations they received from folks in town. There were, apparently, a few (*very* few!) who gave money to Barney to shut him up. But Isadore had figured out from the ledgers that there was money coming in that could not be accounted for, with only a code for the entries. And there was money going out, too, that was likewise given code names.

Some of the outflow could likely be explained by how the prophet was living when not at the encampment. Besides the Pop-Tarts and Funyuns, there were booze bottles, fast-food wrappers and condoms, a satellite TV, video gaming systems, and lots and lots more. But the extra money coming in . . . there was no source listed.

"What would be your best guess?"

"Offhand? Maybe there's some connection between the prophet and an illegal drug supply Baxter has been having trouble tracking a source for," Virgil murmured. "I need to have another look around that whole compound. Might be touchier now that Voorhees and Barney have been released."

Isadore was puzzled, she said, by gaps in the ledgers. Some were missing. She'd try to find out where they were, and she'd try to find out what the codes in the books meant.

"I hope she doesn't get herself in trouble," I fretted. "I have this feeling that I know something but can't remember it, or figure it out," I said. I told him everything I had heard or seen that day. "Maybe it will come together in my sleep and I'll wake up with a revelation."

"Hallelujah," Virgil said, and kissed me.

I was exhausted and fell asleep wrapped in his arms long before we had covered everything from our tumultuous day.

Morning inevitably arrived, and as I made us both breakfast, I told Virgil about Lynn, and also more coherently about the conversation I overheard in the hospital cafeteria. He nodded but was silent. There was a lot he had to cover that day, but I could tell he was disappointed that they hadn't discovered anything to do with Glynnis's murder. So far at least.

It was best to leave him to brood when he was thinking things over like that.

I poured him another cup of coffee in a tall travel mug, reminded him we had dinner guests coming, then ran back upstairs to our lofty bedroom as he departed. I had a shower and planned my day. Dewayne, Patricia, Sheriff Urquhart and his girlfriend, ADA Trujillo, were coming to dinner. I needed the makings of a good meal, and wine, and dessert, which I was not going to prepare; that was going to be all Binny's European Bakery.

But first I had phone calls to make. I called Zee and some others who I thought might like to know that Lynn was okay. Sadly, most were interested — it was a good piece of gossip — but not enthusiastic enough to make the long trek from New York City to western New York State to sit by her bedside. I had counted on the sadness of her story to make up for all the harm she had done and bridges she had burned, but it didn't.

Lynn had hurt me badly, and given her accusation against me of grand theft, it could have easily ruined my life if she had been more believable. And all because she had pawned that necklace — it wasn't hers, it was on loan—and was so stoned she either forgot or was ashamed and blamed its disappearance on me. Would I, hearing about her plight from a distance, come so far for a woman who had damaged me so deeply? I'd like to think I'm a good enough soul, but I'm not sure.

Seeing her in person made it more real; I *felt* how lost she must have been to first, try to find me, and second, end up in the hands of that cult. I was deeply ambivalent about the whole thing. I'd have to see how I felt when Lynn was well enough to talk. If it was the same old Lynn, making excuses and blaming everyone else for her behavior, then I'd help her, of course, but I'd probably keep my distance.

Fortunately, I could rely on my darling Pish, the very embodiment of kindness. He has a soft spot for lost souls. He was going to the hospital armed with notes on the book he had just finished writing—he is actually a fairly well-known author now, after two well-received nonfiction books on financial scams and cons—to think over his editing. He would make sure she had a phone and television, and whatever personal supplies she needed. There was no better person to sit at a hospital bedside, and it freed me to do what I needed to do.

And what I needed to do was a lot of food shopping. I dressed carefully in a fallish outfit. Though I often go shopping for plus-size clothes, most recently with Patricia, Dewayne's wife and my surprising new friend, to an outlet mall, I also do more shopping online than I should. A gal has to look her best, after all. I had found an awesome new-to-me clothing company called VENUS; their plus-size selection is cool, casual, and budget-friendly. I threw on a mock-neck keyhole olive green top over floral-detail embroidered jeans, and slipped my feet into leather clogs. I grabbed a dark gold pashmina, my Birkin bag and keys, and away I went.

I headed to Ridley Ridge first for beer, none being available in Autumn Vale. I already had wine, but Dewayne and Virgil are beer guys, and I supposed that Sheriff Urquhart is too. As I grabbed a case of Pabst, Virgil's favorite, and Miller, for variety, I saw one of the truckers I had met in the Ridley Ridge café a few days before.

He was yakking at the cashier, a typically vacant-eyed RiRi gal, lacking any ambition but a joint and a pizza on Friday night. "Those cops got it all wrong," he said, his loud voice full of village braggadocio. "Those gals out there at that religious compound . . . they know what they're doing. Women like a strong hand at the plow, y'know what I mean?" He did that wink and click-click of the mouth to indicate the sexual prowess of a commanding alpha male.

I sighed and plunked down my cases of beer on the counter.

"Buyin' a little something for your man?" Trucker Guy said.

I wanted so badly to say it was supplies for my weekly sewing circle. Or for the orgy I had planned for later. I did want to shock and correct him, but I only lie in emergencies. I remained silent, and Trucker Guy ignored me, gabbing on to the bored cashier as she rang through my purchases. I added a stack of fashion magazines to drop off for Lynn at the hospital.

"Those gals are just following nature. Lookin' for a man to tell them what to do and take care of them."

I suddenly remembered the guy's name . . . Bob. Swiveling from my goodies on the counter, I stared at him. "I thought you said those are religious nuts out there, communists and the like? You said that just a few days ago in the coffee shop."

He glared at me. "Hmph."

"No, come on, that's what you said. Which is it? Are they nuts, or do they have the goods?"

"Figures," he grunted in disgust. He tossed back his greasy hair and jammed his trucking company ball cap down on his head. "A woman finally listens to me and it's just to throw crap back in my face."

"You seem to know a whole lot about the religious group."

"Not me!" he said. "Don't know a thing about 'em."

"Oh, come on, Bob, you sold them a piece of your land!" the cashier said with a sly glance.

"Is that true?" I asked, astonished. "Why would you do that?"

"Who'd you hear that from?" Bob asked the girl with a squinty gaze.

"It's not like it's a secret," she said, back to being bored again. "Everyone knows. That's old gossip from two, three years ago." She thumbed through one of the fashion magazines, stopped to ogle a TV star, then scanned it, the beep blending with her voice as she said, "Everyone and his mama knows you sold them twenty acres for a song, that patch along Marker Road." She looked up at him and squinted her eyes. "You and Walt own the land, right? I heard he wasn't too happy with you over that."

I cocked my head to one side and stared at the shaggy guy, who was scritch-scratching his three-day growth of stubble. "Why would you sell your land to those religious nuts, as you call them?"

"None of your beeswax," he said, then stomped out of the store.

The dull-eyed cashier snickered as she watched him go, then looked back at me. "That'll be twenty-four ninety-five."

"On debit," I said. "Do you know him well? He was really jawing at you."

She slid the card reader across the counter to me. "He's bored."

I tapped and said, "Doesn't he work?"

"Yeah, but he's a trucker, so it's sporadic, you know? He's always got a wad of cash, so I guess he's doing okay. My cousin dances at the Randy Goat and says he's always in there and tips good."

"My friend Emerald works there sometimes as a cocktail waitress." The Randy Goat—the name was new, the bar was not—was a dive bar, and not one of the fun ones. It had intended to be a cocktail lounge but sank in status until it was now a greasy dive with bad lighting, all the ambiance—and odor—of a back alley.

"I know Emerald! She's nice."

"So, who is Walt? And why does he co-own farmland with Bob?"

"Walt's his brother. It's the family farm, you know?"

Walt . . . the name rang a bell. Aha! The current Millicent had spoken of a Walt who was a mechanic and had his own shop. I asked the cashier and she said yes, that was the same Walt, a mechanic and a welder. My purchase completed, the cashier bagged it all.

There was a television over the checkout desk tuned to a local news channel. I glanced up and saw a tearful couple on-screen. "Can you turn that up?" I said, pointing at the TV.

She did, and we both listened.

"We want to know what happened to Glynnis," the man said, his voice trembling with anger as the woman sobbed into a tissue. "She was our daughter. Someone killed her, beat her to a pulp. The sheriff isn't telling us a goddamn thing!"

I recognized where the man and woman were standing; it was outside of the Ridley Ridge sheriff's department. This was Glynnis Johnson's parents. I felt a deep welling of pity for them and their pain. As the reporter droned on for a minute, giving a capsule explanation of the girl's body found by the side of the highway, a photo flashed on-screen of Anokhi Auretius.

Someone shoved a microphone in Glynnis Johnson's mother's face. Haltingly, she said that the composer had called her just that morning to offer her condolences. "She told me what my daughter said," the woman sobbed. "Glynnis said, 'Am I safe?'" Her voice choked with tears, and she wailed, her mouth stretched into a rictus of pain, such *deep* pain that it overwhelmed everything else. It took her a moment to get herself under control. "I guess she's safe now, in heaven," she finally sobbed, snot running from her nose.

The news channel went on to different news. The cashier sniffed. "Be nice if they cared as much about Glyn when she was alive as they do now that she's dead."

I examined her face, spotty and plain, but with the unthinking fresh healthfulness of youth. "Did you know her?"

"She was friends with my little sister. Glynnis was a nice kid, but her parents preferred their son always. He got everything he wanted and she got nothing." She leaned across the counter. "And her dad is a creepola . . . the kinda dad no one from soccer wants to drive them home, you know? My sister said he's a perv. Always staring at the girls in shorts."

I tried to get her to expand on that, but she just shook her head. If there was more, she would have been happy to divulge it. "What about the other missing girls lately?" I asked. "There have been a few, right?"

"I guess. But they're just dropouts. You know the kind, girls who take drugs, or run away from home, or hang out with the wrong people." She shrugged. "Those kinds of girls get in trouble." She had nothing more to say as a couple of friends came in. After that, she only had eyes for them as they chatted and giggled and whispered about what drugs they were going to try on the weekend.

Seemed to me she was exactly the kind of girl she was dismissing so easily. I picked up my bags.

"Have a nice day," she said as I headed to the door. I turned to look at her, but no smile lightened that most trite of sales phrases.

Some folks might write off the missing and dead girls as runaway troublemakers, but there was a pervasive feeling of dread in the larger community, I had heard. On social media locals were sharing sightings of "weirdoes and prowlers." People were watching each other closely, and doors were locked tightly; security cameras had been installed around homes, the local locksmith had more business than he could handle, and teenage girls were being given stricter curfews by diligent parents.

The newspaper had devoted many news stories and had even detailed all the young girls and women who had either gone missing in the last few years or whose bodies had been found. It was a stark reality, seeing it in black and white, and the chorus of questions was growing in the wake of Glynnis's death: What was Sheriff Ben Baxter doing? Was he even fit to do his job? Where were the missing daughters of Ridley Ridge? The national news cycle had so far ignored us; there was a political crisis in the capital going on. Isn't there usually, these days? I wasn't sure if several dead and missing girls not even making the national news was good—who wanted to be on CNN constantly?—or sad, that it was too everyday an occurrence for it to be front and center.

I dropped the magazines off with Pish, but Lynn was sleeping. She was zonked out as they adjusted her meds to work with the gallons of IV fluids they were pumping into her. I worried . . . did they know how to treat a bulimic oxy-dependent aging-out supermodel? But Pish was there and he could be imperious when necessary.

I told him what I had seen on the TV news, and how Anokhi had apparently called Glynnis's parents. One part of my brain wanted to accept what she had done as a lovely gesture, one mother to another. But the cynic in me recognized it as a savvy public relations move to stave off suspicion and criticism. I didn't know Anokhi well enough to know which was the real answer to why she had reached out, but then, it wasn't my call, or my business. I was sad that my cynicism had surfaced. Maybe I should accept a kind gesture at face value and leave it at that.

I returned to my car and sat for a long moment outside the hospital, haunted by Glynnis's mom's face, her eyes, her pained wail, mouth stretched wide and downturned, the inhuman howl that erupted from her. I remembered well how that kind of extreme pain felt, how it twisted your body, made muscles ache you didn't even know you had, caused every biological function in your body to act up. After Miguel died I spent hours howling in such pain, wishing with every atom of my being that I could join him. It took months before I could even function, before I could get up in the morning and make coffee and wash my face and comb my hair.

Glynnis's mother clearly hadn't slept since her daughter's body was discovered. Her eyes were rimmed in red and swollen, tears a constant stream down her cheeks. I hoped for their sake the crime would be solved soon. I knew enough now about crime detection to understand that a whole lot of slow work would be done before the solution could be found. Coroner's report, DNA analysis, fingernail scrapings, witness interviews, alibi investigation and much much more that I would never know about.

I started the car and pulled away from the curb, but then saw someone I wanted to talk to. It was Mariah's sister, whom I had overheard in the cafeteria the day before.

Chapter Sixteen

She was sitting on a park bench smoking a cigarette. She lit a fresh one from the butt of the old one, which she tossed in a receptacle designed for that function. I didn't know how to approach her, but decided it didn't really matter. Either she'd speak to me or she wouldn't.

Thin, with a halo of frizzy bleached blonde hair pulled back in a scrunchie, she smoked determinedly, like she only had so long and wanted to get in as much nicotine as she could to hold her until the next break. I walked up to her and smiled. "Hi. You don't know me."

"Thanks, Captain Obvious."

I chuckled politely and ducked the cloud of smoke. "I heard you talking about your sister, Maria, yesterday in the cafeteria. I think I've met her out at the Light and the Way Ministry compound."

"Yeah, so?"

"I thought you might like to know that she seems to be doing well."

Grudgingly, she said, "Okay. I guess that's good."

"But I'm really trying to wrap my head around what makes women join the group. You seemed to have some trouble with that too. I have a friend there . . . in fact, my friend introduced your sister to me as her sister-wife of Barney. What . . . why do you think women would be drawn to a guy like that?" I was trying to think of a way to ask a question more sensitive than that.

"I got no clue," she said, dragging deeply on the cigarette and lighting another, then butting out the second of her break-time cigarettes.

"Have you spoken to her since she moved out there? How are they living? Making money? It looks like such a tough life."

"I think she went out there because she was worried about her son," the woman said, her gruff voice. "Johnny was getting into trouble. She tried to keep him on the straight and narrow but . . ." She shrugged. "You know what kids today are like."

"What kind of trouble was he getting into?"

"Fighting, girls, drugs, no job, no goals . . . you know. The usual. She hooked up with that prophet when he was still living in Ridley

Ridge. I thought it was a phase. So did her hubby, poor jerk. But then they moved out to that place and never came back."

"And she married Barney?"

"Can't be married to him . . . not legally. She's still married."

"But what is she getting out of it . . . being married to Barney, with a sister-wife?"

The woman grew impatient, and I didn't blame her. She tossed her third cigarette down on the ground and stomped it. "Heck if I know," she groused, glaring at me. She picked up the butt and tossed it in the receptacle. "All I know is, in the old days my sister wouldn't have stood for that kind of life, being bossed by some man. I don't know what's going on, and I don't know what she's getting out of it, but whatever it is must be pretty important. I keep thinking . . . she's trying to protect Johnny from something. But I don't know what."

"This Johnny . . . what does he look like?"

Her expression shuttered. "That's none of your business," she said. "Why do you want to know?"

"Uh, I—"

"I gotta go back to work." She whirled and headed inside, through the outpatient entry.

I drove out of Ridley Ridge thinking of what little I had learned; Mariah was never a pushover who would let a man be her boss. But she was getting something out of the group, and it seemed to be protection for her Johnny. I'd need to find out who Johnny was. Maybe Gordy would know, though I didn't want to make another trip out to the compound. Maybe Cecily had met Johnny; I didn't even know how old he was or what he looked like.

I headed back to Autumn Vale and stopped in at Binny's. I had ordered a raspberry cream-filled cake. It was ready, and Binny boxed it up for me. She's a nice person, but her natural expression is not just RBF, it appears to reveal a disdain for all of humankind. That was especially evident today.

"What's up, Bin?" I asked.

She shrugged. "Just feeling off today," she said as she slid the box across the pass-thru to me.

"I know what you mean," I said. Cecily's account of her time at the compound was weighing on me, and the people we had left behind had me deeply concerned. If the police had managed to keep Voorhees and Barney locked up it would have been easier, but they were back among the others. I had been worrying at a few pieces of information all day, since the night before, but it was like a knot I couldn't undo. I needed to find the right end of the tangle. I felt if I found the right spot to tug, it would all unravel and begin to make sense.

There were bits and pieces that felt off. I told her about being out to the encampment a couple of times, and my worry about Gordy. Though she was about Gordy and Zeke's age, she hadn't grown up in Autumn Vale. Her mother had taken her away when she was young, leaving behind Binny's now-deceased older half brother with their dad, Rusty.

But she had gotten to know the two fellows since moving back after culinary school. She frowned, a worried grimace on her face. "Gordy's a nice guy, but he's so easily influenced. I hope no one convinced him to do something he ought not to have."

"What do you mean, Bin?"

"I don't know what I mean." She shook her head. "I have a bad feeling about it all."

"You're scaring me, Binny. What do you *mean*?"

"I wish I knew," she said, tears in her eyes. Teary-eyed, she nodded and went back to work.

I stared at her for a long minute as she bustled around in back, throwing pans and utensils about, the set of her shoulders letting me know she could feel me watching. I finally exited. Butcher shop next, a new business owned by a local farmer, Garth Owens. He was in the shop, which was not the usual case. It was most often one of his kids running the place. He was a lean fifty-something, grizzled and with a lined face, but quick moving and quick thinking. He had his own recipes for sausage, including a maple garlic that was so good people were starting to come from Batavia and even as far away as Rochester and Buffalo.

"Hey, Garth," I said. He looked up from his phone. "I called ahead for steaks."

"Yup; we got 'em. Virgil's grilling, huh?"

"He is. We've got company coming."

The bell rang over the door and Janice Grover, my dear friend and our ally in getting locals on board for the arts center, huffed in. We hugged. I hadn't seen her in a few weeks; she and her hubby, Simon, had been away, attending a wedding. I knew they were back, having seen Simon in the coffee shop the day before. As usual she wore a caftan-style dress, this time in autumnal shades, with a border of sunflowers along the bottom edge. She had topped it with an elaborate crocheted poncho in shades of gold, red and orange. She will *never* blend in with the crowd.

We exchanged pleasantries as Garth packaged my steaks, and she told me about the opera she had attended in Toronto, put on by the Opera Atelier group. "It was glorious," she sighed. "I have some names I think you and Pish should investigate."

I told her we'd welcome input, and then conversation inevitably turned to local news.

"So, what's this I hear about all your intrigue at that encampment . . . those batty Light and Way folks?" she asked.

"It's a mess," I said. "It wouldn't bug me if they were doing their own thing—to each their own and all that—but . . ." I lowered my voice and leaned in to her. "I'm worried they're tied up with the missing girls, and the death of Glynnis Johnson." I told her about Anokhi and her family finding Glynnis's body. "She was found on the highway pretty close to the encampment." Garth went into the back for a new roll of butcher paper. "I'm worried. I can't help but think that it's one of the men from the encampment. There are a few possibilities: the prophet, Arden Voorhees; Barney, that awful street preacher . . . he's the worst, with vile views on women! And even Nathan, the boy who roomed with Gordy right here in town . . . he gives me the creeps. Remember we had to get him fired for stalking Shilo." I shook my head. "He seems to keep to himself out at the compound though, along with Gordy. It's the prophet and Barney who get to town the most. It's deeply upsetting."

Janice nodded, her chins quivering. "It's terrible. I heard that the girls at that place are treated like servants. I don't like that. I was talking to Helen this morning—Glynnis Johnson's father is a cousin of hers. She said Reverend Maitland's Sunday sermon is going to be about those who use the name of the Lord to do the devil's work."

"So *you* knew about that encampment, too? How did I miss hearing about it, if it's been there for years?"

"I have friends in Ridley Ridge, which is how I know. And with my antiques business, I keep up on who is getting rid of what and where. Those folks started buying up lots of junk . . . you know, household stuff. They started out at a big rented house near Ridley Ridge. Kept a low profile for the longest time, even after they bought that land."

Garth had returned and was bagging my wrapped steaks. He gave a loud *humph* of displeasure. "Couldn't believe it when Bob Taggart sold some of his family land to those looney tunes."

It seemed that many people, like the cashier in Ridley Ridge, were still mystified by that. It made me wonder too. "You know the trucker, Bob?"

"Sure. Grew up with him and his brother, Walt. Walt's a welder; runs his own garage in Ridley Ridge."

"Yes, I heard of him from a waitress at the coffee shop. He's a mechanic, too. I heard today that he was not totally on board with his brother selling land to the Light and the Way folks."

"The Taggart farm and mine . . . they're right across from each other on Silver Creek Line. Bob told his brother to worry about his shop, that he'd run the farm like he ought to. Then he goes and sells twenty acres to that weirdo, Arden Voorhees, and his crazy crew."

"Did he have his brother's permission?" I asked.

"I guess he musta, even if Walt gripes about it now and then," Garth said, sliding an elastic band over the top of the plastic bag. "Walt still spends a lot of time at the farm, though. He's got a big welding shop there . . . all kinds of trucks coming and going. I guess he fixes 'em out there, rather than in town. We all grew up together, me, Bob, Walt, Lloyd Mackenzie . . . he's another neighbor; he's got land on the next line, behind Bob 'n Walt's land. Bob shouldna sold to that bunch, though."

"How could Bob know what Voorhees was going to do with the land, Garth?" Janice said.

"Come on, now, how could he not? Anything involving those Voorhees boys was gonna be trouble. Always were." He handed me my bag and I paid as he kept talking. "We went to school together. I always thought Bardo was the trouble. Arden more or less kept his nose clean. He was married, a good woman, Essie Palinkas . . . nice family. Good values. Then Bardo dies, after which Essie disappears and Arden goes bonkers. He was so medicated that he couldn't even come to his own brother's funeral! Pissant turnout anyway."

I had heard that refrain before, that it was Bardo's murder that set Arden off on the wrong path. But no one goes off the rails at fifty-something. "Are you sure Arden wasn't troubled before that?"

Garth snorted. "Nah. Well, maybe. He was a skinny runt afraid of his own shadow. Bardo bossed him. Oh, Arden did things, sure—killed a neighbor's cat once, and got in trouble for spying on the girls in the locker rooms—but it was always Bardo put him up to it."

It seemed to me that people blamed Bardo for whatever Arden did wrong. And they still were, in a way, blaming Arden's current weirdness on Bardo's death. "So why do you think Bob Taggart sold the land to Voorhees? It does seem an odd move."

"I'll tell ya why . . . Bob has always looked out for his own self."

"What do you mean?" I asked, putting my wallet back in my Birkin. "How was selling land to the ministry folks looking after himself?"

"Free labor. Bob never did like working. He sold that Voorhees fellow the land dirt cheap, and in exchange he has guys to work his acreage and look after his animals—leaves him free to truck, rather than work the land—and gals to clean his house, do his laundry and cook his meals. Perfect setup for a lazy-ass jerk like that."

"I guess it's a symbiotic arrangement."

"Sure, if by that you mean using each other. Not the way to live, if you ask me, getting other people to do all your work for you. Why don't he remarry, have kids, have someone to pass it all down to? Selfish, if you ask me."

I hesitated, but I was troubled still about Shilo's reluctant admission that there was some connection between an abused woman and either the ministry or someone connected to it. "Garth, have you ever heard anything about Bob mistreating women?"

He looked up from his cash register and frowned over the counter. "Now, what would make you ask that?"

I didn't want to be more precise. "Just wondering. As one does. Have you?"

"Bob was married once upon a time. This is going back twenty years or more. When his wife divorced him she claimed he beat her, but she never charged him or anything. Probably made it up to get out of the marriage or she *would* have charged him."

I stiffened, but breathed through it. As much as I wanted to rip him a new orifice, I resisted the urge. It's a hard lesson in life that not every battle can be won. I simply said, "Garth, I hope you don't believe that. She may have had private motives for not charging him."

He shrugged. "Doesn't make sense to me. If someone beat me up, I'd sure as hell charge him."

"Perhaps she was concerned that if she did charge him, and he got off on the charge, he'd retaliate."

Garth frowned, started to shake his head, but then stopped. "I don't know. I don't understand it, I guess."

So Bob Taggart was likely an abusive jerk as well as being a misogynistic creep. Was he also a serial murderer of young girls who landed at the cult situated on his land? It was possible.

I waited as Janice bought some of the sausage and then walked out with her, down the two steps to the sidewalk. "Bob and his land seem to be a sore spot for Garth." I was uneasy. "I mean, even though Bob's marriage failed, and he might be a wife beater, Garth believes he should remarry, have kids and pass the farm down to them. Some people are better off alone. It's none of anyone else's business."

"Garth is a by-the-books kind of guy," Janice agreed. She grabbed me in a bear hug. "Honey, I know things are grim right now — no one feels worse for the parents of that poor girl than me — but you keep chugging along."

A hug from Janice goes a long way toward making one feel better. We parted ways and I headed home. I got a text from Lizzie; she and Cecily wanted to come out to talk to me. Perfect. As I pulled into the parking area, I texted back to meet me at the castle. Becket, who had been lounging in the fall sunshine on the terrace, followed me in and all the way to the kitchen.

I made some lunch, a plate of sandwiches for the girls and myself, as well as some fresh-baked muffins from the pail of batter I had stored in the big professional fridge. I heard the girls enter but knew Lizzie would give Cecily a tour, first, before coming to find me. I put on the pot for coffee.

When they joined me I stared; Cecily looked like a different girl. Her plump figure was dressed in leggings, a long shirt with a blue jean jacket over it, and boots I recognized as some of Emerald's. But it was her hair that was the real kicker. She had cut it shorter and dyed the blonde a fabulous magenta. "Wow," I said, examining her. "From *Little House on the Prairie* to punk goddess in two days."

She smiled. "It all feels . . . weird. I've been out of it so long."

We sat at the central trestle table in the kitchen and had lunch, as Becket twined around our legs begging for food. I fed him—again—and brought out the platter of muffins. Cecily tried and failed to get Becket onto her lap. She had coffee, while Lizzie preferred her bottle of water with lemon.

"This is so good," Cecily said with a sigh, draining the last of her coffee to wash down the last bite of muffin. "When I saw you guys at the camp I knew I wanted to leave. I was so tired . . . and tired of being afraid."

"Why were you afraid? Did anyone threaten you?"

She frowned and flicked a muffin crumb off her plate. Becket scooted to claim it off the floor, pouncing on it like it was a bug. "I can't explain it. We had to stay up all night for prayer, you know, and there were these long boring tapes we had to listen to. They were of this old guy from way back . . . I mean, they were, like, cassette tapes!"

"What did he say in the lectures?"

"That there was one way to salvation, and that was to follow his word."

"The guy on the tape?"

She shrugged. "I guess. I never thought of that. Mother Esther said it meant we had to follow Prophet Voorhees."

"Was the prophet around much?"

"Not really. He was there sometimes, but other times Mother said he was praying and couldn't be disturbed. She'd tell us what he'd said we were to do, like, stay up all night scrubbing the kitchen shack, or doing laundry by hand."

Lizzie snorted. "Bet that all came from her. Bet Voorhees never said anything of the kind. And I'll bet *she* did nothing."

"No, she . . ." Cecily paused and cocked her head. "I guess

you're right. I mean, she'd say she was going to do something, and would check in on us, but I don't think I ever saw her actually working."

"Who is she? Do you know?"

"Mother Esther? She's just . . . her."

I got out my phone and texted Hannah, asking if she could find out who she was. "So what else did the tapes say?"

"The preacher said that women are made from a tiny piece of man, and she is formed to tempt and betray men. He said that women were created by God but were corrupted by Satan. If she isn't kept under control, she will lead to the downfall of the United States." Cecily's plump cheeks colored faintly. "It sounds so stupid now that I'm away from it."

I put my hand over hers on the counter. "Not stupid, honey; it's mind control. Tell me . . . you said you were scared. What . . . or *who* were you afraid of?" I wondered if she would say anything about Bob Taggart. Had he been hanging around the camp?

"I don't know why I was scared," she whispered, frowning. "I mean, no one beat me, you know?"

"If you were scared, why didn't you leave?"

Cecily shook her head and knit her thick brows together. "I don't know. It's like I can't remember what kept me there. I mean, I *knew* I couldn't go home; my dad won't have me. But I felt like . . . like I was bad, and I needed to be punished. So I stayed. I kept hoping I'd be judged . . . I don't know . . . *worthy* or something." She sighed and rolled her shoulders. "I don't understand myself. Seeing you guys . . . it woke me up, and I knew I had to leave. But I'm still kinda scared. Even now, I keep looking over my shoulder. It was . . . it was those *tapes*."

"What else did they say?"

"A lot." She picked at a fingernail and frowned, biting at the skin along her thumb. She stopped and looked up at me. "I don't know if you'll understand. What the prophet said, and the preacher on those tapes, that women needed to stay home and raise babies . . . it made a weird kind of sense after a while. The world's messed up, right? I mean, there are all kinds of troubles in the world today. I started to wonder . . . is it because none of us are living right? Especially me. I'd been smoking, and doing weed, and stealing money from my dad's wallet, and drinking his booze. I didn't obey my dad. What if the mess my life was in was because I wasn't following the real way? I mean, maybe it's harsh, but maybe that was the way it was supposed to be."

"Who benefits by women staying 'in their place'?"

She looked down at our joined hands. "Well, men, I guess."

"Right. When people tell you some way is the only way, always consider the why of it . . . who benefits?"

She nodded slowly. "I don't get why what the prophet said made sense to me when I was there, and doesn't now. And Mother Esther said that we needed to replenish the earth with . . . with white babies. Or whites were going to disappear." Her cheeks turned a bright crimson.

Mother Esther's "mongrel" comment about Lizzie came back to me. I took a deep breath and let it out slowly. "*You* know that's wrong, though."

She nodded. "I never believed it. And I didn't want to marry, like, Nathan, or Barney, or whoever. I hated them *all* after a while!"

"But the prophet made you feel guilty for wanting something else beyond having kids and obeying a husband."

"It wasn't the prophet, it was more Mother Esther. Whenever we would talk, Arden—the prophet, you know—would say he didn't really give a crap. Except he didn't say crap. *She* was the one who kept hammering away at it. I mean, I told her, yeah, I want kids. *Some*day." She grinned. "Just not *now*."

We all laughed. I was relieved by the spark of humor I had seen in Cecily. I found it interesting that Arden Voorhees didn't seem to be overly committed to his Light and Way Ministry philosophy, as put forth by Mother Esther. "I'm proud of you for breaking free, Cecily. It took courage. Now . . . why did you guys want to come out here?"

The girls exchanged looks. "Cecily was wondering . . . she wants to *try* to go back and live with her dad, but they left things on bad terms. I said you'd talk to him for her."

I felt a moment of consternation . . . I didn't know Cecily well enough, and didn't know her dad at all. "I don't see why me talking to him would help. I'd say . . . get reenrolled in school to prove you're serious, *then* try to talk to him yourself."

"They don't care, my dad and stepmom," she said, tears welling in her eyes. "They're never going to talk to me. We left things on bad terms, you know, like . . . real bad. I'm scared they hate me."

I sighed. "I know how you feel but trust me, your dad loves you. I'd bet they'll take you back in."

"So you won't talk to him?" Lizzie said, immediately going into combative mode, as usual.

"I didn't say that. Let me think about it."

"You don't *have* to," Cecily said glumly. She cradled her coffee in both hands. "Maybe I'll head for New York, like I was going to. I could probably hitch."

"Okay, I'll *talk* to him! I promise." The thought of this girl, damaged already by what she'd been through, heading to New York City on her own was too much. I wasn't sure she had learned her lesson at the Light and the Way compound and could easily step from one abusive situation into another. From my own experience it takes successive hard knocks to get it through the thickest of skulls; Cecily and I were very much alike, I was afraid. When I was her age I was exactly that same blend of knowingness and naïveté. However . . . as I noted another look between the two of them, I thought I may have been scammed into agreeing.

"Cecily, do you mind if we talk more about your experience out at the encampment?"

She shrugged. "I've already talked myself hoarse with the cops."

"I still have a lot of questions, and some of them may not be ones the police thought of. I suppose they asked you about Glynnis?"

She nodded. "I don't know what happened to her. She disappeared one night."

Disappeared; I wondered where she had been before she was found by the highway. "How did she get along with everyone?"

"The older women didn't like her as much as they liked me. She was so pretty. There was even talk that the prophet was going to marry her."

"How did she feel about that?"

"She wasn't happy, but it would have been better than marrying Barney or Nathan."

"Aren't there other men there?"

"Yeah, but they're not around much. Some of them work for the construction company, some of them work on the farm. Most of them live somewhere else."

"That's weird," I said. I was puzzled by so many aspects of the Light and the Way camp, but that explained why there were so many women and children and so few men around the camp.

"I never thought about it much. It was just the way it was. The prophet doesn't let them marry, not until they prove themselves, anyway. That's what Gordy is trying to do, prove himself worthy. The guys have a lot more freedom than the girls. Even when some of them did come for prayer meetings, we didn't get to hang out with them much. Mother Esther kept us separate, though it was Barney who really enforced the rules."

"So Barney is the boss?"

She shook her head. "He still has to listen to the prophet. But he's around us more, so we have to listen to him."

Lizzie growled under her breath; she was still anxious about Felice and Alcina, as was I. "Do they have cars? How do they get to the construction site?"

"Barney or the prophet drives them into town in the van. Or they stay off-site. Like I said, most of them only come back to the encampment on weekends."

"So the women didn't like Glynnis as much as they liked you . . . maybe there were other reasons than that she was pretty?"

Cecily shrugged and turned her mug in her hands. "She was snoopy, too . . . she got caught listening in on conversations, and she would go through people's stuff."

That was more likely why people didn't like her. "Did anyone threaten her? Did she ever confide in you anything she had found out by snooping?"

Frowning and twisting her lips, Cecily thought that over. "She was really smart . . . smarter than me. She said . . . lemme think."

I tapped my fingernails on the table as she stared off into space. She met my gaze.

"She said something like . . . anyone who thought the prophet believed any of his own lies was full of sh . . . sugar."

"Is that all?"

Cecily rolled her eyes. "I had a few other things on my mind, and Glynnis . . . you had to know her. I really liked her, but the girl was a drama queen. She liked to say mysterious stuff and then just look mysterious when you asked her to make it clearer."

That worried me. What did Glynnis know? And had it led to her death? "When Glynnis disappeared, did anyone say anything to you all?"

Cecily shook her head. "She had talked about running away," she whispered. "She said there was something wrong about the Light and the Way. She told me she was going to leave, but I didn't tell anyone, I swear. But that's why I didn't think anything when she was gone."

Plus, there wasn't time; she was gone, but then she was found by the highway soon after, maybe the very next evening. "You may not have been the only one she told, right? About thinking there was something going on at the encampment?"

"I guess not."

"Is there anything else you can remember about her? Maybe about her snooping?"

"She was caught a few times away from the women's camp. That wasn't allowed."

"You had boundaries?"

Cecily nodded. "We could go as far as the church hut, but no farther, supposedly, though I saw Mariah wandering back in the field at times. She said she was looking for herbs." She sniffed in disgust. "If so, she never found any."

I thought of the prophet's hut, with its stock of "luxuries" like Pop-Tarts and electronics. They couldn't have anyone telling the girls what they were missing, I suppose. "But if she found anything, she never told you."

"No." Cecily looked off into the distance. "Mother Esther used to take her aside all the time and talk to her. That's why some of us thought Mother was getting Glynnis ready to be the prophet's next wife."

"Did he ever seem to take a special interest in her?"

"It was all Mother Esther. To us girls she said Glynnis was good breeding stock, whatever the heck that means. Sounds gross to me. She never said that to Glynnis that I know of. Anyway, like I said, the prophet wasn't around much, except to lecture us about once a week, and I didn't think he paid any attention to Glynnis."

"How do you think the prophet would have taken it if Glynnis *did* try to run away?"

"He would have found out. He had snitches."

"Like Barney and Nathan?"

"More Barney than anyone, but Mother Esther, too."

Lizzie's phone rang and she answered it. After talking for a moment, she looked up. "We gotta go, Cecily. Grandma needs her car back. I sure hope Mom comes back sometime soon so I can use her car. Grandma's always wanting to go to church or shopping."

The girls left after I promised to talk to Cecily's father. Our conversation had left me with a vague sense of unease. Nothing about the Light and the Way Ministry added up.

Chapter Seventeen

But I had a dinner party to prepare for, and talking to Cecily and Lizzie had put me behind. I tidied the castle kitchen and returned to my own house, talking to Pish on the phone as I did some prep work for dinner. Lynn had been awake for a while and had told him what she remembered. She had, a couple of months ago—or more, she wasn't too clear on times—decided to come find me. She swore I asked her to. That was clearly impossible because I hadn't spoken to the woman in years. During the time I worked for her Lynn often imagined she had spoken to people and that they had promised her things. She was a pathological liar, I thought, but I was starting to wonder if she had very real mental health issues that had gone undiagnosed. Instead of becoming exasperated with her all those times, I wish I had tried to get her help.

Lynn did say one interesting thing that Pish passed on to me: one night, not long before she was rescued, she swore she heard a girl screaming. She didn't know when it was. She was prowling the encampment looking, she admitted, for drugs, even weed, which she assumed *someone* would have. She seemed to think she was in some 1970s-style hippie commune, Pish said. She thought the prophet was like the hippie king, or something, a guru maybe, when it was more like a fundamentalist/survivalist camp.

A girl screaming. I vacuumed the living room and replaced the scented candles, wondering . . . what did that mean? Was Lynn hallucinating? Was she lying? The police were coming to interview her from her hospital bed. They were, of course, intent on finding out if Glynnis Johnson's murder could be attributed to anyone living at the Light and the Way Ministry compound. So far there was no evidence either way, and neither Sheriff Baxter, whose jurisdiction the encampment was in, nor any other police service could prove a link. Already facing lawsuits for his ill-timed and poorly planned raid, Baxter had to be sure before going back in.

But given the last few months of Glynnis's life, it made sense to think that those at the compound were most likely to have killed her. Or did it, given the deaths of other girls going back several years? If she was running away, as Cecily said she had been planning, it could have been misfortune; perhaps there was a serial killer driving the back roads of our area, just looking for easy victims, and she had tried to hitch a ride away from there.

Pish, in full protective bulldog mode, was staying at the hospital to make sure the detectives didn't bully Lynn. I said to come join us at my house when he got back, if he felt up to it.

• • •

Our company had arrived.

I love my Craftsman house. We have a long covered front porch that is wheelchair accessible; I was thinking of our friend Hannah when I insisted on that. When you come in the front door, there is a smallish office to the left, and then you enter the great room from the foyer. It is spacious and comfortable, open concept for the most part, with natural wood built-ins, glass-doored shelves on both sides of a stone fireplace that hold books and treasures from both Virgil and my life. You move from there naturally into the large kitchen, and from there the eating area, overlooking the stone patio out back.

The lights were dim and there was a fire in the fireplace, so it felt cozy, and conversation was flowing. We have a U-shaped leather sofa with soft cushions in every corner, and our visitors looked supremely comfortable, propped up against the cushions drinking scotch and wine in cut-crystal glasses. It was nice to have company in our new house. As much as I love the castle, entertaining there always felt like it was either a grand affair or we were letting the place down. Here in our human-sized abode we have a gorgeous kitchen where people can gather at the breakfast bar while I cook and Virgil grills on the patio off the kitchen.

After cocktails I moved to the kitchen to put the finishing touches on dinner. Virgil grabbed the container of steaks that had been coming up to room temperature for about an hour. Our guests, lonely for our fascinating company, trailed us. I set out canapés on the island, and Urquhart nabbed some shrimp, then followed my husband out the back door into the chilly evening air.

There is a lovely seating nook in a bay window that overlooks the patio, all framed in the natural wood that dominates our Craftsman home. I had custom cushions and curtains sewn for the nook, so the windows were framed in natural shades, lots of olive green, burnt umber and sienna. Dewayne and Patricia sat there with ADA Elisandre Trujillo, who had insisted we all call her Ellie. They chatted in an animated fashion, laughter rising and falling. Dewayne is a natural raconteur, and his stories range from pathos to humor, as he easily assesses the proper temperature of the conversation.

Urquhart was still out on the patio having a beer with Virgil as he grilled the steaks. We were serving standard Autumn Vale fare: t-bones and baked potatoes, with a big green salad. It doesn't do to stray too far off the beaten path. I had worried that Ellie might be vegan, as my friend Shilo is, but I needn't have worried. The assistant DA called herself a hypocritical carnivore, and I confessed I was the same. We both love animals and yet consume meat. Maybe someday I'll come to terms with my hypocrisy and become a vegetarian.

I had also made another protein, though, for anyone who wasn't fond of steak. Ahead of time I had prepared boneless skinless chicken thighs stuffed with a delicious blend of cream cheese, cheddar and green onions. I popped those in the oven with the baked potatoes (which had already been baked once; this was their second delicious bake stuffed with cheddar) and set the timer.

Ellie slid down from the banquette seating and sat on the floor near the breakfast bar crooning into Becket's fur; my cat was milking it for all it was worth. "I've heard the stories about him surviving in the woods for a year." She looked up at me as I used a mandoline to sliver red onions. "How is that possible?"

"I've never been sure," I said, watching my marmalade cat stretch luxuriously and roll over, his lovely ginger fur contrasting with the dark wood flooring. "He knows these woods a lot better than I do. I've begun wondering if he used the fairy tale houses as shelter in the worst of winter."

Ellie cocked her head to one side. She's a lovely woman, petite and brown-eyed, with curly, almost frizzy, hair. She's the kind of woman people underestimate, I'd bet; she looks cute and fluffy, but her voice is mesmerizing, and there are flashes of deep intelligence. "What do you mean by fairy tale houses?"

I explained how there were structures in the woods behind our house that I didn't know what to make of at first. There was one built of river rock, like a cobblestone tower about seven feet tall, and another of now-rotting wood cut with a skil saw to resemble gingerbread. "Then a young friend, Lizzie Proctor, was going through some of the old photo albums left in the castle attic. There was a photo of me, with my father, grandfather and great-uncle. It was going to be a fairy tale woods for me, a kind of elaborate playhouse." I shook my head and tossed the slivers of red onion into the salad bowl. "I never knew," I said softly.

"Wow!" she said, ruffling Becket's thick fur. "Did you get to play in it?"

"Not that I remember. Unfortunately, my grandfather died in an accident, and my dad blamed my great-uncle. There was a big fight, and my dad and mom went back to New York City. My dad died before he ever got to make up the quarrel, and my mom, being a spitfire herself, only brought me out here once, after my dad died. She had a big fight with my uncle Melvyn and we left. I didn't remember that until I came out here. I never knew that this was my legacy—the castle and the property—until after Melvyn died and the lawyers found me."

"That's amazing." She stood and dusted off her bottom. She was wearing a long flowy skirt in a moss green, with a billowy floral top in soft greens, rose and taupe. She leaned on the breakfast bar and watched me chop romaine. "Didn't your uncle try to contact you all those years?"

"He was looking for me, but I was married and had legally changed my last name to Paradiso. My husband and I traveled a lot, and then after Miguel died I still moved around. I was . . . restless. Sad. Disconnected, even though I had—have—a couple of good friends who kept me grounded. This is the longest I've lived anywhere since my Nana and mother died within six months of each other when I was just twenty-one." I finished with the veggies and rinsed my hands in the breakfast bar sink. "What about you?" I asked, drying my hands as I examined her face. "What brought you to this area?"

"How do you know I wasn't born here?"

I smiled. "Well, for one thing everyone knows everyone around here. I know exactly when you arrived eleven months ago. But also . . . you have New York City in your voice. So do I. I didn't realize it until the tenth time a local told me."

She laughed. "Ambition brought me here, believe it or not. I came here for the job. It was either struggle along in the prosecutor's office, just another grunt in New York City, or become ADA here. This was going to be short-term, while I got some experience." She looked out the back window at Virgil and Urquhart, both with bottles of beer in their hands, earnestly talking. "It was *going* to be."

Hmmm . . . did that mean things were more serious than I realized between her and Urquhart? I wanted to ask what she saw in the sheriff, but there was no polite way.

"Can I help, Merry?" Patricia Schwartz, now married to Dewayne, had become a good friend and shopping buddy, both of us favoring plus-sized women's stores and outlets. She first came to Autumn Vale to help her mother, one of a group of women who invaded the castle for a time—the Legion of Horrible Ladies, as I had named them—but she came back after returning her mother to the city, and had stayed. She made the lightest, most delicious cakes, and had made a business out of it, named after her nickname as a child, Pattycakes. She's a big woman, handsome, sweet-natured, over-the-moon happy with solid, handsome Dewayne. Tonight she had on a flowy caftan-like dress in olive and tangerine, with floral earrings and her hair up in a turban. She was starting to dress like Janice Grover; maybe they even shared a wardrobe.

"I think I'm good for now, but as soon as the food is ready it will be great to have some help toting everything to the table."

Virgil popped his head into the kitchen. "Put some music on, will you, Dewayne?"

His friend headed into the living room. I expected Motown or old R&B, but he went to his other favorite, some soft jazzy blues. He came back and grabbed Patricia, whirling her around and dancing with her, her silky caftan billowing, his dark-eyed gaze never leaving her face. They were rhythmic and graceful, matching each other's steps with effortless ease.

Ellie sighed. "You guys are all couple goals for me," she said, eyeing them and then turning back to me.

"You wait until I pick a fight with Virgil during the dessert course and Dewayne falls asleep on the sofa after dinner," I said, tossing the big bowl of salad.

"Still," Ellie said, turning back to again wistfully watch Dewayne and Patricia, "hashtag couple goals."

Dinner was great. Wine flowed; conversation too. Worry had been nagging at the back of my mind all day and evening, but I made a concerted effort to let it go for a few hours. My friends deserved that much from their hostess. We ate, Virgil and I cleaned up and served drinks, and we retired to the great room again.

After an hour of laughter and intent chatter, we entered that phase of the evening when all of the partiers, worn out from a week of work, became earnest and philosophical. Urquhart, Virgil and Dewayne headed out on the back patio again and started a fire in the firepit Virgil had built. I thought it was too cold, but if the guys wanted to talk in private, that was okay with me. They had already divulged one of the many treasures Isadore Openshaw had found at the prophet's hidden lair and pointed out to them, a stash of stolen merchandise, which possibly explained a rise in break-ins at stores and shops lately all over the area. There was more, Virgil had hinted to me, but we hadn't had a chance yet to talk about it.

Ellie, Patricia and I sat in comfort in the big great room off the kitchen. I put the giant TV, which was mounted over the fireplace, on to something innocuous—the weather channel, I think—and we drank even more wine, the alcohol breaking down any social barriers of age or experience we may have felt. Wine, the great social lubricator!

After a few minutes of chat, getting to know each other (much about Patricia's cake business and Ellie's move to Autumn Vale, and how jarring that had been for a city girl), the ADA finally fixed me with a gimlet lawyerly stare and said, "So, I understand that you have a long and troubled acquaintance with our newest gal mixed up in the Light and the Way Ministry investigation, Miss Lynn Pugmire."

I smiled wryly. "Yes . . . aka Leatrice Pugeot." I briefly told her of our tangled history. "I'm the reason she's even here. She came looking for me."

"What's up with her? Our investigators tried to interview her this afternoon but even when the nurse swore she was not on any meds that might make her confused she was . . . confused. Your friend Pish was wonderful—a translator, you might say—but . . ."

She shook her head. "We're trying to find evidence to arrest some of the men at the encampment, but she was zero help, despite saying she was trying to remember. And that she'd been there for weeks. Or months. She wasn't even sure about that."

I sipped merlot and stared into the fireplace. "Lynn is a long-term addict. She was on oxy and dabbled in meth; she mixed and matched drugs to try to make her feel better without wanting to eat. She had a fear of gaining weight." I smiled and glugged some merlot. "I think she hired me as a kind of example of what not to do, you know? An example of what could happen if she let go and ate whatever she wanted."

Ellie rolled her eyes. "Please, as if a donut or two or three would hurt that woman. Was she always that thin?"

"Mmmm, I'd say she's probably lost ten or twelve pounds since her modeling days. It doesn't sound like a lot, but ten pounds down from one-o-five is scary-thin, not healthy-thin."

"So the drugs were to keep her thin?"

"God, no. The drugs were because she didn't know how to be okay without them. The drugs were so she wouldn't have to feel anything, or care about anything. The times I managed to keep her clean she was worse: abusive, manipulative, whiny, a people user."

"Why did you stay with her so long?"

"I was a mess too." I stared into the merlot, swirling it in my wineglass, thinking of the past. "It took me a long time to climb up out of the hole of depression after my husband died. Years! My friends kept me alive and sane, but just barely. I think I stayed with Lynn so long because . . ." I took a long drink, then frowned down into my almost empty glass. "Maybe because it made me feel better to know there was someone worse off than me." I wanted to change the subject. "Off the record, Ellie, what do you think is going on at that encampment? I'm so confused; is it a genuine religious organization, or is that a cover for other activities?" Again, something tugged at my mind, something to do with that question.

"We don't know. Your husband's information, and that given to us by Ms. Openshaw, leads me to believe—off the record—that the Light and the Way Ministry is a front for some illicit activity."

"Maybe drug smuggling?" I asked.

"Maybe. Or a theft ring. Or prostitution."

My eyes widened, and Patsy and I exchange glances. "Is that . . . do you think the girls who have disappeared . . . I mean . . ."

Ellie shook her head. Her lips clamped together. Finally she said, "We don't know anything yet. Honestly. I'm speculating, and I shouldn't. I'm going to blame the wine and shut my mouth."

I went to get another bottle. Somehow that didn't feel right, prostitution as a solution. Some of the folks seemed sincerely to believe in the religious mission of the group. I was trying my best to tie it all together—the prophet and his hideaway with the stolen goods, luxury living and messed-up books—and the missing girls, and Glynnis's murder. But maybe it didn't go all together.

At that moment Pish arrived, letting himself in. We greeted him with glad cries and wine. I hugged him hard, holding him close. He rested his head on my shoulder, then kissed my cheek. I led him to the sofa and ensconced him next to Patricia, then poured him a glass of his favorite pinot noir. He was weary and troubled, but the good wine started to relax him and the forehead lines smoothed out as he sat back on the comfy sofa.

"I was telling Ellie about Lynn and my background. How is she, Pish?"

"She's . . . confused."

"Ellie was just saying the investigators for the DA's office can't get much out of her. You said she's talked about hearing a woman screaming. Does she have any better idea of when that was?"

Her wine haze completely worn off, the assistant district attorney was sitting on the edge of the sofa now. "How reliable is this woman?" she asked. "Merry says not very."

Pish cocked his head. "I was talking to one of your investigators, Ellie . . . Detective Sanchez—"

"I thought you two would hit it off," she said with a wink toward me. "Sanchez is a great guy. When he first joined the county prosecutor's office a few months ago I was interested in him, even if he is a bit old for me—this was before I met Urquhart—until I realized he was not attracted to my . . . type."

"Detective Sanchez was most professional," Pish said with a stern look at Ellie.

"Okay, all right. So, back to my question: how reliable is Lynn Pugmire ultimately?"

"I don't think she knows when she's lying, sometimes," I said. "I'm beginning to realize that all the years she screwed me around, told blatant lies—ones that could be verified or disproved in five minutes or less—and told two different and opposite stories within a ten-minute conversation, she was probably suffering mental health issues. It could explain a lot, including her addiction issues."

"But she could be telling the truth this time," Pish said, a worried look on his lightly lined face.

"Why do you say that?" Patricia asked. She glanced around at us and made an apologetic face. "I only ask because I knew someone like that once, and there were . . . oh, in poker we'd call it tells that let you know when she was lying or telling the truth."

Pish nodded. "You've got it," he said, pointing a finger at her. "That's the thing . . . I'd swear she at least *believes* this is true, about the girl or woman screaming."

Ellie grabbed her purse and got out a notebook, scribbling what Pish had said. The ADA in her was most definitely emerging. She shot a rapid-fire round of questions at Pish, which he answered, concerning Lynn's assertions. He and Sanchez had gotten much more out of her than the local police had been able to.

It was late in the night and Lynn was wandering the encampment. She had been living alone in the hut I had found her in because none of the other women would put up with her. She didn't help out, she didn't cook or clean, and she wouldn't even do her own laundry. Night terrors meant she woke up screaming fairly often, and she occasionally sleepwalked. She was thoroughly miserable, and decided that she was ready to leave. Wandering, trying to figure out *how* to leave, she sat down on something, lost and afraid. She said she heard multiple male voices and one female screaming. She had no one to tell, no one to run to. When the screaming stopped, she got up and tried to find her way back to her hut.

That was the story she told. At first.

Much of this was new, gotten by Sanchez and Pish after an hour of delicate probing. But by the end of the hour her story had changed subtly. She did intend to leave. *That* was true. And she did hear screaming, but there was more to it. She finally—reluctantly, appearing afraid—admitted that she saw two men carrying a girl who was now silent. She could not identify either man, since it was dark, but both were tall. And there was, she believed, a woman nearby who spoke to the two men. That was all she recalled, Pish told us. She could not say what day it was, except that it was not long before she was rescued. She swore it was the truth.

I was stunned; if it was true, it *could* be solid proof that Glynnis had been beaten at the encampment and was moved, or she had been knocked unconscious, beaten, then left by the highway to die, or she had escaped her killers and made it to the highway. "Did she say *where* this was in the camp?"

Pish frowned. "She didn't know; I believe that. According to her she had started across a field, trying to make her way to the highway. She didn't say why she didn't try to escape in daylight. I had a sense she was afraid of someone there, but she wouldn't say who. She had been walking a few minutes when she heard the screaming, and then that stopped. She then headed toward a distant light that she thought might be a farmhouse or a truck stop on the highway. The clouds parted, and she started to see shapes. That's when she saw the men carrying the girl."

Like Lynn, it was confusing.

"I'll get the official report from Sanchez later," Ellie said. "But this gives me something to think about. Pish, do you think she's telling the truth?"

He sighed and grimaced. "I told the detective this, and I'll tell you . . . it *feels* like it's an actual memory. I think she's telling the truth, as she knows it."

"Which part, her first or second story?" I said, my tone caustic. It was classic Lynn to confuse issues so much, but this was vital.

"The second," he said. "But who knows?"

"How did she get back to her hut?" I asked. "And *why* did she go back?"

He shrugged. "She's not sure . . . in fact, she's downright vague on that part. She wandered, and found her way back. Once she got there, she passed out and didn't wake up until broad daylight."

"I hate to ask, Pish, but could it have been a dream?" I asked.

"The screams fit with what we know," Ellie said. "We have to assume that at least some of it is true. We know that Glynnis was at the encampment, and she was badly beaten. It's likely that what happened to her was at the hands of someone or more than one person from the encampment."

"I hope her information helps. When I saw her in the hospital, she was afraid that 'men' were coming to get her," I said. "I wonder if that's from that night? Didn't anyone else there hear any of this?"

"We're going out to that encampment tomorrow morning," Ellie said. "Our investigators have been out there several times, but they have to go easy. We don't want to frighten anyone into taking off, and unless we're willing to take people into custody, we don't want to start throwing our weight around. We're hoping for cooperation. But we can't force these women to talk."

"You've been investigating the missing girls in connection with the encampment, I assume?" She nodded. I had been obsessing over everything I had seen and heard in the last while, so I told her as much as I could remember, and Pish added more from our visit to rescue Lynn, and his talk with Mother Esther. She jotted it all down. I felt like there was something more I knew or suspected, but either my brain was tired or I had merlot memory.

Dewayne, Virgil and Urquhart had joined us as I talked. Dewayne, working pro bono for the family of Glynnis Johnson, listened intently.

Virgil, who had already told Ellie what he and Dewayne had discovered—the place where Voorhees spent most of his time, in the hut with wifi and satellite TV, as well as the stolen goods and the ledgers Isadore was working on, with the unaccounted-for income—and then Dewayne looked around at all of us.

"This stays among us, okay?"

When Dewayne said something like that, we listened.

"The trucker who owns the land and sold that piece to the Light and the Way Ministry . . . Virge and me have a feeling there is something going on that involves him. The hut that Voorhees hides away in . . . it's just a football field away from Bob Taggart's farmhouse. I think that's why he sold Voorhees the land, that there is some agreement between them."

I spoke up with the explanation I had heard from Garth that Taggart was lazy, and his agreement with Voorhees allowed him cheap farm labor and women to clean, and who knew what else. I added what Cecily had said that confirmed what Garth said. Virgil nodded and said that she had told the police that.

Dewayne looked unconvinced. "I think there's more to it. I'm still going to have a look around Bob's place."

Ellie was about to speak, but Dewayne held up one hand. "You don't know about that, and never heard this," he said with a slow smile. "If I find anything out, you may get an anonymous but well-informed tip from a concerned citizen."

I wondered aloud if Mother Esther was innocent, or complicit in whatever had happened. "If there was a woman there when the girl was screaming, as Lynn says, I would bet it was her."

"But we don't know if the screaming girl was Glynnis," Ellie said.

"We don't know who the men were, either," I said. But I wondered . . . Barney, maybe? And the prophet himself? "We know that Glynnis was there, and Cecily too."

"Both of their own free will," Ellie pointed out. "There's no crime in joining an organization, and both girls are over eighteen."

I nodded. "But so far we haven't located any of the other missing girls. They could still be there," I said, thinking of Peaches. "We need more information."

"We're working on it," Ellie said. "We're still trying to find a way to identify other girls at the encampment, but without their cooperation . . ." She shook her head. "No one has said that any of the girls appear to be there against their will."

Dewayne chimed in, his deep voice a growl of anger. "All those missing girls, and that unsolved murder from last year of a girl in the same age group . . . Ben Baxter ignored the problem for too long. At first I think he was afraid to look into it too deeply, worried about reelection."

"That's horrible!" I interjected.

"I know, I know. It sounds bad, but I'm not saying he *completely* ignored the murders or missing girls," Dewayne said. "He and his department did investigate."

"He did . . . the DA's office kept on him about it," Ellie said, glancing among us all. "I've been here less than a year, but I know our men and women were on it."

Virgil nodded. "Ben didn't connect them together like he's

starting to now. He's convinced that Voorhees is behind the girls' disappearance. I'm not so sure."

"Why not?" Trujillo asked, her tone sharp.

He exchanged a look with Dewayne. "You can explain better than me. You've been studying this longer."

Dewayne nodded. "We were just talking about it. He's lumping all the missing girls in one lot now, and we can't get him to slow down and examine these cases one by one. Glynnis and Cecily were both runaways, right? *And* showed up at the Light and the Way Ministry. Cecily is fine, but Glynnis was murdered. However . . . we don't have a speck of proof that there are other girls from the list there . . . yet!" he tacked on the end, holding up one hand as I was about to break in to speak of my suspicions of Madison Pinker. "And there is zero evidence that the two girls found murdered four years ago and Yolanda Perkins, found murdered two and a half years ago, had anything to do with Voorhees and his crew," he continued. "Then there is Delonda Henson; she's been missing ten months, but she had been talking about leaving town for a long time. She was estranged from her family, had a quarrel with her boyfriend, and I suspect she just took off. But now Ben just wants to lump them all in together."

"It sounds . . . worrisome," Patricia said. "I don't know the sheriff, but it sounds like his judgment is compromised. I was involved in a charity benefit board once, and the chairwoman was so stressed she began to make rash decisions. She had to retire finally when complaints began to pour in. She was actually harassing the singer who had agreed to perform."

I had had my run-ins with Sheriff Ben Baxter, but this sounded like a whole new level of trouble. I got what Patricia was saying, that sometimes stress can get to someone. Maybe she had a point. But who could get the duly elected sheriff to step down?

"Anyway, I want to use data from the Murder Accountability Project to map all area unsolved murders," Dewayne said.

"What is the Murder Accountability Project?" I asked.

"It's a group that collates data on unsolved murders across the whole country," Ellie said. "It shows patterns that otherwise might go unnoticed."

"What complicates this investigation is, many of these missing girls can't be assumed murdered just because they're not here," Dewayne finished, spreading his big hands and shrugging. "We have a few, but connecting them together is a long task. We have to collect all the data on cause of death, DNA, fingerprints, hair . . . all of that."

"That's what police are doing right now, trying to connect the unsolved murders we have," Virgil said. "But it's not a quick job like they show on TV."

Except when I get lucky and solve it with some fluky guesswork, I wanted to say but didn't. This was not a topic for levity.

Someone banged on the door and I glanced around; almost everyone I knew who would come to my house was already here. I jumped up and trailed Virgil to the front door. He opened it.

Lizzie charged in, followed by Cecily, who hugged herself, tears in her eyes.

"What's going on?" I asked. "What's wrong?"

"Nothing's wrong," Lizzie said. "Something's finally right." She grabbed my arms, her fingers digging into the flesh of my upper arm, and hauled me away to the staircase. "Cec and I went to the encampment and got Alcina," she muttered furtively. "I have her in the car. *Now* what'll I do?"

Chapter Eighteen

"What do you mean you've got Alcina in the car?" I hissed, pulling myself out of her grip. I took hold of her wrist and dragged her through the murky foyer into the office. Cecily bobbed after us and Virgil followed, looking grim, but I caught his eye and shook my head. I did *not* want the others to hear this until we figured out what was going on.

Virgil, his lips firmed into a straight line, rolled his eyes and went back to our friends, closing the office door behind him. I telepathically tried to tell him to say that Lizzie was here with some teenage emergency.

"Tell me what you mean?" I asked, shaking her. I released her and turned on the desk lamp, the light greenish through its banker-style shade. Cecily collapsed on the leather love seat, put her elbows on her knees and covered her face with both hands.

"I was worried," Lizzie said, staring at me through narrowed eyes. "After the day before yesterday and all that crap, I wasn't going to let Felice keep Alcina there just because she's a brainwashed moron who—"

"Lizzie, hush!" I said. "Now, from the beginning. Tell me what happened."

"She did the right thing," Cecily said from the sofa, hands now on her lap. She thrust one through her magenta hair and sobbed, her breath coming in panicky gulps. "I told Lizzie . . . we *had* to do it. I didn't tell the cops, but I *saw* one night when Nathan grabbed a girl and tried to get friendly with her."

"What?" I collapsed on the love seat beside her. Anger flared. "How could you not tell me this?" Especially after our long, friendly chat.

Cecily was trembling. "I'm sorry. I'm so *sorry!*" she sobbed. She grabbed my arm, clinging to me. "I was scared," she said, staring directly into my eyes, pleading for understanding. "Nathan is about as bad as Barney, and he said if I told anyone, he'd make sure the prophet let him marry me. Until I left I was scared."

"I can't believe you didn't even tell *me!*" Lizzie shrieked, stomping back and forth and finally looming over the other girl.

"Lizzie, shut up. You're not helping. Okay, all right. Let me think." I took a deep breath. This could get messy. Alcina was fifteen, and her mother was her legal custodial parent. But surely if she was in imminent danger no law in the land would force her to stay. I had a sheriff in the other room, and I could right now get his help. But . . . the encampment wasn't in his jurisdiction. I was caught between my growing trust in Urquhart and yet knowing that by handing Alcina over to him I would be putting him in a legal bind and perhaps traumatizing Alcina. The poor child had been through enough.

And ADA Trujillo? I didn't know her at all. I *liked* her, based on our conversations this evening. I *felt* I could trust her, but I wasn't sure. She was bound by the law, and Alcina was in her mother's custody.

Nathan Garrison: was he one of the two men with the girl Lynn claimed to have heard screaming? I had thought Barney and the prophet. My mind raced in circles, like Becket high on catnip.

"I can't leave her out in the frickin' car," Lizzie said, gesticulating wildly. "Merry, what are we going to do? I can't take her back to Grandma's place."

"No, I agree. I need to talk to her." When I cautiously emerged from the study, peeping in both directions, it was to find Pish pacing in the foyer.

He raced to me and caught and held my gaze. "What's going on? Virgil told me to come here and wait for you."

My husband . . . he always knew *exactly* what to do. Pish was the one who could be trusted with the information I had. "What did he tell the others?"

"He said that Lizzie came rolling up with some teenage crisis that only you could solve."

I took a deep breath. Marital telepathy—or Virgil's own excellent sense—was magical. Lizzie peeked out the study door, her eyes widening when she saw Pish. I put up one hand to stay her, then explained to Pish what was going on. He took it in, and nodded. I asked him to go back to my guests and make some excuse for me because I was going out to talk to Alcina, and then figure out what to do from there. He nodded again, retreated, and I motioned to Lizzie and Cecily, who peeked out behind her, to go out the front door.

Lizzie's grandmother's car sat in the drive in front of the house. I followed my teen friend and got in the backseat, where Alcina cowered against the far door. I turned on the dome light. "Alcina, honey, are you okay?" I said gently, like I was speaking to a frightened kitten.

She had never been especially attached to me, but in that moment myriad emotions fluttered over her pale, tearstained face and she threw herself into my arms. I held her close. She was like some tiny forest creature, her heart beating a mile a minute against my chest. It slowed, calmed. We sat like that for a long time, with me crooning nonsense and rocking her. When it felt like she had settled, I drew back slightly. Lizzie and Cecily talked in low voices in the front seat.

"Honey, I need to ask you some questions," I whispered to Alcina. "Is that okay?"

She nodded.

"Are you physically well? Has anyone harmed you?"

She shook her head.

"Did you come willingly with Lizzie and Cecily? Lizzie didn't bully you to come?"

Lizzie yelped in dismay and glared at me over the seat, but I shot her a look. A kid with that strong a personality can sometimes overwhelm other more easily influenced kids.

Alcina sniffled. "I was so relieved when I saw her, Merry," she said, her light voice trembling. She explained that Lizzie had crept through the camp, calling her name. "I was so happy. It was like a dream. She said she'd get me out of there, and I went."

"So you wanted to leave your mother?"

Alcina started crying. "No, I didn't! She's not been feeling well. I'm worried about her. But I've been begging to go for months . . . asking to *leave* that awful place. I've been dodging those men, keeping away. Hiding. But she wouldn't *leave*. At first . . . at first it was because she thought it was best for us. But then—"

"Yes? Then?"

"She's scared," Alcina said, wide-eyed.

"What is she scared of?"

"I don't know. I'm hoping that when she realizes I'm gone she'll come looking for me."

"Okay, all right. Let me think."

"Merry, what are we going to do?" she asked, her small hand trembling within mine. "If she doesn't escape, how can we get her out of there?"

I chafed it, trying to warm her. "Let me think about that tonight. I'll figure something out."

Satisfied that Alcina had cooperated in her flight from the camp and was happy to leave, that solved my moral worries. Nothing was more important than Alcina's safety. But now there was a legal dilemma.

"Honey, I have a couple of questions to ask. Just answer as best you can." She nodded, her pearly skin dewy with a film of perspiration raised by fear. "Do you know what the custody agreement is between your parents?"

"Daddy has Teddy, and Mom has me."

"Does your dad have a right to have visits with you?"

She nodded.

"Is it up to you, to visit him?"

She nodded.

"But you haven't visited him for a while?"

She shook her head. "He tried to come see me at the encampment, but Barney turned him away."

I wondered why her father hadn't gotten the sheriff's office involved. "So you haven't seen your little brother in all this time?"

She shook her head, tears dripping down her face and off her chin. "I miss him," she said.

"Where does your father live?"

"With my Aunt Sally and my cousins, her kids. Aunt Sally is Daddy's sister."

"Where, in Ridley Ridge or Autumn Vale?"

"Ridley Ridge."

"He's a trucker, right?"

She nodded.

"There is always someone at the house to look after Teddy?"

She nodded again.

"Do you like it there?"

She nodded, a child of few words but firm opinions.

My mind made up, I asked her, "So what do you think of going there to stay for a few days while we try to help your mom? Can I call them and arrange it?" I wasn't going to send Lizzie to the woman's door in the middle of the night unannounced, Alcina in tow.

She nodded, her eyes puffy from tears, her whole slim body sagging from exhaustion. I hugged her, holding her close, gently. "It'll be okay, honey, really," I murmured against her ratty hair, that lovely golden hair that had always been so silky and soft. "We'll all help you get your mom back and sort everything out. I promise." I hoped I could keep my promise, but for now, it was enough that she was safe.

I commandeered Lizzie's cell phone, and in the darkness of the car interior I made a difficult call. To the woman's credit, though I had woken her out of a sound sleep—with young kids she was probably exhausted—Sally agreed without hesitation to take Alcina in. She adored her niece and had missed her. They shared a special bond of loving fairies and gardens. Teddy missed her terribly, too, she told me, unprompted, and longed for his big sister.

I explained the legal situation, but she understood it better than I did. I had a sense it had been the subject of discussion between her and her brother for some time. She confirmed that, telling me that her brother had intended to go to the police for help in enforcing the custody order that allowed him parental rights. He was worried about his child's living arrangements, but until now he hadn't wanted to get his ex-wife, whom he still loved, in trouble. He had been hoping to work something out, and had tried repeatedly when he was home to contact her. In the last month or so he had become frantic enough to consult a lawyer, who was going to help him apply for custody of Alcina unless Felice would agree to leave the encampment.

I was relieved. It was Happy Families, it seemed, with everyone wanting the best for Alcina. I told Sally a teenage friend was going to deliver her niece to her door. She'd have hot chocolate and cinnamon rolls ready, she said. I put Alcina on the line, and she sobbed to her aunt in weepy bursts of speech that both seemed to understand.

I took the phone, said goodbye to the woman, then handed it back to Lizzie. Alcina was already asleep, bundled up with Lizzie's grandma's old soft plaid car blanket. I'd bet it was the warmest she had been in a month or more. "Cecily, you have to tell me what you meant when you said you saw Nathan trying to get friendly with a girl," I whispered to the teenager. "What does that mean?"

"He was touching her. And holding on to her."

"What girl was it?"

"I don't know."

"*When* was it?"

"I don't remember!" She was weeping and hiccupping. "I was s-scared to tell the cops everything!" she said. "I told Barney, and he called me a liar and said to shut my mouth. Barney's a jerk. What if he comes after us? What if he—"

"I understand, Cecily. I do!" She had been in trouble before and the police were not her friends. I pondered my next words; I had to trust my gut. "Cecily, inside is the assistant district attorney. So far, they haven't had enough to arrest anyone there. You say you didn't tell them the whole truth last time about what is going on at the encampment; do you want to do that now? Tell them about Nathan and Barney? It could help the other girls and women at the encampment. It might even lead to justice for poor Glynnis."

Cecily looked doubtful.

"Her name is Elisandre Trujillo. She's a nice woman, and only concerned with helping all of you who have been taken advantage of. You could come in right now and talk to her, but I won't pressure you to do it. It's truly up to you."

Her eyes unfocused, I could see the thoughts churning.

"Cecily, you aren't in trouble," I said, hoping that was true. "My husband is inside. You know he was a cop, and he's a good guy."

"It's true, Cec. He helped me out when I was in trouble. Virgil's okay." Lizzie hugged her friend across the center console, then let her go. "But whatever you want to do is okay," she added.

The teenager took in a deep breath and looked up at me. "I'll talk to her if . . . if you think it'll be okay."

That made me think seriously. I couldn't guarantee anything. Except . . . "I don't know how all of this is going to go but I can guarantee one thing: you can count on *me*. I'll stay by your side the whole time." I took her hand and squeezed it, then released. "If what you've said to me is true—and I do believe you—then you've done nothing wrong."

She nodded. "Okay. I'll talk."

Cecily and I got out of the car and I sent Lizzie off. Alcina's aunt had texted the address in Ridley Ridge and directions. I turned with Cecily and walked her back into the house and ushered her into the living room, where my guests were chatting. Ellie was talking with Urquhart, waving her phone around. Something had happened.

"What's going on?" I asked.

Ellie turned to me. "I got a text from Sheriff Baxter. Another girl has disappeared, and he's worried. It took him this long to take it all seriously, but now he's concerned. She was seen at the bus station this evening, but she apparently never got on the bus."

"It could be that she decided to stay with a friend instead," Urquhart said. "Has he put out an Amber Alert yet?"

"They can't. She's eighteen. She had a fight with her mom and left, saying she was going to LA. She was seen in the bus station, and she bought a ticket, but she never used it." Ellie looked around, then her gaze settled on Urquhart. "None of us can do anything yet," she said.

There was a feeling of consternation among the group, a sad way to end a lovely dinner party. But then they saw Cecily, who shrank behind me, cowering. I felt for her, but she was getting to an age when she had to take responsibility. "Friends, this is Cecily," I said, taking her arm and pulling her to stand beside me. "Until recently she was living out at the Light and the Way Ministry encampment." I turned to the assistant district attorney and said, "Ellie, she'd like to talk to you in person. She'd like to amend her police statement. Can she do that with you? I feel like it's important that she do it *now*, especially in light of another young woman missing."

Patricia and Dewayne left, as did Pish. I was true to my word with Cecily and stayed with her as she amended her statement to ADA Trujillo, who was all business. She videotaped their interview using an app on her phone, and also took copious notes. Sheriff Urquhart remained—he was Ellie's ride—but he and Virgil stayed in the great room talking about the missing girls' case, letting Cecily and me and Trujillo have the office to conduct our business.

Ellie Trujillo and Urquhart finally left, and I put Cecily in our guest room. Don't judge me, but I gave her a shot of sherry to relax her and help her sleep.

• • •

I told Virgil all about Lizzie and Cecily breaking Alcina out of the encampment as we whispered together in our bed, aware that we had a houseguest for the first time since building our house. Virgil was supportive, but said that eventually Alcina would have to talk to authorities. I agreed, but at least now she would have her dad's support.

For the rest of the night I tossed and turned as Virgil snored, worrying over what I was missing, and the teenager who had disappeared, and Alcina and Felice and everything else. Cecily was low-key the next morning when I got her up. She was not normally a morning person, I would have bet, and she had been through a lot the day before. But we had to decide what she was going to do . . . where she was going to live.

Fortunately Ellie called early, sounding bright and chipper, with news. She had been in touch with Cecily's father, who was deeply relieved to learn his daughter was alive and well. He also seemed contrite that he had not been more supportive of her transition to her new situation with his new wife and her kids. It had been difficult, he admitted, but he wanted her to come home. He had a room fixed up for her. He had *not* thrown out her stuff as she feared, and in fact had preserved it.

I put the phone to my chest and told Cecily that, and she yipped with happiness, then skipped off to have a shower. I had some clothes for her, ones that were a little tight for me but would be right for her, a pair of designer jeans and a Lane Bryant slashed yoke tee in the same magenta as her hair, with a jean jacket I had grown out of—in other words, too tight over the bust and arms. She was so enthused about the clothes I promised to go through all my stuff and send her a big bag.

I came back to the phone and Ellie told me that because of Cecily's amended statement, they would be going to the encampment later to pick up Barney and Nathan for questioning. I was happy about that. I had realized that morning something that had been nagging at me for days. Something that didn't make sense. I considered what I thought I might know, taken along with Hannah's text to me that very morning giving me her opinion (after research) in answer to my question about who Mother Esther might be.

"Ellie, before you go, I have a question: can you find out how Bardo Voorhees died?"

"The prophet's brother? That was what . . . three years ago? I've heard about it. It's a cold case, of course, his death. I know he was beaten and his body left in the woods. Sure, I can look into it, but I'm going to be kind of busy. Why are you asking?"

I told her what I was thinking, and she exclaimed in shock, making notes as we spoke. Something else fell into place; for a moment I was silent, and then I told her what else I was thinking.

"You may have something," she said, scribbling furiously in the background. "I've got to go. I need to see the coroner about a body."

Chapter Nineteen

Virgil was fixing himself a second cup of coffee and crunching on the overcooked bacon he so dearly loves. "How did you figure all that out? What you told Ellie?" he asked, spooning sugar into his coffee.

"About the Voorhees brothers?"

He nodded.

"It's been bugging me all along. You know that nagging feeling, knowing there was something but not being able to pin down what it was? I had it, in spades. Garth, the meat guy, was talking about the Voorhees brothers, how he knew them as kids. He said Bardo was trouble, but he always thought Arden was okay."

Virgil nodded. "I've heard that. Bardo was fresh out of jail when he was murdered, his sentence reduced because of good behavior, meaning he snitched on someone while inside. Baxter figured a jail associate caught up with him and killed him for snitching. They actually picked up a guy but had to release him. No evidence. As far as I know, they're still working on that angle."

"Okay," I said impatiently, "but Garth described Arden as a runty little guy, and someone else said he had thin hair. Not like the guy who is now Arden, who has abundant hair; he keeps it up under a wrap a lot of the time, but I've seen it down. He's got hair. And everyone said Arden went off the rails after his brother was murdered, that he became reclusive. They also said Arden's wife disappeared." I paused. "*After* the murder."

Virgil's cloudy gaze cleared. He stopped dead and set his cup down. "So . . . if Arden became reclusive, no one saw him after his brother was murdered?"

I nodded.

"I wonder who identified Bardo's body, after it was found?"

"That's what I want to know. But I'll bet Arden was so 'laid up and upset' that it had to be Arden's wife, Essie. As in, maybe, Esther?"

"As in *Mother* Esther," he said.

"Exactly. Hannah did some investigation into it, and it hit her . . . the woman involved in the case, Arden's wife Essie Voorhees, was the right age and had disappeared—supposedly she left town— around the same time as Mother Esther came into being."

"Goddamn. Right in front of us this whole time. Clever," he said, nodding his head. "So Bardo killed his brother, Arden, and took his identity. Arden's wife ID'd her 'brother-in-law's' body because her 'husband' was too upset. I remember now . . . the body's face was smashed in, but the ID was made positively by a family member. She ID'd him, then 'disappeared' herself, after telling people she was leaving."

"It makes sense," I said. "I'm pretty sure I'm right about this. But wouldn't they do fingerprinting to prove it was Bardo?"

Virgil sighed and swiped a hand over his face. "You know, I'd like to say yes, but if a family member positively identifies someone there is no reason to go further, to fingerprints or dental. It saves time and trouble."

"Okay. I thought I was crazy for a while, when I started putting this together. I thought for sure the police would ID the body with fingerprinting at the very least. But deliberate misidentification makes a lot more sense than a fifty-year-old man suddenly growing four inches and getting lots of hair when he just had thin wispy hair before. That's why Bardo, pretending to be Arden, had to stay out of town, off the grid, suddenly. The Ridley Ridge house they started the Light and the Way Ministry in wasn't enough, they needed to get out of town. Even the farmhouse they went to next probably wasn't far enough away. They needed somewhere that would protect Bardo, that people couldn't see him up close.

"I'm thinking Arden and Bardo resembled each other enough that seeing him driving a van where you couldn't compare height, the visual similarity would be enough to convince you that Bardo was Arden. The only thing I can't think of is *why*? Why would Bardo want to take over Arden's life?"

"It's probably a simple matter. Maybe Esther and Bardo were having a fling, or maybe there was money or property in Arden's name, and Esther and Bardo wanted it for themselves. It was simpler just to keep it, as Arden, rather than have Arden die and go through the courts for Esther to inherit. Some minds work that way . . . easier to kill and take than inherit legally."

"You're probably right. It's usually money, isn't it?" I squinted out the back window as Becket curled around my feet, mewing to be let out. I strolled to the back patio door, opened it, and he jauntily trotted out, looking back over his shoulder at me and blinking once, before disappearing into the woods. "Something else has been bothering me," I said, turning back to him. I circled the kitchen island to where Virgil sat on a high stool, sipping his coffee. "Did Barney give his full name to the sheriff when he was picked up the other day?"

"I know he gave them a name. I don't know what it is, or if it's his *actual* name. And before this, on the street, he always skirted the law, pulling back when a cop challenged him."

I nodded. "Yeah, that's what he did in Ridley Ridge when the female police officer told him to take a hike."

"So, no, I don't think he's ever been pulled in."

"I've been thinking and thinking." I searched my husband's brown eyes and frowned, trying to express what I was thinking. "He doesn't seem like the *type* to espouse a doomsday type of religion."

"What are you saying?" He put his hands on my hips and pulled me closer.

"I'm just wondering . . . who *is* Barney, really? Maybe he's hiding out at the encampment. Good place to disappear, off the grid."

"You could be right. I'll check it out," he said, pulling me onto his lap.

We canoodled for a moment, but I pulled away. "Hopefully, then, since they're picking up Barney and Nathan, we'll get some definitive answers," I said, breathless and rearranging my clothes. "You had better go."

He checked his phone. "I'm already late."

Virgil and Dewayne were getting together with Urquhart and Baxter to discuss progress on the list of missing girls and women. Their task force had been approved by the DA's office. Cecily's information might help. I had, of course, shared with Virgil my fear that Peaches was Madison Pinker, and they were meeting to decide how to proceed, how to identify her without making trouble at the encampment. With the latest possible missing girl, it was urgent that any connection to the Light and the Way Ministry was explored.

Virgil had been checking in with Baxter's office. Though deputies had already gone out to the encampment, neither Nathan nor Barney had been taken into custody because they simply weren't there. Both were being elusive. That was troubling.

Cecily joined us. I handed her a muffin for her breakfast and we headed outside. She was clearly ecstatic in her new duds and excited to see her dad. Virgil and I kissed goodbye lingeringly while Cecily watched with a pink-cheeked grin. Then we got in our vehicles and headed out, me with Cecily nonstop chattering about what her dad had said, and hoping she could start fresh with her stepmother and stepsiblings.

We drove into Ridley Ridge and I got out of the car when her dad came out to greet her. I was reassured by the tears in his eyes and the way he hugged Cecily. He thanked me profusely and shook my hand, but I said the girl he should be thanking was Lizzie Proctor, and I hoped that their friendship would continue. Lizzie is a strong-minded independent woman, and a good friend. Cecily agreed. I watched as they entered the tidy ranch-style home and the door closed behind them, then closed my eyes and said a silent prayer.

I headed back to Autumn Vale and down the side street to the library. Hannah had texted me repeatedly and wanted me to come in; she and Zeke had more information beyond the Esther/Essie riddle. I was in luck. Zeke was at the library with her, working on setting up three donated computers in an unused corner of the library. It would become a resource center for locals to use the internet and do research.

He left his work and joined Hannah and me at her desk. There were no patrons, so we could speak without reservation. After greetings, I told the couple a little of what I had learned, and about finding Lynn, about Cecily and Alcina being safe, and about my plans to go out to the encampment to talk Felice into coming away with me.

Now that Ellie was on the track of the Arden/Bardo Voorhees mystery, it could ultimately result in murder charges. I didn't tell Zeke and Hannah about my surmise about Esther and Bardo killing Arden Voorhees, preferring not to spill the beans before it was proved. We chatted, and they were happy Alcina was safe. Zeke asked me to try again to talk Gordy into leaving, but I was pretty sure I'd be spinning my wheels.

I was curious about Voorhees's hideaway shack, so Zeke explained to me some technical facts, like how Voorhees was able to get cable and cell service even though the Light and the Way Ministry property was off the grid. He must have a generator, Zeke said, but also he had what we saw in Lizzie's photos of the distant building: a satellite dish.

Hannah and Zeke exchanged a look, and Hannah said, "Merry, there is something else . . . what we called you here for. Zeke did some asking around among friends, and a fellow, Eddie Owens, whose family owns property on the same road —"

"Oh, is that Garth Owens's son, maybe? The family owns the new butcher shop in town?"

"Yes, that's them . . . anyway, he told Zeke there is a lot of coming and going near where that shack of Voorhees's is, but farther back in the woods, shielded from the road and even from the shack."

"What do you mean, a lot of coming and going? What's out there? *What*, exactly, is coming and going?"

"Trucks," Zeke said. "*Lots* of trucks."

I thought of the times I had been out there, how a truck had almost run me off the road, and how one whizzed past me at full speed. Down a gravel road, for heaven's sake! "On the cult's compound?"

Hannah nodded. "Maybe . . . or the property right next to it."

"The property next to it . . . but it takes up a corner of Bob Taggart's land, right? So you're saying *his* property could be involved?"

Zeke nodded. "Yeah. There's this parking area down a lane in the woody part, and I can't tell if it's on the Light and the Way property or Bob Taggart's."

"How do you know about this?"

"One of Zeke's friends . . ." She exchanged a look with Zeke. "He won't tell the police about this, because he has his own . . . uh . . . secrets. He grows pot on a little patch of land nearby."

"Is this maybe that same friend, Eddie Owens?" I asked.

"I'm not allowed to say," Hannah primly answered. "But look, he got curious," she said, bringing up a video on her computer. "So he flew a drone over the property. This is what he recorded."

She hit the little arrow and the drone footage played.

"This is Silver Creek Line," Zeke said, pointing on the screen with a pencil at the road the drone was flying over. "Just off Marker

Road, around the corner from the Light and the Way encampment. That is the prophet's shack there," Zeke said, pointing to a flat-roofed shed with multiple vehicles parked around it and a satellite dish prominent on the roof. That would have been the shack Dewayne and Virgil broke into, where they found Isadore already rifling through the place. "But look over here, shielded from the road by all this brush . . ." He pointed as the drone footage dipped closer to earth.

You had to go a ways. Deep in the woods was a clearing reached by a winding lane. Through the leafy canopy I could make out white rectangles, and squinted. From the ground you might not even be able to see the clearing, it was so densely foliaged, and the lane twisted in a snaky S. Every turn of the lane would have concealed what was beyond it, just as my own twisting lane leading to my castle did. As the drone dipped closer, though, I could identify something interesting. The clearing was an expansive graveled parking area; what appeared just as white rectangles from above were, upon closer inspection, trucks and truck trailers parked in a long row near a big fuel tank, and an industrial-sized generator. What was going on?

"What's that over there?" I asked, pointing to a ramshackle house.

"Bob Taggart's farmhouse. See what we mean? It's hard to tell where the Light and the Way property ends and Bob Taggart's farmland begins."

"But it sure looks like those semis are being stored on Taggart's farmland, directly behind his farmhouse, not on Light and the Way land."

Zeke's friend thought the prophet was likely running drugs, Hannah told me, which meant that the semi trailers could be full of contraband. That was quite possible. There is a thriving industry in drug smuggling between the U.S. and Canada, and we're not far from the border. Even I knew that there was a booming business in cocaine and meth flowing from Mexico, through the States and to Canada and back. Fentanyl and ecstasy flow back. Something tugged at my brain, something involving the generator, but I shook my head. It would come to me, but only if I left it alone.

There were *other* possible items they could be smuggling:

weapons, booze, cigarettes . . . Surprisingly, one of the biggest smuggling rings busted locally was so-called buttlegging, the smuggling of cigarettes from out of state into New York, where taxes on tobacco are sky-high compared with other states. There was also another commodity that was always in demand: women. I considered Barney's well-known habit of meeting girls at the bus station. He had been run off from the Ridley Ridge bus station, but had he just moved on to Batavia, Henrietta, and beyond? I had an uneasy feeling. Especially now, with yet another girl missing.

"I have a feeling a tip to the sheriff's department is in order," I said.

"You don't think . . ." Hannah's soft voice held a thread of worry. "You don't imagine there are girls . . . that they're smuggling girls or women? If there are girls being kept there, maybe there is no one to let them out."

"I'm going to call the sheriff's office and give them the info. I won't say where I heard it, but you're right . . . with everything going on in the world, we can't take a chance." I called the sheriff's office, gave my name, and told them what I was worried about. Then, to be sure, I texted Virgil with Hannah's fear. She sighed with relief. She had a hero-worship faith in Virgil, which I completely understood.

"Now, how do we get Gordy out of there?" Zeke asked.

I sighed. He was not going to leave it alone, and they were going to hate what I had to say. "Hannah, Zeke, I've tried talking to him. But he's a man, an adult, it's up to him now. It's time for him to take responsibility for what he believes."

"But *Felice* is a grown woman," Zeke said, pushing his glasses up on his nose. His acne-scarred face was becoming red with emotion. "Shouldn't you be letting her live there if she's made up her own mind?"

Hannah put one hand on his arm to calm him, but he had a point. I was treating the two differently, though I thought I had good reason. "I get what you're saying, Zeke, truly, I do," I said gently. "But the Light and the Way Ministry is a cult that specializes in making women believe that they are to be submissive. They expend a lot of energy in sermons and rules to make women knuckle under. Felice appears to have bought into it."

I still had a feeling Felice was hiding something. I was hoping she'd freely tell me whatever it was she was holding back, but I didn't know. "I have to go," I said, standing, then leaning over and hugging Hannah. I was heading to the door, saying goodbye over my shoulder, when we were dramatically interrupted.

There are certain people who seem destined to be forgotten. Isadore Openshaw is one of those, a woman so mute and reserved she disappears in a crowd. I had heard from Virgil, of course, that he had come across Isadore in the prophet's secret shack, but I had once again forgotten her and the mission she had embarked upon. So it was enormously surprising when she burst into the library, her strawlike hair sticking up all around her head and her eyes wide and bulging.

"Isadore, what is it?" I cried, bolting toward her.

"You . . . you have to come," she said, panting and clutching the door frame. "Out to the camp . . . Mr. English. Mr. Dread. They're headed out there to get Gordy!"

Chapter Twenty

I clutched the steering wheel hard and cursed fluently. Of all the harebrained . . . what the hell were those two old dudes doing heading out to the encampment? I followed Isadore, but she is a poky driver. I honked loudly and roared around her, taking off like a rocket. Doc English is my only connection to my past and he is a dear old soul I love like the grandpa I had never known. I'd be damned if I was going to let him go out there with that skunk Nathan, weird Barney, and the possible murderer Prophet Voorhees and scary Mother Esther about.

I didn't think that Doc would even be able to make it through the fence, but he was stubborn as a goat, and twice as feisty, so who knew? Nor was I aware that Hubert Dread still drove; *that* was a chilling thought. His eyesight is almost as bad as Doc's. I knew he had a car, but as far as I knew he had not driven it in three years, he just loaned it out to various family members who took him places.

I pulled up behind an old Skylark—the car I knew was Hubert's from seeing it in the Golden Acres parking lot—parked haphazardly on a crazy angle half in the ditch. It was empty. "Oh no, oh no, oh *no!*" I muttered. I was not dressed for this, and a cold wind shuddered along the road as I scrambled up the rise to the gate, which had been damaged badly by Virgil and Dewayne charging through it the other day. It hung haphazardly but had been resecured with ropes and a chain. I shinnied again through the gap between the gate and gatepost, my jacket catching on a nail. I pulled hastily on it, ripping it away. I was fated to ruin many a sweater and jacket on that nail, it seemed. As I topped the rise and started across the grassy expanse I saw a confrontation.

Nathan, the jerk, had Hubert Dread, who was a foot shorter than he, by the shoulder and was yelling into his face. Hubert is hard of hearing, but not deaf. I ran the whole way, noticing at the last minute that Gordy Shute was also running toward us. I'd like to say I knew he'd step in, but I was not so sure of Gordy anymore, sadly.

"You take your (and here I swore, a *lot*, and proficiently, something I haven't done for years) hands off that man!" I yelled, coming in hot.

Women were heading toward us, and a gray-haired guy from

another angle, as Gordy reached them at the same time as me. I was panting like a bulldog running a marathon; Gordy was red-faced but fine. The gray-haired dude turned away. I felt like I recognized him, but I didn't have time to think about it.

"What's going on?" Gordy said, looking between his great-uncle, who—fists clenched at his sides, corduroy trousers hitched up to his chest and elbow-patched cardigan flapping in the breeze—was defiantly staring up at Nathan.

I reached out to Doc, who, a gappy grin on his puckered face, looked up at me. "Hey, Merry . . . ain't this the bee's knees? I haven't had this much fun since Dotty Levitz lost her teeth in the soup pot!"

"I thought you had more sense than this!" I hissed, clutching him firmly to my side.

"Nah, sense is for the birds," he said, leaning on his quad cane on the uneven terrain. "If I'm gonna go, I'll go out swinging."

"Nathan, what gives?" Gordy said, prying his so-called friend's fingers off his great-uncle's shoulder.

The stiffening breeze fluttered the fellow's perfect hair and he swept it off his forehead, turning to glare at Gordy. "He started it, telling me we're a bunch of commies!"

I almost snorted in laughter. Whenever Hubert didn't like someone he called them a commie pinko, the worst criticism he could think of, I guess.

"These old men are on our private land," Nathan continued. "What the hell are they doing here?"

Where *were* the police when you wanted them? Earlier they hadn't been able to find him, and here he was. This was the perfect time to nab him. I spied Mariah, lingering nearby with a couple of children, who were wide-eyed and frightened, clinging to her, but I didn't see Felice, nor did I see Barney or the prophet, who was probably off in his lair getting stoned and eating Funyuns while he waited for his next prophecy to come to him on Facebook.

"This is my Uncle Hubert!" Gordy yelped, smacking Nathan's hand away and placing himself between his uncle and erstwhile friend. "He can visit if he wants. And that's his buddy," he finished, hitching his thumb over his shoulder at Doc English, who, having broken away from my hold, was still grinning and shadowboxing shakily, his quad cane swinging on his bony wrist.

Mariah tried to intervene, her expression one of deep worry, but Mother Esther had arrived on the scene and held her arm in a hard grip. "All of you girls go back or risk the wrath of the prophet!" she said sternly to the gathered younger women. Some obeyed, sulkily. This was probably the most interesting thing to happen in a while. My gaze flitted over them, looking for Felice, wondering if any more of these girls were among the missing, but I still didn't see her. I was seriously alarmed, and disturbed by Mother Esther's behavior. Some of the remaining women looked frightened, retreating but not disappearing, and others looked mutinous.

Isadore stomped up to us across the grassy expanse. "Hannah is calling your husband," she muttered. "And Zeke is following me."

"Good. Something is going on here, and I'm not sure what." There was something more beyond two old men and two young men in a standoff. There was a feeling in the air, an aura of turmoil. The women were upset about something, but because they were accustomed to deferring to Mother Esther, those left did nothing but stand in groups and talk softly to each other. It looked like they were arguing.

Peaches broke away from the other girls and approached Gordy. She stood on tiptoe, whispered something, and he nodded.

"Nathan, you leave my uncle and Doc here alone," Gordy warned.

I liked his firmness.

Nathan got an ugly look on his face, a sneer that mingled contempt with dislike. "Who died and made *you* boss, Gordy?"

"Who said you had the right to grab an old man, Nathan?" Gordy shot back.

I wanted to cheer. *Go, Gordy!*

Peaches stepped up to the two men. "Mr. . . . I mean, Doc English?" she said, touching my old friend's arm. "Are you really a medical doctor?"

He straightened and peered at her through his ever-smudgy glasses. "I am . . . or I was for fifty years. Dr. Theodore English, at your service," he said with a courtly bow. He is ever a gentleman, especially with a pretty young lady.

Peaches, tears welling and dripping down her cheeks, sobbed, wringing her hands. "Can you help? I'm afraid one of the women is really sick. She's been throwing up blood, and we don't know what to do, and Mother Esther won't let us take her to the hospital!"

"Take me to her," he commanded, even as Mother Esther shrieked her disapproval, her long robe flapping in the chill wind. Doc looked back to me; my goofy friend had disappeared, to be replaced by an elderly but professional medical doctor. "Call an ambulance, Merry, right now. Vomiting blood is potentially lethal. We can't let her stay here untreated." He said that loud enough that even Mother Esther heard. She balled her fists at her sides and fumed, at least now in silence.

Gordy half supported, half carried my beloved old friend to the hut and I followed, dialing 911 and giving as precise directions as I could, telling them to contact the police for help, since Baxter and Urquhart both knew *exactly* where this encampment was. I was furious that Esther had tried to block the woman from getting help, and proud of Peaches for being bold enough to do the right thing.

It wasn't until I got into the hut that I realized, with horror, that the sick woman was Felice Eklund. Barney hovered nearby, looking uncertain. I didn't say a thing, afraid to scare him off, but the first chance I had I would be telling the cops that *both* Nathan and Barney were now at the camp. I wondered, did they have the prophet yet? Was the raid going ahead on the prophet's shack? I needed to tell someone what I suspected, that there was illegal activity going on not just on the Light and the Way Ministry property but also on a portion of Bob Taggart's farm!

"Who are *you*?" Barney said to Doc. "What are you doing here?"

"Oh my god, Felice!" I cried, scooting across the creaky hut floor. It was cold in this shack, and she shivered, pale and writhing in pain. There was red all over her nightgown, and the metallic tang of blood drifted in the frigid air. I whipped off my jacket and laid it across her, feverishly hoping the ambulance came quickly.

Doc could not physically help Felice—he had worn out every last bit of strength he had, and collapsed on a chair, supporting himself with his cane—but he did tell Peaches and the other women how to help her. I was a weeping mess, afraid Felice was dying, a million fears coursing through my brain. How would I tell Alcina? How would she feel, if her mom died?

Isadore Openshaw patted my back and muttered *"there there"* every few seconds. It was oddly comforting. I put my arm around her and squeezed, making her yelp in disapproval and back away.

"What's going on?" Barney said. "What are you people doing here?" Suddenly his head went up and he froze. The wail of an ambulance in the distance pierced through the muttering and weeping. "What the hell . . . ? Who said you could call an ambulance?" he asked, directing his ire at me, logical since I still had my phone out. "She's *my* wife. She's not going anywhere!"

I strode over to him, and said, through gritted teeth, "So help me God, if you get in the way or object, I will peel the skin off your body with tweezers, a skinny strip at a time!" I do not, to this day, know where that threat came from, but I stand by it.

The ambulance arrived. Like Dwayne and Virgil, the ambulance driver pulled right up through the gate to the encampment, turning and backing closer, directed by one of the women, the beep-beep-beep of the backing alarm shrieking through the jabber of the women as Barney melted away and disappeared. The paramedics swiftly cut through the babble and assessed Felice with the aid of Peaches and one of the older women.

I waited until they had Felice on the gurney, IV hooked up, monitoring equipment telling her medical story, and trotted up to it, tears still streaming down my face.

She opened her eyes and saw me. "Merry!" she cried, grabbing my hand. "Merry, where is Alcina? Is she safe?" She was deadly white and shivering.

"Yes, Alcina is safe and at her dad's place. I should have gotten you a message," I babbled, sobbing. "But it's all been so chaotic. She *is* safe, Felice, and it was her choice to leave. I hope you know that and don't blame Lizzie."

"I know. It's okay," she said, tears running down her face into her hairline. "I should never have c-come here! It's been so awful, and I was so s-scared—"

Of what, I wanted to ask . . . but it was not the moment. "Don't worry about anything but getting better right now, Felice," I said as her ice-cold hand was tugged from mine by the paramedics, who loaded her into the ambulance. "I'll make sure Alcina knows you're at the hospital!" I called out. As the doors closed, I added, for my own comfort, "You're going to be okay now, Felice! Everything's all right."

But as the ambulance pulled away and I followed out to the clearing, I could see the drama continued. Hubert Dread had his great-nephew by the shoulders and shook him, his arthritic grasp surprisingly strong. Gordy was stubbornly looking off into the distance. Nathan was pacing in the background. Peaches avoided Nathan.

"Gordy, you gotta listen to me!" Hubert said, his crackly voice louder than I had ever heard him. He stared up at his nephew, his dark glasses shielding his rheumy eyes. "My boy, all those stories I told you when you was a kid . . . it was all fun and games! I been telling tall tales my whole life. You gotta believe me now . . . I never meant you to take 'em seriously."

Gordy shook his head and firmed his lips, still looking off into space. He appeared unwilling to argue with his uncle, but was still firm in his opinions.

"*Listen to me!*" Hubert said again, his tone becoming frantic. "Dontcha think if Elvis was really an alien he woulda gone off on a spaceship, not died on the john?"

My young friend finally met his uncle's gaze. "Uncle Hubert, I don't believe Elvis is an alien; not anymore," he said with withering sarcasm. "But there is so much more going on in the world that none of you know about. Our government is experimenting on us, *poisoning* us with chemicals to make us easy to control. Big Pharma is proof! Antidepressants, vaccinations . . . all that crap that's in them . . . they want to *poison* us! And the worst of it is chemtrails!" he said, pointing up to the sky where a contrail lingered. "What do you think that crap is, if not chemicals sprayed down on us to make us easy to control?"

"Gordy, think about what you're saying!" I had to chime in to support poor Hubert, who was clearly perplexed and exasperated. I jammed my hands down in my sagging sweater pockets—I had left my jacket over Felice—and steadied myself against the stiffening breeze. "You're saying that all the leaders in the world got together and agreed to use chemicals to control their citizens. How would that even work? How would they keep it a secret?"

"They haven't, but some people are too naïve to believe what's in front of their own eyes," he countered.

That was rich; he was accusing *me* of naïveté. "Gordy, come on . . . how would the chemicals not fall on their own people, their families and friends and loved ones?" I said.

He shook his head. "I don't know. Those people have an antidote, or something. You don't know like I do. You've clearly never investigated like I have the New World Order! It started with the Bushes . . . the 9/11 attack was our *own people*!" His voice was rising, the wind whipping his words back and forth as he got louder and more shrill, his eyes wide with alarm. The contrail above us was feathering into oblivion, much like Gordy's poor evaporating sanity. "That's why there was no debris at the Pennsylvania site where the supposed plane crashed! Those so-called families of the victims were all crisis actors. It's been *proven*! I've seen the *pictures*! I've *done* the research. There is *so* much evidence! You're all just . . . just *sheeple*."

I fell silent and stared at him, tears in my eyes. Much of what he said was a mystery to me, but I had done some research on conspiracy theories while trying to figure out how to combat Gordy's growing disaffection. What he believed appeared to be a stew of many of the most prevalent crackpot theories. We had lost the Gordy I had first met three years ago; we had left it too long. Even attacking the logic of his beliefs wasn't working because he shifted to another conspiracy theory, or another, all connected in some vast monolithic New World Order mishmash conspiracy. As if anyone could get governments to agree on *anything*, even combating climate change, for heaven's sake. Afraid to correct him, loath to be combative, we had let Gordy go on with his "research," what we thought was harmless. After all, everyone has a crazy uncle who thinks that nobody landed on the moon, or the earth is flat, or Elvis never died; we thought Gordy was speculating.

But it led to this.

Zeke had arrived in the meantime and heard the last bit. He eyed his old friend — they had known each other since grade school — with pity, and with love. He stepped up, inserting himself between our friend and Hubert. "Gordy, I'm sorry you thought I abandoned you," he said, tackling one of their more recent conflicts. "I never meant for you to feel that way. I got caught up in things, and didn't spend the time with my best friend, like I should have."

Nathan surged over to Zeke, pointing and yelling, "You think you're better than us."

"Nathan, *shut up!*" Gordy yelled, his hands on his head, pushing back his wispy hair.

But Nathan was not about to be silenced. "You got no right to be here," he screamed at Zeke, shaking a finger in his face. "You with your precious cripple girlfriend and stupid computer job!"

Nobody spoke slightingly of Hannah to any of her friends, least of all her boyfriend. Zeke punched Nathan so hard he fell backward and curled up, blubbering like a baby. Zeke turned to Gordy, rubbing his knuckles. "I love you, buddy, and I hope we can still be friends. Let's get together. Maybe we could take a road trip to Rochester to the World Video Game Hall of Fame."

"Just you and me?"

"Just you and me."

Gordy stared at his friend open-mouthed. "Okay, yeah . . . I'd *love* that."

"We'll do it!" Zeke smiled. "Next week. You free on Saturday?"

Gordy nodded. Nathan had scrambled to his feet, tears in his eyes, his nose red and bloody.

"But not while *that* jerk is your pal," Zeke said, gesturing to the other fellow. "No one who talks about Hannah like that could be a friend of yours. You're too nice a guy, Gordy." He clapped him on the shoulder. "And I know you love Hannah too, as a friend." He turned on his heel and walked away, back to the gate.

Meanwhile, some of the young girls had clustered together, and a bunch of them came to me. Peaches was their spokesperson.

"Merry, we w-want to leave, but we're scared," she said, wrapping her arms around herself and looking over her shoulder at Mother Esther, then swiftly back to me. "Can we go with you? Like, *now*?"

I smiled. "How many of you are there?" There were six, plus Peaches, and one older woman, Mariah. We could fit four in Isadore's car and four in mine. "We're good to go," I said. "By the way, Peaches, what's your real name?"

"Madison Pinker," she said.

Chapter Twenty-one

I took in a deep breath and nodded. "How do you do, Madison? I think your parents are going to be glad to see you."

She started crying, her chin down on her chest, her whole body shaking.

Gordy, distraught, came to her. "Peaches, no! What about our plans? Don't you want to stay with me?"

"Gordy, I can't live like this anymore!" she cried, her whole body shuddering. "I'm tired. I'm done with washing clothes and looking after kids and running away from creepo Nathan! I w-want my mom!"

"It's okay, Madison," I said, patting her shoulder. "Gordy, let her go. Her parents have been worried sick for months. They want her back. And Gordy . . ." I stared at him, but decided I had to tell him like it is. "Look, she's underage, barely sixteen. You could be in a whole lot of trouble, my friend."

"We didn't do anything!" he stormed. "What do you think I am?"

The kind of guy who'd marry a sixteen-year-old? "Just let her go. Madison, get your things together. We're leaving."

I found Zeke and asked him to help get Doc, who had clearly used up every bit of his strength, out to Hubert's car. He readily agreed and we went to fetch my old friend. Between us we made a sling of our arms for Doc to sit in. He didn't weigh much more than a hundred and twenty or so, and I'm a strong woman. He put his stringy arms around our necks and we carried him to Hubert's car, putting him in the front seat. I kissed his cheek and gave him his quad cane. Hubert grumpily agreed to make sure the doctor had a look at Doc when he got back to Golden Acres. I could tell the old dude was upset at his great-nephew, but after seeing Zeke work his magic, I thought there might be hope for Gordy yet.

As Hubert revved his motor and took off down the dirt road, I turned to my young friend. "Zeke, how did you know to say what you did to Gordy?"

He grinned, blinking, his eyes owlish behind his glasses. "Come on, Merry . . . how do you think?"

I put two and two together. "Hannah told you what to say."

"Kinda. Yup. She said if you can't push someone with anger, sometimes you can lead them with kindness."

That was Hannah in a nutshell, leading with kindness. I should pay more attention to how she gets things done. I motioned to the gathering of girls and led the way to my car as Isadore silently trudged along with a gaggle of teens and young women behind her, a grumpy Mother Goose. I talked to those who would speak as they walked, trying to find out if any other girls on Urquhart's list were present. Some of them had only recently joined the compound, a couple from other states who had been hitching or taking the bus and had been convinced by Barney to come stay at the camp. The most recent to join I sent along with Isadore. All of these girls had been here too long to be the most recent missing teen. But the young women would be interviewed by the police, I was sure, and if she was among them, she would be discovered.

When we reached the cars, Isadore and I sorted things out. Her car full, she chugged away, headed to the women's shelter. I texted Shilo and asked her to meet them there, knowing that my good-hearted friend could help acclimate the girls to their new situation, and help the shelter managers. I texted Reverend Maitland, too, because I knew he could help with finding them suitable clothes and other items from the Methodist church clothes cupboard, something they kept stocked with items for families burned or flooded out of their homes. I hurriedly texted Virgil with a few questions that had come up from Zeke's friend's drone footage.

"Zeke, could you do me a huge favor?"

"Sure," he said. "You know I'll help any way I can, Merry."

I wanted to hug the guy. He's such a sweetie. "Can you take some of the girls in your car?"

His eyes widened, and he looked alarmed. "Look, I've already set up help through the women's shelter. You just have to take them and drop them off."

"O . . . okay." Some piled in his car and he followed Isadore down Marker Road toward town.

But I had cut Peaches and Mariah from the herd. I wanted them to myself, with no distractions. We got in my car, and I turned to view the women in the backseat. "Madison, why don't you introduce me to your friend?" I said, eyeing the woman, who was stroking the seat leather and examining the details. "Even though we *have* kind of met before."

"This is Mariah."

I nodded. Barney's plural wife. "Your sister works at the hospital in Ridley Ridge." She looked up quickly and frowned. "You told her you liked the idea of having a sister-wife; it was someone to share the chores with, and talk to."

She eyed me with suspicion. "How do you know that?"

"I'm a mind reader," I said lightly. "Were you taken to clean and cook at a man's place . . . a man named Bob?"

She nodded.

"Was there anything weird going on there?" I caught a moment of shrewd calculation in her pale eyes as I asked.

But then she looked down at her clasped hands. "Not there, but . . . but at the *other* place—"

"The other place?"

"Yeah. Another trucker's house. It's just back on Quarry Road, off Silver Creek Line."

"A trucker?" I thought of the other trucker, the guy named Mack. I described him. "Is that who you mean? Did you go to his place, too?" She shuddered. "You can tell me the truth, you know," I said. "I'm not a cop."

Peaches frowned and stared at her in puzzlement. "I never heard of any other place," she said.

"Mother Esther wasn't going to tell you little girls about it," Mariah said. She then described in shocking, salacious detail what went on at the place.

I turned and stared at her. "Are you . . . are you positive?" It was everything I had feared.

"Would I make something like that up? It's horrible."

She told me how to get there, and she told me who might be there.

My alarm grew as she talked. Panicked and disgusted, my hands shaking and my stomach lurching, I texted Virgil and Dewayne and told them to have police there to meet us. Virgil texted back immediately.

He had acted swiftly on my information. In a joint operation with both counties' cooperation there were two simultaneous raids occurring at the Taggarts' farm and Prophet Voorhees's shack. Drugs had already been found stored in the truck trailers hidden back in the woods. My surmise was absolutely correct, he said. Now I knew more about how some of it was connected. Those truck trailers were not only in that clearing as storage, they were also being converted to cunning drug-carrying vessels, with hidden compartments welded into place by crafty Walt Taggart. That's why there was a huge fuel tank and a big industrial generator on Bob and Walt Taggart's land; that was their hidden work area in the woods.

Also . . . Voorhees—Bardo Voorhees, if my logic was correct—had been taken into custody. Virgil didn't think Urquhart or Ben Baxter would be available to meet me, but he'd make sure *someone* was. If I was right yet again, they would need multiple units. I was shaking, worried about what we'd find next, but I did text him back that I had seen both Nathan and Barney at the Light and the Way Ministry encampment. I didn't know if there were any police available given all that was going on, but I hoped they'd be able to catch the elusive two.

Virgil texted that he'd get whoever he could to meet us and for me to stay out of sight until they arrived. I couldn't guarantee that, not when someone was in danger. With Peaches and Mariah in my car, I followed Mariah's directions. I was tempted to take Silver Creek Line, the most logical route, but it would be swarming with police and I wasn't sure I could get through. I had to go back to Connaught Line, and head to Quarry Road that way, to a lonely farmhouse.

It looked every bit like a country house out of a slasher movie, a sagging, peeling clapboard house, two stories, with overgrown grass and weeds growing wild. I pulled up the long lane and sat staring at it, waiting, wondering what to do. Dare I do *anything*? Virgil had told me to wait.

And yet, given everything Mariah had told me, how could I not do something, now, before it was too late? I could be saving someone's life if I found a way into that farmhouse. It looked so tranquil on the outside . . . run-down, yes, but in a kind of charming way, with a sagging porch, a swing hanging from the porch rafters, and a tumble of flowering weeds rambling up and over the railings. And yet . . . it concealed such darkness.

I turned and looked at Mariah and Peaches. Mariah was huddled in her heavy handknit sweater, her graying hair tied back in a kerchief. Peaches was wide-eyed and frightened, shell-shocked by what Mariah had told me. With great dramatic flair she had told me that the trucker named Mack was the owner, and ran a house of perversion for other men using kidnapped girls, even one or two who had run away from the harsh conditions of the Light and the Way Ministry camp.

"We're supposed to wait for the police," I said. "I guess I can tell you this now . . . Prophet Voorhees has been arrested."

Mariah nodded and sniffed. "I think he's behind it all! *Such* an evil man," she said, her voice shaking. She let her head sink down until her chin was resting on her chest. Hands clasped, she began praying for the prophet's salvation.

It must be hard for a believer to see their prophet's feet of clay, I thought.

Peaches, aka Madison, finally said, in a small voice, "How did I not know any of this was going on? I thought . . . I thought the prophet was genuine, that he r-really cared about us. I thought, like, those long meetings were meant to . . . to break down our walls and let love in." She sniffed. "Gordy said we were . . . uh, trailblazers, or something like that. That we were ready for the trouble to come, while everyone else was sleepwalking through life."

I twisted in my seat again and opened my mouth to say something, but Mariah spoke instead.

"The prophet also said it was up to us to take back America and repopulate it with godly people who would be ready when the end-times started."

"Yeah, I can imagine," I said, resisting rolling my eyes. I turned back and watched the house, still tangling with my growing desire to bust in there and break up whatever could be going on this very second. I thought of what Isadore had discovered in the ledgers she had found, all the money flowing in. I eyed the farmhouse, still waiting, but it was beginning to get on my nerves. "So, Peaches . . . Madison . . . were there girls at the camp who disappeared?"

She nodded, tears in her eyes. "There was a new girl who came a few weeks ago. I met her, and we talked, and then the next day she was gone."

195

"What was her name?"

"Cara."

Cara Urquhart! I texted Virgil, telling him what I had discovered.

Mariah looked up from her prayers. With a panicked expression, voice still shaky, she said, "We should leave. What if the trucker comes out with a gun?"

"I don't think he's here," I said. "I don't see a vehicle."

"It could be parked anywhere . . . behind the barn. Somewhere else. We should leave. Let's go back."

I eyed the house again. I saw someone moving inside, whisking back a curtain. Screw it. I couldn't just sit and wait. "You two stay here," I said, opening the car door. "I'm going to see if there *is* someone here. I won't go in, I'll just knock." I walked slowly up the drive, then up the creaky porch steps and to the door, my heart hammering in my chest. This was crazy, maybe, to be doing this, but it didn't look to me like the guy who owned the house was home.

That moment a pickup truck roared up the drive and a guy jumped out and charged toward me, leaving his truck door open, the open-door signal pinging. "Who are you? What are you doing here?" he hollered.

I turned to face him. "Your name is Mack, right?" I said, my heart thudding. I felt sick. I had hoped to have everything resolved before he came back. I examined his face, thinking he had seemed kind of nice when last I saw him in the coffee shop in Ridley Ridge.

"What's it to you?"

"I just . . ." Crap. There was no way to ask what I needed to ask, or say what I wanted to say, or do what I needed to do. I took a deep breath, considering my options. I looked over to my car; the two women sat watching. I needed to be brave, to show them courage, like they were exemplifying by leaving the encampment. I thought, *to hell with it.* I took a deep breath and looked him in the eye. "Do you have a girl here, a missing girl?" I said, hitching my thumb over my shoulder, indicating his farmhouse. "One who Barney convinced to join the Light and the Way Ministry, and then gave to you?"

"Mack, if you're keeping one of the girls here, you gotta give her up." Unbeknownst to me, Mariah had approached from behind and spoke, her tone harsh, her voice trembling as she joined us. Her anxious gaze flicked back and forth between me and him.

"You can identify him, right?" I said, turning to her.

"Like I told you, I came here to clean sometimes, like we did at Bob's place. I thought Mack was okay, but last time I was here . . ." She shook her head. "He's dangerous."

"What the good goddamn are you talking about, woman?" he said, his wild gray eyebrows drawn down together.

I looked at her, and then turned to Mack. I didn't see a weapon. He looked harmless and baffled. "Last time Mariah was here she found out that you were giving drugs to girls, and abusing them. And I'm here to tell you . . . you had better let the girl you have inside go, or you'll be in big trouble." He was going to be in trouble anyway, but he didn't need to know that.

"What the living hell are you talking about?" He turned to Mariah. "You're mad 'cause I wouldn't sleep with your bony, ugly ass!" Mack blurted out, glaring at the woman. "I told you then, and I'll tell you again," he said, poking his finger at her. "I don't like no flat-chested woman."

"What does he mean?" I said to Mariah.

"He's *lying*!" she yelled, red-faced.

"Am not! You said Voorhees sent you to please me, and I said you couldn't please me if you was the last woman on earth."

At that moment an Autumn Vale PD car roared up the drive and Sheriff Urquhart pelted from the driver's seat, followed by my husband from the passenger's side. "What's going on here?" Urquhart said, hand on his gun, but the holster still domed shut. Other sheriff's department vehicles roared up the lane, too, and officers got out.

The farmhouse door burst open and a young woman raced out and directly at Urquhart, throwing herself at him. "Uncle Cam!" she shrieked. "Will you take me home?"

Chapter Twenty-two

Cam? So that was Urquhart's first name? In the years of knowing him, I had only ever called him Urquhart.

"Cara!" Urquhart exclaimed as the girl dashed at him. He hugged her to him, tears streaming down his chiseled cheek and jaw. It was a touching reunion.

It seemed to me that Cara seemed perfectly fine, just peeved. I had an *aha* moment; I had seen this particular young woman before, when I went to watch hockey at the arena. Mack had his arm around her. But because I had only known her as lackadaisical Millicent, working at the coffee shop, I hadn't recognized her out of uniform except for a vague *I should know this girl* sensation. When I saw her at the arena she had slunk away because she knew Urquhart was on the team, and she hadn't wanted to see her uncle. Not then, anyway. She was not a prisoner, and never had been. This was her choice, but she was tired of her new life and wanted out.

As Virgil approached, I turned and glared at Mariah. "Was *anything* you told me true?"

She glared right back, and slunk away to the other side of the car.

"What was this all about?" Virgil asked.

I sent a frightened and bewildered Madison—the girl had followed me, timidly, when I went closer to the house—back to sit in the car and related to my husband what the woman had told me. Mariah's lurid tales of bizarre sexual practices and girls held against their will by the devious trucker Mack were clearly not true. Officers were searching the trucker's farmhouse, but one came out shrugging. They not only didn't find any other girls, they soon learned, as the girl babbled her story to her Uncle Cam, that Mack had actually *sheltered* Cara Urquhart at his farmhouse when she ran away from the Light and the Way Ministry encampment.

She had swiftly (like, overnight) become fed up with the lifestyle: drudgery, little sleep, bad food and a den mother in Mother Esther who continually harangued the girls about their duty to provide white children to the cream of the crop white men, aka Barney and—presumably—Nathan, Voorhees and Trucker Bob, among others. She had taken off before the repetitive sermonizing and haranguing had time to take effect on her psyche.

I was left puzzled by so much. As a cult the Light and the Way Ministry was mismanaged. It felt like no one was united in any kind of belief system; all were there for their own purposes. Even the prophet didn't appear to believe a word of his own crazy religion, though he seemed to have some of his adherents fooled. He clearly preferred to farm out the religious responsibilities: sermons were old tapes, Mother Esther shepherded the girls, and the congregants did all the physical labor, while he snuggled comfortably in his electronic hideaway. Even as I was listening to Mariah's wild tales, I knew that as far off the rails as Gordy had gone, he would *never* have stuck around if there was rape, drugging and sexual torture involved. He was misguided but not evil.

Virgil had retreated to speak to some of the other sheriff's deputies. He returned to my side. "They're packing up here. Nothing to see. They've taken some of Mack's porn collection into custody but I doubt they'll find anything out other than that he is a pretty normal joe."

I leaned against my car and watched Mariah, who was sulking and glaring at Mack. "I'm not buying any of it," I said suddenly. "This whole religious angle . . . it's weird. It's a fraud."

"Yeah, well, we've kind of figured that out."

"No, I mean . . ." I sighed and shook my head. "I guess that's self-evident now, right? But still . . . *some* of them thought it was genuine. They all poured their own convictions into the so-called religion. That's why I couldn't get a handle on it. It felt like each one of them had their own interpretation of what the Light and the Way was all about. But I would bet that not one of the congregants was aware that this was all a cover for a convicted felon, Bardo Voorhees—masquerading as the brother he murdered and hiding out so he would not be recognized—to run a drug smuggling ring close to the Canadian border."

"It worked for a while, right?" Virgil's handsome face was wreathed in a weary smile. "They were betting that local law enforcement would be afraid to tangle too deeply with the boundaries of a religious organization. Baxter was suspicious, but he knew he had to be careful."

"And yet he mounted a raid that turned up nothing."

Virgil, suddenly tight-lipped, nodded. "I'm worried about him.

He's not been acting rationally for a while. Kelly says that her dad has changed even in day-to-day behavior, not just his job."

Virgil's ex-wife, Kelly, still called him from time to time, and I was okay with that. They had split years ago, and she had caused him real problems with unfounded accusations, but my husband is a good man and had forgiven her. They were family once, and those ties don't completely dissolve.

I hugged him. "Maybe Ben will step down as sheriff."

He nodded. "Maybe."

Everyone was packing up. Mariah wasn't arrested. So far, lying to another citizen wasn't against the law even if, this time, it had led to a waste of sheriff's department time. Virgil strolled over to talk to Urquhart, so I approached Mariah, examining the sour look on her face. "Why all this?" I waved my hand around at the assembly of police cars and Mack the trucker scowling at her from fifty feet away.

"You wouldn't understand."

"Try me."

She stared at me. Her expression was cold, her pale eyes steely. "I was married, you know that?"

"Okay."

"All I was to him was cook, housekeeper, nurse. I was fed up, so I left."

"And went to the Light and the Way Ministry. Was living in dirt and squalor and being a sister-wife to Barney better?" All she was there was a cook, housekeeper and nurse, it seemed to me.

"Better to make my own choices in life. People suck, you know that? Women, men, girls, boys . . . they all suck."

Okay. Misanthropy was alive and well. "I'll give you a ride back to the encampment if you want. Or . . . where do you want to go?"

She sniffed in disdain and looked me up and down. Succinctly, she told me what I could do to myself and then said she'd find her own way back. She marched off across a field as I stood watching.

What an odd duck. Her lies had been brazen and bizarre, and to what purpose? Just to give Mack trouble, it seemed, for his sexual rejection of her. Now that she had achieved her goal, she was off. Her figure, tromping purposefully across the field, became smaller and hazier. She appeared to know exactly where she was headed.

Some people have an unerring sense of direction. Having come by road I had no idea how to get back to the Light and the Way property across country, but she headed toward woods at the back of Mack's farm with a firm and certain step.

I turned away, bewildered once again by the oddness of some local folks. I'm sure they would have felt the same if they were plopped down in the middle of my muddling, befuddling, beloved New York City. There were odd ducks everywhere.

I had not forgotten, nor had Virgil or Urquhart, that there was still a murder left unsolved. The sheriff had suspects to question (Urquhart had been tasked with helping Baxter's investigation), but first he was taking his niece back to his sister. Mack was asked to come into the station to shed some light on Mariah's accusations, and he agreed to be there the next morning, though he was as puzzled as anyone as to why she had made such bizarre and outrageous claims.

Virgil and I took Madison home to her parents, who wept and hugged and consoled and loved on her. There would be much more to come; the girl had been there a long time, over a year, and she was changed. How she reintegrated back into her family, how they came together, how they mended the rifts and sorrows, would take time and professional help. I hoped they had both.

Virgil and I sat in the car after dropping her off. "Do you think she'll be okay?" I whispered, watching the house. Another car raced up the street and screeched to a halt at the curb. A woman got out and raced up the front walk and bolted inside. Probably a relative relieved to find out that Madison was alive and relatively well.

"I know some folks who can help," he said. "There's a counselor at the women's shelter. I'll call her tomorrow and make sure the girls from the Light and the Way can get help."

The shelter. I searched his eyes. "Virgil, this is in confidence, but Shilo told me there was a woman at the shelter who had escaped the compound. She might have important information, but . . . but being a survivor of abuse, she might not come forward on her own. Is there any way . . . I mean, can she be contacted to give information? Or testimony?"

He thought about it for a long moment. "Let me talk to my contact. I'll see what I can find out. At least Voorhees is in custody.

But some cops have been back to the camp . . . neither Nathan nor Barney was there. Those guys have an uncanny ability to evade the police."

"There one minute and gone the next," I murmured. I frowned and tapped one finger on the steering wheel. "I wonder where Barney went? He was there, trying to keep us from taking Felice to the hospital, but then he was gone. You'd think he would have been there right to the moment she was taken away. Why would he try to keep us from helping her?"

Virgil squinted and stared down the street. "He was losing control over her, right? Those kinds of creeps don't like their women getting away from them, having choices. Maybe that's it."

"Maybe," I said. But something bothered me about that. "What is Barney's last name?" I asked.

Virgil brought up a file on his phone, where he keeps all his notes. "We never got a last name for him. No one seemed to know it and he refused to answer when asked."

"That's weird." I looked over at him. "You know, it once occurred to me that the compound would be a great place for an escaped felon to hide out. Do you suppose he's wanted?"

"Maybe. Let me look into it."

• • •

The exhausting events of Saturday were behind me. I called Lizzie. She told me that Alcina had been able to visit her mom in the hospital. All tests had indicated that Felice had a bleeding ulcer, which was why she had been throwing up blood. She had a transfusion and was on medication, and was going to be okay. Alcina's dad had taken their little boy to the hospital to see his mother, too. Lizzie, who had gone with Alcina, reported that it was a teary reunion. It seemed that there was hope for the Eklund family. Alcina's dad had rented a house near his sister's, and that was where he, Alcina, and Teddy were going to live; Felice, too, once she left the hospital.

It was Sunday morning, and I wasn't sure what to do with my time, so I cleaned my kitchen and vacuumed while listening to a recording of the LSO doing Vivaldi's "Autumn." Virgil had left early; he wanted to talk Urquhart into interviewing his niece, convinced that the girl might know a lot more than she had so far said about her time at the camp. They were still doggedly trying to solve Glynnis's murder.

I reminded him about my own questions, particularly about Barney. He was always out there, shouting at people berating women. But other than that, what sign was there that he was truly religious? It always felt like he was going through the motions, maybe for his own ulterior motives. I had thought about it a lot, about how there was scant indication the group was a religious organization other than Barney and Nathan and their insult campaign against women and the taped lectures they used to indoctrinate their followers. Were they using religion as a front to keep people away from the Light and the Way Ministry? Locals wrote them off as nuts, and, other than Sheriff Baxter's hasty and ill-planned raid, the police were wary of interfering lest they be hit with a lawsuit against them for interference with religious freedom. The bottom line was, the group had been left alone for years with no oversight.

Something was tickling my brain, something I had been thinking about, and had even said at one point. It went back to when Hannah looked up the FBI list of most wanted criminals. I sat down at the kitchen breakfast bar with my laptop and found the site she had showed me, the FBI wanted list. There was a name I remembered, one I had remarked on at the time. I found it, and looked more carefully at the photo attached, thought about the name, and considered Barney. I really looked, examining the face and the wound that cut up into his hairline. What would that look like healed?

I called Virgil, asking him if they had found Barney yet.

"He's taken off. They have a BOLO out on him. Urquhart got Baxter to have a deputy go out to the compound this morning to ask some questions, but he came back and said the place is virtually deserted; folks are leaving the Light and the Way Ministry. All of us want to talk to Barney, given how much control he seemed to have, and how he was the most active recruiter for the cult, but he's gone."

My heart pounded. "Virgil, I think I know why. I'm looking at a photo on the FBI's most wanted list." I told him the name and clicked to send the link to his inbox. "The guy looks like Barney might look if he had a beard and longer hair, and he has a wound on his forehead. Virgil, Barney has a scar that would match the cut! The mug shot would explain why Barney was short-haired and clean-shaven when the rest of the Light and the Way guys have scruff, beards and long hair. He needed to look as little like his wanted poster as possible, given how much time he spent in public, on the streets."

"I'll look." He disappeared off the phone for a long minute, then came back. "I think you're right." He's accustomed to facial recognition, to being able to identify people regardless of changes in hair or dress.

"So you agree. Barney is likely literally John Doe, wanted for armed robbery?"

"I'd bet on it. What made you connect the two?"

"I've been thinking for a while that the encampment would be the perfect place to hide if you were a wanted felon. I didn't figure it would be the one guy who is out front and on the streets! It was chance that Hannah and I were looking at mug shots, and I saw the one of the guy with the forehead cut. But I didn't connect it with Barney until this minute." I hesitated. "I suppose he could be Glynnis's murderer. Cecily said Glynnis was a snoop. Maybe she figured out who he was."

"It's possible. I'll hunt him down if it's the last thing I do."

My heart calmed; Virgil is very *very* good at hunting criminals, and with the connections he has with police departments across our area and the country, I knew I could count on him.

I finally sat down with my coffee and reflected on the murder of Glynnis. What I knew was, she had been at the Light and the Way Ministry cult camp, and had, it seemed, either been beaten and escaped, or escaped and been beaten by someone else or—the most likely fate, in my mind—had been beaten at the camp and then taken away to be dropped on the side of the highway, presumably dead.

I made a list of the possible suspects, something I usually do much earlier when I am involved in a tragedy like this. So much else had happened, and there had been such a confusing set of personal involvements in this, with Felice and Alcina and Lizzie's concern over them, our rescue of Cecily, Gordy's predicament, which had involved me initially, and finally finding Lynn there and rescuing her.

It seemed to me that there were several possibilities in the murder of Glynnis:

> *Prophet Voorhees:* now known to be Bardo, not Arden. He was such a shadowy figure. I didn't have a clue if he'd kill, but he had a lot to lose if Glynnis had, perhaps, in her "snooping" (as Cecily called it) come across information indicating who he really was.
>
> *Mother Esther:* aka the real Arden's wife; that woman was a coldhearted bitch and, I thought, possibly the only true believer in the cult message they were selling. If a girl had decided she no longer wanted to live like that, and perhaps did not want to be the mother of the next generation of neo-Nazis, the woman may have killed her, rather than let her leave.
>
> *Barney:* Voorhees's next in command. With what I now knew, I thought his motives for killing Glynnis could have been similar to ones I considered for Voorhees. Maybe she could have figured out who he was. If she had threatened to turn him in, he would have killed her. The venom he spewed toward women seemed genuine; I could imagine he would beat a woman to death.
>
> *Trucker Bob:* now known to be tied up in the illegal side business of the Light and the Way. They were up to their necks in drugs, and in altering trucks to carry them across the border into Canada. Had Glynnis figured it out? She had gotten in trouble for leaving the encampment, and so may have wandered as far afield as the prophet's shack, or even Bob's farm, and may have seen what she ought not to have, and paid the price.
>
> *Mariah:* That woman, that piece of work, was as vile a liar as I had ever met, and as venomous as Mother Esther. She appeared to be a jealous witch,

taking revenge on Mack for not falling under her sexual spell. Who knows what conflicts she may have had with the other women? Glynnis was pretty, Cecily said. That may have been enough for Mariah to become even more unhinged than she already was.

And it was also quite possible that the assailant was someone I had not met, or hadn't figured out yet. This case didn't have the cut-and-dried closed circle of suspects I was accustomed to. I needed to know more . . . *much* more.

My phone rang and I picked it up. Pish! "Hey, my love," I said. "What's up?"

"Lynn is home from the hospital."

"Already? I thought she'd be there a week, at least."

"She's doing better than they expected. I brought her here, to the castle, and a nurse is going to check in twice a day, to make sure she's okay. She wants to see you. Can you come?"

I sighed and set the phone down. This was not on my agenda for the day, making my way through Lynn's labyrinthine ability to lie, manipulate and blame-shift. I picked the phone back up. "Okay. I'll be there in ten." This was not for Lynn, this was for Pish. I could not bear to look like a lout in his eyes.

"See you in ten," he said.

I was nervous, regressing to the old me. I understood it; I was going to be faced with someone who in the past had the ability to manipulate me, make me ashamed and guilty and upset. She had used me for two years and had delighted in humiliating me. But that was over. I would combat those old feelings and come through even stronger.

I slipped on a tawny Zelie for She skirt and sweater set. The skirt was mid-calf and form-fitting, and yet so comfortable I could have done a cartwheel in it . . . if I had ever been able to do a cartwheel, which I never have. The clothes from that designer are fashion-forward and very chic, and I adore them. I twisted my long dark hair up into a messy bun, slipped on a pair of black Louboutin booties, got my Birkin bag and donned Cavalli sunglasses and headed out the door, armored by designer labels. I'm shallow enough that that alone gives me confidence.

Becket rode with me, leaped out of the car when I parked, and pranced into the castle at my feet. No pocket puppy for me; I prefer a tiny tiger. I headed to the kitchen and entered, removing my sunglasses, still filled with trepidation.

Lynn was at the long center table. She rose when she saw me come in, her eyes filling with tears, almost mewing in distress. Pish put his arm around her shoulders and guided her around the table toward me. I didn't know what to do. I examined her, how thin she was still, how gray, the bags under her eyes, the tissue-thin look of her skin, under which threaded blue arteries. Was it safe for her to be out of the hospital? Despite Pish's reassurance, I was deeply worried. It was strange, but in that moment I realized that I had missed her. As miserable as our two years as boss and gofer had been, there had been good moments, or I wouldn't have stayed so long. I had just forgotten — or blocked out — those good moments.

I walked to her, set my bag and sunglasses aside and took her in my arms, hugged her gently, then tried to let her go. But she clung to me and laid her head on my shoulder — not easy, since she is fairly tall — taking a long, deep breath. "You smell so good," she said after inhaling my Houbigant Quelques Fleurs l'Original. "It felt wonderful this morning, having a shower. I forgot how good a shower feels, the hot water, the soap. That camp . . . it was so dirty, and I was cold all the time." She shuddered, then finally stood on her own.

I watched her a moment. Reed-thin as always, painfully bony, still . . . she seemed calm and steady. That was a good start. "Lynn . . . Leatrice . . ." I frowned. "Which do you prefer?"

"Just Lynn," she said. "Leatrice Pugeot died in a puddle of her own vomit at that horrible place." She shuddered but stuck her chin up. "I'm never going to be Leatrice again."

I nodded, not trusting her transformation. She had vowed to change before. She had sobered, gone into recovery, gone to rehab, escaped from rehab, ended up in a shooting gallery in the Bronx, back to rehab, OD'd on prescription pain meds, been committed to the psych ward . . . she had been through it *all*. It would be a long time before she could be considered sober or before I would trust her reformation. We sat down next to each other at the table, sipping some of Pish's wonderful coffee and talking. I examined her bony face, the high cheekbones, the pale green eyes and full lips; all those features had come together to make her something special as a model, catlike, mysterious. Photographers had loved her. Light loved her, etching shadows and mystery over her. I could still make out the Leatrice she was for the camera.

As cautious as I intended to be, still, as we chatted I realized all I had been harboring for so long. When I first arrived in Autumn Vale that anger had kept me moving forward. It had kept me going, fueled me, but now it served no purpose. I let the weight of years of resentment slip from me. "How long were you there, at the camp?"

She shook her head and frowned, stroking the smooth wood surface of the kitchen table. "At least two months, maybe more." And yet nobody had tried to find her, not one of her so-called friends.

"So, were you taking drugs while there?" I asked, watching her.

There was a pulse in one temple, a heartbeat rhythm. "I was."

"What kind?"

"All kinds. Anything I could get. You know me," she said with a grimace. "I'm not fussy. Oxy is my choice, but beans, bath salts, blow, crank, molly, smack . . . I'll try anything, with a side of Jack or Patron. Doctors here said they'd never seen such a soup of chemicals as they found in my blood!"

I bit back a response. It had almost sounded like she was proud of it for a moment, but there was no pride on her face, just tired acknowledgment. "What was it mostly?"

"Cocaine. It got me through every day, I guess. It's a miracle I lived there for as long as I did. Still, I've woken up in worse places." She cracked a weary half smile.

I knew from experience how true that was. "How did you get it?"

"There was a guy who would sneak it to me . . . some fellow in a newsboy cap and golf shirt."

Barney. Hmm.

"Do you think they knew who you were?"

Lynn has a narrow, cunning little face. When she was modeling, she was ethereal and fairy-like, but that had transformed into a feral foxiness now. "I'm pretty sure they did," she said, eyes narrowed. "I *knew* they might recognize me. That's why I hid my purse. I didn't want them getting a hold of my credit cards."

Which Felice had known how to find, fortunately, for her ID and insurance card.

"You think someone recognized you?"

She nodded. "Some of those poor girls had old fashion magazines from, like, ten years ago, hidden away to read when no one was looking. I was in a few of the fashion spreads. I'd bet they knew who I was and someone told that prophet guy."

"Did he try to get money out of you?"

"Omigawd, all the *time*! That fellow, Voorhees . . . huh!" She rolled her eyes and shook her head. "At first I was his private pet. That old fraud said he could help me cure my addiction even though he knew they were feeding me drugs. Catch was, I had to be willing to give up my worldly goods. Hah! I told him I'd give up my worldly goods when he did. I knew that putz had a crib somewhere with booze, drugs, video games and girls. How else did he make sure I got all the pretty poison I wanted? He's not the first horny guru I've met."

I laughed, remembering that when she was sober, Lynn could be a hoot. Though she was apparently taking drugs pretty much the whole time she was there, she still noticed and remembered a lot. As we chatted, and she gave her thoughts on all the members of the Light and the Way, I realized something: I had dismissed one person from being in the circle of suspects in Glynnis's murder. I was disturbed that in many scenarios he was there, in the background, leering with evil intent and warped view, close enough, and yet not bringing attention to one aspect of his behavior, his vile view of women and their place in society, and their utility if they refused his advances.

Could he be the answer? Surely it wasn't that simple.

My phone buzzed. It was Hannah. As Lynn and Pish chatted, I walked out into the great hall to talk to my librarian friend.

"Merry, Gordy is in trouble!" she said after the briefest of salutations.

"What's going on?" My voice echoed in the huge marble-floored hall.

"Sheriff Baxter arrested him out at the camp. Gordy phoned his uncle—not Mr. Dread, the other uncle, Richard Shute, the one he worked for—and his uncle phoned Zeke. A woman at the encampment said that Gordy knew everything that was going on and helped the prophet lure women into the cult! She said Gordy stole money, and drugs, and . . . she told the sheriff that Gordy was involved in Glynnis's murder!"

A woman? Mariah, I would bet on it! That lying *witch*. Why would the police believe her, after what she had said the day before? But . . . I took a deep breath. That tip, of the supposed sex maniac trucker Mack, had come from me, not her. Maybe the connection, in Baxter's sheriff's department—that Mariah was the source—was not made.

"And Merry, we found something else out."

"What is that?"

"We know who Nathan is now."

"Really? I hope it's someone unsavory. I'd love someone to nail that creep to the wall. Who is he?"

"He's Mariah's son."

Chapter Twenty-three

"Mariah's son?" I screeched. "But her sister said her son's name is Johnny . . . oh, wait. Nathan could be short for Jonathan, and maybe some in the family called him Johnny. I never would have thought of that." At first I didn't think it mattered, even given the direction my suspicions had begun to lurch in. But then my busy mind got busier. I thought back to what Binny had said about Nathan, what Zeke had said about how Gordy met the guy. I remembered that Urquhart had banished him from Autumn Vale, and that Nathan had lured Gordy out to the camp soon after.

Damn. My suspicions were already there, but with this new knowledge, I felt them sharpen. Mariah, with her lies, had now effectively gotten rid of Gordy. And getting Gordy arrested for Glynnis's murder would take the heat and any shadow of suspicion off . . . her son. How could I have dismissed Nathan as a suspect? "I'll call you back in a minute," I said. "I have to check in with Lizzie." I looked at my messages, knowing my phone had buzzed a few times as I talked to Hannah.

There were a string of messages from Lizzie that became increasingly frenzied.

Merry, need 2 talk.

Mer, where R U????

Going 2 camp 2 get stuff 4 Al and Fe.

Where the (expletive deleted) R U???

No. *No!* Lizzie was on her way to the camp to retrieve Alcina and Felice's stuff, and Nathan and Mariah were there. I hit the speed dial for Lizzie's phone, but it rang and rang. I left a frantic *Stop what you're doing!* voice mail, then texted her the same. No answer.

I looked up at Pish, who had followed me. "Lizzie is on her way to the camp," I said. "I think I know now who killed the dead teens, *including* Glynnis. And he's been right in front of us the whole time. I have to go. If Lizzie gets there and meets up with them—"

"Them?"

"Lying witch Mariah and her scary son, Nathan."

"Son?"

"Yes, *son*. I don't know how I missed him as a suspect, but his mother, Mariah, has been covering up for him the whole time. If I'm

211

right that is one sick, twisted pair, and they will kill Lizzie in a heartbeat if we don't stop them."

Lynn was sitting on the kitchen floor talking to Becket when I retrieved my bag. She looked up at me with shining eyes. "I never knew cats were so smart!" she said, then went back to crooning to him. I smiled, and I'll admit my eyes were teary.

"I'm not letting you go alone," my dear friend said.

"What about Lynn?" I muttered, gesturing to her. She was too fragile to leave alone.

"Becket can take care of her. The nurse is due in ten minutes; she texted me she's on her way, and she has instructions to just come in if I don't hear her. It'll be all right. We can't take a chance that Lizzie will get in trouble."

I called Virgil on my way out of the castle, Pish trailing behind me. My husband told me under no circumstances was I to go out there to that camp without him. I propped the phone between my ear and shoulder as I opened the car door. "I will *not* leave Lizzie to deal on her own, and I can't get her to answer the phone, which may mean she's already there and left her phone in the car. If you want to meet me there, fine, but I'm *not waiting*."

I ended the call and drove at record speed, Pish clutching the dashboard in fear or worry, I didn't care which. Lizzie's grand-mother's car was, indeed, parked along the road. I parked behind her, then climbed the rise and squeezed through the fence—for once not ruining my clothes in the process—a silent and worried Pish hustling along behind me as I trotted across the open expanse. If I'd known I'd be hiking, I would not have worn the Louboutin booties, which were likely going to be ruined by the damp dead grass and dirt.

The camp was deserted, a chill wind blowing the dead weeds and grass to almost flattened stems, and no fire in the pit. I got a sick sense of unease in my belly. I stopped and let my gaze travel over the encampment. "Where is everyone?" I whispered. I knew some had left, but in the wake of the arrests and desertions had *everyone* vacated the Light and the Way Ministry compound?

Pish, beside me, said, "I don't like this . . . it feels too still."

The wind shifted, and I heard voices. "That way!" I said, pointing toward the Quonset huts.

There was a loud report, and an outcry. In a flash I pictured all kinds of things . . . worst of all, my dear Lizzie on the ground spilling her teenaged blood into the yellow weeds and dirt. I ran, scooting between the red and blue Quonset huts, and came out into an open area to find a scenario I had not expected. I skidded to a halt like a cartoon character, digging a trench in the dirt under my heels.

Lizzie, gun pointed to the sky, was facing off against Nathan and Mariah, the deadly son and mother duo. Nathan had dropped to his knees by a hole in the ground, a shovel still upright in its depths, but Mariah, the more deadly of the two, I now thought, faced Lizzie, hands outspread. She was talking quickly, but Lizzie was shaking her head.

"What's going on?" I asked, and Lizzie whirled.

Big mistake. Nathan lunged from his knees, knocked Lizzie down and grabbed the gun, rolling over on his side and coming up to his feet in a flash. He stood and held the gun out at us, his dirty hands clutching the weapon and shaking as he backed up a few steps. His mother still had her hands raised and spread, but she was now facing her son.

"What the *hell* is going on?" I muttered.

"Why'd ya hafta distract me?" Lizzie howled, shaking her fists in anger as she climbed back to her feet.

"How was I supposed to know what was going on?"

"I had the gun, *that's* what was going on!"

"I'm *sorry!*" I hollered. I took a deep breath as I watched Nathan. Tears streamed down his dirty face, leaving mucky trails as he moved slowly, holding the gun on each of us in turn, but stopping as he pointed it at his mother.

"Nathan, honey, give me the gun," Mariah coaxed.

"No, Nathan, you dolt!" Lizzie shouted as Nathan wavered, the gun drooping in his hand. "A minute ago she was making you dig a grave and was going to put you in it!"

"What?" I screeched.

Lizzie batted at me with her free hand. "Shut up!" she hissed.

"I was *not* going to put him in it," Mariah said, her tone scary calm. "It was . . . it was a trick to fool you. Why would I do that to my own son?"

My mind cleared . . . the two of them had been working in concert before now, or one was covering for the other. Which was it? Was Nathan a killer with a worried mother who covered his tracks, or was she the killer with a desperate son trying to save her? Or . . . was it a weird mother/son team? I took deep breaths, letting them out slowly, glancing at Lizzie, who was clenching and unclenching her fists in anxiety.

Pish had retreated. He is a wise man; it would have been pointless for him to be trapped here too, at the point of a gun. He could guide Virgil or whoever else he managed to get to help us. With a gun in the equation we needed a professional.

"She's off her rocker," Lizzie muttered, gesturing to Mariah.

"He doesn't look a whole lot saner," I said, watching Nathan, his whole body quivering.

"Nathan, honey, give me the gun," Mariah said, her tone a crooning hum. She stretched out her hands and beckoned, curling her fingers in a *come to me* gesture.

The guy looked confused. "But Mom, you said—"

"Never mind," she said, "Never mind, honey. Just a misunderstanding. Give me the gun and we can work this all out."

"Oh, man, this is not good," Lizzie said, sidling to me and grabbing my hand. "Honest to gawd, two minutes ago she was holding the gun on him and had him digging a freakin' grave for himself."

"I don't understand."

"I think Mariah or Nathan killed Glynnis," Lizzie muttered.

"Yeah, I got that much. I think they were in on it together," I said. The two tallish men Lynn had seen carrying a limp girl's body were actually Nathan and his mother, who was almost as tall as him, and thin and bony. If she was wearing pants and had her hair up, in silhouette she could easily be mistaken as a man in the dark. That's why Lynn heard a woman's voice as well. I had been fooled into thinking it was a trio made up of Barney, Voorhees and Mother Esther. "Or one was covering for the other; I'm not sure which yet. What happened?"

"I just came here to get Alcina and her mom's stuff. There was no one around . . . I thought. I was collecting up their stuff when Nathan grabbed my arm and hauled me out."

"Did he have the gun?"

"No! He was mad, said I was snooping, threatened me in a kind of vague way. He's stronger than he looks. He bent my arm behind my back and I couldn't get away from him."

My stomach twisted; he was strong from experience grabbing girls, I thought. "He's a wiry kind of strong. Easy to underestimate," I said as I watched the two. Mariah was still trying to talk him into giving her the gun.

"Then his mother—who knew she was his mother?—came tromping in looking like she was off her meds and told me—us—to get out and march to the back. Nathan looked confused but did as he was told, hauling me with him. Then she drew a gun out of her pocket, threw a shovel at him and told him to dig, so he did. I was *sweating*! Thought I was a goner. Thought the grave was for me. I couldn't even make a break for it, afraid I'd get shot in the back."

I nodded . . . we were in a clearing. It would have been an easy shot.

"Then she told *him* to kneel in front of the hole. I didn't know what to think. I still don't. He sniveled, and asked why, and then you blundered in."

"Wait . . . *you* had the gun when I blundered in."

"Oh, yeah. I forgot the part where I leaped at her, grabbed the gun, shot it in the air and told them *both* to stand by the hole." She gave me side-eye. "*Then* you blundered in, startled me, he lunged and got the freakin' gun. And now we're in a fix."

"Okay, all right, I'm sorry." I watched the mother and son duo, transfixed. It was like something I saw on the nature channel once, a cobra and a bunny, one holding the other with a fixed gaze and hypnotic movement. Until the cobra devoured the fluffy bunny. Not that I'm comparing Nathan to a bunny, given that he was the one who had the gun, but Mariah was *definitely* a cobra. I heard the distant sound of a heavy, throbbing motor; that was Virgil arriving. Pish would guide him to our aid. The small hairs on the back of my neck prickled; I felt like I heard stealthy footsteps, but I wasn't sure if it was real or my wishful imagination.

I had to distract them. "Hey, you two . . . so what really happened? Who killed Glynnis?"

Nathan whirled, the gun drooping, and Mariah made a feint toward it, but he steadied and pointed it back at her.

"Shut up, you," Nathan snarled.

Maybe there were two cobras and no fluffy bunnies.

"And . . . and the others?"

"It was him," Mariah said, glaring at her son. "He's a pathetic loser and couldn't get a girl without strangling her."

"Shut up . . . just shut *up*, Mom!" Nathan said, waving the gun around.

It was the weirdest thing, between them, so typically mother and son, and yet so very twisted. His face was contorted with anger, suffused with red. Mariah, on the other hand, was dead calm, no emotion on her plain face.

"It was all him," she said.

"Glynnis was only the last," I said, trying to keep my voice from shaking. I thought of the bodies found four years ago, and the one of poor Yolanda Perkins, found two and a half years ago. And if I recalled, there was still one missing girl from a couple of years ago, and one missing currently. I gulped. "There are more, going back several years."

Nathan was weeping, snot dribbling from his nose and the tears coursing down his cheeks. How could he see to hold the gun? But he did. "It's all her fault!" he shrieked, waving the gun toward his mother.

I ducked and bobbed, afraid the gun would go off. "Mariah, did you kill those girls?"

"What are you doing?" Lizzie muttered.

"Go with it," I hissed out of the corner of my mouth. I could hear rustling and what sounded like a booted footstep; I needed to keep them focused on me and their mutual antagonism. I motioned slightly with my head back the way we had come.

Her eyes widened, and she stuck a hand in her frizzing hair. "Crap. Okay." She stood taller. "I don't think it was her. It was all you, wasn't it, Nathan?"

"No . . . it's the mom," I argued. "Mariah, why did you kill those girls?"

She glanced my way as her son, still holding the gun and still weeping, moaned in agony, his free hand pressed against his stomach. "Little witches needed to be taught a lesson," she growled.

"What kind of lesson?"

"If you're gonna tease a guy, you got a duty to come across with the goods."

"Was that why you killed Glynnis?"

She smiled, but it was a weird, tired, disgusted smile. "She'd have told the cops what Nathan tried on her. He liked her, but she wasn't having none of that. She was going to leave so he grabbed her to have a little fun, but she screamed." She shrugged. "It didn't go so well after that. He was gonna do what he'd done before, but he was being slow about it, so I had to shut her up."

My stomach lurched. "What about the other girls? The ones in the past? You said he was going to do what he'd done before."

She sighed heavily, the much put-upon mother. "He's never had much luck with women. He's such a good-looking boy . . . what's wrong with girls today? So damned picky. I've always just tried to help him find a girlfriend. But he just can't keep his hands to himself . . . can't be gentle." She turned and glared at her son. "Now look, Nathan, this woman is going to blame it all on you, all those girls we took care of."

"But Mom, you told me . . ." He looked confused and worried, and the gun drooped even more.

I had no pity in my heart for him, but in that moment he looked so young and afraid. I wondered how she had raised him, how she had warped him. I'm *never* for blaming the mother—I think moms get a bum rap—but in this case . . . I blamed the mother. "You killed any girl he tried to do anything to. Any girl he assaulted."

"Oh, *he* killed a couple. The first ones, anyway, coupla hitchhikers."

"Mom, that was an accident! You *know* that," he whined. "You told me it was okay!"

She glanced at me with a smile, like, *kids . . . what are ya gonna do?* "He was just a kid, messing around . . . like a cat with mice, you know?"

My eyes widened and my heart thudded. *Messing around . . .* how could she put it that way?

"But then he wanted to drop that Yolanda girl off on the road, alive, but I told him she would have told the police and the cops would have put him away." She turned back to her son again. "You and me need to stick together," she said sweetly. "Nathan, honey, give me the gun. I'll kill 'em both and we'll make sure no one blames you for *anything*."

"Nathan, keep the gun. Your mother is the one who is going to blame you for it all," I said, my gaze flicking back and forth between the mother and son. I kept hearing sounds, and I needed to keep them at odds so they wouldn't notice the help that was coming for us. "She's going to kill us and blame it *all* on you." Staying at this encampment, the Light and the Way had been their shield for so long. Seeing them interact I now had no doubt who the mastermind was. Mariah/Maria had pretended to a womanly submission to stay at the Light and the Way camp under Mother Esther's dubious leadership, but underneath she was a seething cauldron of dangerous brooding emotion.

"*We* know you're innocent," I said to Nathan. I'd say *anything* to make him keep the gun, because I thought that if Mariah got hold of it she'd kill us in a heartbeat. "We believe you; your mother did it *all*."

"Shut up, witch," she hissed, turning a furious wild-eyed look on me. She pushed her kerchief back on her head and wisps of hair escaped, fluttering in the breeze.

"Mariah, why did you marry Barney?" I asked, casting about for topics to keep her busy and talking. Where *were* Pish and Virgil and the others? It felt like hours had passed, but it had probably only been five minutes. I felt like they were near, but I didn't see anyone!

"Now, don't you ask interesting questions!" she said. "You think I didn't know who Barney was?" She smiled. "I knew from the start, the minute he dragged into Ridley Ridge, running from the law and hiding out in that farmhouse Bardo Voorhees had as the Light and the Way. We got to be friends. *Good* friends. He confided in me . . . like another son in a way."

"You knew who he was all along? *And* you knew that Arden Voorhees was really Bardo?"

"Who do you think showed Barney how to clean himself up so he didn't look anything like his wanted photo? Hah! Get his real name . . . it's John Doe! I thought that was a hoot. And who do you think taught him how to act so folks wouldn't be suspicious?" She snorted in derision. "That man . . . I knew he was a felon from the get-go, the moment I met him. He *stank* of it, of fear, of deception.

But he was helpful. Good cover. We kept him safe, and he acted the crazy street preacher who kept folks from wanting to look into the Light and the Way more closely. All my idea. I told Bardo my plan, and he approved." She sighed and shook her head. "But after a coupla years Barney was getting cocky, full of himself; he felt safe. He was bored with living out here, and being without a woman."

"But he had you, right?" I said.

Wrong thing to say. Her cheeks flushed a deep wine, and red blotches broke out on her neck. "He didn't *want* me," she spat out. "After all I'd done for him he wanted to leave the Light and the Way! But I knew how to get him to stay. The stupid sot fell in love with Felice; she's so *pretty!*" Mariah snarled, jealousy darkening her tone. "I told him I'd help him marry that prissy little tramp Felice, make her trust him. I told her that she was destined for great things, and that she had been chosen for us as my sister-wife."

I shivered. How close had Felice come to being murdered by a jealous Mariah? Pretty close, I would bet.

She snickered. "Fool. The woman's an *idiot*. All Barney wanted was to get her in his bed. He woulda gotten tired of her pretty quick."

I'd had it, that casual reference to poor Felice, now in a hospital room, and I literally saw blood red, a blinding flood of fury that sent me rocketing at the woman, clawing and scratching, as Lizzie — with me all the way — lashed out. It was a melee in the midst of which was a loud report, a deafening bang. I screamed, as did someone else. All I could see was Mariah's hair, the kerchief pulled askew, and her patterned dress. I pushed her off me and she grunted, a groan of anguish or pain, I didn't know which. I was helped to my feet by a pair of strong hands as I wept in fear and anger, my gaze slewing around. "Lizzie!" I yelled, flailing, feeling like the world was spinning out of control. "Lizzie, where . . . ?"

Virgil had grabbed hold of me, binding me tightly in his grasp. "Sweetie, are you all right?" He kissed my brow, the warmth and comfort of his arms infusing me with strength. "I've got to help Dewayne, honey, I have to let you go. Are you okay?"

I nodded and pushed him away, confused and scared and worried for Lizzie. Shuddering with the adrenaline flow, my vision cleared and I took in the scene. Dewayne had Mariah in his strong grip and had pulled her to her feet, bending her arm behind her back and holding her firmly. She was wailing, and I looked in the direction she was staring; Nathan had used the gun on himself. He lay bloody and dying on the ground by the hole that was intended as his grave by his mother, who, paradoxically, was now weeping in anguish for her dead son. Lizzie stood nearby, arms wrapped around herself, tears flooding her eyes and dripping from her chin.

I muttered that I was okay and dashed to Lizzie, taking her in my arms, pushing her head on my shoulder. "Don't look, honey, don't look."

After a few minutes of heaving tears she stilled. Lizzie took a deep breath and pulled away from me, her wet, shimmering eyes full of wisdom and pain. "I'm okay. Truly, Merry. I'm alive. You're alive. Alcina and Felice are okay."

In so many ways Lizzie was a stronger woman than I, and I loved her for it, but she needed to know it was okay to break down. I looked deep into her eyes. "It's all right if you're not okay, you know. This was a lot; you don't have to be strong. You can lean on me."

She nodded, and the tears came again, welling and running, dripping down her face. "I'm . . . I'm kinda horrified, you know? But . . . God, it sounds awful. I'm relieved, too, that he offed himself."

"I get it. Just let yourself feel whatever you feel, honey."

Pish, his face lined with weariness, came to us and took us both in his arms. He was, as I had figured, responsible for getting Virgil and Dewayne to us so quickly, guiding them to our location. I had felt them near, but it took a few minutes, likely, to figure out how to get us safely extracted. My precipitous launching at Mariah had hurried the event.

"I'm sorry I wasn't here for you, my darling girl, but I was worried that if I rushed them, or . . . or tried to help I'd be worse than no help."

"Pish, you brought Virgil and Dewayne. You did the right thing."

Even if the police had allowed us, I couldn't leave. There was still something nagging at me; Lynn had claimed that while she was wandering, looking for drugs, she had heard screaming. I shielded my eyes from the brilliant cold sun and looked into the distance. There was the other abandoned shed I had noticed once before, and that I had seen in some of the drone footage . . . the abandoned one I had never searched because I had found Lynn before I had a chance to.

I had a bad feeling, a sickness in the pit of my stomach. Without a word I skirted the dug grave and the dead body of Nathan, and I took off at a run over the grass, toward it, stumbling and staggering in my anxiety. Virgil and the others yelled, but it was as if I was possessed. Something about that shed in the drone footage had bothered me; there was a trail leading away from it, but it went back across the land, toward the far woods, through which there was a path. That was, I would bet, the woods that Mariah so confidently knew the way through when she left Mack's farm on Quarry Road, the next road over.

I raced to the outbuilding, grabbed the door, and shook it; the whole shed shuddered, but the door wouldn't open. I stood back. There was a shiny new padlock. Who puts a shiny new lock on an old, rickety shed in the middle of a field? I heard a noise inside. I shook the door again, and put my ear up to the door as the others came to me.

"What's going on?" Virgil said.

I turned to my husband. "There's someone in here! I hear a noise, a muffled moan."

He put his ear to the door and grunted. "Yup." He said more loudly, "Hello! We're here to help you! Stay away from the door and cover your eyes, if you can."

I expected him to pull out his gun, like in the movies, and shoot off the padlock, but instead, he backed up and gave a powerful kick at the plank door. It shuddered, and the wood cracked, splintering. He did it again, and again, finally breaking through the wood with his booted foot. He pulled away boards, ignoring the cuts and scrapes he was inflicting on his bare arms, and kicked more of the door apart. He pulled out his cell phone and tapped the flashlight app, shining it inside as he pushed his thick body through the opening he had made.

Something in a far corner sparkled, reflecting the light, which I saw as I followed. My shape is a little different than his, but I can get through where he gets through. He held up his cell phone, hunching down, probably knowing how intimidating he would look, full height.

I looked over him. Cowering in the corner was a girl confined by duct tape, dirty, hair matted, shaking with fright and choking with fear, her eyes wild over the duct tape that covered her mouth.

Chapter Twenty-four

I moved forward, pushing past my husband. "Honey, you're safe," I said softly, my voice quivering. "I promise you. Whatever has happened, you're safe now. We have the people who hurt you. This is my husband, and he's a good man," I said, gesturing toward Virgil, behind me. "We'll get you out of here as fast as we can. Do you understand?"

Her eyes full of tears, she nodded as Virgil knelt by her and with his penknife cut the tape over her mouth and that bound her hands and ankles.

By now the ambulance drivers knew their way well to the encampment, and the young woman, the missing girl, was taken directly to the hospital, the ragged ends of duct tape that had gagged her still clinging to her filthy hair. And of course *we* couldn't go home. We had to talk to the police.

They were puzzled by how I had zeroed in on that shed, and how I had connected so many random occurrences — Lynn hearing the screams, the drone footage of the shed, Mariah walking, unerringly, through the woods as if she knew the way — and came up with the latest missing girl being held in that cabin by the weird duo. I couldn't explain it myself; it sounded dumb, no matter how I put it.

But that's how my mind works. I've always been like that, random images and thoughts coalescing into one gleaming idea that takes hold of me. It's what I was like as a stylist, and designing our home. Everything I had been thinking pelted into my brain and I knew that was where Mariah and Nathan had kept their victims, and probably where they had murdered them. One detail stayed in my mind from finding that poor missing girl in there just now. "Detective Sanchez," I said to the handsome fellow who was from the DA's office. "I saw something in that shed . . . something that I'm wondering about. I heard that poor girl, Glynnis Johnson . . . she had one sparkly barrette in her hair, but it looked like another had been torn out. I saw one in that shed just now, sparkling from my husband's cell phone flashlight app. I'm wondering . . . could it be the one missing from Glynnis Johnson's hair?"

He assured me they would check it out, and I told him

everything else I knew and had seen and thought and heard. There was an old truck visible behind the shed, I remembered, from the drone footage. Something Ford Hayes always said came back to me: it didn't matter what a car or truck looked like, it was what was under the hood. When police investigated it they found that that "old truck" was in perfect working order, despite its broken-down, rusted-out appearance. That's how they had picked up their other victims, those who didn't come to the camp willingly, and that is likely how they transported victims like the girls who had been found partially buried, like Yolanda Perkins, driving them away from the encampment to dispose of when they could.

We talked and talked at the site, of course. Lizzie and I both took the New York State Police detectives through the confusing narration of the crimes by Mariah and Nathan. It sounded like they had both killed, Nathan the first two girls, and Mariah poor Yolanda Perkins. Lizzie, Virgil, Dewayne and I—among others—then went to Baxter's sheriff station to talk some more with the FBI, and the New York State Police, and anyone else who wanted to listen. We talked for *hours*.

Finally we left, free to return home, even as the police set up camp at the Light and the Way Ministry because they suspected that behind that awful shed, where there was some indication that the ground had been disturbed, was the grave of at least one girl, Ashley Walker. She was the one from the list who had been missing for two years. Maria/Mariah was not talking, and had been put on suicide watch. Which of them had killed who would be sorted out eventually, I supposed, taking into account what we had heard and the evidence gathered by the forensic team. The NYSP were coordinating with the FBI because of the complicated nature of the multi-county, multi-state murder and drug smuggling case.

I had shared a thought with the police, but I didn't know if they would be following up on it; I would bet that the prophet knew about the pair's murderous proclivities but didn't see fit to turn them in, as that would have brought law enforcement down on Voorhees's head and disrupted his tidy little drug smuggling ring. I would bet that the day I was there he was alarmed enough to warn them to get rid of Glynnis, if she was in that shed, because he may have suspected, knowing my husband had been a cop, that there would be police following my visit. That was likely the turmoil that Isadore had witnessed, Mariah's agitation, though we might never know.

The one thing that buoyed me over the next few days was a beacon of light shining through the awfulness: we had saved that poor girl in the shed. She had been beaten, but if Nathan and Mariah had stayed alive and free they would have undoubtedly killed her. As good as *that* thought was, it wasn't enough comfort to counter the confirmation I received through the grapevine that the barrette in the shed was Glynnis's. That poor child had been through so much; there was evidence found that she had been beaten, then taken from the shed and dropped off in some bushes—Mariah and Nathan assumed she was dead—but that she had dragged herself to the side of the highway to be found by Anokhi and her daughter and son-in-law. I'd never get over that, the knowledge that the poor girl may have been close at hand even as I wandered the camp.

Among all the horror I *had* to focus on the positive. Felice was okay and out of the hospital. Gordy, free and exonerated of any criminal actions, was back in Ridley Ridge, living in the apartment above Binny's bakery, recovering from a broken heart and a wounded spirit. Lynn was doing as well as could be expected, and Pish was, I think, enjoying having company in the castle again. And I knew he loved having someone to take care of, to father and nurture.

I was weary of it all, and sick at heart at the awfulness of humanity, at times. But for every awful part of the story—and it was drenched in horror, for me—there was redemption in how the towns, both Autumn Vale and Ridley Ridge, had come together, for once, sharing information, helping the families of the victims . . . it was inspiring. And I hoped not the last time everyone would come together that way.

I think Sheriff Baxter was relieved to have the state and the feds take over. He was tired and, in news footage, appeared bewildered by all that had happened. And I believe he was more than a little ashamed that he had let the ball drop on the Light and the Way Ministry, which he should have been more watchful of. But I did get how the so-called cult—more of a criminal enterprise, really—had managed to fly under the radar so long. Who wanted to confront a band of oddballs unless you had to? They had kept a low profile, with Barney making just enough ruckus in public to discourage anyone wanting to check out their "religion."

It was all so horrible that I did not sleep that first night; Virgil stayed awake with me, just holding me tight in our big comfy bed. I had Lizzie stay in our guest room, but eventually she came in and crashed on the floor of our bedroom in front of the warm glow of the fireplace, fluffy comforter pulled over her, Becket, seeming to know what she needed, curled up at her side, ready to hug and snuggle. I was relieved the next morning to find that Barney — the real John Doe — on the run, had been caught and extradited to Ohio. He was not being considered for bail as he was clearly a flight risk, having fled the system before and evaded capture for years.

It was odd how many criminals that cult had sheltered. Besides Barney and Nathan and Maria, there was Bardo Voorhees (masquerading as his brother, Arden) and Trucker Bob, who had helped in the drug smuggling enterprise, and his brother Walt, the welder, who had altered the trucks to create cunning compartments to conceal massive amounts of cocaine that then found their way from Mexico through the States and into Canada. That border drug bust I had read about in the *Ridley Ridge Record* was of trucks altered by Walt the welder. Forensics was likely having a good time connecting all the dots. Isadore basked in her share of the limelight because it was her shrewd assessment of the ledgers being cooked that had made us think of the Light and the Way being a cover for criminal enterprises.

Virgil discovered and was able to tell me that the woman who had ended up in the women's shelter decided, finally, to press charges. She had entered into a relationship with the prophet, but had run from the encampment when she was beaten so badly she ended up with a concussion. Voorhees was not the one who did the beating, it was Mother Esther, she said, after she mouthed off to the prophet's "wife" and tried to run away. It made me wonder . . . which of the two, Bardo or Esther, actually killed Esther's husband, Arden? That would certainly be a case for the courts. Charges had been filed against both in the Arden Voorhees murder, but each was blaming the other.

A couple of evenings later we gathered in the castle with Hannah and Zeke, Pish, Lynn, Lizzie and Urquhart. From an initial phase of buoyed good spirits, Lynn had become subdued and introspective, which worried Pish. I thought maybe her quietude was a good thing, a period of readjustment she needed, and I trusted it more than her glib chirpiness. Her body had gone through so much from the toxic soup of chemicals she had been flooded with. With Pish watching over her like an anxious robin on a nest of fragile eggs, she would be fine.

Or not. At a certain point an addict has to take responsibility. I hoped she would.

We were sitting in the parlor, one of the few human-sized rooms in the castle. Sometimes I forget how much I love my castle, with all its grandeur and space, but I never forget how much I love the parlor. It is an intimate space, with a fireplace at one end, and antique sofas and chairs set around a low coffee table on which the Wynter family antique tea service usually sits. But Pish had a retro bar cart that held scotch, soda, bourbon, Crown Royal whiskey and many other alcohols. He made everyone—except Lynn, who was drinking tea—a signature drink, a new one he was working on he called an Autumn Mist, with the whiskey and cinnamon schnapps. It was delicious and warming.

Urquhart brought Ellie with him. He had, of course, given her a tour of the castle—everyone has to see the whole thing before they sit down or they seem distracted wondering about the edifice and its history and layout—and then they joined us. She was quiet too, mostly because she couldn't talk about the cases as they were before the court, and yet, of course, all of what had happened was all anyone wanted to talk about. The state police investigation had widened to the property the Light and the Way Ministry had rented before buying the land from Bob Taggart. Using GPR—ground penetrating radar—they had found what they thought were graves. These were troubling indications that there might be other victims of the deadly mother and son duo, perhaps girls from out of state. It was a sobering and sad thought, but we tried to set aside the sorrow as we came together.

After an hour or two of drinks, hors d'oeuvres and nonsense chat, all designed to lift people's spirits, Pish served coffee and tea to the drivers. Some (and by "some" I mean me) drank more wine.

Lizzie, with the resilience of teenage-dom, her eyes sparkling, had recounted our adventure at length, standing in the middle of the room, dramatizing it for effect. She is an amazing kid, with a buoyant personality and the strength to bounce back even after seeing Nathan kill himself. I intended to keep an eye on her, though. These things can come back to haunt us when we least expect it, as I know from experience.

One little mystery was solved for me when she threw off her jean jacket, revealing the racer-back tee she was wearing. On her left shoulder, over her scapula, was a tattoo—that first of which we had spoken—of a camera with wings. It was perfect!

I had my part to play, of course, in telling how I had figured out about Nathan and Mariah, and especially the discovery in the shed. I told them some of what I told the police, downplaying it a bit and simply saying everything just clicked, and I figured it out. I don't know if I ever would have if Lizzie hadn't gone to get Alcina and Felice's belongings and stumbled upon Nathan and Mariah. I shudder to think of what would have happened if she hadn't. She was the real hero of the event, I said, and I meant it.

"What puzzled me from the beginning was how disjointed the group felt . . . not like a group at all, but like warring factions," I reflected. I stared into my wine. "No one seemed to be working together for the same ends. Mother Esther was the only one who appeared to have any ideological beliefs that she steadfastly followed, as horrible as her misogyny and racism is. Voorhees's main preoccupation was finding a way to disappear in plain view, creating a drug empire while protecting it with the gleaming halo of a religious commune."

"And everyone who was attracted to it had their own ideas, and their own motives," Hannah said.

Ellie, eyes glowing with interest, nodded, but didn't say anything.

"But it all fell apart for me," I said. "Runaways were attracted to the Light and the Way as a convenient place to get away from parents or authority figures. Felice was troubled by her marriage breaking up, and the struggle to keep her farm going on her own. Mariah convinced her that her destiny was to be with Barney, who promised to take care of her and Alcina." I shuddered, grateful afresh that they had escaped from harm.

"What a collection of crazies," Virgil said, stroking my back. "I swear, only *you* could look at that mess and sort it out."

I knew too well how lucky I had gotten in some guessing, some information that connected with other information, and the help of strong and smart people around me. I shook my head. "Normally I can figure it out from who was where when, but I didn't have any of that information this time. I got lucky, and I heard and saw more than some were able to."

"Access is everything," Ellie agreed, holding up her glass for more wine. "It would have taken some time to get all the warrants and talk to all the people out there."

Pish poured and said, "It all could have been prevented if Sheriff Baxter had been operating at his proper level."

We were all silent for a minute. It was supposed to be a secret for now, but we all knew that beyond not running in the next election, Sheriff Ben Baxter was retiring for "medical reasons," and his second in command would be taking over until the next election.

"So *many* crazies!" I said, shaking my head. "Mother Esther was a racist wanting to start a neo-Nazi baby factory. Mariah and Nathan . . . they were hiding a brand of family madness that defies belief. Bob and Walt Taggart weren't crazy, just crafty. They were in with Voorhees from the beginning to hide their drug smuggling." I paused, but then said, "And Gordy . . . our poor friend was just looking for someplace to fit in. Hannah, Zeke . . . didn't Gordy want to come out here tonight?" I had invited him personally when I saw him after giving my statement to the police.

The two exchanged glances.

"He's, uh . . . he's not ready yet," Zeke said.

"He's . . . embarrassed," Hannah said softly.

"And resentful?" I said. "Angry, maybe?"

Biting her lip, Hannah nodded. "I hope you understand. He feels like he had a good thing going, and he was looking forward to marrying Peaches . . . uh, Madison. And now it's gone."

"It was all an illusion anyway," I said, irritated. "He needs to come out of his dream world and face reality. It was never real, none of it. It was a con man's game to hide his drug dealing and smuggling. Voorhees never lived like they did. He had his own lair with heat, video games, pot, pizza and satellite TV. And Madison was a runaway who clung to Gordy to avoid being mauled by Nathan."

"You have to see it from his viewpoint, Merry," Hannah said. "Maybe Voorhees was a fraud and others were crazy, but what that community was building felt real to Gordy."

"Including repopulating the earth with white babies?" I snapped.

Zeke looked hurt, and I felt bad immediately. I sighed. "Look, I know Gordy's not a racist or a bigot," I said. "I'm sorry. But I do wish he'd wake *up*." I couldn't help being exasperated.

Virgil patted my back, then took the whiskey Pish handed him. "Relax, Merry. I think Hannah and Zeke have a better chance to deprogram Gordy than anyone else."

Hannah smiled. "I've been doing a lot of reading and research. Virgil helped; he knows people and is getting us books."

I looked at my husband in surprise. The firelight played over his handsome face, his eyes looking hooded and mysterious under his thick dark brows. He took a sip of the whiskey and winked at me. I felt a warm flush and smiled.

"Hey, I know a few people," he said. "Actually, it's a contact of Dewayne's, someone in a cult recovery network."

"We're taking it on, Zeke and I," Hannah said, looking at her boyfriend with warmth and love. "He's going to make sure Gordy and him do the things they used to, you know . . . play video games, watch movies, take road trips. Binny promised him a permanent job with Turner Construction, to start when he's up to it, hopefully soon. And together with his uncles we're going to do what the anti-conspiracy sites say works. But we're going to take our time and show Gordy the compassion he needs while he reevaluates everything he has come to believe."

I reflected on that; how many people can reevaluate their whole worldview and come through it? I needed more of that compassion in my heart. "I think like Virgil says, if anyone can do it, you two can."

They had a plan, and they were committed to helping their childhood friend.

I sighed, peace stealing into my heart. I had held on to anger toward Gordy, anger that he had let himself be so heavily influenced

by theories and notions I considered idiotic. But simply saying that
to him would not accomplish anything. It wasn't up to me, after all.
I looked at Zeke and Hannah and smiled. "I promise, when I see
Gordy I am going to use the same methods; just kindness. You're
good people, you two." I hesitated, but then added, "And tell him,
from me, that I truly believe that with his care and concern for her
he kept Madison safe from Nathan and Mariah. I really do. He may
have saved her life."

Chapter Twenty-five

It was early November, getting chilly, but still beautiful. Wynter Woods was clearer, most of the leaves having fluttered to the ground, except for the occasional old oaks, the leaves of which hang on longer than most of the others. Everything was brown and crunchy underfoot.

It was a Saturday morning. Pish, Lizzie and I were at the entrance of the woods where the performance center was going to be built, and I was nervously pacing. This was stage one of our campaign to win over the hearts and minds of the various factions in Autumn Vale. First up: the Autumn Vale Methodist Church Choir.

"They're here," Pish said.

I turned. There, across the landscape, following the lane that had been created by the heavy construction vehicles as the work crew dug the foundation and installed the services to the site, bumped a school bus full of Methodists driven by Reverend Maitland himself. The bus stopped and the group of about thirty, most of them choir members but a few others, too, who were church group leaders, disembarked. Shepherded by Graciela and John Maitland, they approached, looking about with unfeigned interest. Graciela had shown me a path to local acceptance and I hoped I was smart enough to take it.

Pish and I would gain the approval of Autumn Vale and Ridley Ridge folk alike, and bring them to realize that the Wynter Woods Performance Center was going to be good for everyone, locals and outsiders. The Maitlands smiled at me, and Graciela nodded, motioning with her hands, encouraging me to start.

"Hello, everyone," I said, clasping my hands together in front of me and wringing them anxiously. I looked over the gathering; the congregation was a diverse group of local business leaders and regular folk. It included many people I knew, and many more I didn't. I smiled and nodded to them all. "My name is Merry Grace Wynter, and this is Pish Lincoln, my business partner and longtime friend. Welcome to our project. We are going to walk this path, and what you will see is a big open space in the woods, but someday . . . someday *soon*, we hope . . . there will be a domed performance center, with professional sound engineering, sound studios, and practice space for talented musicians and singers. We have artistic renderings of the finished product, but it will require you to use your imagination. Come with me."

Lizzie, snapping photos for our website-to-be, followed the crowd, their heads bent together in chat. They followed Pish and me down the woodland path, leaves crunching underfoot, coming out finally to the opening, where a wooden stage had hastily been built and huge billboards, ordered swiftly from the company who would build the dome, depicting the performance center had also been erected. On the stage, with a microphone and nothing else, stood Liliana Bartholomew, majestically zaftig in purple choir robes. She had graciously acquiesced to Pish's plea to help us win over locals.

"This," I said, sweeping my hand to point to her, above us, "is the magnificent Liliana Bartholomew, soprano for the Lexington Opera Company, who has agreed to be one of our first performers at the Wynter Woods Performance Center."

With no musical accompaniment other than her magnificent voice, she belted out "Amazing Grace," sounding like a cross between the sweet and powerful lilt of Jessye Norman and the flavorful runs of the recordings I had heard of Mahalia Jackson. The church group was spellbound and surged, as one, toward the stage, swaying in time with her powerful voice. As the song ended and the echoes of her performance melted into the woods, they broke out into applause. And when she sat down on the top step of the stage, they crowded around her, thanking her and begging for an encore and asking questions.

As I stood, tears in my eyes, I beckoned to Graciela. She came to stand with me. "Thank you so much," I murmured, putting one arm over her shoulders. "I feel like we have a chance now." I hugged her and released, then eyed the billboard, which showed a domed theater with a stone entrance and depictions of people gathered waiting to enter. "I feel like we might be able to make it happen."

The crowd had worked its magic and an encore was coming; Liliana remounted the stage and looked over to her sound engineer, also known as her famous son, Mojo, who stood at a mixing board and amplifier with headphones on. She murmured something to him, and he smiled, nodded, then twiddled with the sound system.

"What I will sing next is an old spiritual song, a classic sung by the incomparable Mahalia Jackson. What you may not realize is, the very *first* recording of this song was done by an African-American singer by the name of Dorothy Maynor, the daughter of a Methodist minister. She was also the founder of the Harlem School of the Arts." She swept her hand over the gathered choir members and said, "I *know* you all will know it. Will you join me on this stage, those who can, and sing *with* me?"

They all eagerly climbed those wooden steps, the younger helping the older, the infirm making their way on faith-strengthened limbs. Even the church deacons, ladies' auxiliary director and Reverend Maitland joined in. As they clustered behind Liliana, she started slow, low and soft . . . *"Go, tell it on the mountain . . ."* and the rest joined in joyfully, once they realized that they did indeed know all the words. It was amazing; they swayed and clapped and chorused with her. I had shivers all over my body and tears in my eyes in the great temple of my forest. I'm not a religious person, but this was a holy experience.

Lizzie was busy snapping photos and taking video footage. Pish was standing silent, tears running down his cheeks. I babbled out a weepy thanks to Graciela for her idea, blowing my running nose and weak with gratitude. I would never, for the rest of my life, forget that moment, and how it felt like our temple of the arts had been blessed not just by Liliana's magnificent voice, but by these openhearted people who had taken me into their lives. I would do my best to give back to them.

• • •

Later in the day our phone would not stop ringing. Someone (ahem . . . Lizzie) had videotaped the performance and loaded it on social media; Liliana's performance of "Amazing Grace" had gone viral as "Holy Moment, Holy Voice." Wynter Woods Performance Center was trending on Twitter — as was the Autumn Vale Methodist Church Choir and their backup on "Go Tell It on the Mountain" — and Pish had bookings lined up for the year following our construction finish date and beyond. My mother-in-law, Gogi, called to tell me it was all anyone was talking about in town, in the coffee shop and new yoga studio that opened a week before.

I was under no illusions; there was still a lot of work to be done. There were negative Nancies and naysayers aplenty, still. But there was time, and I was determined, and there were good people all around wishing us success.

• • •

The next morning I took a walk in the woods behind our house. Becket followed, and we headed deep into the Fairy Tale Forest. I heard their voices before I saw them, and was smiling as I came into the opening where the stone structure stood, one of the remaining decrepit but amazing structures my father, grandfather and great-uncle had started building for me.

Alcina and Lizzie—together again, the best of friends—were working on a scene. My photographer friend was snapping photos as Alcina, fairy wings in place, long, rippling blonde hair shimmering in waves over her shoulders, and a long white gown from a thrift shop—a dress that may have once been a wedding gown—dragging on the forest floor, as she built a tiny scene of toadstools and acorns and mouse figurines at the base of the cobblestone structure. Alcina was now fifteen, but I hoped she would never grow out of her fairy wings and gnome homes.

Becket crept up to them and dashed forward, stealing one of the fuzzy mousies and taking off into the woods, Alcina racing after him, her laughter floating back over her shoulder. Lizzie turned and looked at me, a radiant smile on her face. "She's back," she said, glowing with joy. "My friend is back."

I smiled. "Go find them. When you're done, come back to my place for lunch and show me your photos."

I left them and returned home, grateful that the eighteen- and fifteen-year-olds still felt able to play in the woods, their childlike wonder intact after all they had seen and learned. I had been reminded that the sense of play and fun is resilient and, in the best people, cannot be vanquished by the evil men and women do. Jim Henson once said that the most sophisticated people he knew were still children inside, and who could argue with the man who created Kermit and Miss Piggy?

Not I.

Recipes

Cheese-Stuffed Bacon-Wrapped Chicken Thighs

These are delectable and company-worthy. They are a little tedious and finicky, but you can prepare them ahead of time, then put them in a container in the fridge until they need to go into the oven.

¾–1 cup shredded cheddar
¼ cup parmesan
Pinch of Old Bay or your favorite seasoning blend
1 cup cream cheese
3 green onions
12 boneless skinless chicken thighs
12 – 24 slices of thin-sliced bacon (depending on how 'wrapped' you want these!)

Mix the shredded cheddar with the parmesan, tossing it lightly . . . this keeps the shredded cheese from clumping. Then blend well the seasoning, cream cheese, shredded cheddar and parmesan mix, and finely chopped green onions in a bowl. Set the cheese mixture aside; I would cover it and put it in the fridge while you do the next step, since the cheese handles better chilled.

Using the flat side of a meat tenderizing hammer, open out and flatten the thighs, being careful not to tear them up too much.

Scoop a good-sized dollop of the cheese mixture and put it in the center of the inside of the thigh, then wrap the thigh around it, tucking in any bits and pieces of the thigh meat.

The bacon wrapping is highly individual. I like these bundles nice and neat, so I wrap a half piece of bacon around the thigh end to end, and then use another full piece of bacon to spiral-wrap the whole thigh. I use super-thin bacon for two reasons: it stretches slightly, so like a good pair of tights it keeps everything snug and eliminates bulging (Spanx of the meat world, I salute you!), and it crisps up well.

These, once done, can be put in the fridge until dinner.

Bake in a 350 degree oven for 35 minutes, or until done. Add a minute or two extra to the time if you are baking them from the fridge. If the bacon isn't crisp enough, stick them under the broiler, but watch them carefully!

These are even good heated up the next day for lunch, with a salad!

Merry's Mandarin Orange Cranberry Chocolate Chip Muffins

Have you ever had a Terry's Chocolate Orange? I don't know if you can get them here, but a British friend of my grandmother's used to bring them back in her suitcase when she visited "over 'ome," as she called England still, after forty years in the States. They are a milk chocolate treat in the shape of an orange and with orange flavoring, and you whack it on the table to break the "orange" segments apart! These treats were the inspiration for the flavor combination of chocolate and orange.

Makes 12 Muffins

1 10-ounce tin mandarin orange segments, diced, liquid reserved!
½ cup sweetened dried cranberries
½ cup all-purpose flour
½ cup sugar
2½ teaspoon baking powder
¼ teaspoon salt
½ teaspoon spice blend (mixed spices: cinnamon, cloves, allspice and nutmeg) OR ¼ teaspoon each cinnamon and nutmeg. *Note: next time I make these I may boost the spice blend to a whole scant or level teaspoon to get more of the spice flavor!
1 cup milk chocolate chips
1 egg
¾ cup milk
⅓ cup vegetable oil

Preheat oven to 400°F. These are very moist muffins; I did use muffin liners, but if you do so, the muffins must cool completely before serving or they stick to the liners. Alternately, you can spray a muffin tin with oil and flour lightly.

Drain the mandarin segments and set them aside. Heat the nectar from the mandarins in a microwave-safe bowl—not boiling, just fifteen or twenty seconds on high will do. Soak the dried cranberries in the warmed nectar for about fifteen minutes (or as long as it takes to put together the rest of the recipe!) to plump them.

In a large bowl, combine flour, sugar, baking powder, salt, and spices together. Toss the cup of chocolate chips in with the flour mix.

Dice peeled orange segments.

Beat the egg, milk and vegetable oil together.

Add to the dry and stir just until combined.

Fold in the diced orange pieces and the plumped cranberries, discarding the liquid. (Pish says the liquid, strained, might make a good simple syrup–type sweetener for a cocktail!)

Pour batter into prepared muffin tins and bake for about 23-25 minutes, just until a toothpick inserted in the center comes out clean. Check at 23 minutes . . . ovens vary so much!

Remove muffins from muffin tin and allow to cool before serving.

Serve with butter, jam, or orange cranberry conserve!

About the Author

Victoria Hamilton is the pseudonym of nationally bestselling romance author Donna Lea Simpson. She is the bestselling author of three mystery series, the Lady Anne Addison Mysteries, the Vintage Kitchen Mysteries, and the Merry Muffin Mysteries. She is also the bestselling author of Regency and historical romances as Donna Lea Simpson. Her latest adventure in writing is a Regency-set historical mystery series, starting with *A Gentlewoman's Guide to Murder*.

Victoria loves to read, especially mystery novels, and enjoys good tea and cheap wine, the company of friends, and has a newfound appreciation for opera. She enjoys crocheting and beading, but a good book can tempt her away from almost anything . . . except writing!

Visit Victoria at: www.victoriahamiltonmysteries.com.

CPSIA information can be obtained
at www.ICGtesting.com
Printed in the USA
LVHW030740200120
644151LV00002B/658